The Manhattan Secret

Marie-Bernadette Dupuy is the author of more than 30 novels that have gone on to sell over 4 million copies, making her France's most successful saga author.

MARIE-BERNADETTE DUPUY

The Manhattan Secret

Translated from the French by Deniz Gulan

HODDER

First published in the French language as *L'Orpheline de Manhattan* by Editions Calmann-Lévy in 2019

First published in Great Britain in 2020 by Hodder & Stoughton
An Hachette UK company

1

A CIP catalogue record for this title is available from the British Library

Paperback ISBN 9781529338249
eBook ISBN 9781529338256

Typeset in Plantin Light by Hewer Text UK Ltd, Edinburgh
Printed and bound in Great Britain by Clays Ltd, Elcograf S.p.A.

Hodder & Stoughton policy is to use papers that are natural, renewable
and recyclable products and made from wood grown in sustainable
forests. The logging and manufacturing processes are expected to
conform to the environmental regulations of the country of origin.

Hodder & Stoughton Ltd
Carmelite House
50 Victoria Embankment
London EC4Y 0DZ

www.hodder.co.uk

To my friend Philippe Porée-Kurrer

Do you remember, my dear friend? It was over a good meal in New York that we talked so excitedly and fondly about this gigantic and beautiful city of lights and evoked its past, its shadows, and its intrigues. There was so much laughter and emotion as we shared these ideas. It is in memory of those unforgettable moments that I dedicate this book to you.

PART ONE

PART FOUR

I

A Family Torn Apart

Guerville Castle
Friday, October 15, 1886

"No, no, and no! I will not accept your leaving! It's sheer madness!" hollered Hugues Laroche, slamming his clenched fist so violently on the table that the crystal glasses shook.

A clap of thunder responded to his furious outburst.

The storm had hit the county about half an hour ago. It was now in full force, and the windows vibrated with each rumble. The sky was a leaden grey, streaked at times with long white flashes of lightning.

"Let your husband pursue his seafaring adventures, if that's what he wants, but you, Catherine—you must stay in France, on the land where you were born!" added the master of the castle.

"Father, I would follow Guillaume to the end of the world and back if I had to, so please stop shouting. We are not going to change our minds."

With one hand placed on her protruding belly, the young woman smiled quietly at her father. She gazed worriedly at the estate's hundred-year-old oak trees, whose red leaves were swirling madly, at the mercy of the gusting wind.

The child she was carrying was restless, as if troubled by the apocalyptic atmosphere.

"Don't worry, my princess, we're safe here," she told her six-year-old daughter, sitting next to her.

Jerome, the butler, had placed a cushion on the chair, so that she was now the right height to sit at the table to eat. In front of her was her dessert, a meringue tart. But her wide-eyed gaze expressed panic.

Her mother took her in her arms and cuddled her, whispering words of comfort in her ear.

"She's no longer a baby, Catherine," protested Adela Laroche. "If you mollycoddle her too much, you'll make her weak."

"But Mother, Elizabeth is frightened. I know her better than you do. She's distressed by the storm, and Father's shouting."

"I have good reason to shout!" he intervened sharply.

Catherine's father was of slim build, with strong features, and rather obsessed with his social status. A wealthy landowner, in charge of some very fine vineyards, he was accustomed to imposing his will.

"Yes, I have every right to be furious," he exclaimed, "after that announcement! I was so looking forward to having you here for dinner tonight . . . And all the time you were merely waiting to stab me in the back!"

Hugues Laroche pointed an accusing index finger at his son-in-law.

"Guillaume, you have overstepped the mark," he said. "For my daughter's happiness, I accepted her marrying beneath herself, but enough is enough. This time you've gone too far! You're taking my only daughter on a dangerous and ridiculous wild goose chase to America—New York! Do you really think they need more crummy carpenters over there?"

Elizabeth, still huddled against her mother, could not take her eyes off her grandfather. He reminded her of the ogre in the fairy tales read to her by her parents, or the devil who, according to an old woman in the village, used to kidnap disobedient children.

The master of the castle had neither horns nor cloven hooves, yet the little girl was sure she could see a greyish mist around his head, as though he were emitting smoke.

"Grandpa is angry, don't be afraid," whispered Catherine, squeezing her even tighter against her.

Guillaume Duquesne saw that his daughter was overcome with fright and became indignant. "Please, Sir, let us talk about it later, when Elizabeth is in bed," the thirty-three-year-old member of the Carpenters' Guild confronted his father-in-law firmly. "She shouldn't have to witness our quarrel. Moreover, your fury is in vain. Nothing will stop us from going. In four days' time, we will be boarding the liner *La Champagne*, from Le Havre. It would be preferable to part on good terms."

"Father, I agree with Guillaume," added Catherine. "I beg you, let's not leave each other on bad terms."

The young couple had anticipated the scene that was unfolding in the vast dining room. Hugues Laroche pursed his lips. He gazed coldly at his only daughter. At almost twenty-nine years of age, this young lady was so pretty. Her blonde hair was in perfect harmony with her milky complexion and her regular, delicate features. Her beautiful green eyes shone with courage and determination.

Full of bitterness, he asked himself once more why and how she could have fallen in love with this raven-haired Guillaume, with his sun-tanned complexion and grey eyes.

The third offspring of a miller, he thought to himself. *I had hoped for a son-in-law capable of replacing me on the estate, and not a jackass like him.*

He was about to continue his attack when a violent and prolonged thunderclap erupted with such force that everyone froze. At that moment, the rain intensified. Adela Laroche made the sign of the cross, while trying to maintain a blank expression.

"What an evening!" she lamented. "It's enough to make you a nervous wreck! Nevertheless, your father is right. It's utter folly. Think of your daughter, Catherine, and the discomfort and unpleasantness of the crossing! The roll and sway of the sea, the seasickness, the bad food, the inevitable seasickness and the overcrowded and squalid conditions! I assume you'll be in third class?"

"The voyage lasts about ten days," said Catherine. "My pregnancy isn't giving me any problems; I'm in my seventh month. I'm sorry for causing you so much pain. I admit that we deliberately left it until the last minute to tell you, but only to avoid endless discussions and accusations. We have already sold our furniture and a piece of land that belonged to me, to pay for the tickets."

"We are expected in New York," explained Guillaume. "A friend of mine has promised me a job, on a building they're constructing on 23rd Street. They're looking for skilled carpenters."

"That's a joke, Duquesne! As if they don't have any there already!" shouted Hugues Laroche at the top of his voice.

He threw his arms up in the air. A new rumble interspersed with ominous crackling sounds resounded, leaving Elizabeth convinced that her grandfather's rage had caused it. A sense of imminent yet inexplicable danger came over her.

"I'm very scared, Mummy," she whispered.

"Don't be, my darling. As I said before, we're quite safe here," Catherine whispered back, before kissing her tenderly on the forehead.

Guillaume looked gloomy as he ruminated over Laroche's harsh words. If he'd been able to, he would have taken his family away there and then. But the infernal lightning display was continuing outside, and the windows were awash with rain.

"It will be worse in the middle of the ocean," remarked Adela Laroche spitefully, as she dabbed her lips with the tip of her white napkin.

A silhouette appeared from the adjoining corridor. It was the butler, checking that dinner was progressing smoothly.

"You can clear away now, Jerome," ordered the mistress of the house. "Catherine, an idea has just come to me: leave Elizabeth with us. She will receive a good education, in her ancestral home. Our granddaughter will brighten up the rather stern atmosphere of this old house."

Elizabeth's blue eyes darted over to her grandmother. She hardly knew her, and the idea of being entrusted to this blonde-bunned, hook-nosed lady made her grip her mother's neck tightly.

The decor of the massive dining room, to which the child had paid little attention, now appeared strange and oppressive, as if it were ready to close in and hold her prisoner. Her dismayed gaze went from the heavy green velvet curtains and the paintings depicting sullen-looking characters, to the white plaster ceiling, which was adorned with embossed rosettes representing bunches of grapes, foliage and extravagant flowers and the dark oak panelling, that Elizabeth was certain concealed secret doors leading to damp cellars.

"My sweetheart, you're clutching me so tightly that I can hardly breathe," protested Catherine with a chuckle. "Elizabeth, my child, have no fear. You're coming with us to America."

"Mummy, I don't like the castle," she whispered. "I prefer our home and Grandpa Toine's."

Elizabeth had grown up in a charming little dwelling on the banks of the Charente river in the village of Montignac. Her other grandfather, the miller Antoine Duquesne, lived half a mile away, upstream. It was a child's paradise, where she was doted on and able to roam freely from dawn till dusk in the small garden.

"Don't worry, my princess," Catherine replied in her ear. "You're coming with us, I promise you."

"And why?!" fumed Hugues Laroche. "Adela is right, we could at least keep Elizabeth. She won't want for anything. I'll leave everything to her."

Guillaume struck the table with the flat of his hand. This time, his fury had no measure.

"Don't even think about it!" he exclaimed. "Our daughter will grow up on American soil, well away from the tainted values of this old-fashioned continent. I am more than capable of providing for my family. Let's not talk about it anymore, please."

As Elizabeth calmed down under her soothing touch, Catherine grabbed the opportunity to say her piece. She was radiant, her soft golden curls cascading over her delicate shoulders.

Guillaume could not help but smile at her. He loved her with all his heart. Initially drawn in by her sheer beauty and delicacy like that of an antique sculpture, he had soon been won over by her warm heart, her intelligence and her vitality.

"Mother, Father, this discussion is exhausting me. We will write to you, I promise. My husband and I are eager to follow our dream. Why would you oppose it?"

The butler busied himself around the table, on which the silverware and crystal glasses did their best to outshine each other. The wind was howling in the chimneys and, despite the fires lit in the dining room and the adjoining large drawing room, it sounded as if a pack of wolves were prowling around the castle.

A torrential downpour was now streaming down the high slate roofs, cascading from the zinc guttering and swamping the lawns.

"Dear Lord, this is no longer a storm, but a tempest! You should really stay here tonight," proposed Adela. "It will soon be nightfall. Jerome, ask Madeleine to prepare a room, with a lit fire and warmed sheets, and tell her to make up a bed for Miss Elizabeth in the nursery."

"Yes, Madam," answered the servant.

"Mother, stop making our decisions for us!" protested Catherine. "The horse-drawn carriage that the doctor lent us has a wax-covered canvas hood which is virtually waterproof. We had intended to return to the Duquesnes' house. But I am happy to spend the night at the castle. Tomorrow morning, we will have to say our goodbyes, and perhaps we will all be in better spirits then."

Adela was delighted at the extra time she had gained. A lot could happen in a few hours; it might be enough to change their minds.

A truce was established, over liqueurs to aid digestion of the golden-crusted roast veal and meringue tarts they had just eaten. While sipping a blackcurrant liqueur, Hugues Laroche was silently seeking ways in which to prevent his daughter and granddaughter from leaving. He refused to imagine them at sea, let alone on the streets of New York.

"Guillaume, son-in-law," he began, having emptied his glass, "I apologize to you. Put yourself in my shoes. As soon as we sat down at the table, you announced to me that you would be sailing from Le Havre in four days' time. I had every reason to be upset! This is such a serious undertaking that I would have appreciated discussing it with you and Catherine beforehand. The harm is done, and I have made some unpleasant remarks about you. Please forgive me."

"I forgive you, Sir."

"Let me be frank. I was upset and most disagreeable at the beginning of your marriage. However, you must grant me one thing: I gave in when I saw that it was a love match. Now, let's get to the heart of the problem."

"What do you mean?"

"What if I were to offer you a future on the estate? You would become my partner, and move into the castle, which has some very comfortably furnished rooms. My daughter would return to the lifestyle to which she is accustomed and the baby would be born in the best conditions. We would share both the workload and the profits."

Catherine was astounded. She understood the magnitude of her father's proposal. The intransigent winegrower had never made such an offer in the past. He usually made no secret of his contempt for his son-in-law.

Guillaume would be stupid to refuse such an offer, thought Adela to herself, her eyes gleaming with hope. *My Lord, they are going to stay, I am certain of it.*

"That's very generous of you, Sir," replied the carpenter politely. "But I don't wish to run your vineyards or to avail myself of your generosity. I love my job, and the New World is beckoning me. My wife, our children and I will build a new life there for ourselves, without relying on anyone else. I'm sorry."

Catherine, feeling relieved, straightened up. She could almost feel the sea breeze on her forehead and cheeks. Her rush of joy didn't go unnoticed, but her father concealed his irritation with a resigned smile.

"Deep down, you are an arrogant man, Guillaume," he said, "which is often a key to success. You are proud, too, and I cannot reproach you for that. I had hoped we would find some common ground, but well, we'll have to leave it at that."

Guillaume nodded in agreement but gave Catherine an amused look. Nothing could have changed the minds of the young couple, who shared the same desire for freedom and discovery.

Elizabeth returned to her chair. She finished her meringue tart, comforted by the certainty that her parents loved her and would take her with them.

Every evening for the past two weeks, she had listened to them explaining how their grand sea voyage would unfold. Catherine had enchanted her with epic descriptions. She had shown her pictures of the immense blue-and-green ocean, with its waves of white foam. There were images of seagulls too, a species unknown in Charente.

Guillaume had found a photograph of a liner, to explain to his daughter that they would spend ten days on a gigantic boat, akin to a huge floating house.

Elizabeth's new-found peace of mind vanished when Madeleine, the Laroches' housekeeper, pulled her chair back. The twenty-eight-year-old robust peasant woman had a piercing gaze. She wore a small white bonnet over her chestnut hair, which was tied at the nape of her neck.

"I must put you to bed, Miss," she said.

Catherine, used to putting her daughter to bed herself, made a gesture in protest, but Adela intervened:

"Madeleine will take good care of Elizabeth; the two of us need to talk. You were raised that way, have you forgotten? Children this age need to go to bed early to get enough rest."

"I remember it perfectly," retorted Catherine. "In the summer, I spent my evenings bored in bed whilst you received guests in the garden, under the lanterns. I could hear the music, and I felt sad about being left out of the festivities. It was even worse in wintertime, when I used to be very afraid, up there alone, with the wind howling in the fireplace, just like it did this evening. In fact, I felt less alone at boarding school."

"Is it my fault that I couldn't give you brothers and sisters?" complained her mother. "Please, don't be so sensitive. Say good night to Elizabeth."

Disgruntled, Catherine yielded. At dawn, they would be leaving. Never again would anyone impose such silly rules on her.

"Elizabeth, my darling, you follow Madeleine. Do as she tells you, say your prayers and go to sleep. I'll come and see you when I come up to bed." Then she cuddled her daughter and kissed her repeatedly, in an effort to comfort her.

"Mummy, you will come, won't you?" Elizabeth asked worriedly.

"I thought our little doll had lost her tongue," guffawed Hugues Laroche. "But no, she can talk, all right."

"Elizabeth is no doll, Sir," said Guillaume with indignation. "With us, at home, she is very talkative and curious about everything. We are proud to say that she can now read simple phrases without our help."

The winegrower was about to reply, but a dreadful noise prevented him from doing so. It was as though a section of roof had caved in, or doors and windows had been smashed.

"Good God, what was that?" cried Adela, panic-stricken. "I thought the storm was over!"

"Something has obviously been struck by lightning," replied her husband.

The butler ran towards them, pale-faced and wide-eyed. He bowed to his employers.

"Sir, Madam, I have just heard from Vincent, as he was coming back from the stable, that the great fir tree has fallen against the turret!"

"Good Lord, that tree was two hundred years old!" lamented Laroche as he jumped up. "Forgive me for being pessimistic, but this doesn't bode well. I need to examine the damage."

"I'll come with you," offered Guillaume at once.

Adela did not move but reached out towards Catherine and grasped her hand. Madeleine, unfazed by these events, led the little girl out of the dining room and towards the Laroches' grand entrance hall—a 12th-century Romanesque reception room which provided access to the drawbridge. The Laroches never missed an opportunity to remind their guests of the rich historical legacy of the former fortress, which the locals of Guerville respectfully called "the castle".

Elizabeth turned to look at her mother one last time. She would have liked to stay on her lap or go upstairs with her. The unwelcoming dining room suddenly seemed like a cosy refuge to her. Oil lamps cast a soft yellow glow on the heavy wooden furniture.

"Come on, Miss, we must hurry," ordered the housekeeper.

Once they got to the entrance hall, which was decorated with potted plants and mirrors, the little girl slowed right down. The walls, covered in panels of red velvet, featured a collection of hunting trophies. Elizabeth had not noticed them upon her arrival. There, under the flickering candlelight, she gazed at these poor, unfortunate beasts with frozen eyes of coloured glass.

She could see a wild boar, a deer and a few roebucks. Reminded of the graceful creatures that often wandered near the castle to drink from the river there, she grew even sadder.

"It was the master of the castle, your grandfather, who killed them, Miss," added the housekeeper reverently. "But he stuffs only the finest ones!"

As she climbed the countless steps leading to the bedrooms, Elizabeth was overcome with exhaustion. She couldn't stop yawning on the way up to the first floor. Eventually they arrived at the nursery, and Madeleine pushed her inside. Now that she was far away from the stern glances of her employers, her sweet manners and docile appearance had vanished.

"Get to bed quickly," she said harshly. "You've been such a nuisance to us tonight."

The fire, lit only five minutes ago, had not had time to warm up the room, which was illuminated only by a nearly burnt-out candle.

"Of course, you'll need a nightshirt," said the housekeeper impatiently.

"I've got one on under my dress."

"Oh, so you've found your tongue, have you? Yes, that'll do, take everything else off. I put two blankets on your cot, so you won't be cold."

"Are you angry?"

The frankness of the question surprised Madeleine somewhat. She was wary of the little girl.

"Angry or not, I don't have the time to take care of you. I have more than enough work to keep me busy from morning to night. Besides, Vincent is waiting for me for our card game."

"Who is Vincent?"

"The stable hand, who also brings the wood up to the bedrooms. Have you finished interrogating me now, you nasty little girl?"

Elizabeth had to hold back her tears, distressed by the housekeeper's attitude towards her. Without a word, she let Madeleine undress her. Suddenly she let out a cry, as she glimpsed two people a few steps away—a woman and a child, who were moving around, handling clothes.

"Look over there," she stuttered. "People!"

"I despair of you, child. How silly you are!" scoffed Madeleine. "It's only you and I in the mirror, you simpleton. Have you never seen a mirror before? Move forward a bit."

The child knew what a mirror was, but the one used by her parents was round, and the size of a dinner plate. Catherine showed the girl her reflection in it every Sunday morning, before going to church, which amused her.

This time it was different. She could see herself from head to toe, in her white strappy nightdress. Her eyes looked bigger, her cheeks and chin fuller. She observed her brown curls, the pink ribbon that held them back from her face, and finally recognized herself.

"There's nothing to be afraid of," laughed the housekeeper. "Now, go to bed."

"But I have to say my prayers!"

"You will say them in your bed—do you hear me? I'm in a hurry."

Madeleine helped her get in between the icy sheets, which had not been touched by a warming pan. Then she crouched down near the fireplace, and energetically worked the bellows. Bright yellow flames flared up.

"I'll blow out the candle, but the fire will serve as a night light," she called out. "You are not to be pitied, child! There are those who are worse off than you. And I'm warning you, if you tell your mother how I've spoken to you, then heaven help you! I know some bad spells, to punish children who talk too much. Oh yes, I can pull maggots out of your mouth and earthworms out of your ears. Do you understand?"

"Yes," whispered the terrified little girl, as she hoisted the blanket up to her nose.

She was struggling to understand Madeleine's apparent anger towards her but decided to put her stern voice and nervous gestures down to the rumblings and fury of the evening's storm.

Deep down inside, Elizabeth blamed the sinister castle for all her misfortunes. No good could ever happen here. She had seen enough proof of that, be it her grandfather's hollering and banging on the table, or her grandmother's frostiness.

"Mummy," she called out softly. "Mummy, please come."

Madeleine heard her from the doorway of the nursery and scowled at her sternly.

"Your mother has better things to do! Now get some sleep."

She closed the door behind her. The fire sparked and crackled, but this was of little solace to the child. Her wide-eyed gaze took in the huge white curtains that obscured the windows. She thought she could see them shaking slightly, so she stopped looking at them. Her eyes focused on the decorative plasterwork adorning the four corners of the room instead, but amidst the arabesque swirls she imagined she could see spiders crouching.

Finally, she sought comfort from a tall wardrobe with a triangular front pediment. The doors shimmered in the shadows and then slowly opened. Elizabeth was terrified. Her little body heaved with sobbing.

"Mummy! Daddy!" she moaned.

Nobody came to her rescue.

Catherine, who had joined her husband and father in the small drawing room they referred to as the smoking room, was oblivious to her daughter's torment. Despite the unpleasant stench of the tobacco smoke, she snuggled up to Guillaume, always eager to be at his side. Both men had just returned inside, their hair glistening with rain.

"I am sick to the stomach," said Hugues Laroche. "That mighty fir tree was the emblem of our estate. To think that it was already in the ground when Louis XIV, the Sun King, visited our castle!"

"It is quite possible—the tree was more than two hundred years old," confirmed the young carpenter. "But it broke only halfway up, so it won't die."

"Regardless, it will have to be cropped right down to the ground, to preserve the beauty of the park," sighed Laroche. "I'll plant another one, even if I won't live to see it grow to that size."

"Father dear, I'm so sorry. Please don't be sad," exclaimed Catherine.

"My only consolation would be to keep all three of you and the unborn child here with me," he said solemnly. "If you have a son and Guillaume accepted my offer, I could die in peace, knowing the castle and vineyards were in good hands."

The young woman smiled. She broke out of her husband's embrace to give her father a hug.

"You're only fifty-two years old, Father. You'll be running this estate for a long time to come!"

"How can I be sure, my dear? Remember the words of the Gospel. We know neither the day nor the hour when the Lord will beckon us. But anyway, I've given up trying to convince you. The die is cast, and I know perfectly well that nothing will keep you on French soil."

Adela entered the room at that moment. She flapped her hand in front of her face, to indicate her disgust at the cigar smoke. At once, Hugues Laroche tossed his cigar into the fire.

"Let's return to the dining room," he said. "Jerome will bring us some champagne. We might as well toast your departure."

Catherine and Guillaume exchanged a relieved glance. The evening had ended on a positive note for them.

"I hope Elizabeth isn't waiting for me," lamented the young mother. "I'm sure she would have been happier sleeping with us."

"Good heavens! A child of her age, sleeping in your bed?!" said Adela, outraged.

"Just this once, we wouldn't have minded," exclaimed Catherine. "In our home in Montignac, I set up a small room for her, adjoining our room. She's not been sleeping well for days now."

"It's not surprising. The prospect of the voyage has undoubtedly unsettled her," commented Guillaume.

The conversation dried up after this. Hugues Laroche embraced his daughter, putting an arm around her waist. He had a profound need to touch her, to feel her physical presence and smell her delicate lavender scent.

"And if you need anything," he whispered in her ear, "write to me, Catherine, and I'll see you're looked after. You can come back whenever you want. My offer stands for as long as I have any breath in my body."

"Father, you have such a kind heart underneath your suit of armour," she replied softly. "Thank you very much. Don't worry about a thing. We are so excited about discovering New York together. Yesterday morning, we had a good laugh about this extraordinary honeymoon!"

"Your honeymoon!" repeated Adela bitterly. "Was it our fault that you refused to go to Italy? It was our gift to you, but no! You preferred to spend a week on the banks of the Charente river, renovating that shabby house you were going to live in."

Catherine refrained from answering her mother, who she suspected was on the verge of tears of anger and frustration. She simply kissed her on the cheek.

Obeying Adela's mumbled order, the butler rushed to get the champagne. Madeleine ran into him in the hallway. She winked at him before entering the dining room.

"Madam, Miss Elizabeth has recited her prayers and is already asleep," she announced, staring at Catherine.

"Thank you for taking care of her," said Catherine politely. "I was afraid she would be scared, all alone upstairs."

"Oh no, Madam. I sat by her bedside, but she was tired," lied the housekeeper, doing her utmost to ingratiate herself before leaving the room.

Indeed, nothing could have been further from the truth, for on the first floor of the castle, in the nursery, Elizabeth was experiencing the fright of her life. She was convinced she could see the doors of the wardrobe open and close at a steady pace. At first, she hid under the sheets, calling out to her mother repeatedly. But then, she started watching the piece of furniture in fascination through the lacquered wooden bars of her cot, lying in wait for the mysterious back-and-forth movement of the doors.

She no longer had the strength to scream or shout, convinced that at the slightest noise, a monster would emerge and pounce on her. She couldn't stop herself crying and sniffing, and tried to stifle the sound of her sobs by covering her mouth with a trembling hand.

To make matters worse, the orange flames of the fire were dying out. The child, faced with the onslaught of darkness, began to pray. She could have tried to get up or run away, but she didn't dare to leave her refuge.

She panicked as one of the wardrobe's doors truly did open. The hanging clothes stirred and a hand emerged.

"You're crying," said a barely audible voice. "Don't cry!"

Elizabeth clumsily drew a sign of the cross in the air. The tales her Grandpa Toine used to tell her while sitting around the fire sprang up in her frightened little mind; the Montignac miller had conjured up all sorts of dangerous creatures.

There was the witch with the iron hook, lurking at the bottom of the well, who would catch any curious little children who were leaning over the dark abyss. Despite Guillaume's objections, he would also tell the girl that some men turned into werewolves at night and devoured anyone they caught in the woods.

And yet, Elizabeth wasn't sure if a monster would speak in such a soft voice and tell its victim not to cry. She sat up and scrutinized the figure that slipped out of the wardrobe.

"I think I frightened you," murmured a boy in a long white shirt.

"Yes, you did!" she whispered.

"I wanted to see you up close, so I hid. If my aunt discovers me here, she will whip me, so please don't scream."

"Who is your aunt?" inquired the little girl, still trembling.

"Madeleine the housekeeper, of course. Shh, don't move. I'll take care of the fire. It's about to go out."

Already, Elizabeth was breathing more easily. She rubbed her eyes and wiped her wet cheeks. Sitting up in her cot, she watched as the boy crouched down in front of the fireplace, used the bellows and put a log on the fire. Soon, beautiful bright flames began to flicker. He got up quickly and went to have a closer look at the girl.

"I saw you earlier, when you arrived in a carriage with your parents, but only from a distance. My aunt said you were a stuck-up little madam, but I thought you looked sweet. So why are you crying? You were calling out for your mother a short while ago."

"I was afraid. Very afraid."

"Yes, and then my aunt was mean to you—she can't help it. Is it true your name is Elizabeth? I'm Justin. I'm eight years old."

They stared at each other in silence. Justin admired her dark-brown curls, her round chin, rosy cheeks and large pale-blue eyes. He gave a dazzling smile.

"I didn't mean to frighten you. Will you forgive me?"

"I forgive you," answered the little girl.

"How long are you staying in the castle? I won't be allowed to play with you, but tomorrow night I could come back to talk to you."

Elizabeth was not used to other children. One of her uncles was married, but she didn't have any cousins yet and was accustomed to being around adults. All of a sudden, she felt sad at the thought of leaving.

"We are departing tomorrow morning," she said. "First, we'll take a train, then a giant boat. Daddy is going to work in America."

Dumbfounded, Justin nodded. He had no idea where America was, but the name sounded familiar to him.

"It sounds very far away," he sighed. "If you're going to sea, I must give you a gift. There are lots of old toys here. I come here in secret, to play with them."

Justin trotted towards a wicker trunk, with its lid against the wall. He rummaged through a cardboard box, from which he pulled out an object that he held tightly in his hand.

"Here you are: a tin soldier, my favourite. He plays the drum. He'll protect you during the journey, and if you're still scared, you can tell him to send for me. I shall come and save you."

"You won't be able to," she protested, grinning. "But I'll keep it, and it will remind me of you."

She grabbed the tiny figurine. The metal felt warm in her fingers, warm like the boy.

"Thank you, Justin. I will never lose it. I promise."

"Will you promise to come back someday?"

She hesitated because, despite her young age, her parents had instilled in her the importance of not breaking a promise. But she found Justin so charming, with his blond hair and his dark eyes, that she whispered:

"Yes, I promise."

"Well, it makes me sad that you're leaving tomorrow. I must go upstairs to bed now. If my aunt sees I'm not there, she'll have my guts for garters."

"Where do you sleep?"

"In the loft. My aunt has a room, and I sleep behind the partition, on a straw mattress. Goodbye, Elizabeth."

He looked at her for a moment longer, then, after taking a deep breath, he leaned over and kissed her on the cheek.

"Goodbye," she said, surprised and comforted by this sign of tenderness. "Look, can you not stay a little longer? Mummy usually stays till I fall asleep—could you do the same?"

"All right. But just five minutes. They're probably playing cards downstairs in the pantry."

"Who do you mean by 'they'?"

"My aunt, Vincent and old Leandre, the gardener. And tomorrow, if I can, I'll watch you leave, from that window there, the one on the right. You'll give me a sign, won't you?"

She nodded yes. Justin knelt down by the cot and took her hand between the bars.

"You're so kind," said Elizabeth, yawning. "Where is your mother? And your father?"

"They're both dead. I don't even remember them."

"You must be so sad," said the little girl faintly. "But they are in heaven, with the angels and baby Jesus."

"Yes, of course they are. Go to sleep quickly, so I won't be punished."

Elizabeth closed her eyes, her fingers intertwined with the boy's. Suddenly she was overcome by sleep, a delicious deep sleep that left a cheerful expression on her face.

And that was how Catherine found her, half an hour later. Justin had left no trace of his presence. The young mother stroked her child's round forehead, her silken curls, and pulled the sheets up a little. Then she placed the fireguard in front of the pink-marble fireplace and tiptoed out of the nursery.

I will praise Madeleine tomorrow morning, she thought. *She took good care of my little princess.*

Guillaume was waiting for her, sitting on the edge of the four-poster bed in their room. He was looking with astonishment at the luxurious setting around him.

"This is the third time in five years that I've spent the night in this castle," he remarked to his wife when she entered. "Yet, it still bothers me to think that you grew up among all this beautiful furniture and these expensive tapestries and ornaments. You say you liked our simple home in Montignac, but how will you feel once we get to New York? You won't have a garden anymore, and Elizabeth loves roaming around outside. I hope you won't regret coming with me, my dear. Your father has sown the seed of doubt in me. What if the life I'm offering you there proves to be nothing but miserable?"

Catherine shrugged, laughing, and turned her back to him.

"Instead of talking nonsense, you'd better help me get my dress off, and most importantly, undo my corset. I can't take being squeezed like this any longer."

"Does it hurt the baby?"

"No, but he's been moving around a lot."

Soon Catherine was dressed in a white cambric shirt. She massaged her stomach and sighed with pleasure. Guillaume put his lips to hers, and they shared a long, passionate kiss.

"As long as we're together, I'm happy," she said, catching her breath. "Our children will grow up on American soil, they will become perfect little New Yorkers, and we will make a fortune, by our own means and the force of our love."

Deeply moved by her declaration, Guillaume kissed her again. Catherine was the light of his life.

Less than an hour later, Catherine woke up with a start and shook her husband by the shoulder.

"Guillaume, did you hear that? It was Elizabeth shouting, I'm sure of it. I'm going!"

"What are you saying?" he asked in a muffled voice.

"I think our daughter has had another nightmare. It wouldn't surprise me, given my father's yelling and tonight's storm."

The young woman was already up. She rushed out of the bedroom and up to the nursery, from where loud screams were coming. She found her daughter in tears, panting, and gasping for breath.

"I'm here, my darling. What's wrong?"

"A bad dream, Mummy, I was so scared! And I didn't have my doll."

"Come on, you're coming with me. I should never have let you sleep here."

Guillaume joined them. At once, he picked up the girl, who wrapped her little arms around his neck.

"It's over now, Daddy's here," he reassured her. "I'll bring you to our bed and you'll stay with us, sweetheart. Tell us what you saw, you'll feel better then."

"I can't remember," Elizabeth struggled to express herself. "It was raining hard, and . . . everything was dark."

They walked along the corridor, which was lit by a wall-mounted gas lamp. Catherine was upset.

"I shouldn't have bowed to Mother's will. I should have put our beloved daughter to bed myself, alongside our bed, and not in that icy nursery," she complained quietly.

"Our departure is unsettling her—she's losing her bearings. Cathy, it's normal at her age. She's not able to look forward to it like us," reasoned her husband. "Everything will be fine—don't worry."

At that very moment, Adela Laroche emerged from her room. She cast an irritated glance at all three of them.

"What are you doing? Take the girl back to the nursery! You should have punished her for screaming so loudly!"

"Punish her, Mother?!" said Catherine indignantly. "And you wanted us to leave her here with you? Dear Lord, she's having nightmares—it's hardly her fault."

"Spoiled children do their utmost to attract their parents' attention," preached Adela in a stern voice. "What's that she's holding? It looks like one of my great-uncle's tin soldiers!"

Guillaume glanced at the toy his little girl was clutching and shrugged his shoulders.

"Justin gave it to me," said Elizabeth boldly, sniffing. Nestled in her father's arms, she felt safe; so much so that she added: "Justin is nice."

"Who are you talking about?" asked her grandmother suspiciously. "You're telling lies. I won't tolerate that. There is no one called Justin in this castle."

"Yes, there is. He's a little boy—Madeleine's nephew—and he comforted me."

"Good Lord, what story have you invented, Elizabeth? I am well informed about my servants, and Madeleine has neither brother nor sister, and therefore no nephew. Moreover, there aren't any little boys living under our roof. You're making it up, child. I hope we can all get some sleep now!"

"Mother, do you want the tin soldier back?"

"No—the collection has been incomplete for a long time; your daughter can keep it."

Elizabeth hid her face in Guillaume's neck. He squeezed her tighter, kissing her silky brown hair.

"You mustn't tell lies, my darling," said the young mother. "You must have dreamt about this boy, Justin."

The girl refused to answer. She was well aware of the difference between a dream, a nightmare and the real world. Too bad if her parents didn't believe her. At least she would be able to spend the rest of the night in their bed, safe from harm.

2

The Departure

Le Havre, four days later, at dawn
Tuesday, October 19, 1886

Guillaume helped Catherine off the train before picking Elizabeth up by the waist. The railway line ended at the quayside of the port of Le Havre, a major boarding point for the crossing to New York and other faraway destinations.

"Look, my darlings, the sea!" he cried, pointing to the vast blue expanse with shades of grey, stretching all the way to the horizon. "And all those seagulls in the sky! We can see the four masts of our liner *La Champagne*, which is waiting for high tide."

"Good Lord, how beautiful!" exclaimed an ecstatic Catherine.

Her husband had worked in Brittany and in the vicinity of La Rochelle while touring France with his Carpenters' Guild. He had often described the vastness of the ocean to Catherine— the way its waves, crowned with white foam, crashed down on the rocks or washed over the sand.

"Elizabeth, are you feeling a little better?" asked Guillaume. "Don't worry—you won't have to get back on a train any time soon."

"Yes, Daddy, I'm a little bit better. I'm sorry I was ill."

The couple exchanged a worried glance. They were concerned about their daughter's behaviour. She'd been extremely anxious before boarding the train at Saint-Lazare station.

"I don't want to!" she had kept crying angrily, her eyes wide with inexplicable fright.

Even though they had reassured her and asked her why she was afraid, Elizabeth had clammed up, trembling. Her father had to carry her inside the train compartment while Catherine watched the scene with sadness.

Luckily, our little girl calmed down quite quickly once her head was on my lap, she recalled. *Guillaume is right. It's because her world has been turned upside down. She was used to my father-in-law, her dear Grandpa Toine, and her uncles. She even had to see her youngest uncle—Jean—cry, as we were saying farewell.*

Catherine was roused from her thoughts when her husband gently stroked her cheek.

"We can't stay here, Cathy—we're in the way," he whispered.

There was a crowd around them and a hive of activity. The noise was deafening, amidst people calling out, voices shrieking, and people shouting orders at the top of their lungs. Staff in grey coats were pushing carts overladen with luggage, others noted down the numbers written on large wooden crates.

"Well, we're getting close," said Guillaume. "In a couple of hours, we'll be on the ship's deck. Don't worry, Elizabeth—we're going to have a nice trip. Here in Le Havre we're on the edge of the Channel, but soon we'll be on the ocean, you'll see. There will be big waves, and probably whales and dolphins."

The little girl gave a faint smile. Her father continued:

"We need to get closer to our boarding bridge. Third-class passengers board first, to be registered. We should be able to avoid the health check, thanks to our doctor's certificates."

"What about our trunks?" asked Catherine worriedly.

"Wait for me over here, out of the wind, will you," he said, leading mother and child to a bench next to a wooden warehouse. "I think I should go and find out about the trunk transfer."

As soon as Elizabeth was seated, she sought refuge in her mother's arms. A stench of tar, rusty metal, and rubbish was coming from the warehouse. Seagulls circled over the docks with high-pitched cries.

"Everything will be fine, my darling," said Catherine soothingly, having felt her daughter tremble with nervousness. "Let's not forget that we're adventurers! It's important to observe everything around you and appreciate it."

"Yes, Mummy."

Strangers walked past their bench. Catherine politely greeted the eldest of a group of travellers whose clothes, hats and hairstyles made her think they were Jews on their way to New York. Then another family – three adults and six children – marched by.

But she was feeling weary. She was thinking about the moment she had said goodbye to her parents. She remembered with sadness how her mother had kissed her at least six times, while slipping an envelope of banknotes into her coat pocket, her eyes filled with tears.

Catherine banished the harrowing memory with a stoic movement of her head. Her nostrils expanded to inhale the fresh sea air that was blowing in on the wind, intoxicating her. It overpowered the pungent smell of the docks, just as the gulls' piercing cries drowned out the travellers' voices.

Elizabeth eagerly awaited her father's return. She had experienced a strange sensation when she'd watched him walk away in his grey corduroy suit.

"Why has Daddy left us?" she asked.

"He won't be long," answered her mother. "I'm here to protect you. Are you afraid of crossing the ocean, sweetheart?"

"No, I'm not afraid, I just want Daddy to come back."

"He'll be back in a minute," Catherine assured her.

The girl slipped her hand into the bottom of her coat pocket. She felt the tin soldier and clasped it tightly. She wondered about Justin, who, according to her grandmother, didn't exist. Yet he had given her this toy, proof that she had not dreamt any of it.

Time was running out, and the excitement and clamour were growing on the quayside. Catherine checked the silver watch hidden in her skirt pocket. Guillaume seemed to have been gone a long time already.

She got up from the bench to walk a few steps. Her green eyes took in the four masts and two large funnels of the passenger ship *La Champagne*, launched by the Transatlantic General Company in May of that year.

Sailors were running about on the decks. Catherine saw a great number of people boarding the ship in an unbroken line of bustling figures.

"Where has Guillaume got to?" she muttered to herself, one hand on her heart, feeling its beat getting faster.

She hid her anguish so as not to alarm her daughter. With a glance, she checked that the large leather case containing their basic necessities was still there.

A man in a sailor's uniform, probably a senior officer, came to greet her. He raised his cap, which bore the name of the Transatlantic General Company.

"Would you happen to be a passenger on *La Champagne*, Madam?" he enquired politely.

"Yes, Sir."

"You should make your way to the pier with your child, then. I assume you are booked into a second-class cabin?"

The young woman's refined appearance and speech had deceived him. Modest as she was, she told him the truth at once.

"No, Sir, we're travelling in third class. Thank you for your kindness—but I prefer to wait for my husband. He's gone to take care of our trunks."

"All the luggage has been brought aboard, I believe. If you are in third class, Madam, you'd better hurry up."

The officer then quickly made his way to the dock. Catherine looked all around in vain.

"Come, Elizabeth. Daddy will find us by the boarding bridge."

"But Mummy! We must stay here!"

"You heard the gentleman, darling. We must get ready to board. Daddy will work out where we've gone and join us."

Catherine grabbed the leather case and adjusted the canvas bag on her shoulder that contained their provisions. The wind was getting stronger and stronger and blew a lock of blonde hair out of her hat.

"Give me your hand, Elizabeth, and hold on to me. I don't want you to get pushed."

They finally arrived at the foot of the third-class gangway, after squeezing through the crowd.

Catherine continued to search for her husband, but this was extremely difficult amidst the hordes of people milling around. The men were all wearing the same kind of clothing: a jacket and brown or grey trousers.

Two members of staff were checking the names of the last third-class passengers in a large logbook before allowing them to board.

"Guillaume, please come back," murmured Catherine.

Elizabeth heard her. Small as she was, she couldn't see the faces of those around her, but she carried on looking for her father. Suddenly, there was a loud and deep breathing noise, followed by a rumbling, close behind her. A strange smell wafted over the little girl as she turned.

"Mummy, help me!" she shouted at the top of her voice.

Catherine whirled around and screamed with fright upon catching sight of the bear facing Elizabeth. The animal was sniffing the sea air. There was a ring through its two shiny wet nostrils, and it was connected to a sturdy chain held by the animal's master.

"Don't be afraid, ladies and gentlemen! Garro wouldn't hurt a fly," he exclaimed. "His claws and teeth have been filed down."

The man had a dark complexion and spoke with a gravelly accent. He wore a black hat and had a long moustache, his free hand leaning on a stick.

Awestruck by the spectacle, people moved out of the way, so that the area around the beast and its master was cleared.

"I'm going to entertain the New Yorkers," he shouted to anyone who would listen. "I'm not the first and I won't be the last. One of my brothers left three years ago and makes a good living out of it, so I'm having a stab at it, too."

"Where are you from, Sir?" Catherine asked, holding her daughter close to her.

"From the Ercé valley in the Pyrenees, of course!"

An officer from *La Champagne* pointed a peremptory finger at the mountain dweller. "You'll have to muzzle your bear, my friend, or I can't let you board."

"Aye, aye, Sir. I have the necessary equipment. Don't fret, I took his muzzle off to give him an apple to munch on."

Elizabeth had already seen pictures of bears in books, but the animal's imposing physique made her back away.

"Don't be afraid, little girl!" laughed its handler. "Wait until you see him dancing!"

The incident had distracted Catherine, but she was growing restless again. Her husband's lateness was becoming truly worrying. The bear handler, who was also travelling in third class, stepped onto the boarding bridge, followed by his beast.

"Madam, your tickets!" demanded the clerk in charge of counting the passengers.

She took them out of the inner pocket of her coat. His fingers were shaking.

"Sir, I can't get on board without my husband. He must have been delayed. I beg you, please give me another moment."

"That will be difficult, Madam. We have to open up access to the second-class decks. It'll be high tide in less than two hours."

"I beg you!" insisted Catherine.

The man saw the state she was in and compassionately gave a nod of approval. He was not indifferent to the beauty of this pregnant young woman, nor to the frightened face of the dark-haired child next to her.

"Five minutes, no more," he retorted.

"Thank you, Sir, thank you!"

Elizabeth scanned the teeming crowd of strangers gathered along the quayside. Judging by their style and elegance, most of them were wealthy, but she soon lost interest in them. Just then someone came round the corner of the warehouse.

"Daddy! Over there! Mummy, it's Daddy!"

"There he is! Thank God!" exclaimed Catherine.

But her relief was short-lived. Guillaume was staggering towards them as if he were drunk. His jacket sleeve was torn, as was his shirt collar, and his face was covered in blood. Elizabeth let out a stifled wail.

"Daddy's bleeding, Mummy! Look, he's bleeding!"

Catherine ran to her husband. Instinctively, she kept one hand on her belly, as if to protect her unborn child.

"Guillaume, what on earth has happened to you?!"

The carpenter was panting and bent over. She saw that he had nasty bluish bruises on his forehead and chin; his lower lip was split and his nose was bleeding.

"Good God, you've been in a fight!" she said, alarmed.

"No, Cathy—I was beaten up! Some fellows jumped on me from behind. They were after my wallet, and also robbed me of my father's pocket watch, my wedding ring, and the gold medal my brother gave me last month. I did my best to defend myself, but three against one, I couldn't win!"

"Guillaume, my love," she whispered. "I'm so sorry you lost your family mementoes, but we have to board immediately. I'll tend to you when we're settled in. I feared that there might have been an accident, but you are here now, that's all that matters."

"I didn't have time to clean myself up. I hope my appearance won't scare Elizabeth."

"No, we'll talk to her. Come quickly! How fortunate that I had the travel tickets with me, or they would have stolen them as well."

Catherine managed a smile through her tears. Guillaume grinned painfully; his assailants had also punched him in the stomach and the ribs. And yet, he was joyful at the thought of boarding, and did his best to forget his inner torment.

On the deck of La Champagne
Two hours later

The ship's siren resounded, followed by shouts and yells from all directions. Plumes of smoke rose from the liner's funnels. Many passengers were standing on the large deck, leaning against the rail, some hoping to catch a last glimpse of a friend or relative.

A smaller crowd of people were walking along the dock, waving white handkerchiefs. Farewells and goodbyes were flying thick and fast. Travellers and those on the dock were weeping, smiling and calling out to each other.

"Nobody has come to see us off!" moaned Elizabeth.

She glanced up at her parents, who were standing beside her, locked in an embrace. They smiled at her sweetly.

"No, because all three of us are leaving," replied Catherine.

"Why didn't Pops Toine and Uncle Jean come, then?"

"The train journey to Le Havre would have been too expensive for them," explained Guillaume.

Elizabeth sighed. She would have liked to be enthusiastic about the trip, but something was weighing her down. Aside from that, she could hardly bring herself to look at her father's face, which was covered in blood.

A young sailor walked by and smiled at her cheerfully as he adjusted his white beret.

"So, Miss," he said, "it looks like we're going to discover America, aboard the 'Lord of the Seas', as the Captain calls it! It's my first long voyage too."

"'The Lord of the Seas'—that has a nice ring to it," Catherine remarked, exhilarated at the thought of setting sail.

The sailor saluted her and moved on. A modestly dressed man also came up to the couple.

"You've got to admit, this is a pretty impressive ship," he said, holding his hand out to Guillaume. "Hey, you look like someone beat the living daylights out of you!"

"I'm afraid so. I was robbed on the docks, near the warehouses."

"Bah, that happens a lot, in the hustle and bustle of boarding, between the train and the docks. You need your wits about you. Could have been worse, though," said the stranger.

"A rail worker turned up, and the thugs took off. But it left me in quite a daze. Any worse, and we couldn't have boarded."

The vessel was about to set sail for the vast ocean, and Catherine had hoped to share this special moment with just her husband and daughter. Unfortunately for her, the stranger seemed eager to chat.

"The company wouldn't even have reimbursed you," he said. "It would have been a real pity to miss the departure. You do realize that we are standing on a 6,726-ton ship with a 9,000-horsepower steam engine? Apparently, it can carry more than a thousand passengers and two hundred crew members. I've been doing some research."

La Champagne raised anchor, and the heavy vessel shuddered throughout. In the distance, the horizon was a blurry mass of sky, water and bluish-green haze.

Catherine took her husband and daughter further along near the ship's bow, and laughed cheerfully.

"I'm so happy! Guillaume, we're finally on our way. Elizabeth, darling, look at the seagulls! They're as free as we are."

Seagulls were diving over the deck, zigzagging between the four masts. The deafening noise of the engines caused a stir on the dock, as the ship's enormous hull pulled away.

"And in ten days' time, we'll see New York and the famous Statue of Liberty," said Guillaume excitedly. "Elizabeth, my princess, say goodbye to your homeland!"

"But how, Daddy?" replied the child, fascinated by the thumping of the waves against the ship's gigantic flank.

"You can wave goodbye with your hand!"

She hastened to obey, and her bright-blue eyes strayed towards the docks, which were slowly disappearing, the figures growing smaller and smaller. Full steam ahead, *La Champagne* thrust itself into the vast Atlantic Ocean.

Guillaume hugged his wife and daughter. He felt confident and hopeful: they were about to embark on their new life.

The passengers gradually left the deck. Depending on their social status, some were headed for first class, others for second. Catherine was delaying the moment when they would have to climb down to the lower level, reserved for the poorest travellers. The ship's crew were busy all over the ship, working in synchrony.

"Let's find our berths," whispered Guillaume. "Then we can clean ourselves up a bit, especially me."

Catherine nodded. She wasn't going to falter now, well aware that her husband was trying hard to put on a brave face, despite the bitterness he was feeling. Though he didn't complain, the loss of his watch and his gold Saint Christopher had shaken him.

"You, you're the epitome of goodness," she whispered in his ear. "It's so unfair, what they did to you."

"Who knows? Perhaps it was a sign that we shouldn't leave," he replied softly. "My dearest Cathy, you were born with a silver spoon in your mouth, as my father used to say when he was teasing you. Because of me, you had to give up all your privileges. We could have travelled in second class, but it would have taken all our savings."

"I won't let you blame yourself, Guillaume. We made all our decisions jointly. We're in this together, for as long as we live. Now, let's go downstairs."

Elizabeth was still gazing at the port of Le Havre and the church towers in the distance.

"Mummy, I want my doll," she said, overcome by a sudden urge to hold her toy.

"Be patient, my darling," Catherine said kindly. "We need to get settled in first. Daddy will pick up our trunks later."

With dismay, the couple examined the third-class dormitory in which their berths were located. It could only be reached via a steep staircase with slippery steps.

An alarming kerfuffle was going on. Dozens of passengers were moving around and yelling at each other in the smoke-filled atmosphere. The women were unfolding blankets and unpacking their luggage. The cries of children and babies could be heard amidst the din.

A pungent smell of unwashed bodies and sweat emanated from the mass of passengers crammed in there, below the ship's waterline.

"It's poorly ventilated down here," murmured Catherine, whose delicate sense of smell was troubled by the human stench.

They could feel the deck beneath their feet vibrating with the ship's heaving machinery. It was almost as if the vessel was being rocked by roaring monsters. Elizabeth sought refuge in her mother's skirts.

"Come along," said Guillaume.

The narrow iron bunks, which took up every available space, looked very uncomfortable. They all looked occupied already. Elizabeth clung to her father's hand.

"Don't be afraid, my darling," he said firmly. "It's the turmoil of the ship's departure, that's all. Things will calm down soon, and then we'll have our own little corner."

"I really hope so," said Catherine, alarmed. "I'm getting tired."

"You will soon be able to rest," he promised.

They had huddled together to hear each other better over the background noise and commotion.

A woman called out to them in a raspy voice, gesturing for them to move aside:

"Hey lovebirds, don't block up the gangway! I need to go to the conveniences. My goodness, there are only two of them for one hundred people in these quarters! I don't want to miss supper time, either!"

Catherine stepped back so hastily that she hit her back against a large metal post. Guillaume saw her wincing with pain.

"Cathy, my darling, are you hurt?" he asked, hugging her.

"No, no. Please, let's find our bunks, I need to lie down. Then you can find out where to get water, as I can't clean you up otherwise."

After a tedious search, Guillaume finally identified their bunks. He picked up Elizabeth and sat her down on the top bunk.

"You won't be jostled up here," he said, stroking her hair. "Now, let me go and get your doll."

"I'd rather go back outside, Daddy. It smells horrible in here."

"We'll go back up to the deck later, but right now your poor mummy is tired. Be a good girl."

Elizabeth lay down in a foetal position on the brown blanket. From her pocket she took the tin soldier that her friend Justin had given her and held it tightly. She was exhausted from the train journey and the excitement of the morning and dozed off in no time.

As for Catherine, she pretended to be asleep to avoid the curious glances of her neighbours. Guillaume, who had gone in search of a water point, had been careful to hide the large leather case under the bottom bunk.

"Hey, pretty lady, it's not wise to travel in your condition," shouted a voice.

Catherine was startled. She blinked and saw a grim, ruddy face staring at her.

"Excuse me, Madam, I fell asleep," she claimed.

"If you can snooze in this bedlam, then good for you. The ship isn't pitching too much at the moment. But once we're on the high seas, we'll be shaken like plums on a tree. Where are you from?"

"Charente."

"Uh, I don't know where that is. Me and my man, we left Valence with our four little ones. They closed the pit down, so we decided to try our luck in America. I'm Colette, but you can call me Coco."

"Catherine Duquesne."

Colette, a red-headed and busty woman, was rummaging through a wicker trunk. She grabbed a black bodice, put it back in the trunk and then took out a woollen knit.

"I'm freezing, aren't you?"

"No, I've kept my coat on, it's so cold."

"Your husband has been in the wars, hasn't he! Was he fighting?"

"He was attacked and robbed, shortly before our departure, at the warehouses on the dock," explained Catherine as she sat up.

"That's really unfortunate, my pretty lady," sighed the woman, looking sorrowful.

"Where are your children, Madam?" enquired Catherine, trying to make polite conversation.

"I sent them up on the deck, my husband too, to get a moment's peace," laughed Colette.

Guillaume came back holding a small bucket of water. Catherine immediately straightened up, greeting her husband with a massive smile.

"Sit down, I'm finally going to be able to nurse you. Grab our bag, I have everything we need. This is our neighbour, Colette. Madam, my husband, Guillaume."

The carpenter greeted her amicably enough, although inwardly he was already hating the overcrowded, squalid conditions where drudgery, gossip, fighting and appalling sanitary conditions appeared to be the norm.

Sullen-faced, he let Catherine clean his wounds and apply a comfrey balm to them.

"I'm going to start sewing," she announced. "Remove your jacket, please."

"There's no hurry," he sighed. "You look very pale. Lie down."

Colette had moved away. Guillaume took advantage of this and kissed his wife on the lips, then gazed at her tenderly.

"My beautiful wife," he said. "It makes me sad to see you in the middle of this mayhem."

"Why?" she asked calmly. "Because I was born in a castle? Guillaume, I love you. I proved my love for you by following you to Montignac and marrying you, and I wouldn't let you sell our little home, because of all the wonderful memories I have there.

Your brothers will rent it out and it will give them a small income, but it's still ours."

"But who cares? We have no intention of returning to France! That money would have kept you away from this squalor, these people, their cries and smells. It stinks in here."

"Ten days, Guillaume—the journey only lasts ten days, according to the shipping company," said Catherine. "We're together, and we'll ensure Elizabeth doesn't come to any harm. Please stop worrying and give me your jacket. I don't want a scruffy husband."

An hour later, Catherine was reliving the same drama she had endured on the docks: her husband had gone to seek their two trunks and had not returned. During that time, she had been able to sleep for twenty minutes, nibble a slice of bread from her bag, and repair the jacket.

"Do you know where they store the luggage?" she asked her neighbour Colette, who was changing a small boy's soiled vest.

"Not far away, my dear—the room next to the refectory. See, my man brought mine to me right away."

The woman pointed with her chin at the wicker trunk near her bed.

"Which was lucky, since I've gotta slip a fresh vest onto this little squirt. He's my youngest, Paul—three years old. My eldest, who's ten, brought him downstairs. The poor thing had thrown up. They say it's quite rough up there on deck."

"Even down here you can feel the waves rolling," Catherine remarked. "I had no idea you could get seasick on such a big ship. My daughter hasn't noticed anything. She's sleeping well, I'm glad to say."

"She won't sleep a wink tonight, though," replied Colette. "Right, young lady, I'll take this lad to the conveniences, otherwise it'll be his trousers he fills next."

Watching Colette through the maze of beds, Catherine caught Guillaume's gaze as he returned. He looked desperate, and his swollen face didn't help. She waited, sitting on the bunk.

"Cathy, fate must be against us," he declared, sitting down beside her. "I had to ask to see the Captain."

"Why?"

"Our trunks have disappeared. They can't be found anywhere. A member of staff helped me search for them, and he thought there'd been a mistake. But no, our luggage has gone astray somewhere between the train and the ship's hold. We'll arrive in New York with nothing. In your trunk were your clothes and Elizabeth's, and the baby's layette. In my trunk were my carpenter's tools engraved with my name, my work clothes, our books, and the little one's doll."

The news left Catherine speechless. Her husband took her hand.

"The Captain is aware of the situation. He apologized and said such problems only rarely occur."

"But what are we going to do?" she asked indignantly. "The company should pay us compensation. Are we the only ones this has happened to?"

"Maybe not—I'll find out tonight."

"Thank God we still have the leather case. I put some clothes in it for Elizabeth, a few sewing items, and our identity papers."

"I just don't understand it," said Guillaume, dismayed. "I wanted to tell you before going back up to have another look. The ship is huge; maybe they placed our trunks in a second-class cabin."

"No, please—don't go back up again. I'm sick of being alone. The people have calmed down a bit now, but I don't feel safe here without you." In hushed tones, she pointed out that some of the passengers looked shady. "You should eat something, Guillaume—you haven't had a bite to eat since this morning. I can give you some bread, cheese, or an apple?"

"I'm thirsty more than anything, Cathy. A man advised me not to drink the water from the cistern. He travelled on another liner two years ago and nearly died of dysentery. Sanitation is not a priority in third class."

Catherine remained silent. She handed him an enamelled mug into which she poured the last water from a bottle.

"I brought some sweet tea with us," she whispered. "After that, we'll have to drink the ship's water."

"Lord, I had no idea we'd have this much trouble! I hope Elizabeth doesn't get ill," said Guillaume, worried.

"None of us will get ill," said the young woman determinedly. "We simply have to be practical. Too bad about our trunks—I can sew, I'll make us a whole set of new clothes when we get to America."

"And my tools?"

"We'll get you a new kit with the money my mother gave us. Thank goodness I accepted it! I know you didn't want my family's help, but there comes a point where you have to swallow your pride. We no longer have a choice. I have enough to see us through a few weeks in New York. As for the baby's clothes, I'll work something out. And if we lack anything, I'm sure that some kind souls will help us out during the journey."

She smiled confidently, but Guillaume perceived a twinge of sorrow in her dulcet tones. It made him admire her all the more.

"You're the most extraordinary woman in the world," he said, kissing her.

Elizabeth had heard every word. She had been awake for a good quarter of an hour. Happy to hear her father's voice, she was about to lean towards him when he mentioned the disappearance of the trunks.

What about my doll? she thought, ready to burst into tears. *Pops Toine wouldn't be happy to hear that I'd lost her.*

She stifled her wailing, but Catherine's ears pricked up, and she gestured to her husband to get up.

"We need to talk to her, Guillaume. She hasn't been herself for three weeks now. I should have put her dolly in the leather case."

Two small feet clad in woollen socks appeared on the edge of the top bunk.

"Mummy, Daddy, I want to get down," she called out. "Can you pick me up, Daddy?"

"Of course, my princess!"

Her arms wrapped around her father's neck. She felt secure at once. Guillaume covered her face with kisses.

"I'm afraid we have some bad news, my precious one," he whispered in her ear. "Our trunks have disappeared."

"I know, Daddy."

"You will be sad without your doll, but we'll soon be able to buy you another one, when we get to America."

"Or I could even make one right here on the boat," added Catherine brightly. "Pops Toine made yours from wood and pieces of fabric—I can do the same."

"Would you really, Mummy? I love you very much!"

"We love you too, darling," said her parents in unison, and all three of them laughed.

A faint snatch of music echoed their cheerfulness. Someone was playing the violin. At first, everyone grew quiet, but soon the chatter resumed, mingled with the squealing voices of children and the crying of babies.

People were to-ing and fro-ing, climbing up to their bunks, jostling and shoving each other. The dull rumbling of the engines at the bottom of the hold barely drowned out the continuous hullabaloo of a hundred people, many of whom were fretting or vomiting.

"I wonder where the bear handler is," remarked Catherine.

"Not in this part of the steerage," replied her husband. "I've been told there are over a thousand passengers, Cathy, not to mention the crew. And more than five hundred of us in steerage."

"Good Lord—we'll never get acquainted with everyone!"

"Mummy, when are you going to make my new doll?"

"How about right now, darling? It'll force me to stay seated," said the young woman. "I have to warn you though—it will be small, very small."

The little girl nodded happily. Her parents looked at each other with relief. Elizabeth seemed to have recovered and was calm and composed, ready to cope with the trials and tribulations of the crossing.

On the deck of La Champagne
The following morning

Guillaume put his hand on Catherine's shoulder, as they watched the sea in awe. The sheer vastness of the ocean stretched out before them all the way to the horizon. Though his face still bore purplish bruises from the blows he had received, his gloomy gaze revealed a glimmer of pride. In spite of the bad luck they had suffered, he was beaming with joy at being on board the liner.

"We made it, Cathy darling," he said affectionately. "Elizabeth slept like an angel last night."

"Yes, what a relief," agreed his wife. "Her new doll must have something to do with it."

They laughed quietly as they watched their daughter playing with Colette's little boy, Paul. Their neighbour was sitting on a wooden stool, knitting. The two children were happily throwing a ball to each other.

Guillaume had prudently tied it to a string, which in turn was tied around the railing.

"This will stop it falling into the sea," he'd explained. "If you lose it, we'll have little chance of finding another one."

The weather was clear, with a pale-blue sky. Exhilarated by the sea air, Catherine was enjoying the warmth of the sun on her fair skin.

"Wouldn't it be wonderful if we could sleep on the deck?" she said. "When I woke up this morning, the stench of vomit was unbearable. I couldn't help feeling nauseous, too. We should stay up on deck as much as we can. The weather is good and the sea is calm, so let's make the most of it."

A man came up beside them. He was quite young and was wearing a tweed cap.

"We shouldn't crow too soon," he declared as he lit his pipe. "*La Champagne* will be navigating colder waters from tomorrow, which could mean heavy squalls."

"Squalls?" repeated Catherine with surprise. "What are they?"

"Heavy rain and strong winds arriving unexpectedly at the same time," explained the stranger. "But I can assure you, Madam, that this sort of vessel has nothing to fear. I couldn't help overhearing you mention the stench down there, in third class. We mustn't forget that it's not as bad as it used to be. Only a few decades back, the ships carrying emigrants were known as 'coffin ships'."

The young man lifted his cap to them and continued his stroll. Elizabeth had stopped playing. Paul was waiting for her to throw the ball, but she held it tightly between her hands before abruptly dropping it and running to her parents, seeking refuge in her mother's skirt.

"What's the matter, princess?" asked Guillaume. "Be nice to your little friend, he's waiting for you."

"I don't want to play anymore, Daddy. I'd rather go for a walk."

"All right, let's take a walk together," he said.

Paul had picked up the ball and was throwing it up in the air, under his mother's puzzled gaze.

"Don't worry, little lad. Girls can be fickle," she said loudly as she carried on knitting.

Catherine, sitting by herself, thought she should apologize for her daughter's attitude.

"I'm sorry, Colette—Elizabeth is unhappy about leaving. It's not easy for her. She's been uprooted from her home, from the people she grew up with, her grandfather and her uncles. We also had to give our cat to a neighbour."

The woman shrugged her sturdy shoulders. She wondered what the pretty Catherine, with her upper-class accent, was doing travelling in third class.

"Good heavens, I'm not offended! We can't stand on ceremony for things like that. Nippers, you never know what's going on in their heads! And please call me Coco, as I told you before."

Catherine nodded her head and smiled, but resolved to stick to "Colette", "Coco" being too familiar for her liking.

She turned to look at the vast expanse of the ocean, carved in two by the ship's bow. Towering waves appeared to be galloping away from the horizon that *La Champagne* was approaching at a brisk pace.

"New York, America . . ." she muttered dreamily. "I can't wait to get there, even though it'll be tough when we arrive."

She'd been dwelling on the impending difficulties, such as the language (though she did speak a little English), and where they would live. It certainly wouldn't be as comfortable as their little home with a garden in Montignac.

I'll be alone all day and I won't have the help of my sister-in-law when the baby is born, so I'll have to take care of it and my little princess by myself.

Her thoughts drifted towards gentle Yvonne, the wife of Guillaume's eldest brother Pierre. Yvonne had been a huge help to her when Elizabeth was born, and during the first few months afterwards.

"I say, pretty lady," said Colette, glancing at her, "you must be worried about what's happened to your trunks. I suppose the layette was ready for the little one?"

"Yes, it was. I'd spent all summer working on it, with my sister-in-law," replied Catherine, turning to face her. "I'll have to start all over again. I have no choice."

"That's such a shame! But, as long as you've got your health and a few pennies set aside . . . I suppose you'll have to go shopping once we're ashore."

"Yes, but my husband has been hit the hardest. He's lost all his tools."

The trunks did not turn up, despite the crew's efforts. Guillaume was trying hard to put on a brave face, but Catherine sensed how bitter and disappointed he was.

By the time they returned below deck, night had fallen. It was relatively calm in the dormitory. The children had been put to bed early, as soon as they had devoured the meagre meals handed out by the Transatlantic Company, and were already asleep.

A rumour was circulating that there were in fact nine hundred people in steerage, and not five hundred, as declared by the Captain.

Catherine couldn't fall asleep. The ship resounded with almost unbearable noises. The rumbling of the machines beneath their feet made her nervous, and from the multitude of people around her came sighs, whispers, snoring and coughing. Finally, further away, above their heads, they could hear quick footsteps, cries, and even some music from afar. The young woman imagined the first-class travellers dancing in the large and lavishly decorated lounge after a gourmet dinner. She wasn't envious, just annoyed.

When will all this change? she wondered. *People are treated according to their financial resources. The poor suffer from hunger and lack of sanitation, as if it were their destiny, and the wealthy don't care and make merry, as if entitled to privilege and glory.*

Her principles and her loathing of any form of injustice had prompted Catherine to embark on a new life, and she was proud and happy to have married for love, despite the virulent protests of her parents.

"Farewell, my childhood castle, farewell to my family's contempt for Guillaume, farewell to the Old Continent," she muttered under her breath.

Catherine felt comforted by the sound of her husband's steady breathing, as he lay on the bunk next to her own. She felt an urge to touch him, to make sure he was really there.

Just then a whine followed by a high-pitched scream interrupted her thoughts.

"Mummy! Mummy!" sobbed Elizabeth.

The little girl was tossing and turning, causing the mesh bunk base above Catherine to grind and creak. She jumped up.

"My darling, I'm here, everything's all right," she whispered. "Shh, don't shout so loudly." The little girl was breathless from crying. Her trembling hands clung to her mother's neck.

"I'm scared, Mummy, I'm so scared," she wept.

"There, there. Come down, my darling. You can sleep with me tonight."

"Damn it, when will this bloody noise stop!" yelled Colette's husband, furious. "She needs a good hiding, then she'll stop whimpering."

"Excuse us, Sir," muttered Guillaume, whom Elizabeth's screams had also awakened. "Our daughter has been suffering from nightmares recently."

The man grumbled an insult and then said no more. Catherine, whose heart was pounding, stroked her daughter's forehead.

"What is it that makes you so afraid, my darling?" she sighed softly. "Lord, if I only knew."

3

In the Middle of the Ocean

On board La Champagne
Friday, October 22, 1886

The fourth day of their journey was about to begin. The weather was mild, but the waves were rough, and an icy wind prevailed. Sailors were handing out extra buckets to third-class passengers, many of whom were suffering with seasickness.

The stench in the dormitories was unbearable.

"Let's spend the day outside," said Catherine to her husband. "I don't understand how some people can stay locked up in here, from sunrise to sunset."

Barely awake, the young woman was desperate to groom and wash herself. She brushed her hair while Guillaume went to fetch her some water.

How lucky I was, to be given a bowl, she thought. *It makes washing Elizabeth and myself so much easier.*

An old Jewish lady had given it to her. The unfortunate woman had been bedridden ever since the ship's departure, suffering from chest pains.

"One of your neighbours, who calls herself Coco, told me you've lost your trunks," the elderly woman had said. "I thought I would need the bowl, but I don't have the strength to use it anymore. My daughter-in-law is doing her best to take care of me."

The kind octogenarian was called Rachel Bassan. The woman's extreme pallor did not bode well.

"You're expecting a child!" she had said ecstatically. "A gift from God. I'd also love to meet your little girl; I hear she's adorable."

Before long, the two women had become engaged in a lively discussion, ignoring the shouting and swearing of a group of men playing cards nearby.

As time went on, all of the passengers had gradually became acquainted, whether by instant affinity or chance meeting. And those who were incompatible sought to avoid one other, nipping quarrels in the bud.

"I'll take Elizabeth up on deck as soon as she's ready," said Guillaume, looking up.

Their daughter had woken up from yet another nightmare, covered in sweat and tears.

"I'm hardly surprised," said Catherine. "Food is in short supply and it's poor-quality stuff. People are complaining and keep getting up to be sick. How can Elizabeth get a good night's sleep in such conditions?"

"But darling, she's not the only child on the ship. Colette's sons and many other children are sound asleep," replied her husband. "We both know that her nightmares began in Montignac, before the dinner at your parents'. I wonder what's wrong with her . . ."

The couple looked at each other in sorrow. The village doctor they had consulted just a week before their departure had said their daughter was perfectly healthy. "It's her age," he had said, smiling. "It will pass. Give her lime blossom or chamomile tea to drink, make sure she is very active during the day, and she'll soon be as right as rain."

These words of comfort were whirling round in Catherine's head. She had followed the doctor's advice, but the herbal infusions he had recommended hadn't had the desired effect.

"It doesn't matter if we're cramped, tonight she's going to sleep by my side," Catherine announced.

"As you wish. But right now, our princess is catching up on her sleep. I have noticed she sleeps better in the morning," remarked Guillaume. "Let me try to get you a cup of hot coffee in the meantime."

"Thank you, my love," she whispered in his ear, giving him a quick peck on the cheek, for the sake of modesty. They couldn't so much as think of intimacy until they reached America. As if to prove this point, Colette returned from the refectory at that very moment.

"Oh, my goodness, can you believe such a thing!" she wailed, her hands clasped together in front of her ample bosom. "That poor woman! What a shame!"

"Who are you talking about, Colette?" asked Guillaume, puzzled.

"Why, that poor lady Rachel, who gave you her pretty enamelled bowl. She's dead now! Passed away at sunrise, her eldest son David said."

"Good Lord, she was so nice and kind," sighed Catherine. "I was planning to visit her with Elizabeth at noon. I'd told her to call the ship's doctor."

"I hear her heart gave out," sighed Colette. "And to think, she was eighty-two years old. She wanted to emigrate with her family. I must get back—I offered to wash her."

Shocked, Guillaume stood up. He had met David Bassan several times on deck and rather liked him.

"What will happen next?" he wondered aloud. "We won't touch land for another six days."

"The Captain must go down and talk to these poor people, but don't you see what must happen, Mr. Duquesne?"

Shocked, Catherine took a small vial of cologne from her bag and moistened a handkerchief with it. She breathed in the scent, eyes half shut.

"Mummy!"

The young woman gathered herself upon hearing her daughter's voice. Guillaume grabbed Elizabeth from the top bunk and brought her down. Dressed in a nightgown, with her messy dark hair, the child looked exquisite. She stared at her mother with her bright-blue eyes.

"Mummy, it smells good now."

"Come to Mummy," Catherine beckoned. "Where is your doll? Have you left her all by herself?"

"Yes, Mummy, she's resting."

Colette nodded to Guillaume before leaving. He followed her at a brisk pace.

"Why is Daddy going?"

"He'll be back very soon, my princess. I need a big hug right now."

Elizabeth didn't need to be asked twice. She hugged and cuddled her mother and they rubbed cheeks, revelling in tenderness and kisses, as they had done every morning in Montignac. Just feeling her daughter's soft, warm arms gave Catherine courage, and she told herself not to think about the deceased old lady with the angelic smile.

"Elizabeth darling, I am going to style your hair and dress you, so we can take a stroll along the deck. It's important to get some sea air and exercise. Daddy is busy. He will join us later. I still have some cinnamon biscuits left—let me give you one with some water."

"I'd rather drink milk, Mummy."

"We'll find some, I promise. I'll buy you a can of condensed milk—they sell it in the refectory."

Familiar routines were a comfort to Catherine. She brushed her daughter's silky curls, which naturally turned into ringlets at the ends, and tied a blue scarf over her hair.

"Otherwise you won't see a thing if it's windy," she laughed. "Put your woollen coat on and get your doll. Oh, so you hid it under your pillow, you cheeky monkey!"

Elizabeth cherished her new doll that had been skilfully and lovingly crafted by her mother, just as she did the tin soldier from Justin. To fashion the doll, Catherine had had to sacrifice three of her husband's large linen handkerchiefs from the bottom of the leather case. They had enabled her to create a rather appealing figure; as for the face, all she had to do was embroider eyes and a mouth, using coloured threads. For the doll's hair, the young woman had had no qualms about cutting the fringes off her shawl.

"You haven't given your doll a name yet, have you?"

"I wanted to wait," replied the child dreamily. "Maybe I'll call her Cathy, after you. I like it when Daddy calls you Cathy."

"Why not?" replied her mother.

A few minutes later, they were climbing up endless steep and slippery steps. Sea spray was blowing into the steerage, which was already drenched, and the climb was treacherous if you didn't cling tightly to the banister.

Catherine had to stop for a moment, one hand on her belly. The baby was moving a lot. She was almost relieved, as it had not made its presence felt the previous day.

"Are you in pain, Mummy?" asked Elizabeth.

"No, my princess. It's nothing. We need to hurry."

The sky was bright blue, dotted with snow-white clouds. Massive waves crashed along the ship's majestic black hull. Catherine marvelled at the turquoise hues of the ocean.

"I never tire of looking at the sea," she sighed. "I don't think I've ever seen anything so beautiful!"

She held her pretty face up into the offshore wind, making the loose blonde tendrils of her hair flutter.

"Daddy said that we would see whales," exclaimed Elizabeth. "But there aren't any."

"Be patient, my darling."

The young woman turned to observe the crowd standing about thirty feet away. A sailor in a dark-blue pea jacket and cap was moving around in the background. It was then that she spotted the reddish-brown body behind the people who had gathered.

"It looks like the mountain bear is out," she said to her daughter. "Shall we get nearer? Or are you afraid of it?"

"No, I'm not afraid of him, Mummy. Nor of the man with the big black hat."

"Oh, good. I was wondering if the bear had caused your nightmare last night."

Elizabeth shook her head. She was unable to tell her parents what her nightmares were about. The images that made her scream with terror at night were often just a confused blur when she woke up. She would wake up feeling sad, without knowing what she had dreamt.

A voice with a gravelly accent rang out. The Pyrenean bear handler was lashing out at the sailor.

"What do you mean, my animal can't dance? People need cheering up around here! Even first-class folk are eager to see Garro perform."

The bear handler twirled his iron stick towards the upper-deck gangways, where rich passengers were watching the scene from the terrace of one of the lounges. Catherine took in the extravagant jewellery, sumptuous fabrics, and hats decorated with fine feathers.

"The Captain is the sole commander of the ship, mate," insisted the young sailor. "He doesn't care for any entertainment this morning. We've had a fatality, with all the problems it entails—do you understand?"

The bear then suddenly stood up on his hind legs. Properly muzzled, he began to swing, lifting one foot and then the other.

"As you can see for yourself," shouted the hillbilly, "Garro needs to stretch his legs."

A woman burst out laughing, and a small child whistled. A few coins were thrown at the animal, which feigned a bow of gratitude. Catherine watched, pitying the submissive beast.

"Cathy, my love, you're here! I've been looking for you."

Guillaume slipped his arm around his wife's waist. As Elizabeth seemed enraptured by the animal's performance, the couple stepped aside.

"Oh God, Cathy! I was with Rachel Bassan's family. They're praying at her bedside. A service will be held tonight," he whispered in her ear. "It's dreadful! They're going to follow maritime tradition, wrap her body in a shroud and toss it into the sea."

"Good heavens, that's monstrous!" she muttered.

"The Captain says he has no choice, as the cause of death is unknown. He fears an epidemic that could spread—after all, we're in the middle of the ocean."

Gripped by fear, Catherine crossed herself. Guillaume pulled her closer and kissed her.

"I'll put in an appearance," he said, "and you must stay in the dormitory with Elizabeth. She's so nervous these days, we have to handle her very carefully."

Elizabeth ran towards her parents with lifted spirits, holding her doll.

"Garro is going to perform tomorrow evening, too!" she shouted. "We will go and watch him, won't we, Mummy? There will be music, too."

"Of course we'll go, my darling. Now Daddy will try to find you some fresh milk and bread," said Catherine affectionately, making it clear she wanted to go to Rachel Bassan's bedside herself and that Guillaume would stay with Elizabeth. Catherine hurried back down to their dormitory, which was a hive of activity, as usual. But once she got closer to the Jewish family's berths, she was struck by the silence, which was only interrupted by people murmuring prayers that sounded like sad litanies.

As she stepped forward, she glimpsed the old lady's body. She was wrapped in a sheet; only her sallow face was visible. Her sons, their wives, and two children stood next to her bunk.

I am not of their faith, thought Catherine. *I barely knew this unfortunate woman. I hope my presence doesn't embarrass them.*

Yet, she lingered, quietly reciting the Lord's Prayer. With a heavy heart she wiped away a tear, not daring to approach further.

On board La Champagne
The same day, in the evening

Guillaume could not take his eyes off the dark waves that had just swallowed the sad oblong package. The currents were pounding against the hull, and the moon was gleaming in the sky, as it did every evening. But tonight, a body had been cast into the ocean, sewn into a thick cloth shroud and held down with cast-iron weights.

The Captain was still standing to attention, one hand level with his gold-braided cap. Some of the crew members had attended the short and gruelling service, under the yellow glare of the oil lamps.

David Bassan nodded to the Captain with due respect, but like the young carpenter, he was also staring into the murky waters. This was where his mother would rest—a random point in the middle of the Atlantic Ocean. They would never share a single day in the New World.

A grave-faced Colette and her husband Jacques came to lean against the rail. Catherine was looking after their two sons.

"I wouldn't want to end up like that," murmured Colette. "Gives me chills all down my spine."

"Yeah, feeding the fish doesn't do a lot for me," added her husband, in his Northern drawl. "There was no way around it, though. Maritime law—I spoke to a sailor. But I've got to say, you have to watch your tongue here!"

The former miner winced, revealing the pitiful state of his teeth, and added:

"I made the mistake of telling him that I bred rabbits down there, in Valence. Apparently, it's forbidden to say the word 'rabbit' on board, or 'hare', or 'rope', or 'string'. And above all, Mr. Duquesne, never harm a seagull! Those birds are said to be the souls of drowned men."

"Bah, no such danger!" snarled Colette. "You don't see any seagulls on the high seas."

Guillaume stepped away, nodding in approval, pretending to be interested in their conversation. He was impatient to be reunited with Catherine and to kiss Elizabeth, who undoubtedly was already asleep.

Thank goodness the ship is fairly new; the company has invested in certain things, he thought to himself. *I wouldn't want my two princesses to travel on an emigrant ship that has been in service for twenty years already.*

Their dormitory was practically deserted, as most of the passengers were in the refectory. Catherine was lying down, telling Paul a story.

"Elizabeth fell asleep as soon as she'd finished her bowl of soup," she explained. "Paul is being good, but his brother is scampering around somewhere, despite me telling him not to go off."

"He's probably just hanging about near the galley, don't worry. Leonard is a big boy of ten, don't forget that," said Guillaume. "His parents won't be long. Have you eaten, Cathy?"

"Yes, some soup, like Elizabeth. I've brought you your serving, with a slice of bread."

Catherine could see from her husband's gloomy face that he was trying to contain his emotions. She did not question him; they would talk later. She took his hand tenderly, and Guillaume sat next to her. Little Paul, perched on the opposite berth, was sucking his thumb, eager to hear the end of the story.

"I'll read the rest to you tomorrow," Catherine promised. "I'm only halfway through, and Guillaume is here now. You should lie down a little and get some much-needed rest."

Catherine's sweet voice worked wonders on young children, as did her pretty face. Paul obeyed her at once.

"He's an adorable little boy," she admitted. "I hope to give you a son this time, with dark eyes and hair, like yours."

"I'd rather he had your golden hair and green eyes. Elizabeth inherited my father's ocean-blue eyes—a stroke of luck."

"How poetic you sound, my darling. 'Ocean-blue eyes'— that's so pretty," she whispered in his ear. "One thing is sure— our baby likes the pitching of the ship."

"Imagine him getting seasick," joked Guillaume. "His beautiful mother hasn't been affected, thank God."

Catherine could feel her husband's desire when he hugged her, quivering slightly. He began kissing her more passionately.

"We can't—not here!" she muttered.

"Other couples have less qualms," he replied, stroking her nipples through the fabric of her blouse. "Please, my darling. I miss you—it's been a whole week!"

In hushed tones and overcome by the heady scent of her loose hair, he confessed his need for her. Troubled, Catherine peered around.

"I have an idea," Guillaume said. "Come quickly—we'll only be gone for a few minutes."

"But I have to look after Paul, and Elizabeth might come looking for us."

"They are both sleeping, my dear—come."

Luckily, Colette returned at that very moment and found them standing there, arm in arm.

"Ah, perfect timing, Colette!" said Guillaume. "I'm taking my wife to the conveniences. I need to accompany her—there are drunkards hanging round at this time of night."

Colette grumbled a sleepy 'All right.' The young couple took refuge in the storeroom for the trunks, which would remain deserted until the ship reached New York. The largest trunks, stacked in rows and separated by a narrow aisle, concealed their presence.

Sneaking off together in the dark had dispelled Catherine's fear, and she had become as excited and aroused as her husband. Their mouths locked passionately as they gasped for breath, hungry for each other's bodies. Hands slipped under clothes, and fingers trembled when they finally touched bare flesh.

"Don't be too rough," Catherine urged, as Guillaume lifted up her skirt and petticoat. "The village nurse said no sex beyond the sixth month of pregnancy—it could bring on labour before full term."

"When you were expecting Elizabeth," he panted, "we knew no such thing, and you were delighted to welcome me inside you, my darling. Lean against that chest—I won't hurt you."

She surrendered to his will, swept away by waves of desire and fascinated by the ecstatic expression on her husband's face. He stroked her inner thighs, tantalizing the most sensitive spot of her body. With his eyes half shut, he savoured the moment.

The young lady of Guerville and the son of the Montignac miller had married for love—a love so intense that it paid no heed to social convention, or the rebukes and misgivings of others. Catherine and Guillaume had been lovers for six months already when they were joined in matrimony. Their secret meetings had been going on from the autumn through the spring, marking them for life as kindred spirits whose bodies were destined to become one.

The young woman could not contain a low moan, while her husband moved in and out of her pregnant body. He didn't thrust too deeply, since she was leaning against the luggage wall in front of him, but he was content.

Once they had climaxed, they kissed each other tenderly, grinning at their own cleverness.

"This reminds me of our old hide-outs," he said as he cuddled her. "My brother's hayloft, and the cellar of the dilapidated house by the river."

"And the castle's hunting lodge, the night it snowed," she added, amused. "I had to wait until my parents were asleep. I remember what fun it was, the two of us under those thick blankets!"

"You managed to steal wine and biscuits from the pantry. My darling Cathy, you're such an adventurer, and a beautiful one at that."

"Let's hurry back to the dormitory," she replied, begging for a last kiss.

Colette greeted them with a stinging glare, not fooled by their ploy.

Catherine avoided her gaze, but Guillaume couldn't prevent himself from smirking.

"My man is playing cards in the refectory, and some of them are out there dancing," Colette grumbled. "Oh well, you might as well have a good time, before you end up six feet under or at the bottom of this bloody ocean. Me, I can't wait to get off this horrible boat!"

"Good night, Colette," whispered Catherine. "Thank you for keeping an eye on our daughter."

"Good heavens, I was merely returning the favour. Good night."

The night lights were flickering, low on oil. Happy and fulfilled, Guillaume lay down. He knew where this sudden and overwhelming desire had come from: his mind was trying to block out all thoughts of the body tossed into the sea, and of the grieving family's prayers. Life was for living—with gusto, love and joy.

On these thoughts, he fell into a deep slumber. The great passenger ship continued its voyage, packed with hordes of passengers—some rich, some poor, but all eager to discover New York or start a new life.

Beneath the chandeliers in their luxurious lounge, first-class passengers were dancing the waltz. The ladies wore beautiful silk gowns and diamond necklaces, the gentlemen were dressed in black dinner suits and white shirts. Champagne flowed into crystal flutes, and exquisite pastries were served.

Two very different worlds existed side by side, each with its own joys and tribulations. They had very little in common. Catherine lay awake, too excited to sleep—thinking about reaching America, and seeing thousands of unfamiliar faces. She could feel the baby dishing out little kicks and giggled silently, massaging her belly to calm her unborn child.

"Patience, you mad little one—stay there and out of harm's way. If you only knew how much I love you already . . ."

The next day, Saturday, October 23, 1886

No one on board *La Champagne* had escaped the news of the death of the old lady, whose body was now lying at the bottom of the ocean. Even the wealthiest passengers commented on the sad event and talked about the brief religious ceremony organized by the Jewish family.

The thought of her death troubled some; others managed to brush it aside. In an attempt to ease the atmosphere, the Captain allowed the bear handler to give a little show.

The third-class passengers and the sailors would have the front-row seats, but the Captain knew very well that many of the wealthier passengers would enjoy the spectacle from the covered terrace on the upper deck.

Delighted to have been given the opportunity, the bear handler, Alphonse Sutra, began to entice the crowd gathered around his beast. He took a harmonica from his pocket and brandished it in the air. The metal reflected the rays of the setting sun.

"We're rehearsing for the New Yorkers," he shouted, smoothing down his moustache. "Hey, Garro, give them your best performance! Tonight we have a real fiddler with us!"

He pointed to a young blond man with rosy cheeks who was en route to the New World, hoping to make his living with his only legacy, a fine-quality violin.

Catherine, Elizabeth and Guillaume were sitting on the edge of a hatch. Colette stood beside them, giggling. She was keeping an eye out for her sons, but you could sense that she was ready to start dancing at the slightest jingle.

"Jesus, if I'd known that I would be seeing a real bear on this boat!" said Leonard, her eldest son. "Last night, I brought him a piece of bread in the hold where he sleeps. The old fella ties his chain to a pillar, to stop him from bolting."

"Can't you speak any better, in front of Madam Catherine?" scolded his mother. "You don't say, 'the old fella', but 'the gentleman'."

Elizabeth was barely listening. Her bright-blue eyes were riveted on Garro's body. The animal was waddling around on its hind legs, stretching its brown head towards the violinist.

"Have you noticed that Sutra has tied a tambourine to one of the bear's front legs?" murmured Guillaume.

"I suppose he's taught him how to play it," said Catherine.

Then came some lively music. Sutra played a polka on his harmonica, backed up by the violinist. The crowd cheered enthusiastically, and the children were clapping.

"Go, Garro!" ordered Sutra, rolling his *r*'s.

The bear began to spin around. It was swaying, its mouth partly open, despite the leather muzzle. Finally, it made the tambourine jingle.

The crowd applauded and laughed at the performance, especially when the hillbilly, with his wide-brimmed black hat, started warbling a song from his homeland, in his local dialect.

"Now, that's my kind of man!" laughed Colette. "Maybe we'll run into each other again in New York."

With this, she winked mischievously at Catherine. The young woman smiled back. She and Guillaume were thrilled to see their daughter so happy. The little girl had gone to join the circle formed by Leonard, Paul and two other girls. Her dark-blue twill skirt fluttered around her legs, and a few dark-brown locks had escaped from her calico bonnet. She didn't seem to have a worry in the world.

Each time Elizabeth came face to face with the bear, she smiled at him kindly. Garro continued to dance to the rhythm of the music. His audience was cheering him on and the huge beast, used to receiving applause and bravos, started bowing.

"Thank you, ladies and gentlemen," cried his trainer. "You're applauding the fearsome wild beast of the Pyrenees, who has terrorized both shepherds and their flocks! Look how clever he is, my dear friends—he's the best!"

To captivate his audience one last time, the hillbilly hugged the bear, which wrapped its paws around him. There were a few shrieks of fear, but it wasn't long before Garro started bowing again.

"Do you have any coins on you?" Catherine asked her husband. "We should give him something, but let's hurry back down afterwards—I'm freezing!"

"You're right, it's chilly tonight. The ship has turned north, to take the fastest sea route," said Guillaume.

He picked three coins out of his pocket. Alphonse Sutra was already passing his hat round. Elizabeth had returned, to snuggle into her mother's arms. She was out of breath but seemed delighted.

"We're having a great time, Mummy," she gasped. "The gentleman who plays the violin mustn't stop, it's so beautiful! Just like the sky. Look at all these stars!"

Catherine looked up at the vast night sky, which was almost black, but dotted with millions of bright specks. The dainty quarter moon looked as if it were suspended on top of one of the ship's masts. For once, the sea was calm; you could barely hear the lapping of the waves against the hull.

Guillaume returned with Colette's husband. The former miner had been drinking. He had seen his wife chatting with the bear handler, who was now counting his takings. He interrupted them at once:

"Coco!" he roared. "I've caught you red-handed, messing around behind my back. You're too close to that miserable lout for my liking. I'm going to give him a piece of my mind. You dirty slut, you can't help yourself, can you!"

"At least he isn't drunk every day that the good Lord gives us," she replied.

Jacques hurled himself at Colette, who managed to dodge him, despite being quite hefty. Their sons cried out in terror.

"And you! Come here and let me rearrange your face!" he snarled at the bear handler.

Alphonse Sutra twirled his iron stick towards the drunkard to defend himself. The bear roared and tugged on its chain in panic.

"Stop it, Jacques, stop it!" cried Colette at the top of her voice, now so ashamed, her face had turned scarlet.

The bear handler hit his assailant on the shoulder, but Jacques got hold of his stick, threw it to the ground, and punched him in the face.

Sailors rushed to separate the two men, but onlookers had begun to take sides, and before long, a riot had broken out.

"Go down to the steerage, Cathy, and take Elizabeth—you could get pushed," advised Guillaume.

"Please, stay out of it!" she replied. "Oh, how peaceful it was just a moment ago. Come with us, please!"

"Yes, Daddy, please come," implored the little girl. "And let's take Paul with us—he's crying, all alone, over there."

Struck by the compassion Elizabeth had shown towards the young boy, Guillaume complied. He lifted the child up and put him on his arm. Catherine, who was holding her daughter's hand tightly, heard loud, scoffing laughter come from the upper deck.

"The first-class passengers are enjoying the fight," she said to her husband. "Listen to them, giggling and taunting! I suppose they think they're better than us, but they merely settle their affairs in private. Really, they're no better than the bear handler and poor Jacques, who started slaving away in the mines as a twelve-year-old."

Outraged, she hastened down the narrow stairs to the steerage. She didn't hold onto the handrail and missed the second step.

"Cathy!"

Guillaume saw her fall on her back, her arms in the air in search of something to hold on to. Her heavy skirt was rolled up when she finally came to a halt, having braced her left foot against the wall. He quickly put Paul down and rushed to her rescue.

"Mummy, Mummy!" screamed Elizabeth. "Are you hurt?"

"No, it's nothing," gasped Catherine, breathless.

Guillaume helped her up. He was as white as a sheet.

"Dear Lord, you gave me a scare! Are you in pain, my darling?"

"I felt the edge of each step along my back, but thank God I didn't fall forward! Please dear, don't worry. It's all my fault, I wasn't paying attention."

"What about the baby?"

"He must be a little shaken up, the poor mite. Guillaume, you look so pale! I'm sorry. Please help the children down the stairs."

Catherine proceeded cautiously towards the corridor that led to the dormitories. She had lied: her stomach had hardened, and a sharp pain was pounding in her lower back. Even as she reached her bunk, she continued to pretend she was all right.

"I'll get Elizabeth washed and ready," said her husband. "I think you should lie down quickly. There's some water left. Paul should go to bed straight away. Take off your shoes and your jacket, little lad. You've had enough excitement for one night."

The boy was used to sleeping in his clothes, and obeyed without putting up a fight. Catherine took advantage of the opportunity.

"Please Guillaume, put our little princess in her nightgown while I go to the conveniences."

"All right, but shout very loudly if someone bothers you," he said, still worried about her.

Elizabeth was yawning. She rubbed her eyes, then held her arms out to her father. He cuddled her tenderly.

"Tell me, Daddy—what were the gentlemen fighting about? They're not going to hurt Garro, are they?"

"Garro? You mean the bear? Of course not, my Lisbeth."

"Lisbeth?"

"When we arrive in New York, I'll call you that, or Betty—both sound more American. I've heard that those are the short versions of your first name, on the other side of the pond!"

"Not Betty, Daddy—I prefer Lisbeth. Will other people call me that, too?"

"Probably," he replied, absentmindedly.

Guillaume couldn't stop picturing his wife lying flat on her back across the steps. His forehead was covered in beads of sweat, and he was barely able to conceal his emotions while he took care of his daughter. He tucked her in with a kiss.

"You left your doll under your pillow," he noted. "Good idea, it kept her warm."

Guillaume noticed how cold the air had become, as if the offshore wind was gusting down into the depths of the ship. He gazed at the other berths. Those who were already settled in for the night had pulled their blankets right up to their chins.

"Can you sing me a nursery rhyme, Daddy?" begged Elizabeth.

"Wait a minute, sweetheart—I'm listening to something."

Guillaume wasn't paying attention to the familiar noises of snoring, squeaking bedsprings, coughing fits, and whispers. He was intrigued by the strange sound he could hear outside, and by the swaying of the ship that grew heavier by the minute.

It's getting rough, he thought to himself. *What's Catherine doing?*

In the foul-smelling cubbyhole in which she had locked herself, the young woman had noticed the same changes. The ship was pitching a lot and she was shivering. She could also hear voices and people running about.

But she was trembling for another reason. Her long lace-adorned cotton drawers were stained with blood. The red smear glared back at her menacingly. Catherine pulled down her skirt and petticoat, and tried to convince herself she hadn't seen it.

4

A Night at Sea

On board La Champagne
The night of Saturday, October 23 to
Sunday, October 24, 1886

Catherine was roused by the noisy return of her neighbours.
The faint glow of the night lights emphasized the miner's
sagging features and badly bruised face. Colette was furious
and shook her husband, hurling abuse at him in hushed tones.

"You should be ashamed, you drunkard! Making a spectacle
of yourself in front of all those people! If I catch you drinking
that much again, Jacques, I'll be off, and you can fend for yourself in America!"

Her husband couldn't keep upright any longer and fell flat on
his face in front of Catherine's bunk. At once, he started vomiting, which woke Guillaume.

"For heaven's sake!" he said indignantly. "That's all we need!
My wife needs to rest—she fell down the stairs earlier. See to
him, Colette—I'll clean up the mess."

The carpenter quickly rose to his feet and helped Jacques up,
stepping over the foul pool of vomit, then rushed to the water
point near the conveniences.

"How did the fight end?" Catherine asked Colette, who
mumbled apologetically.

"That brave bear handler got off with a black eye. He doesn't
bear a grudge, in any case—they even shook hands afterwards.
I hear you had a bad fall, my dear?"

"Nothing serious. I slipped and fell on my back."

"Looks like we're gonna be flung around a bit longer. A deck hand told me that terrible weather is coming tonight," said Colette, pouting anxiously. "Jacques won't be the last one to dirty the floor, I'm telling you. Christ, can you feel how it's shaking? I feel giddy already."

Despite its sheer size and power, the ship had been rudely jolted up and down for the last hour. In steerage, below the waterline, you could hear a dull knocking against the hull. The waves were racing to attack the boat, shaking it with fury.

"You're right, Colette—it's pitching a lot," agreed Catherine anxiously. "I don't feel too good. It must be seasickness, although I've not had it since we set sail."

"It shakes your guts around, all the goings-on out there."

Catherine closed her eyes, indifferent to her neighbour's banter.

She could feel an occasional spasm in her lower abdomen, so she massaged her belly with the flat of her hand under the blanket. To reassure herself, she recalled what the doctor had said two weeks earlier. *The doctor said I'll give birth around mid January. Guillaume has promised me that our new home will be well heated. Thank God I'm not bleeding anymore*, she thought. *If I stay lying down tomorrow, everything should be fine. I shouldn't have rushed down the stairs like that. Oh, that stench is unbearable!*

When her husband returned with a bucket of water in each hand, he found her with a handkerchief over her nose.

"I'm so sorry you have to endure this," he murmured.

"Come on, I'll help you, Mr. Duquesne," said Colette from her bed. "As for the smell, this is just the start—mark my words."

She was spot on. Many passengers were feeling ill and the unpleasant sounds of vomiting could be heard all around. *La Champagne* was continuously swaying, dipping and righting herself. Some passengers had even refused their evening meal. Children were crying anxiously.

"It would be interesting to climb up on deck and take a look," said Guillaume, cleaning up the floor as best he could. "The waves must be gigantic."

"No, don't go!" pleaded Catherine. "You could get blown overboard! What would become of me and Elizabeth then? Please don't!"

"I won't, darling. Luckily, Elizabeth is sleeping through the noise. It must be pouring out there, and the wind is getting up. I'm sure the crew have their hands full."

Guillaume was listening, all tensed up. Catherine knew he was eager to confront the raging elements and assist the sailors, if need be.

"Please don't go up," she insisted.

"I won't, but I'll have to empty the buckets, or there won't be enough for everyone to use tonight. You must rest, Cathy. I'll look after you both."

The ship's increasingly violent rolling made him stagger, as if he were drunk. A man ran towards him in the corridor.

"A storm is on its way!" he cried out. "No one is allowed up on deck—Captain's orders. You'd have to be mad to stay up there anyway—the waves are crashing over the railing!"

"Is it really that bad?" enquired Guillaume. "Who told you about the storm?"

"The Captain's second in command. According to him, it isn't unusual in these waters, due to underwater currents— though I didn't understand everything. I'll have to warn my sister, who's travelling with me."

"Well, good evening—and thank you."

Guillaume headed to the conveniences. They were in a pitiful state, causing him to gag as he sloshed through yellowish, stinking water. He had barely stepped outside, when he was thrown against the opposite wall.

"For God's sake!" he said indignantly. "I can hardly stand!"

Overcome by curiosity, despite the stranger's warning, he rushed down the gangway and began climbing the steps. He hadn't even made it to the deck before the icy rain hit him in the face.

What he discovered, as he stood watching from the top step, filled him with horror. The wind that was blowing in the shrouds sounded like a long and piercing scream. The "Lord of the Seas" was now nothing but a frail little vessel that was being tossed around by the raging sea.

Sailors dressed in oilskins were running around frantically. One of them spotted him.

"Get down from there immediately, Sir! A storm is coming!" he called out. "We must close the hatches and steerage."

"The storm is already here," retorted Guillaume.

"Do as you're told!"

Catherine was anxiously waiting for her husband to return. She knew she would be unable to sleep because that trickle of blood had soiled her nightgown. Without any change of clothing at hand, she was feeling desperate.

"If only we had our trunks—I packed some squares of cloth for the birth. Now I have nothing, nothing at all," she lamented in a soft voice, her teeth clenched.

Her neighbour looked up in alarm and raised herself up on one elbow.

"What's going on, my dear? Anything wrong?"

"Oh Colette—yes, I'm bleeding! It started after the fall I had earlier on, and I can't change my clothes or clean myself, you see . . ."

"Good Lord, I understand! I can help you out, but is this it—is the baby on its way?"

"No, I don't have any pains. I must have injured myself."

"You know, there's a doc aboard this bloody boat. You'll have to get him to check you over tomorrow. If we're still alive by then!"

"Heavens above, don't say such things, Colette!"

The young woman crossed herself. She then became aware of the deafening sound of the waves outside. It was a dreadful rumbling noise that even drowned out the roaring of the engines beneath them.

"Guillaume!" she cried out. "My husband hasn't returned! Coco, the boat is tilting—look, it's tilting!"

At that moment, Elizabeth awoke shouting "Mummy!" as loud as she could. Other terrified children who had also woken up started calling out for their mothers too.

"Calm down, my darling!" exclaimed Catherine. "I can't get up, but Daddy will be here in a minute!"

Guillaume emerged from the darkness, his hair soaking wet. He leaned over his daughter's bed. She was hiccuping, clutching her doll tightly against her chest.

"Don't be afraid, my princess—the sea is raging, but it'll quieten down soon."

The child stared at him, wide-eyed. He stroked her cheek and smiled in an attempt to hide his own anguish.

"Lisbeth, darling—talk to me. Have you had another nightmare?"

She nodded yes. Her father sighed before asking:

"Do you want to sleep next to Mummy?"

"No, you take her, Guillaume," protested Catherine. "I feel sick, please take her. Have you noticed that the boat is tilting?"

"I know, Cathy," he said. "We must have faith in the Captain. He knows what he's doing—it's not his first crossing."

But they weren't the only passengers who were alarmed at the abnormal listing of the ship: it was all anyone could talk about. The women stayed in bed, cursing, while the men got up and dressed anxiously. The word "storm" was on everyone's lips, amplifying the fear and confusion.

"Jesus, I'm quaking in my boots, me," admitted Colette.

Her sons were sitting on their bunk, crying. Leonard, the eldest, had his arm around little Paul's shoulder.

"Look at your father, snoring!" said their mother, enraged. "We could all be drowning while he sleeps off his binge!"

Catherine began to pray. She couldn't bear the thought of losing her baby; if such a thing happened, she would never be able to forgive herself.

"Mummy!" shouted Elizabeth once more. "Mummy, a kiss!"

"But you're with Daddy, my sweetheart—now be good and go back to sleep. I'll be sick if I come over to you."

A subdued sob followed her words. Guillaume did his best to calm the little girl. Catherine could hear him humming Elizabeth's favourite song to her. "*Marianne goes to the mill, to grind her grain, dressed in blue twill . . .*"

Before long, the little girl was revelling in memories of summer days spent on the banks of the River Charente, of golden wheat fields, and the scent of mint and thyme in their garden in Montignac. She wiped away her tears quietly, homesick for the life they had left behind.

La Champagne had been battling against the wrath of the elements for more than an hour already. Guillaume was on edge, while Elizabeth nestled her head on his shoulder. The little girl had fallen asleep again, comforted by her father's presence. Guillaume was not the only one who was agitated. He could see dark figures darting around the dormitory, on their way to the conveniences, or looking after a neighbour. The incessant clamour of voices mingled with the violent sound of waves battering the ship and the howling of the wind.

Just then, the storm seemed to intensify. The ship was now right in the firing line and was dealt a harsh blow. All those who had hoped for a return to normality now realized that had been wishful thinking.

"Lord, please have mercy on us," murmured Catherine. Sleep was just a distant memory now.

She lay curled up in the hollow of her bunk, fingers clasped around her baptism medal. Suddenly, she felt a surge of courage, as if something miraculous had occurred.

It's stopped hurting and I'm no longer bleeding, she thought. *Colette told me she'd experienced the same thing during one of her pregnancies.*

A split second later, all hell broke loose. The passengers were in the dark as to what exactly was going on but they got the distinct impression that the liner was capsizing to port. It immediately started pitching, nose up. The deck was tilting alarmingly.

Random objects were rolling from one end of the aisle to the other.

Curses, shouts and complaints were coming from all directions. Children were screaming in terror. Then, without warning, *La Champagne* plunged downwards, as if a chasm had opened up in front of it.

Had the third-class passengers been able to get to the upper deck, they would have seen the magnitude and violence of the waves. As the ship took them one by one, it was blown in all directions like a strand of straw.

Catherine continued to pray while clinging to the metal bars of her bunk. She heard Guillaume comforting Elizabeth, who had been woken up again by the tremors and the screams.

"Be brave, my darling," said Catherine. "Hold on tight to Daddy's neck. It'll pass—it'll soon be over."

"Yes, Mummy," replied the little girl, "but I can't see you! I wish I could see you."

Most of the night lights were no longer standing, and the few that remained only emitted faint rays of light. An oppressive darkness shrouded the dormitory.

"The sailors should bring us lanterns," shouted one man. "They're treating us like animals."

"They're probably too busy trying to save our lives," snapped another.

Exclamations were flying in all directions. Catherine was aware of the danger they were in. Her daughter's cries tugged at her heartstrings.

My princess needs me, she thought. *She's so young—of course she wants her mummy.*

"Guillaume!" she cried out. "Help Elizabeth come to me. I want her beside me, in case we . . . and beside you, too."

"You're right, my darling," he whispered.

He could read his wife's thoughts. The little girl broke out of her father's embrace, relieved at the idea of being next to her mother. She got out of bed at the precise moment when the ship righted itself, listing to starboard this time. Elizabeth lost her balance and stumbled. She tried to catch herself but fell and slid forward, carried by the abnormal listing of the deck. Colette, who was hugging her boys against her, let out a hoarse cry.

"Good Lord, your lass!"

Startled, Catherine jumped up, and rushed to her daughter's rescue. Guillaume cursed, one leg caught in his blanket. When he was finally up, he searched in the darkness, guided by a loud bump followed by a stifled moan.

"Cathy, Elizabeth!" he called out, sick with worry. A young man he recognized as the violinist tapped him on the shoulder.

"Over there, I think, Sir!"

They rushed in the direction he had indicated, having to hold on to the bed railings and push people out of the way. Many were themselves busy helping their nearest and dearest who had fallen over, or trying to find their scanty belongings which lay scattered all over the place.

"This is a nightmare!" exclaimed Guillaume in exasperation. "Cathy, Elizabeth!"

"Daddy, Daddy!"

He snatched an oil lamp out of a young man's hand.

"You'll get it back, I promise," he muttered.

"There—they're over there!" yelled the musician.

Elizabeth was curled up in a corner, her blue eyes wide open with fright. Catherine was lying next to her, motionless.

"Mummy hit herself really badly, Daddy," stammered the little girl, "on the forehead!"

"Cathy, my darling! My poor Cathy!"

He knelt down. The violinist took the lamp so Guillaume could see better. Cautiously, he lifted his wife's upper body to examine her head. Blood was oozing from her blonde locks. She was blinking at him.

"I'm sorry," she sighed.

"Thank heavens you're all right. My darling, you shouldn't have got up!"

"But Elizabeth could have hurt herself."

"Sorry, Mummy—it's all my fault," the little girl sobbed.

"Of course it's not, my princess," protested her father. "It's the ocean's fault for bringing us such a dreadful storm."

"At least it seems to be calming down," pointed out the young musician. "Let me help you get back to your bunks."

"Thank you, that's very kind," said Guillaume, overwhelmed with relief.

He embraced his beloved wife and covered her forehead in kisses before tenderly stroking Elizabeth's cheek.

"Dry your tears, my darling," he muttered. "The gentleman is right—it's a lot calmer now. Mummy seems to be all right. I bet you that there'll be bright sunshine tomorrow, and the sea will be calm once more. You'll see, my princess."

The next day, Sunday, October 24, 1886

Catherine was lying on a narrow bed in the ship's infirmary. At sunrise that day, in excruciating pain, she had given birth to a small, stillborn baby. She was very pale, but did her best to smile at Guillaume, who was holding her hand. The ship's doctor left them alone.

"Please forgive me, my love," she sighed. "I've destroyed all our dreams with my foolishness."

"Don't say that, Cathy, my darling," he moaned. "It's not your fault! I was the one who couldn't hold Elizabeth back. You simply did what any mother would have done in trying to save her."

"If only I hadn't fallen down the stairs," she groaned. "That's when I started bleeding, but I didn't want to worry you. And then, when I tried to get hold of Elizabeth, I was hurled against a crate and a pillar. It was a boy—the good Lord wanted to give us a beautiful little boy, Guillaume."

Bitter tears ran down the carpenter's cheeks onto his shirt. Catherine gazed at him lovingly. Her husband still bore the marks from the blows he'd taken before boarding, though they had faded a little.

"You're so handsome," she sighed. "Oh, how I love you! I didn't know it was possible to love so much."

"You will continue to love me, Cathy, my beloved. You are my light, my heart and soul. I must ask for your forgiveness, because it was me who dragged you into this mess. I didn't realize how perilous the ocean can be. If only you knew how much I regret it!"

He cast a sombre glance at the porthole. Rays of pink and gold appeared on the horizon. The ship was continuing its journey through the now tranquil waters.

"Guillaume, please, we have little time," said Catherine faintly. "I'm very weary—I'm leaving you, my love. Please let me kiss Elizabeth one last time . . . can you bring her to me?"

"What are you talking about, Cathy? You can't leave me!" he cried. "No, it won't end like this for us. You'll get better, with rest and good food. I'll use the money your mother gave us. We'll take a cabin in second class and we'll have a decent diet."

She no longer had the strength to respond. Guillaume helped her swallow some sugared water.

"Hold on, my darling," he begged her. "You were so brave last night, remember?"

Catherine whispered an almost inaudible "Yes." She was reliving the terrifying moment of her collapse next to her panicking daughter.

Her husband had carried her to her bunk, where she went into labour—but it had all been for nothing.

Colette had used two sheets she had borrowed from another woman to shield Catherine from prying eyes.

"Is Mummy having the baby?" Elizabeth had asked. "Daddy, is the baby coming?"

Worried sick and certain that the newborn had no chance of surviving, the carpenter had sought to reassure his daughter. He would willingly have left her in the care of other women in the dormitory, as Colette had advised, but the little girl had refused, sobbing heavily.

"Now, be a good girl, Elizabeth—I have to take care of Mummy and find the ship's doctor. Please, stay in your bed with your doll and say your prayers!" he had shouted, at the end of his tether.

He had never spoken so harshly to their little princess before. Catherine had heard everything and was panicking, fully aware that it was over for her.

"Guillaume, my love," she said now, in a faint voice, "a difficult task awaits you. You'll have to raise Elizabeth alone, and you must promise to look after her, and protect her from the cold, hunger and fear."

"Shh! Shh! Don't say that!" he wailed.

"Raise her with strong values—frankness, honesty and respect for others. And above all, don't leave her until she's become an accomplished young lady. If my parents offer to take her into their home, refuse—don't let them have her. She'd be unhappy in the castle, I know she would. I want her to be raised on American soil, by your side. Promise me, Guillaume, so I can leave this world in peace."

Her husband gazed at her. Her body was limp, and she had bluish lips and dark circles under her beautiful green eyes. He finally realized that nothing could save her.

"Cathy, this can't be happening to us—to you."

She gave a weak smile. Gradually and relentlessly, her body was giving up. The sheet beneath her was warm and damp.

"The doctor can't stop the bleeding—that's just how it is," she added. "I have one last request, my love. You must offer my body to the ocean, today, on the Lord's Day—otherwise I'll quickly become an abomination. I want Elizabeth to retain a beautiful memory of her mother. Do you remember, you kept telling me that in the summer light, my eyes take on the blueygreen colour of the ocean? Somewhere between turquoise and emerald. I'll have the most beautiful resting place in the world."

Guillaume collapsed on his knees next to the bed. He pressed his forehead against his wife's chest, kissing her hands delicately. She could hardly articulate her next words.

"You have the money that Mother gave me. Sell all my jewellery, but give Elizabeth my baptism medal."

"Catherine, my darling, I can't do it without you!"

"I'll watch over you from heaven, my love. Please, go and get Elizabeth before it's too late."

After placing a trembling kiss on her lips, it took him a superhuman effort to turn away from her. Each step cost him dearly, as he dashed through the gangway, hardly noticing the doctor, bumping into him.

"Excuse me, Doctor," he stammered, his throat choked up. "Is there really no hope for her?"

"I'm sorry, Sir," he replied. "A premature birth is very risky. Your wife was exceptionally brave. I'm on my way back to her bedside."

"Catherine wants to see our daughter. Thank you for all your efforts, Doctor. It was good of you to have my wife transferred to the infirmary."

"The Captain and I thought it was best, both for your daughter and the other passengers in the dormitory. I also wanted to give your wife the best treatment—but unfortunately, fate decided otherwise."

Guillaume nodded, looking dazed. The doctor patted him sympathetically on the shoulder.

Elizabeth had just woken up. Her parents were still not back. She had been calling out to them for ages, crying and shouting, until she dozed off with exhaustion. Colette was a nice woman and a good mother, but her attempts to calm Elizabeth's sorrow had proved fruitless. She had found the doll belonging to the little girl, who snatched it from her with a pitiful scream. The pieces of fabric the toy was made of smelled of Catherine's cologne.

When Guillaume reappeared, he discovered Elizabeth lying face downwards on her bunk. Colette guessed what had happened, from the distraught look the carpenter gave her.

"Daddy, are you there?" muttered the little girl, raising her brunette head. "What about Mummy? Why haven't you brought her back here to be with us?"

"Come, my darling—Mummy is waiting for you. You're going to give her a very big kiss," he said.

He took her by the hand. Colette watched with sympathy, as did her husband Jacques, who had just woken up. Elizabeth was relieved at the thought of seeing her mother again. In her night-gown, with her messy dark hair, she was the embodiment of childhood innocence and purity.

Guillaume carried her to the ship's infirmary. The doctor was waiting at the door for him to return. From the look on his face Guillaume understood at once that Catherine had died.

"Already?!" he cried, aghast. "No, God!"

His body trembled with shock, for deep down, he'd still had a glimmer of hope. The child could feel her father's acute distress and noticed how sorrowful the doctor looked. She didn't ask any questions, sensing impending grief. The expression of joyful impatience had vanished from her face, and her blue eyes glazed over.

"You must kiss Mummy," said Guillaume, dazed.

The doctor let them in. A nurse was busy near the narrow bed where Catherine Duquesne, *née* Laroche, lay. She'd been born twenty-eight years ago, under the slate roofs of Guerville Castle. The young woman looked like she was sleeping, hands crossed on her chest. Her blonde locks had been combed in a hurry.

Elizabeth's whole body was shaking. She prayed to baby Jesus—whose story she knew and whom she thought was so sweet—that he would wake up her mother. Then everything would revert to the way it was before. Maybe the three of them would even return to France, to their house by the river.

"Mummy has gone to heaven, my princess," breathed Guillaume in her ear. "She promised me she'd watch over us."

"But she won't stay there for too long," Elizabeth replied, to reassure herself.

She refused to accept the truth; it was too painful. She knew very well that death had struck, and it frightened her. The smell of the infirmary was repulsive. Never would she forget the scent of the blood and the black soap the nurse had used to wash the linoleum.

Guillaume put his daughter down and led her to the bed with shaking hands. Elizabeth caressed her mother's forehead, which was still warm, then stood on tiptoe to kiss her on the cheek. The doctor coughed nervously, his throat knotted at the tragic scene before him.

"Mummy is in heaven, my darling," said the carpenter desolately. "With your little brother. We must pray for them every day."

"Yes, Daddy."

Elizabeth sighed deeply. Tears were welling in the corners of her eyes. Breathless, she raised her pretty face up at the two men. Overcome with emotion, the nurse, a young sailor, bent down to the little girl.

"If your Daddy allows it, I can take you onto the deck," he suggested. "The sun is rising, and I think I heard a sailor say he's spotted dolphins. They are sea animals, but they jump high above the water. You're not wrapped up warmly enough, but I can put a blanket around you."

"Thank you," sighed Guillaume, distraught. "There's no need for her to stay here. And I'll use the opportunity to spend a moment alone with my wife."

As soon as the door closed behind them, Guillaume broke down.

The sad news had spread rapidly, from the first-class quarters to steerage. The tragedy was summed up in a few words: "A woman and her baby have died in childbirth, victims of the storm."

Many people were moved by the plight of the widower and his six-year-old daughter. There was also talk of the bodies of the ill-fated young woman and her newborn being thrust into the depths of the ocean, like the old Jewish lady's two days before.

The appearance of the sailor carrying Elizabeth, who was wrapped in a thick shawl of tartan wool, immediately aroused curiosity. It was very early, but the crew was already working hard to repair the destruction caused by the storm.

The hillbilly in his black hat was walking his bear along the deck. He had permission to walk his beast once in the morning and once in the evening, for a quarter of an hour each time. The bear was sniffing the salty spray, ambling steadily behind its master, who was smoking his pipe. He turned around at the sight of the child, whose pallid face betrayed the distress she was in.

Elizabeth didn't pay attention to them. She was overwrought and couldn't stop sobbing, which greatly saddened the sailor who was holding her.

"So, where are the dolphins hiding?" he said, attempting a cheerful tone.

Mute with grief and tears, the little girl stared blankly at the horizon. She was carrying a dreadful burden, and even though she was very young, Elizabeth was aware of the enormity of the loss she had just suffered.

"Mummy wanted to see whales," she suddenly whispered in a faint voice.

"Oh, whales! We'll surely encounter some, but further north," replied the sailor. "Did you know it's said that they sing, and that their song is very beautiful? Early seafarers thought it was sirens chanting. Do you know about sirens?"

"Yes, Sir. Daddy showed me a picture."

The offshore wind ruffled the girl's hair. With her small fingers clutching the metal railing, she scanned the infinite ocean. The foamy waves were high, and they were banging sharply against the hull, sending up silvery sprays of water that captured the golden rays of dawn.

At last, a grey silhouette emerged from the waves in the distance, followed by many others. The dolphins were performing acrobatics and amazing stunts, letting out high-pitched cries.

Delighted cheers rose from the upper-deck terrace, where some wealthy passengers were sipping their coffee or tea.

"Do you see that, little girl?" asked the sailor. "What a pretty sight!"

Elizabeth agreed again, just to be polite. She couldn't care less about the dolphins, because her precious Mummy was not there to see them. Her entire being was clouded by an oppressive gloom, and she was hurting.

"Please, Sir—I want my Daddy," she stammered.

Guillaume was dreading nightfall. He'd had to leave Catherine's side to tend to Elizabeth, even though it was a wrench.

"I promised my wife I'd look after our little one," he explained to Colette, who had offered to take care of the child. "My Cathy wouldn't want Elizabeth to be separated from the only parent she has left."

He was pondering the dilemma with his daughter snuggled up against him, on his bunk. Elizabeth had cried herself to sleep.

I must be strong, Guillaume told himself. *Getting through this will show Catherine how much I love her, even if right now, I'd rather be dead myself and join her. My beautiful, sweet Cathy.*

The tragedy had shaken him and resonated through his whole being. Catherine had been the love of his life. He wished he could wake up from this nightmare and look into her blue-green eyes, kiss her rosebud lips.

"Mr. Duquesne," called out Colette, who'd just got back from the refectory.

"Yes?"

"You'd better keep the child away from her tonight. The poor girl is very upset, and dragging her up there would only make matters worse."

"Perhaps—I don't know," Guillaume replied. "What could be worse for a six-year-old girl than to lose her mother? I'll have to think about it."

"I understand. You know where to find me if you need me," she added, before getting ready to give Paul a quick wash.

The carpenter contemplated the question at length. A difficult future was in store for Elizabeth.

She might as well face life's harsh realities from now, he told himself. *Once we arrive in New York I'll have to work, so what will she do all day? I'll have to put her in school, even though she doesn't speak the language.*

He had barely made his decision when he remembered Catherine's ashen face as she begged him to look after their daughter.

No, I won't have Elizabeth watch her mother's body being thrown into the ocean, and that's my last word. She's such a sensitive, nervous child. Cathy, I'll do my best, I promise you. I'll find a trustworthy person in New York to take care of her.

It was almost time. He got up quietly, careful not to wake Elizabeth. Colette seemed to be monitoring his every move, and seemingly out of nowhere, she brandished a crumpled white shirt and a black suit.

"You'll be more decent in these, Mr. Duquesne—they're my husband's. He'll happily lend them to you, since you lost your trunks."

"Thank you, Colette, that's very kind. Yes, I've been stripped of my trunks, my tools, my Guild member's cane with its engraved compass, as well as a set square and a ruler, plus my father's gold watch. At the time I thought I had lost everything, but looking back, I realize what a fool I was. Today, I've lost my beloved wife, Cathy. I would give my life just to see her smile at me once more."

"You still have your young daughter, my good man," added the former miner, who had just joined them.

When he wasn't drunk, Colette's husband was a devoted and charitable man. He even went so far as to make the young widower an offer.

"Coco and me are going to be staying in the Bronx. I got the address from one of my cousins, who lived there for two years. Should things get difficult, you could look for accommodation near us, and Coco would look after your daughter with our little ones during the day."

"Thank you, Jacques. I'll need help, that's for sure."

With that, Guillaume changed his clothes in the narrow space between the bunks. Catherine's death had devastated the young man.

I'll write to my father-in-law from New York, he thought. *When he learns of the tragedy that's beset us, he'll come to get Elizabeth. She'll want for nothing in France and will be raised as a lady in the castle. As for me, I'd do best to end my life—this is all my fault!*

Relief overcame him: at last, he had found a way out of the excruciating pain that was ravaging him. It was really quite simple. There were just a few more days of torture to endure, maybe a month, and then he would cease to exist—he'd be erased from the surface of the earth, like his beloved Cathy.

"Let me take care of your tie for you," offered Colette in a low voice. "Don't worry—if your little one wakes up, I'll tell her to wait for you quietly."

"I don't know how to thank you," said Guillaume. "The ship's chaplain must be waiting for me."

"Be brave, my poor man," Jacques said, shaking his hand. "The ceremony won't take long, that's for sure."

Guillaume simply nodded. Slowly, he started making his way up to the deck.

Elizabeth had been listening to them with her eyes closed, her doll pressed to her chest. She didn't understand what was happening but was sick with fear and grief. All she could remember from the conversation was that her father was going somewhere. He was leaving her, even though he was all she had left.

"He wasn't born under a lucky star, that fellow," said Jacques philosophically. "Coco, I think I'll go up to keep him company—a little stroll on the deck."

"Yes, he's all alone, saying his goodbyes to his little lady, who was so pretty too! Leonard and Paul are in bed, and I have my knitting to do."

Jacques went off, racked by a coughing fit. His lungs had been damaged by coal dust.

"Ah, what a wretched life," sighed Colette, leaning over the contents of her wicker trunk, which she had pulled close to her feet.

Elizabeth was nervous. She tried to remember if she'd been put in her nightshirt. It came to her that Guillaume had dressed her in a grey frock that was embroidered with pink scrolls on the collar and wrists. Black woollen stockings and shoes had completed the outfit.

"Yes, woe betide the rest of us," said Colette, while sorting balls of wool.

Without warning, the little girl threw back her blanket. She fell out of bed, jumped up and ran off. Someone alerted Colette, who hadn't noticed a thing.

"The little one is about to escape!"

"What are you saying?"

Colette, who was fairly stout, had trouble getting up. She called out in vain—the child had already vanished from her sight.

Elizabeth had only one aim: to be reunited with her father and never leave his side again. She had climbed up to the deck several times with her parents and knew the way. Nobody tried to stop her as she clambered up the dimly lit staircase. Holding her doll tightly against her pounding heart, she was surprised at how quickly she had reached her destination.

Elizabeth first noticed the starlit sky: its deep-blue colour was strewn with yellow spots. Then she saw the torches, whose flames were dancing in the evening wind. Many people were gathered around what looked like an oblong package wrapped in a pale cloth.

"Daddy," she whispered, "Daddy, where are you?"

Her ears were ringing, and tears were stinging her eyes. Trembling, she emerged from the hatch, but froze at once in astonishment. She had already seen these people dressed in black, and that man wearing a black cassock who was reciting a prayer. Elizabeth gasped for breath. She had to hold back a scream of terror, as she relived the nightmare that had been disturbing her sleep for days. About ten yards away, sailors were lifting the oblong package, pushing it onto the sloping plank that had been placed on a gangway entrance.

When she heard the splash of the package as it fell into the water, her teeth started to chatter. It only took a moment for the ocean to snatch the package and swallow it up.

The splash was echoed by a hoarse sob from Guillaume. Elizabeth was well aware that it was her mother's body that had just been cast into the sea. Memories of happy and peaceful times with her mother in Montignac filled her mind.

In her mind's eye, she could see her pretty Mummy in a floral dress, laughing and picking flowers from the garden. A straw hat was sitting on her long golden hair.

Darkness had engulfed the ship with its masts, its funnels, its silent deck, and the little girl whose beloved mother had just been cruelly taken from her.

Her mouth agape and wide-eyed with shock, Elizabeth finally let out a howl. Her desperate cry chilled the spines of those attending the funeral ceremony.

"Mummy! No! Mummy!"

Guillaume rushed to his daughter. As he grabbed her by the waist and picked her up, he got the impression of holding a rag doll. She was inert, her arms were dangling, and her head flopped backwards. Guillaume fell to his knees, clutching his daughter tightly.

"Forgive me, Cathy," he said. "Forgive me, my princess. Daddy is here now. I will never leave your side again, I promise."

The young widower covered his daughter in kisses. For a few seconds, he imagined his wife's body sinking into the depths of the ocean; then he brushed the image aside. From now on, Elizabeth would be his only concern, his only treasure.

"Come back to me, my darling," he breathed, kissing her cheek and her brown curls again. "We're going to discover America together, and Mummy will be watching over us from heaven."

The little girl sobbed and shuddered. Guillaume held her even tighter, feeling relieved all of a sudden. He was certain that his wife had just given him new strength.

"Thank you, my beloved," he said. "Rest in peace, my darling Cathy."

5

The New World

On board La Champagne
Saturday, October 30, 1886

Guillaume could hear excited gasps, interspersed with the cries of seagulls. He looked his daughter up and down with relief, grateful to have taken care to pack up the most basic clothing in the big leather case.

"We're going up onto the deck, sweetheart."

The liner had finally arrived in New York; it was the end of their voyage.

Elizabeth nodded in response, but looked anxious. She had lain in bed for two days after her mother's death, refusing to eat. Yet, she had slept better than usual, snuggled up to her father. Little by little, she had started eating some broth again and had taken a new interest in her doll. But she had not spoken, apart from the occasional "yes" or "no".

"My princess, I'm afraid I'm going to have to start work as soon as Monday. A friend has promised me a job on a building site. You must be brave, as I'm going to have to leave you with Colette. She's nice, and you get on well with her little boy, Paul."

"Yes, Daddy. I'll be good."

Touched, the young widower pulled her close and cuddled her. It made him happy to hear his daughter speak in full sentences again.

"I know you're very unhappy because Mummy is no longer with us, but she's become an angel in heaven. To please her, we're going to have to get through this together."

"Are you sure that Mummy is up there in heaven?" asked the child, looking worried. "Because the people in black threw her into the sea."

"You shouldn't have seen that," sighed Guillaume. "It must have been a terrifying experience for you. Mummy wanted to rest at the bottom of the sea, but from there she flew up into the clouds, to remain eternally beautiful and to watch over you."

Elizabeth chewed the end of one of her silky brown ringlets, pensive. She hesitated.

"Daddy, I have a secret," she confessed. "I had already seen the people in black and what they were doing on the ship. They appeared in my nightmares."

Her little body quivered; then she got her breath back and finally began to cry.

Her father moved to her side to look at her carefully.

"What—you saw that scene in your nightmares?" he cried out. "But you always said you didn't remember anything afterwards!"

"I was telling the truth, Daddy, but it came back to me when I saw them throw Mummy into the sea."

Seized with panic, Elizabeth started sobbing. Equally distressed, Guillaume cradled her in his arms.

Good Lord, that explains why she was terrified, he thought to himself. *My poor baby!*

Then suddenly, he recalled the confessions his own mother had made several years ago. One evening, as the family was sitting around the hearth, Ambroisie Duquesne began to recount a rather strange tale, in which she described certain scenes from her dreams that had come true, down to the smallest detail.

"Elizabeth must have inherited this gift," he muttered to himself. "But why? What does it mean? Was it written in the stars that Cathy would die during the crossing?"

Guillaume gave up trying to figure it out. As the hullabaloo on the deck grew louder, he clasped his daughter's hand and picked up their leather case.

"I'm sorry, my darling. I hope you won't have any more nightmares from now on," he said, too upset to try to give Elizabeth a rational explanation.

She followed him obediently, like a frightened little animal.

A noisy and agitated mob was pressing against the railings. All eyes were on the magnificent and gigantic "statue lighting up the world" that stood at the mouth of the Hudson river, on Bedloe's Island to the south of Manhattan. The midday sun was shining in a pure, blue sky. Other boats were sailing nearby, their plumes of smoke resembling flags in the wind.

"Did you see the statue? Gosh, it's gigantic!" shouted a man with a beret.

"A work of art," added a stylish gentleman with a monocle on his eye and a newspaper folded under his arm. "We have reason to be proud, as it was a gift from France to the United States on the centenary of American Independence. It was inaugurated two days ago, on the 28th of October, in front of the President of the United States, Grover Cleveland. The Captain told me."

Guillaume felt crushed; fate had dealt him a hard blow. He imagined Catherine standing at his side, marvelling at the famous statue.

"Look, Lisbeth—look at all those people on the docks, on the boats! It looks like they're all welcoming us. Can you believe it? We're in America!"

"Daddy, why are you calling me Lisbeth?" she protested feebly.

"You know why—it's more fitting for New York, and it makes a nice change, my princess. We're on the brink of a new life in the New World!"

The carpenter paused, his throat choked up. He was feigning joy, in the hope of bringing a smile to his daughter's sad little face. He thought how adorable she looked, in her white calico bonnet wrapped around her brown curls, with her dimpled chin and delicate features.

"We *will* be happy, my darling," he insisted, trying to convince himself.

They were being pushed and shoved. Guillaume turned around and noticed Colette's ruddy face next to him. She was rejoicing, all wrapped up, a misshapen hat on her head.

"Mr. Duquesne, you won't see a more impressive sight than that! My Jacques is looking after the lads, so I've come to keep you company. They say a ferry will take us to Fort Clinton, where the Immigrant Reception Centre is."

The intrepid woman mispronounced the American names in her northern French accent. In different circumstances, Guillaume would have been amused, but today, he just nodded with approval.

"I know, Colette. The ship's doctor already told me what will happen when we disembark—more health and identity checks."

"In that case, I won't bother you any further. I was only trying to help!" she replied.

"Sorry—I didn't mean to be unfriendly," he said. "You've been a very good friend, Colette, and I'm grateful to you. Everything is so difficult! I can't stop thinking about my wife, who was supposed to share this moment with me. Her death has been entered in the ship's register—the Captain recorded the circumstances of her death, and the date. I must notify her parents in France at once—they'll hate me more than ever now. They didn't want us to leave—and do you know what? They were right!"

Letting it all out made him feel better. Colette listened in sorrow.

Elizabeth had heard every word. Clutching her doll tightly, she was watching a flock of seagulls. With her free hand, she took the tin soldier out of her coat pocket.

Suddenly she was back in the castle, hearing the storm rage behind the rain-drenched windows; and then she was in the nursery, where that sweet little boy Justin had appeared. If only he could appear on the deck now, to comfort her.

It took several hours for all the passengers to disembark. Finally, Guillaume and his daughter set foot on a wharf on the edge of Manhattan, near South Street, amidst a cosmopolitan crowd calling out and chatting away in a variety of languages.

They were Irish people, Italians, Poles, Jews from Eastern Europe, as well as French folk. The noise was deafening, and brawls had already broken out due to stolen luggage and language problems.

Elizabeth was exhausted and terrified by all these strangers. Guillaume decided to push his grieving to the back of his mind, to concentrate on more pressing matters. He had three priorities: one, being careful with money; two, protecting his child from the crowd; and three, finding Baptiste, his carpenter friend who awaited him in the Bronx.

"Don't be afraid, my darling. We're going to find a room for the night," he said half-heartedly.

The carpenter had got separated from Colette and her husband, who had embarked on a different ferry; he would have appreciated having them around. He had only known them for ten days, but already considered them as friends. New York was overwhelming. Everything looked disproportionately large to him: the height of the buildings, the length of the streets, the ambient frenzy.

"If only your Mummy were here," he muttered, trying in vain to find his way.

When they were preparing for their departure, Catherine, all smiles, had promised she would handle communication, as she was the only one of them who spoke a little English. In the end he was able to make himself understood when asking for the Bronx, and was given emphatic instructions in the form of hand gestures.

Night was falling when he was finally able to put Elizabeth to bed, in a modest hotel room, after changing some money at a grocery store. Guillaume was surprised to find that the shop-keeper was originally from Normandy. He told him about a cheap boarding house, at the corner of a block not far from his shop.

The little girl fell asleep immediately. She had only eaten an apple for supper. Her father was sitting at her bedside, watching her. Never before had he been caught up in such an abysmal situation. Slumped over, with his head in his hands, he mulled over his grief for a good part of the night, shedding bitter tears over the woman he had loved, and whose beautiful, delicate body was now lying at the bottom of the ocean.

He recalled the discussion he had had with two sailors on deck, when his wife's body was cast into the dark waters. They had dutifully wrapped Catherine in cloth and ballasted the makeshift shroud with special lead rings. Guillaume could also see the newborn infant in his mind; his son had been a tiny, bluish baby, covered in blood.

"God in heaven, why?" he whimpered. "Why? My little lad would have grown up in America, and I would have taught him my trade."

In the letters they had exchanged, his immigrant friend had insisted that it was a piece of cake to find work in New York: the city was expanding at break-neck speed. Tall buildings were springing up everywhere and were being built higher and higher, requiring the skills of talented craftsmen. Nationality was of no importance, as eventually all immigrants would become American citizens.

Guillaume Duquesne was clinging to this hope. He would work extremely hard and be the first to arrive on the site and the last to leave.

But what about Elizabeth? he thought, worried. Cathy was supposed to look after her, and had planned to take on sewing work to earn a few extra dollars after the baby's birth.

He trembled with anger and helplessness in the face of this adversity. However, his main concern was to honour the pledge he had made to his wife.

"Tomorrow I'll be meeting Baptiste, and sooner or later I'll find Colette and her family," he said to himself. "At least we're all French—we'll work something out."

Vaguely comforted by this idea, Guillaume drifted off for a

moment, but was soon woken by Elizabeth's piercing screams. Her eyes were still closed, but her hands were clenching her sheets.

"My princess, calm down! I'm here, Daddy is here," he sighed.

He quickly lay down beside her and pulled her to him. Elizabeth's breathing was jerky and her forehead moist.

"Daddy? Daddy?" she called out in a trembling voice.

He gave her a soothing kiss, but did not dare to ask about the bad dream that had terrorized her.

Guerville Castle
Wednesday, November 3, 1886

Hugues Laroche had just returned from a ride. He'd been inspecting his vines, which his farm workers had started pruning. It was the ideal time to get the job done, after a fruitful harvest.

He led his mount to the stables, casting an irate glance at the spot where the immense fir tree had once stood. The ancient tree had damaged the roof of the turret after being hit by lightning. The roof had been repaired in no time, but the tree was no more. Seeing its stump made him wince. He could not forget that disastrous night—the unrelenting violence of the storm, and having to say goodbye to Catherine the following morning.

Vincent, the groom, came running. He grabbed the reins and Laroche dismounted with ease.

"Tell old Leandre to plant lilacs around here—it'll look more cheerful than these remnants!"

"Of course, Sir. Madam is waiting for you."

"Well, she'll have to wait a little while longer. I'm keen to ride the mare I bought this summer—I need the exercise."

The winegrower's emaciated face betrayed the acrimony he still felt about his daughter's departure. Vincent insisted:

"Forgive me, Sir, but Madam has asked me to come and get

you right away. I was about to go looking for you in the vineyards."

Hugues Laroche noted the expression on his servant's face. He'd rarely seen him so embarrassed.

"All right, then, I'll go right away. I hope you're not hiding anything serious from me—you do look rather guilty!"

The groom remained silent, which intrigued Laroche even further. With a shrug, he took off towards the castle. As soon as he entered the hall, his wife rushed towards him with outstretched arms. Adela was not a very affectionate woman and normally concealed her feelings. He was therefore aghast to see her in tears.

"Hugues! Oh, my God!" She threw herself into his arms, sobbing. "Our daughter, Hugues . . ."

The chatelain knew at once that something terrible had happened. He felt like he'd been punched in the chest.

"Adela, tell me—come on, talk to me," he said, tripping over his words.

"I received a telegram from Guillaume this morning, after you had gone out. Catherine is dead, Hugues!"

"Dead!" he repeated, dazed. "That's impossible. No, no! Not my daughter, not Catherine!"

He pushed her back hard and grabbed the first object he could get his hands on: a Chinese vase on a marble stand with a mahogany pedestal. The blue-patterned porcelain shattered over the worn flagstones.

"Show me the telegram!" he shouted at the top of his voice. "I won't believe it until I see it with my own eyes."

Adela Laroche was white as a sheet as she went into the drawing room. She retrieved the creased rectangular piece of paper she had placed on the piano. Her husband snatched it out of her hand, teeth clenched. On reading the text, he cried in horror. Its brevity implied indifference.

"*Catherine died in childbirth on the ship. Letter follows. G. D.*" he read out under his breath.

"We don't even have the date of her death," lamented Adela,

"and no information as to where she was buried. Our daughter, Hugues, our only child—we will never see her again!"

Stricken with grief, she had to sit down. Hugues Laroche was pacing up and down the room. The look of hatred on his face disfigured him.

"We did warn Catherine about the dangers of undertaking such a voyage while seven months pregnant!" he said, enraged. "But no, she would have followed that yokel to China, if he'd asked her! If that Guillaume was in front of me right now, I would stamp on him like a filthy bug. He has killed our daughter—do you hear, he has killed her!"

"Keep your voice down, Hugues! Someone could hear you," moaned Adela.

Madeleine, the housekeeper, who was hiding behind one of the double doors that led into the smoking room, carefully stepped back. Vincent was waiting in the kitchen, curious to know what was going on.

She scurried to the pantry to tell him about the tragedy.

"Miss Catherine is dead!" she whispered in her lover's ear. "Maybe the carpenter murdered her. Yes, maybe that's it!"

"That's nonsense! Mr. Duquesne loved her."

"Well, passion can lead to crime," retorted Madeleine.

"Are you trying to scare me?" he whispered, with a lewd wink. "Anyway, I didn't know Miss Catherine well—I was hired after she got married—but it's still very sad."

"Yes, she had her feet on the ground—unlike her mother," sighed the housekeeper. "I think I'll go back. We need to know if he killed her or not."

Vincent kissed her on the neck, making her giggle with pleasure. No one noticed the silent presence of a little blond boy lurking behind the big wooden chestnut coffer, as discreet as a shadow.

Justin was curled up in his hideout, holding his breath. He contemplated the pink ribbon in his palm that he had kept in memory of the pretty little girl he had comforted in the nursery.

Elizabeth no longer has a mother, he thought, saddened. *Maybe she'll come back to live in the castle.*

Adela Laroche controlled her emotion, anxious not to make an exhibition of herself in front of her husband. Later, in her bedroom, she would weep for the only child God had given her. Catherine had been a beautiful baby with fair hair, whom she had immediately entrusted to a nurse for breastfeeding, and then to an English governess to give her the best education. By the age of ten, Catherine was a boarder at a religious institution.

"I didn't look after her myself much when she was small and even later on, I didn't show her much affection," she muttered to herself, full of regret. "And now she has died, so far away from me."

The tense silence pulled her out of her memories. Her husband stood near a window, hands behind his back and deep in thought. She knew it had hit him very hard. He had cherished Catherine more than anything.

"I'll wait for the letter," he said suddenly. "I don't know how long it will take to get to France, but I want to know every detail about our daughter's death. Adela, you will organize a service for her, so her soul may rest in peace. Our staff must be informed that our Catherine is no longer of this world."

"Of course, Hugues. I'll take care of it."

"It's out of the question that we let Elizabeth stay with Guillaume. He's incapable of looking after her. I'll go and bring her back—it's our duty to offer her an honourable life. I can't bear to think of my granddaughter begging in the slums of New York."

"I'm so glad you said that!" cried Adela as she stood up. "I couldn't protect Catherine, but I can be a mother to Elizabeth."

Laroche turned around, his face contorted in pain. His anger had vanished, and tears welled in his eyes.

"Adela, the pain is unbearable," he confessed. "It's sheer torture."

"We should have stopped her from going, Hugues—from getting on that damn ship."

He didn't reply but hugged his wife, who was grateful for the affection. They stood holding each other for a while. The loss of their child had broken them; they were devastated.

Madeleine was spying on them, through a door that was ajar. Satisfied, she ran back to the pantry, where Vincent was sipping a glass of wine.

"The boss wants to bring the little girl Elizabeth back," she said excitedly. "Jesus! We'll be able to do as we please for weeks, my fella!"

"So, was it murder or an accident?"

"No idea, but Sir and Madam were crying. I've never seen them in such a state."

"That's normal—their daughter has died, Madeleine. You're not a mother, so of course you wouldn't understand."

"And you—have you got a brat out there somewhere?"

"God, no."

He poured her some wine. Still hiding behind the coffer, Justin guessed they were kissing. He took the opportunity to retreat, on all fours, until he reached the wooden wall that concealed a very steep and narrow service staircase. It was dark and cold there, and damp oozed from the walls, but the steps led straight to the attic rooms, which had been used as servants' quarters for centuries.

The child rejoiced at the thought of little Elizabeth returning to the castle.

The Bronx, New York
Sunday, November 7, 1886

Guillaume gazed at the shabby room in which he and his daughter had been staying for the last week.

"We're leaving tonight, Lisbeth," he said, trying to sound jovial. "My friend Baptiste has found us a place on Orchard Street. It's more respectable than round here, for the same money. I see that Colette has forgotten to clean you up yet again."

Despite all his efforts, the young widower could not look after Elizabeth as well as Catherine would have done. The little girl's hair was a dull, tangled mess. Her only dress was stained, and her shoes and stockings were covered in grey dust.

"Baptiste's wife can take you during the day," he added. "She's nice and kind, really. You'll help her a bit with the housework—she has a six-month-old baby."

Elizabeth, sitting on her bed, nodded *Yes*. She was reluctant to talk, which made her father despair.

"Her name's Lea, and she's French, like us," he said. "Are you pleased?"

"Yes, Daddy."

Guillaume inspected the room, to make sure he had not forgotten anything. There was neither running water nor gas lighting here. The toilet was located in the courtyard and was shared by all the tenants. More often than not, the tiny outhouse resembled a vile cesspool.

After the first night in a boarding house, he had finally been able to track down Colette and Jacques, who had moved into the first floor of a building in the Bronx. They had rented a large room, and the former miner had managed to get Guillaume a small, cramped room in the same building.

"I'm glad we're leaving," he said quietly. "I was constantly worried about you in this place, my darling. With Lea things will be different. Besides, I won't have to give her quite as much money."

He closed their big leather case, when he suddenly remembered something.

"Where's Mummy's baptism medal, Lisbeth?"

"I haven't seen it since last night," replied the little girl.

"What do you mean?" Guillaume snapped. "Don't tell me you've lost it! Darling, it's your Mummy's baptism medal—she wanted you to have it. I told you to hide it under your shirt. Did anyone ask to see it? I remember you playing on the pavement with Paul and Leonard—did they take it from you?"

Elizabeth began to cry, pressing her doll against her chest. The hastily made figure already looked more like a bunch of knotted rags than a toy. Guillaume tried to contain himself—in vain.

"Please Lisbeth, try to remember," he said. "It was a piece of gold jewellery, the only thing we have left of Mummy, besides her rings!" he yelled.

"I don't know," she whimpered.

The carpenter was so annoyed that he searched the room from top to bottom, to no avail.

"Well, I guess we might as well ask Colette. She might have taken it off you and forgotten to give it back. Come along—it'll be dark soon and we have a long way to go."

Guillaume reproached himself for having slept through a part of the day, overcome with exhaustion and grief.

"You know, my princess, the work I do is difficult," he explained, as if to apologize.

He could see the scaffolding beams in his mind's eye, several hundred yards above the ground. He could almost feel the vast drop beneath him, the infinite open space, accompanied by the constant fear of falling to his death. Without Catherine there to offer him joy, love and tenderness, he felt trapped, like a prisoner in this oversized city.

Colette was waiting for them in the dark of the hallway. She had her fists on her hips and seemed to be in a foul mood.

"So that's it, Mr. Duquesne—you're clearing off outta here?" she said in her drawl.

"Yes, Colette, I'm sorry—but thank you again. I have been so lucky to have you to look after my daughter. I don't know how I would have coped without you."

He smiled at her, well aware that he had more than paid for her services. His nest egg was diminishing, forcing him to consider selling one of Catherine's rings.

"Well, we all have to help each other," she said. "If you could give me something to cover her meals, I wouldn't say no. My man has found himself a job on the docks, but he won't get paid till next Saturday. The same goes for me—I'm going to be working in a launderette during Christmas week. But we'll still have to fill our stomachs until then."

"I thought the cost of my daughter's food was covered by what I was paying you, Colette," he said, disgruntled.

"Nope, my poor man. It costs an arm and a leg to survive in this bloody neighbourhood. I don't feel safe here at all. You risk your life every time you go out, according to my hubby. Think about it—there's all sorts out there. Irish, Italians, families from Africa and even the Caribbean. Just communicating is an ordeal with all these different languages!"

"We were warned though, weren't we? America has been welcoming millions of immigrants for years, and they usually arrive in New York. Fortunately, we're rubbing shoulders with some French people, too. On another note, Coco—have you seen my wife's medal? It's made of gold, just like the chain. It would be a real pity to have lost it."

"Ah, my poor man, I told the little girl to be careful when she played in the street with my brats. The chain must have broken. I don't think there's much chance of finding it—the place is swarming with thieves."

"Oh God, it was so important to Catherine that Elizabeth wore it! I'll come back Monday or Tuesday, if you happen to find it. I won't have time tonight."

Elizabeth clung to her father's hand. She wanted to get away from Colette and neither see nor hear her ever again. Guillaume, also in a hurry, handed the woman a small sum of money.

"That's the best I can do for now," he said. "Goodbye. Give all my best to Jacques."

"I will, thank you very much, Mr. Duquesne. I'm very sorry about the medal."

As soon as they were in the street, Colette stuffed the coins deep inside her pocket, where she could feel the gold medal that she had stolen from Elizabeth while brushing her hair the previous morning.

"As if the girl needs this on her neck," she muttered with a contented smile. "Good riddance to the Duquesnes. That child was more than I could bear—she never spoke or smiled."

Colette climbed the stairs, panting. She felt no shame, just self-satisfaction. The gold medal would prove useful in hard times.

After walking about twenty yards, Guillaume and Elizabeth spotted Leonard. The ten-year-old was walking towards them, already blending into the constant busyness of the Bronx. Daring and cunning, he fitted in well. Guillaume was certain he would turn into a fully-fledged American in no time.

"So long, Sir!" he shouted to them. "Looks like it's time to say farewell!"

He was juggling a bright red apple, which he suddenly threw to the carpenter.

"For Lisbeth!" he shouted, already hopping away.

"Thank you, you're a good little fellow," replied Guillaume.

He couldn't understand Leonard's reply, as it was muffled by the noise of the horse-drawn carriages on the cobbled street. The Bronx was teeming with the hustle and bustle of a busy Sunday. The shops were lit up and leaden clouds darkened the sky.

"We could take a cab, darling, but it would be an unnecessary expense. You're going to eat well tonight—Lea has invited us."

"Are you sure you know the way to your friends' house, Daddy?" asked the child curiously.

"Yes. We've been here six days now—I don't get lost anymore. We need to walk in the direction of the building site, Lisbeth."

Her father never missed an occasion to use this diminutive form of her name, and she had grown to like it. It allowed her to pretend she was another little girl, and not the one whose mother had been thrown into the ocean. But try as she might, she could not banish from her mind the image of Catherine on the doorstep of their house in Charente, looking cheerful and pretty.

"Keep going, my princess," said Guillaume, "it's quite far still. I promise to carry you on the last stretch."

They walked along a narrower street interspersed with alleyways. A tabby cat ran off as they approached, while a second one jumped from a window ledge. Elizabeth was still upset that they had had to leave their own cat with their neighbour in Montignac.

"Hold my hand tightly, my darling," insisted the carpenter. "I know a shortcut, but we have to hurry."

When following this route alone, Guillaume had sometimes seen figures lurking in the shadows of the doorways. A red-haired drunk had been looking for a fight with him last Friday night. As soon as they entered the passage, he regretted it. The very same redhead was coming out of a brick building, escorted by three cronies.

"Let's turn around," he whispered, but it was too late.

One of the men had already stopped him, breaking out in an aggressive gibberish rant. He was wielding an iron bar. He and his accomplices threw themselves at Guillaume before he had time to think. The attack was quick and violent—Guillaume was dealt the first blow, with no time to defend himself.

"Run for your life, Elizabeth!" he shouted, ignoring his pain and terrified for her.

"Daddy—no, Daddy!" she shrieked at the top of her voice.

One of the thugs had already seized the leather bag which contained Catherine's jewels and the money given by Adela Laroche, inside an inner satin pocket. Enraged, the carpenter threw himself onto the brute and punched him right in the face. Blood gushed from his nose, but the savage immediately fought back, throwing his prey onto the cobblestones.

"Elizabeth, run for it! Please, do as I say! Run, run—go back to Colette's house!"

The little girl stepped back, terrified. She saw the assailant strike her father on the head with the iron bar, then deal him another blow in the stomach. Struck dumb with horror, she obeyed. A hideous groan, mingled with a few words in French, were the last things she heard.

Elizabeth ran down the street they had come from, in the opposite direction. She felt completely disorientated.

In her frenzy, she knocked and shoved people aside, terrified they could hurt her.

"Daddy, my Daddy!" she muttered anxiously. "Mummy, Daddy!"

She felt her will falter. An old woman tried to stop her, but she escaped. With her throat on fire and her heart pounding, Elizabeth was forced to stop. She took refuge behind a cart stowed against a wall. She curled up against one of the wheels like an animal that was being hunted down.

By now it was dark. A cold wind was beating the faces of the countless city dwellers who were still roaming the streets. No one paid any attention to the child. Her brown woollen jacket merged into the brown bricks of the houses surrounding her.

Elizabeth shut down all thoughts. She was cold and hungry, sensations she was now all too familiar with, but they were nothing compared to the intense pain that plagued her at the thought of her father's suffering. One thing she knew for sure: she was all alone, in the middle of a vast city.

This was so hard for her to accept that she closed her eyes and sought comfort from her fondest memories. She could see Pops Toine. She was sitting on the old miller's lap, and he was grinning mischievously, humming her favourite song: "*Marianne's going to the mill …*" Both of them were laughing, while he made her jump to the rhythm of the music. Many a time, uncle Pierre was there too, playing the harmonica. His wife, Yvonne, would sit nearby, knitting. Next, the poor child recalled her garden—the yellow roses, the lilies, which were as white as their cat Mina's long fur. And of course, she saw Catherine in her green dress and white apron, her blonde hair in braids.

"Will you come with me to pick strawberries, my princess? And radishes?"

Elizabeth trembled. She could almost smell the sweet scent of strawberries and the fresh aroma of the earth. She hastily opened her eyes, unable to bear the thought of having to revisit a family scene in Charente in which her father would appear.

"Daddy, my Daddy," she moaned under her breath. "Please come back, Daddy."

He couldn't abandon her. All of Montignac knew him as a strong, fearless and skilled fighter. Elizabeth regained hope, persuading herself that if she waited there patiently, he would come for her.

"Daddy's coming to get me, and we're going to his friend Baptiste's house. Lea's a nice lady, I'll help her take care of her baby."

At the word *baby*, she suddenly remembered that her mother was supposed to have a baby here in America, but it had died. She burst into tears, overwrought with grief and distress.

The echo of her sobs drew a stray dog, which sniffed the tips of her shoes and then left. Elizabeth started to calm down. As time went by, her father's arrival was getting closer in her mind. She told herself that he must have been able to get up and rid himself of the thieves.

Another hour went by, during which the little girl listened out for the slightest sound of footsteps. She had only eaten a bowl of soup for lunch, and her stomach was aching with hunger pangs. Her father had dropped Leonard's apple in the attack.

Two men were walking around the cart that had served as her shelter. The taller of them hung his jacket on a nail. He stepped back, shouting out something in a foreign language. It was just an Italian swearword, but Elizabeth took off at once, terrified.

After about a hundred yards, she noticed a sign and stopped, trying to decipher the letters: *Bread & Cake Shop.* The delicious smell of warm bread made her stomach rumble.

The shopkeeper was watching her. She stood on the doorstep of the shop and asked Elizabeth something in English.

"I don't have any money," replied Elizabeth in French, reassured by the woman's sympathetic smile.

Head down, she continued on her way, but not before glancing one last time at the brioches and round buns in the brightly lit window.

"Wait a minute, please!" shouted a voice behind her.

The child came to a halt. The shopkeeper was holding out an appetising brioche to her. Elizabeth couldn't remember the last time she'd smelled something that delicious.

"Thank you, Madam," she muttered.

"You French? You lost?" asked the baker in broken French.

But Elizabeth fled. She didn't trust anyone anymore. Those who were surprised to bump into a girl of her age at such a late hour didn't bother to enquire further. They were suspicious: for all they knew, she could be from an organized gang who were using her as bait to rob them of their belongings, should they bend down to her in kindness.

Others hardly noticed her, used to seeing orphans roaming around in search of food. There were hundreds and hundreds of them in the streets of New York, abandoned to their fate.

Despite her sore feet and the hunger pangs that tortured her, Elizabeth ran on aimlessly. She finally stopped at the bottom of a flight of steps to eat a piece of the brioche, casting frightened glances all around her.

Finally, having walked for a long while again, Elizabeth spotted trees behind a gate at the end of an avenue. Having seen very few trees since leaving Montignac, she was drawn to them more than anything. Fascinated, she marched towards the iron gate that opened into Central Park.

At Baptiste and Lea Rambert's house

Baptiste Rambert glanced into the stairwell for the third time. Guillaume's lateness was giving him serious cause for concern.

"Your friend may have got lost," suggested his wife. "You should have gone to meet him, Baptiste."

"But he's been here before," he protested. "I even congratulated him on his sense of direction."

"My potato gratin is going to be cold. Never mind, I'll reheat it."

Dark haired, with an olive complexion, Lea was an Italian immigrant. She had been living in New York for about twelve years. When Baptiste met her, he was impressed that she already spoke perfect French and English. They got married a few months later, to legitimize her pregnancy.

"And I was so looking forward to meeting his little girl Elizabeth," she said, worried.

"They'll get here soon, Lea."

"But if Tony wakes up, I'll have to feed him," she complained.

Their son was actually called Antonio, after Lea's father. Just like Guillaume, the couple had switched to the more American-sounding shortened form.

"So was I—I was looking forward to welcoming little Elizabeth into our home," sighed her husband. "The poor child is still reeling from losing her mother. Guillaume is hardly doing any better, but he's holding up for his daughter's sake. Losing your wife in such conditions . . . there's nothing worse. Catherine would have been a friend to you, Lea."

"I really feel for them," she added. "Baptiste, you should probably go check what's happened. They could have had an accident."

"The streets aren't safe at this hour of the day, that's what bothers me."

"I know—you'd better take your stick with you!"

The carpenter put on his coat. He was used to the dangers of New York. After kissing his wife, he set off, armed with his iron-tipped stick.

Lea breastfed her baby and put him back to sleep. She shot a sorrowful glance at the four place settings at the table. Their home was small, but clean and cosy. Through their windows, you could see the lights of Manhattan between the tall buildings.

Baptiste returned looking grave. He put his stick away in the corner of the doorway and took off his coat and hat.

"Well?" asked his wife. "You've been a long time . . ."

"Apparently there was some trouble a quarter of an hour from here, in an alleyway. An old man told me. Four against one. I saw blood on the cobbles, but no body."

"Do you think it was your friend Guillaume?"

"I sincerely hope not, Lea. But unfortunately, I found this on the ground."

He opened the palm of his left hand to show a copper button, engraved with a compass and the initial *G*.

"I'm almost certain it's from his corduroy jacket."

"What about the little girl, Baptiste?"

"The man didn't mention a child."

"Oh my God—the poor little thing!" cried Lea.

She crossed herself, eyes brimming with tears. Baptiste stared at the copper button in despair. They had no illusions about Elizabeth's fate, should she fall prey to one of the gangs that scoured the Bronx at night.

"Tomorrow, you must go to the address they were staying at," she pressed her husband. "Maybe they're still there."

"I'm working tomorrow, Lea. The foreman will fire me if I'm not on time."

"Then I'll go," she replied. "And I'll pray for your friend Guillaume and his child."

Central Park
One hour later

Elizabeth settled under a privet bush to rest for a while. She had just walked down an alley of tall trees and crossed a bridge with a beautifully crafted metal frame.

She was careful to avoid poorly lit areas. Every time she heard a sound, she would hurry to safety across the grass, which was covered in red leaves that crunched under her feet.

Her father had not told her about the vast park that had been built in the heart of the city thirteen years ago, on a site of wasteland and swamps. The little girl wondered how she had got to the countryside so quickly, but the grass beneath her feet and the foliage above her head comforted her. She felt less threatened.

Elizabeth was drowsy but got up and trotted to a wooden bench under a maple branch. She sat there and devoured what was left of her brioche. Then she lay down, pulling up her collar to keep out the cold. She was all alone, at the mercy of the New World her parents had longed to discover.

6

The Lost Child

The sound of birds singing woke Elizabeth at daybreak. She was surprised to find an idyllic landscape stretched out before her. The maple foliage was a beautiful bronze colour. Other trees nearby were bare, apart from some firs and ornamental bushes.

"Where am I?" she wondered, still drowsy.

She sat up, dazed and sluggish, and noticed a vast expanse of water, which reflected the grey sky. At once, everything came back to her.

"Daddy!" she cried out. "They've hurt my Daddy!"

Flashbacks of men beating and hitting her poor father assailed her. She remembered the iron bar, and his cries of pain and his shouts, urging her to escape: "Run away! Do as I say! Go back to Colette's!"

Elizabeth would have been hard pressed to find the building where Colette and her family lived. Her head sank with guilt.

"Daddy, I didn't mean to go the wrong way," she said anxiously. Her little heart raced as she realized that her father would undoubtedly go to Colette's house to find her, and she wouldn't be there. Seeing a skyscraper between the red branches of the oak trees gave her an idea. If she walked towards it, following the same route but in the opposite direction, she would inevitably end up in the right street.

Elizabeth hopped off the bench and started walking. As she ventured further into the immense park, walking by the lakeside, she was deeply moved by the sheer beauty of nature all around her. Squirrels with stripy coats were chasing each other on the grass, performing acrobatics. She observed them for a moment, amused by their high-pitched squeals.

Traumatised, the little girl blanked out all thought of her mother and the disappearance of her father. She had the common sense to know that it would be unwise to give in to her grief that morning.

"My darling Mummy is in heaven, and Daddy will come back to find me," she repeated to herself.

Hearing the echo of a horse neighing and the sound of hooves, she hid behind a bush. A rider trotted swiftly by. She stared after it in awe, but was soon distracted by the throaty growl of an animal that resounded in the distance. Even though she was terrified, she remained within the shelter of the trees.

Without warning, a man wearing a large black hat appeared. He shouted out in surprise.

"Well, what do we have here?" he exclaimed. "What are you doing here all by yourself, little girl? You were on the same boat as me, right?"

Alphonse Sutra smiled at her. Elizabeth recognized him at once.

"Where's your father?" he asked, concerned. "It's much too early for you to be roaming around Central Park."

Reassured by his familiar gravelly accent and his rolling r's, she approached him. The hillbilly noticed that her cheeks were streaked with tears and dirt, and her hair was all matted under her crumpled cotton bonnet.

"You're in fine shape, aren't you?" he remarked. "Strewth, what's happened to you?"

He remembered her mother's death on board *La Champagne* but decided not to mention it.

Though Elizabeth tried not to catch his gaze, he saw that she was looking around, intrigued.

"You're wondering where my bear has gone, aren't you? I've got a routine going already. I let Garro loose at this hour, as there's no one around. Not for long, though—the fine folk will soon emerge."

He pulled a piece of bread out of his bag and bit into it with gusto.

"If I whistle, Garro returns to me. It's very useful. And you, child—have you lost your tongue? Where's your daddy?"

"I don't know—they hurt him last night," she confessed almost inaudibly.

"What—how come? Who hurt him?"

"I don't know," she repeated, whimpering.

Baffled, Alphonse Sutra swallowed a last bite of bread, then took a metal whistle from his pocket and blew on it. The little girl shrank back, startled.

"Don't move when my beast arrives. I'll tether him right away."

The hillbilly rummaged through his canvas bag with a grin and flashed the chain that he used to hold the animal.

"I can see that misfortune has struck you, child," he said. "It's not wise to hang out on the streets of New York at night. I doubt you'll see your father again, you poor mite. But hey, why don't you stay with me? When I have enough money, I'll buy you a nice dress and you can do the collection."

"Collection?"

The word brought back memories of Sundays in church. Her mother would let her wear her pretty pink dress with a lacy collar.

"Here, my darling—here's a coin for the collection."

Elizabeth would carefully place it at the bottom of her small embroidered velvet pouch. When the altar boy handed the basket to the parishioners, she would perform her role with gusto.

"Collection—like in church?" she asked.

"No, silly—I'm talking about the crowd throwing money at me, when they applaud Garro's tricks. You could even dance next to him! You won't starve to death with me, I promise."

A moment later, the bear appeared, trampling over two slender arbutus bushes. The mighty beast trotted on all fours, jaws wide open, baring its fierce teeth. Elizabeth backed away in fear.

"Come here, Garro," ordered his master. "Your stroll is over now! That muzzle is going back on. If you like, you can pet him now, little girl. You need to become friends, both of you. Tonight, we'll go to my cousins' house—I live with them. They rent a stable to house our bears in the winter. Are you hungry?"

"Yes, Sir. I'm thirsty too."

"Why didn't you say so right away, my angel? Finish up my crust and take a drink."

Garro, muzzled with leather straps, was sitting on his backside, staring at the child with his big, dark eyes. Elizabeth wanted to stroke him but something held her back.

Alphonse Sutra held out the crust to her, as well as a white tin mug in which he had poured a reddish liquid.

"This'll make you feel better," he said.

"Thank you, Sir," she muttered.

Despite being a hardened hillbilly, he was constantly on the lookout for anything untoward. He had left his country when life there became too difficult, to make his fortune in the New World. He'd been fascinated by the American Dream, like so many before him. The child would be a bonus for him, melting the hearts of his audience and increasing his takings.

"We must be wary of the police," he muttered. "If they ask any awkward questions, we'll pass you off as my niece, Marie. We'll talk in French and they'll fall for it hook, line and sinker."

"But that's a lie," protested Elizabeth.

"Would you rather they put you in an orphanage?"

"What's an orphanage, Sir?"

"It's where they put children who have no family. You'd be locked up and you'd have to behave all the time. So, you'd better do as I say. Look out, there's two of them over there. Quick—let's move."

Elizabeth didn't much like the hillbilly, but had no desire to be sent to an orphanage, either. But most of all, she couldn't stop thinking of her father, who was probably out there looking for her.

"Hey, where are you going!" grumbled Alphonse Sutra, as she took off as fast as her little legs could carry her.

Her head was spinning from the diluted wine the bear handler had given her. She was still clutching the morsel of bread.

Soon, she arrived at a castle on a hill. Although very different from Guerville Castle, it looked like it was from a fairy tale, and Elizabeth was convinced she'd be offered shelter there. Without further ado, she crossed an alley and cut across the castle's large lawn.

Without warning, a carriage came from a nearby bridge, drawn by a swiftly trotting black horse. The animal was wearing blinkers and didn't see the child—it struck her with full force.

A woman let out a shrill cry—too late! One of the carriage's wheels had just rolled over Elizabeth's body.

The Dakota Building
One hour later

Edward Woolworth paced up and down the sitting room of the luxurious apartment he and his wife had been living in for the past year, on the third floor of the Dakota Building.

His late father, a wealthy New York banker, had convinced him that this magnificent brand-new building, an elegant Gothic-style mansion resembling a Renaissance castle, would surely impress his clients. His wife Maybel had been delighted with their move, especially since their part-time neighbour was the illustrious Russian composer Tchaikovsky.

Trading in cereals and cotton, the thirty-eight-year-old Edward also speculated on the stock market.

He lit a cigar—which he hastily placed on the edge of a crystal ashtray when the doctor entered the room.

"Is it serious, Doctor? I would have taken the little girl to the hospital, but Maybel insisted on bringing her home with us. I'll do as you advise."

"The child will live—rest assured, Edward. I have reset the fracture in her left leg. At her age, the bone will soon heal. The head injury could lead to complications, but apart from that, she has only some minor bruises. I made her swallow a spoonful of laudanum to ease the pain. Given that she was wandering around Central Park early in the morning in such a dirty state, she must be an orphan. Oh Lord, there are so many of them on the streets! Their numbers are increasing, due to the constant influx of immigrants."

"It's quite possible, I agree. But even so, I'll have to conduct some research. We'll know more once she wakes up. For now, Maybel prefers to keep her here, where it's safe and warm."

"I understand, Edward. I'll be happy to provide her with the necessary care in the coming days. Let me return tonight to check on her again."

"May I count on your absolute discretion on this unfortunate accident, John?"

"You may, of course. But between us, Edward, this little girl was very lucky. She could have been killed on the spot."

The trader nodded contritely, embarrassed. They shook hands.

Even if Elizabeth had been conscious, she wouldn't have understood any of their conversation in English. A woman was leaning over her bed, uttering words of affection to her—in vain.

"Poor little girl, it's our fault you're hurting. Don't worry, you'll be well cared for."

Maybel Woolworth stroked Elizabeth's forehead. She had not yet begun to clean up the street urchin, who had dirty nails and matted hair. Her petticoat didn't smell too fresh either—nor did her feet.

"But you're very pretty," she added. "Edward says you have blue eyes, bright-blue eyes. He says they opened briefly when he picked you up from the ground."

Maybel's chest rose with a melancholic sigh. At the age of thirty, she had already suffered four miscarriages. Most recently, she had given birth to a little girl a month before term, only to lose her a few hours later. Her maternal instincts had been rekindled by the beautiful child that fate had placed in her path.

"John has promised to be discreet," said Edward, joining her in the guests' bedroom, where they had put the child to bed. "Oh, Lord, if she had died because of me, I would have blamed myself for the rest of my life. We were lucky, and so was she."

"Lucky, yes," whispered his wife. "Edward, if . . ."

"Don't say another word, Maybel. I know what you're thinking, but we can't keep this little girl. You can look after her until she's well again, but then we'll take her to the Protestant Child Welfare Institution—provided she has no family, of course."

"And they'll send her out west on the Orphan Train, with all those poor, innocent children who have suffered from tragedy, with no one left to care for them. How can we know what will happen to her, whether she will be well treated?"

"Maybel, we don't know anything about her. How do we know she wasn't begging in Central Park? Perhaps she has parents who are sick with worry about her."

The young woman nodded in resignation. Edward sat beside her and held her hand, in an attempt to appease his wife. He loved her very much.

"She's very pretty indeed," he admitted. "She can't be older than five or six."

"Have you noticed how skinny she is? The bottom of her dress is all stiff with dirt and dust. If she still has a mother, the woman isn't taking good care of her."

The couple gazed longingly at Elizabeth for quite some time. She had a white bandage wrapped around her forehead, and a second, more substantial one was wrapped around her left calf.

"I do wish she'd wake up. I've asked Bonnie to prepare a vegetable broth and some boiled ham."

Edward gave her a kind smile. Maybel looked at him imploringly before kissing him on the lips.

Baptiste and Lea Rambert's apartment
Monday evening, November 8, 1886

Baptiste was fiddling with the copper button he had found in the alley. Despondent, he eventually placed it on the table.

"Guillaume didn't show up for work this morning," he groaned. "I was so hoping to see him. Someone not half as competent has already taken his place."

Lea looked wistfully at her husband while cradling their baby. She had rarely seen him so disheartened.

"Yes, that's a bad sign," she agreed. "You did warn him, though. He should have been more careful. Let me put Tony to bed, then I'll serve your supper."

"I'm not hungry, Lea. I'm beside myself with worry for his little girl. If he's no longer of this world, what's become of her?"

"I went to their old address after leaving Tony with my mother," Lea said, getting up. "I was able to speak to their former neighbour, a French woman, who was sitting knitting on the porch steps."

"Now you mention it, Guillaume did speak of a woman called Colette—northerners, with two sons," said Baptiste.

"I can't say I liked her much," shouted Lea from the bedroom. "She didn't give me her name, but if what she says is true, Guillaume and his daughter left two days ago for a hotel."

"It's not impossible," he replied, opening a beer. "We didn't have much time to talk on the site. Besides, Guillaume wasn't the same man I used to know back in France. He looked desperate to me. Oh Lord, all this is my fault. If I hadn't suggested he join me in New York, he would still be living peacefully in his village, with his wife and daughter."

Lea tied an apron around her waist. She wasn't the sort to indulge in self-pity.

"Don't make yourself ill over this, Baptiste. It's nobody's fault. The Lord giveth and the Lord taketh away. If it makes you feel any better, I'll pay the Sisters of Charity a visit tomorrow. Street children often end up there—Elizabeth could be one of them. She knows her last name—I'll ask the nuns about her. Please eat something!"

But Baptiste Rambert threw his cap down. His mousey hair was cropped very short. He could easily imagine that Guillaume had been set upon.

"I did my Carpenters' Guild tour of France with him," he added. "We restored the timbers of a church in the Limousin region. He was a fine companion, in every sense of the word. He and his daughter would have been safe, living nearby. It makes my blood boil to think they robbed him of his last few possessions. He told me he still had his wife's jewellery and some French money. Catherine came from a very different background—her parents lived in a castle and were very wealthy."

Lea shook her head. The ragout sauce had settled in the hollow of his plate.

"I'll write to her family, if you can recall their names and their address," she said.

"That's a good idea, Lea. It's the Laroche family from the Guerville estate in Charente. Let's write to them."

The Dakota Building
The same evening, the same time

Dr. John Foster had just paid them his second visit of the day. One of the many lift operators who worked at the residence escorted him to the nearest elevator. The Dakota Building had four: one at each corner of the sumptuous building.

Elizabeth was suffering from a high fever, so he'd prescribed both quinine and laudanum. "If her condition doesn't improve by tomorrow, she'll have to be hospitalized," he'd warned before leaving, concerned. Maybel and Edward Woolworth had exchanged anxious glances.

"The poor little girl still can't eat anything," sighed the young woman. "Seeing her like this breaks my heart."

"Don't despair, my dear. At least we know that she's French now. She's calling out to her mother in her delirium."

"Yes, the poor child keeps asking for *maman*, and I'm sure I heard her say *papa*, too."

"I'll make some enquiries tomorrow. My secretary Jack is monitoring the arrival of the liners. As far as her well-being is concerned, and even though I trust John wholeheartedly, I think the child is better off with us than in a hospital."

Trembling with hope, Maybel wrapped her arms around her husband's neck. She gazed at him lovingly.

"Edward, if she *is* an orphan, we could adopt her. I know you deny me this joy because you want your own baby, your own flesh and blood. But deep down, you know we will never have one. All the doctors I've seen have been clear about this."

"I'll think about it. If we adopt, then perhaps we could speak to the Sisters of Charity, who take in the very youngest. Newborns are left on their doorsteps every day, Maybel. But come on now—let's have dinner. We'll talk more tomorrow. I've asked Bonnie to keep an eye on the child."

Maybel followed her husband obediently. She was overcome by an inexplicable fondness for the little girl they had run over. Luck seemed to be on her side, for Edward began to be more accommodating once his sexual appetite had been assuaged later that night. The couple were lying on their king-size bed with its satin-draped posts, their limbs entwined.

A bathroom with a black marble bathtub adjoined the room. The Dakota Building provided a level of comfort that was rare in those days. It provided hot water, electricity and central heating on each floor, and there were numerous hallways within the apartments, to save the residents from being disturbed by their servants.

Edward's lips were caressing his wife's rosy nipples. He groaned with pleasure when Maybel slid her slender fingers around his erect penis. She wasn't usually this bold, and Edward was not fooled. Yet, he straightened up to lie on top of her.

"Darling," he whispered in her ear, "please keep going. You know I love that. Gosh, you are so warm and wet."

He spread her thighs apart with one knee, careful not to hurt her, feeling highly aroused. She stiffened, breathing in snatches.

"Do what you want with me," she moaned. "Let me be your sweet little wife."

The trader let out a husky groan, accustomed to submissiveness from the whores he occasionally visited. Maybel knew exactly how to please him.

They were kissing passionately, panting with ecstasy from the climax they had just reached, when a sharp scream caused them to freeze in mid-action. They heard the sound of footsteps, followed by their servant's voice at the door.

"Madam, the little girl is crying a lot. I don't know what to do . . ."

Maybel broke free from Edward's arms. Alarmed, she put on a red silk bathrobe and rushed to Elizabeth's bedside. A yellow bedside lamp lit up a sad scene: the little girl was battling an invisible enemy in the midst of a messy heap of sheets.

"Help, Mummy!" she shouted with her arms up in the air. "Daddy—they're killing Daddy! Mummy!"

"Good Lord, does she still have a fever?" asked Maybel, feeling Elizabeth's forehead.

"No, Madam, her forehead is only lukewarm."

"Bonnie, what was she saying? I understood the words *maman* and *papa*, but not the rest. Your mother is from Normandy, isn't she? You've often boasted you understand a little French."

"She was calling for help, Madam," said the servant. "I understood that, but not much more."

By this time, Elizabeth was crying, anxiously staring at the decor around her. Maybel was amazed by the sheer blue of her eyes and her dark lashes.

"My doll, I've lost my doll, my Cathy," whined the little girl, choking on her tears.

"Bonnie, please try! What's she saying?"

Edward then entered the room, glaring at poor Bonnie, who frantically tried to recall fragments of her long-forgotten mother tongue. "She's asking for her doll—a doll named Cathy," she replied quickly.

"Well, run and get the one I bought for my niece. It's in a parcel, at the bottom of the linen closet," urged Maybel.

"Darling, that doll cost me a fortune! It was meant for Pearl, my brother's daughter," protested her husband. "It came all the way from London. The head and arms are made of Saxon porcelain, and the body is silk and brocade."

"Just let me show it to her. I'm sure she'll calm down afterwards."

But Elizabeth was caught between her dream and reality. She could feel a stabbing pain in one of her legs, and her forehead was also hurting. Worst, though, were the dreadful scenes she kept reliving: her mother's body being thrown into the ocean, and her father being beaten to death. She could still hear the terrible moan he let out at the end.

"Daddy, Daddy!" she shouted. "They've hurt him! He's dead!"

Bonnie, who had just returned with the pink cardboard box containing the doll, caught these last words. She turned pale and crossed herself.

"I understood that, Madam. The little girl says her father is dead."

"Oh, my goodness, what a violent world we live in!" exclaimed Maybel. "They may have killed him in front of her! Quick, show her the doll, Bonnie."

Strangely enough, the doll had an extraordinary effect on Elizabeth. Through her tears, the astonished girl glimpsed a face with bright eyes and a cloud of cascading blonde curls. Three figures were leaning over her bed.

She sighed in relief upon seeing the two young women. But even so, she thought she was still dreaming: in her memory, it was still early in the morning and the bear handler was attempting to snatch her. Then came flashbacks of running madly, of the black horse and the impact of the crash. She hadn't even had time to be afraid.

"Where am I?" she asked softly.

Maybel moved closer to her and smiled gently. Elizabeth studied her soft features, her amber-coloured eyes and cherry-red lips. The pretty stranger had wavy, light-brown hair tumbling onto her shoulders.

Suddenly, Elizabeth felt an unbearable need for her mother; she was desperate to take refuge in her arms.

"*Maman*," she moaned, "I want *maman*."

Edward rubbed his chin in dismay. He left the room to pour himself a brandy. Bonnie hastened to translate Elizabeth's words:

"Madam, she's asking for her mother."

"I thought as much. Try to speak to her in French, please. Her first name, ask for her first name. Tomorrow, we'll bring your mother here to interpret for us."

"My mother passed away last winter, Madam," whispered Bonnie. "You gave me time off."

"Oh, of course—I forgot. Well, please try again. You'll be rewarded."

"Say your name," said the maid in French. "Your name?"

Elizabeth quivered, relieved to have understood something. So far, the words exchanged at her bedside had meant nothing to her. During the past week in the Bronx, she had got used to hearing a variety of foreign voices, most of which spoke English, but she couldn't remember any words in particular.

"Lisbeth," she whispered shyly.

"Oh, that's not a very French name. You are from France, aren't you?" asked Bonnie.

"Yes. Mummy died on the boat. I don't know about Daddy. Some men hit him very hard last night."

"Say your name again?"

"Elizabeth, but Daddy calls me Lisbeth."

Maybel clasped her hands, charmed by the child's delicate little voice.

"Madam, she no longer has any parents—I'm sure of it."

"Thank you, Bonnie. You're a great help to me. I shall get you a French dictionary."

Maybel promised herself that she would keep the adorable little girl that fate had sent her way, no matter what. She was longing to dip the orphan in a warm bath to wash her hair, and to buy her new dresses and a pair of white leather boots.

"Only you know the whole story, Bonnie," she said quickly. "This poor orphan got thrown under the wheels of our carriage during our morning ride in Central Park. Don't tell anyone, though—no one needs to know."

The young servant nodded fervently. She was twenty-two years old, with an auburn fringe which peeked out from her little white cap. Her chubby face and dark eyes exuded kindness.

Elizabeth was starting to become aware of her surroundings and gazed at the enchanting bedroom and the enormous, cosy bed in which she lay. Most of all, she feared being thrown back onto the streets.

"Get her a bowl of soup, Bonnie," ordered Maybel. "And then, place the doll on the other pillow. We'll bathe and tidy her up tomorrow. It will be best to throw away her clothes. I'll go to Broadway early, to buy her new ones."

When his wife joined him in the sitting room, Edward had a big grin on his face. Maybel sat down on the armrest of his chair. She was naked under her bathrobe and her right breast was gaping out of it.

"You won this round, darling," he said quietly.

Guerville Castle
Tuesday, November 16, 1886

The letter arrived on a rainy morning. Adela and Hugues Laroche read it over and over again. At first, they were absolutely devastated, then indignant and disgusted. They couldn't bear the thought of their daughter being "buried at sea", even though their son-in-law claimed it was in accordance with her dying wishes.

"I will never be able to place flowers on her grave," said Adela in despair. "These people are barbaric! Throwing Catherine's body overboard, as though they were disposing of a useless object!"

"If what Guillaume says is true, the liner had only completed half the crossing," remarked her husband, coldly. "I suppose you can't keep a corpse in the hold for several days."

"Hugues, that's our child you're talking about! 'A corpse'— what a terrible thing to call her! At least there was a funeral service for her, if nothing else. Good heavens, my precious Catherine! I can't begin to imagine the circumstances in which she died. The stillborn baby, the haemorrhaging that ultimately killed her . . . If only she had listened to us. She'd be here now, with us, or at home in Montignac. If only I had visited her more. But you wouldn't let me, on the grounds that it would please the Duquesnes!"

"And I was right! After getting acquainted with us, old Antoine would have been only too happy to get his feet under our table."

"Maybe. But I missed out on so many opportunities to spend quality time with our daughter, because of pride—your pride!"

Laroche shrugged, looking down. He picked up the letter again and fought the urge to crumple it up and throw it on the fire.

"Of course, it's all my fault," he grumbled. "But you were very contemptuous of our son-in-law, Adela—don't deny it! Besides, what's the point of torturing ourselves? We've lost our only daughter. Nothing can bring her back. I'll have a headstone placed in the cemetery in remembrance of her, so you'll have a place to go to pray for her soul."

With that, he grabbed the riding crop he had flung down on the marble surface of a dresser.

"Where are you going, Hugues? I beg you, don't leave me! I'm sick to my stomach."

"I'm going to Rouillac, to send a telegram to Guillaume. We have his address in New York. I shall tell him that I will be taking the next ship to come and get Elizabeth. That peasant thought he was earning his stripes as a member of the Carpenters' Guild. I will tell him that his stupidity and pig-headedness have brought about the death of Catherine and my grandson. If the child had been born at full term, here in France, he would have had a bright future ahead, as heir to my estate."

Breathless, Hugues Laroche fell silent. Hatred and pain were choking him.

"I wonder how it's possible to send messages so quickly from one end of the world to another," remarked Adela absentmindedly.

"Humans are clever and resourceful. Who knows what advances we'll make in the future. Europe is now connected to America via submarine cables, through which decoded sounds pass . . . Look, I don't want to waste time explaining it!"

His wife wasn't listening. She couldn't hold back her tears any longer.

"I wish I could have been at Catherine's side to say goodbye to her, to give her one last kiss," she whimpered. "Hugues, do you really think Guillaume will let us have Elizabeth?"

"He will do as I say, Adela," Laroche growled.

He raised his arms up in the air in exasperation and stormed out.

Madeleine heard the hallway door slam. She quietly entered the drawing room.

"Madam, I have prepared some tea. A cup would do you good."

"Good idea, Madeleine. I want to thank you—you've taken excellent care of me since I lost my daughter. Alas, my husband and I have found out a bit more—our son-in-law wrote to us. Catherine's body is lying on the bottom of the ocean. He says it was what she wanted, though I doubt it very much. The baby she was expecting was a boy."

Adela was relieved to be able to confide in her servant and tell her about the shameful events surrounding her daughter's death.

"I was never a very affectionate mother," she said bitterly. "I will be much more loving and affectionate to little Elizabeth, should my husband manage to find her and bring her back. The presence of a child would brighten up the castle. We must pray, my dear Madeleine."

"Oh, I will, Madam—I'll pray morning and night," she asserted. "You look very pale, Madam. Let me bring you the tea."

"Pour me a glass of brandy, while you're at it. I'm in such pain—it will make me feel better."

"Of course, Madam."

Madeleine tended to Adela's well-being with keen devotion, but her demeanour changed as soon as she got back to the pantry. Her hands on her hips, she glanced furiously around her.

"Pray that the little brat will come back—whatever next? Me—why would I pray for her? We certainly don't need that snooty little madam in our way—no we don't. As if I didn't have enough to do already!"

She was furious, and restrained herself from smashing an earthenware bowl that stood on the edge of the table. Vincent, who was watching her through the glass door leading to the back of the castle, knocked hesitantly.

"Oh, just come in!" she shouted furiously.

"Hey, I'm being careful! I know you, my sweetie. When you're pissed off, you're capable of ripping me to shreds," he joked as he joined her.

"Listen, the boss made me saddle Talion, that damned grey gelding of his. He was off to Rouillac. Do you know what's going on?"

"They received a letter from New York. Apparently, Miss Catherine was thrown into the ocean. Her husband didn't kill her, after all—well, in a way he did, because she died in childbirth. Of course, the boss wants the other child back."

"Yeah, that's to be expected," he grumbled, as he kissed her in the hollow of her neck. "By the way, your nephew got out again. I saw him running down in the park."

"For crying out loud! Wait till I catch him—I'll have his guts for garters. I swear he won't do it again. If Madam were to see him . . ."

The groom silenced her with a hungry kiss. Without so much as a protest, she followed him down into the cellar. He grinned silently as he slid the bolt across the door.

The Dakota Building, New York
Saturday, November 20, 1886

Maybel brushed Elizabeth's beautiful brown locks. With Bonnie's help, she had just washed them for the third time in five days. The child couldn't be bathed, due to the plaster cast on her left leg, but she had been cleaned and groomed with bowls of hot water.

Propped up in bed against big fluffy pillows, the child beamed as she breathed in the smell of soap and talcum powder. She felt the softness of the terry towels and the silkiness of the fine underwear.

"My, you have ringlets, Lisbeth!" cried Maybel. "Bonnie, translate."

"Yes, Mummy used to say that too," replied the little girl.

"She's learned the word, Madam," rejoiced the servant. "If you keep her, she'll have to learn English."

"If we keep her! There's not a shadow of a doubt as to that. She has stolen Edward's heart—we couldn't part with her now."

Elizabeth was listening attentively. She started to remember the names of these extraordinary people who were looking after her with such love and devotion. They seemed very wealthy to her—even more so than her grandparents in Guerville.

"The doctor is pleased with her progress," declared Maybel, picking some blue ribbons from a pile of frilly trimmings fanned out on the bedspread. "According to him, Lisbeth will be able to walk in two weeks' time."

"She's already a better colour and her face is filling out a bit," agreed Bonnie. "God pushed her in front of your carriage, Madam!"

"Perhaps—but she could have died!" exclaimed Maybel. "In any case, we must make amends. Edward will ensure that this is put right. Anyhow, I'll hand her over to you now, Bonnie."

"Yes, Madam."

Maybel left the room. Her long red velvet dress swirled with each step, a high bun accentuating her neck and shoulders. Elizabeth let out a small sigh once she had disappeared into the hallway.

"Will you talk to me?" Bonnie asked her.

Since Elizabeth's arrival, the Woolworths' maid had been making great efforts to remember her French. She still had a French uncle in Queens, whom she'd visited as soon as possible. Maybel had been very generous to her, letting her travel by carriage, even going so far as to give her extra pay. Bonnie was surprised at how fast the words and expressions were coming back to her. The bilingual dictionary was very useful, too.

"Madam Maybel wants to know if you are happy here," she said to the child, taking care to speak clearly.

"Maybel," repeated Elizabeth. "You're Bonnie."

"Yes, I'm Bonnie. I work for Maybel and her husband."

"I am happy, but also sad," said the little girl. "Where are my clothes—the ones that Mummy made in Montignac?"

"Montignac? Is that where you lived? Madam ordered me to throw away your clothes."

Elizabeth teared up. She was about to cry, but then Bonnie had an idea.

"I found this in one of your pockets, so I put it aside to return to you later."

She handed her the tin soldier. Elizabeth snatched it out of her hand. The tiny toy was her last remaining attachment to France, Guerville Castle, and her parents.

"I shall keep it under my pillow," she whispered. "A kind little boy gave it to me."

"Madam Maybel will soon buy you beautiful new toys, Lisbeth."

"I'd love to stay here, but if Daddy comes looking for me, he won't know where to find me."

"But you said they killed your daddy!"

"That's true. I think he's dead, like Mummy—I saw it in my nightmare," stammered Elizabeth.

Bonnie didn't understand everything because the little girl was mumbling. She thought it best to end the conversation.

"You must rest, Lisbeth," she advised. "Don't worry—I'll be back at noon with your lunch."

Edward Woolworth got home late that night. Maybel was anxiously awaiting him in the sitting room. She had been leafing through an illustrated fashion magazine.

"Darling, at last!" she cried out. "How did your enquiries go?"

The trader handed his coat and hat to Bonnie, then sat down next to his wife. She kissed him, but without the enthusiasm he had been hoping for.

"I learned from my secretary that they've fished a body out of the Hudson River. The man was in his thirties, severely wounded and unrecognizable, carrying nothing that would have identified him. You know as well as I do that countless people end up like that. This city is getting more and more dangerous, especially the Bronx. Score settling, heinous crimes, rapes, not to mention the wretched plight of the many hundreds of orphans roaming the streets. So how do we know if this drowned man with the smashed skull is Lisbeth's father? There's no clear evidence to support it. The police were intrigued by the buttons on his jacket, though. One was missing; they were copper, engraved with a compass."

Maybel frowned incredulously.

"What does Jack say? You always say your secretary has an answer to everything."

"You're right, Jack would bend over backwards to help me. As it happens, he did come up with something. According to him, these buttons prove that the deceased was a member of the

Compagnons du Devoir, a well-known French craftsmen's association."

"Oh God, he may well be the little girl's father, then. Edward, let's not search any further. She's an orphan. I don't want to lose her. I love her so much! I must be the happiest person in the world, now that I've got a child by my side."

"Maybel, there's nothing I'd rather do than keep and adopt her, but she's an immigrant and probably has family in France. Once she can tell us more about her background, we can search the registers at the Immigrant Reception Centre in Fort Clinton, and . . ."

"No," she cut him short, placing her index finger on his lips. "Please, don't say any more. Those poor people abandon their homelands to seek their fortune here in America, on the other side of the ocean. We can give her a wonderful life, Edward. I beg you, we must adopt her at once!"

"I'm thinking it over, Maybel. I would do anything to see you looking so pretty and cheerful every day."

The couple exchanged a tender kiss. At that moment, they felt invincible, their love growing at the prospect of finally having a child to pamper.

Baptiste and Lea Rambert's home
Saturday, November 27, 1886

Light flakes of snow were falling in New York, much to the delight of Lea, who stood at the window holding her baby.

"Before long, the city will be all white, Tony," she murmured. "Mummy won't be able to take you out for strolls anymore."

Baptiste was watching them. He had left the building site at noon, with the firm intention of spending the rest of the weekend with his family. Tomorrow they would go to church, if the pavements were not too slippery. He frowned with annoyance when he heard a knock on their door.

"There's no peace for the wicked!" he grumbled, which made his wife chuckle.

Baptiste opened the door and was surprised to find a tall man standing in front of him. He had grey temples and looked extremely elegant in his black woollen coat and top hat.

"Sir, you must have the wrong door . . . " Baptiste began, for the upper classes never ventured into his building.

"Are you Baptiste Rambert? I got your address from your employer."

The stranger spoke in impeccable French. His thin face and steely gaze unsettled the carpenter.

"I am. Do come in, Sir—it's cold on the doorstep."

"Thank you very much. I'm Hugues Laroche—Guillaume Duquesne's father-in-law."

"Good Lord," murmured Baptiste.

"Please take a seat, Sir," Lea said.

Then she hastily put their son to bed.

Laroche's lacklustre eyes scanned the room. Though the small apartment was clean and tidy, he was struck by how cramped and poorly furnished it was. It gave away the couple's lack of means.

"It's nice to be able to converse with fellow countrymen," he said, to be polite. "I arrived the day before yesterday, after a harrowing crossing on *La Bretagne*. The ship entered service this year, like *La Champagne*—that damn boat whose name I can hardly bring myself to mention. My son-in-law, my daughter Catherine and their girl Elizabeth had the misfortune to board it in October."

Baptiste nodded; he knew the story. Lea again gestured to a chair, but the visitor seemed too distressed to notice.

"You must know why I'm here?" he pursued.

"I can understand why you came to New York," said Baptiste, "but not why you came to see us."

"That is easily explained. I sent two telegrams to my son-in-law several weeks ago, and received no answer. Certainly, the service is costly. But since my wife gave my daughter a handsome amount of money before she left—without my knowledge—Guillaume could have taken the trouble to give me some news. Catherine's death was a cruel blow to my wife and I, and we're very worried about our granddaughter Elizabeth. May I trouble you for a glass of water?"

Lea, touched by this distressed father's self-restraint, poured him a drink.

"Sir, I can't tell you how sorry I am! Your son-in-law and his child disappeared on the evening of Sunday, the 7th of November, while on their way here. We had invited them to dinner, and Baptiste had found them a place to stay in our street. We have running water in this part of town, unlike their previous lodgings."

Hugues Laroche looked down, clenching his fists in silence.

The calm before the storm, thought Baptiste, aware of the inner turmoil that was ravaging Laroche. He was not mistaken.

"You're *sorry*, Madam?!" the Frenchman exclaimed. "For God's sake, you announce that Guillaume and Elizabeth disappeared as though it were a trivial matter! What happened? Did you notify the police?"

"I forbid you to take it out on my wife, Sir! She's been doing her utmost to try to find your granddaughter. We, too, have been profoundly affected by this tragedy, to this very day. You haven't even given us time to explain."

"Forgive me, Mr. Rambert," pleaded Laroche at once. "I've been beside myself ever since I learned of the death of my daughter. Please, continue."

Baptiste recounted his story with much anguish and produced the statement he gave at the police station. He then took the copper button out of the table drawer.

"Every night, even in broad daylight, people are murdered," he added. "Their bodies are found lying in a dead-end alley or in the Hudson River. I'm afraid I have every reason to believe that my friend is dead! As for your granddaughter, Elizabeth, Lea has tried in vain to track her down. We wanted to keep her and look after her."

Lea sat down opposite their visitor. In French peppered with Italian, she gave an account of everything she had done.

"I have a seven-month-old baby," she began. "My mother took care of him while I was out searching for the poor little girl. I paid the Sisters of Charity a visit, but they mostly take in toddlers and babies. They hadn't heard of a six-year-old French girl, but pointed me in the direction of a Protestant institution called the Children's Aid Society, founded by Charles Loring Brace. For the last thirty years, Mr. Laroche, this gentleman's organization has enabled thousands of orphans and abandoned children to get a better life in the West. Unfortunately, none of the many poor girls there fitted Elizabeth's description."

"Have you seen her before?" asked Laroche.

"I'm afraid I haven't."

"Then how would you recognize her?"

"I knew her first and last names and spoke in her mother tongue," Lea explained. "Given that she is already six years old, she would certainly have responded. An Orphan Train was on its way to Indiana last week, and I took a close look at the children. My goodness, they were so joyful at the prospect of leaving the city for the countryside. You should have seen them—all dressed up and clean, eager to find their new parents on arrival."

Lea's voice was quaking, so Baptiste took over:

"My wife scrutinized the face of every girl who looked around your granddaughter's age. Six were named Elizabeth. One of them was French, but she was twelve years old. The others couldn't understand Lea's questions, and none were brunette with bright-blue eyes and long curls, as Guillaume had described her. To be candid, Sir—I fear the worst. Those who attacked your son-in-law must have got rid of his daughter too."

"No, that's impossible!" said Hugues Laroche indignantly. "I won't even hear of it! Even if you are right and these villains robbed Guillaume, why would they hurt an innocent little girl?"

Laroche loosened his shirt collar. His face had turned crimson, and Lea saw he was having trouble breathing. Full of pity, she offered him a glass of the remaining whisky she'd been saving for special occasions.

"Here you are—it'll do you good."

Distraught, Laroche swallowed it straight down, then banged his fist on the table.

"My granddaughter is alive, I'm certain of it! I'll leave no stone unturned to find her. Yesterday, I went to the address Guillaume gave me in his letter. I managed to string together a few words in English, and a neighbour explained that there had been some French people in that grubby building, but they had moved on. A couple with two boys."

"I've met the woman," piped up Lea. "It was the day after Guillaume and Elizabeth disappeared. She wasn't helpful at all."

"This leaves us with only one solution," sighed Laroche. "The press! I shall post an announcement, offering a reward. Anyone who can tell me something about the whereabouts of my granddaughter can find me at my hotel."

"Put our address in it, too," advised Baptiste with new optimism.

The atmosphere mellowed, despite the prevailing social differences and the anxiety gnawing away at their visitor. They talked for another hour before saying goodbye, imbued with a glimmer of hope.

Alas, no one came forward with information, and Hugues Laroche eventually had to return to France. When *La Gascogne* had completed half the crossing, he wandered onto the deck holding a bouquet of luxurious artificial white flowers that he had purchased on Broadway. He cast the bouquet into the turbulent ocean, murmuring words of love to his daughter Catherine.

The Dakota Building
Saturday, December 18, 1886

Though the Woolworths' sumptuous home had central heating, it still featured a marble fireplace that was the focal point of the sitting room. Maybel was busy decorating the pine tree next to it for Christmas. She loved having an open fire in wintertime, just to bask in the heat while watching the flames dance.

It was snowing heavily. Elizabeth, who had been walking without crutches for a whole week now, stood with her nose pressed against one of the windows, fascinated by the cascading snowflakes.

"How beautiful!" she gushed in English.

Maybel ran towards the child and kissed her excitedly. The English lessons she'd been giving her were bearing fruit. At this rate, her little Lisbeth would soon be conversing with her and Edward. Maybel laughed gaily.

"My pretty little doll," she murmured, and Elizabeth let herself be cuddled. She had no idea that her care-giver had just burnt a newspaper advertisement promising a reward to anyone who had knowledge of Elizabeth Duquesne, who had disappeared on the night of Sunday, November 7 to Monday, November 8, 1886.

Maybel had hurriedly thrown several copies into the fire. Even so, her husband had managed to salvage one, which he then hid at the bottom of his safe.

7

Lisbeth Woolworth

The Dakota Building
9 a.m., Wednesday, December 23, 1896

Lisbeth was putting the final touches to the stunning Christmas tree that had been delivered the previous day. This year, snow was slow to grace the streets of New York. The city was getting bigger by the day, with new buildings springing up against the grey sky. The young girl was daydreaming, a decorated glass bauble in hand.

She was trying in vain to remember her first Christmas in the Woolworth household ten years ago. Nothing would come back to her, except for a vague smell of soap and the sensation of hot bath water on her skin.

"Bonnie!" she called out. "Bonnie!"

The servant ran from the kitchen, ruddy-faced and with a large apron tied at her waist. Now aged thirty-two, she was starting to get a bit plump. She had become a housekeeper, with the pay that went with it, and her job took so much of her time that it required her to stay single.

"Yes, Miss! Do you need me?" she asked, arranging a red lock of hair that had escaped from her bun. There was no need for her to speak French anymore: Lisbeth had been fluent in English for years now. The servant looked her up and down admiringly. Lisbeth was wearing a velvet dress with a plunging neckline.

The orphan from Central Park had grown into a beautiful American lady of high society, whose blue eyes, dark waves and angelic face filled Maybel and Edward with pride.

"You look very pretty today, Miss."

"We have guests coming tonight, and Mom wants me to look my best. Dad has invited one of his social acquaintances, a lawyer called Peter Ford."

"That name doesn't ring a bell, but you definitely look stunning."

"Thank you, Bonnie. I don't know why, but today I keep thinking about the first winter I spent here. I recall almost nothing from that time. You were here, weren't you? Can you tell me about it?"

"Why today, Miss?"

"Why not? I told you, I can't help thinking about it."

"Madam wouldn't like it. She worries so much when you have bad dreams and cry. It's not good to rake up the past."

"Please, Bonnie—just a few details," begged Lisbeth, smiling at her adorably.

"Well, if you must hear about it, you'd better come into the kitchen. I can't risk burning the cakes, or I won't have anything to serve for tea!"

They stood around a heavy oak table whose surface was still covered in flour.

"So. What is it you want to hear about?" sighed the servant. "I've told you time and time again that Sir and Madam ran you over in their carriage, and then brought you home."

"And my left leg was broken, plus I took a blow to the head. Yes, I know that part by heart. But who were my real parents? Did I talk about them at the beginning? Oh Bonnie, sometimes I have such strange dreams!"

"You were scared and very unhappy and said that both your parents were dead. Please, Lisbeth, you must let it go. Before long, you grew to love Madam and Sir."

"How could I not—they've only ever been kind and loving to me. I remember a magnificent doll with blonde hair and fine clothes."

"Ah, the doll—that was your first night here!" Bonnie chuckled. "You calmed down as soon as I showed it to you. Sir had bought it for your cousin Pearl, and he ended up giving it to her. Madam bought you an even more beautiful one the next day."

Lisbeth traced the letter *P* in the flour. A strange feeling overcame her.

"I'm sorry, Bonnie—I don't feel very well. I think I'll go and lie down for a while."

"Proof that I was right, Miss—it's not good to venture too far into the past! You're white as a sheet."

The young girl hastened to leave the room. She reproached herself for interrogating Bonnie, for she loved her dearly.

"What's wrong with me?" she asked herself in a low voice.

Maybel and Edward Woolworth had told her countless times that her background was nothing out of the ordinary. They had not been blessed with the joys of parenthood, which was why they had decided to take in the emaciated, dirty orphan they'd run over in Central Park.

I was carrying nothing that could have helped them identify me, and without them, I would have been sent out West, crammed into a train with other orphans, she thought to herself, relieved to be back in her own bedroom. *I've been very lucky.*

She flung herself across the bed, the beautiful surroundings consoling her. Floral fabrics made from chintz imported from London comprised most of the decor, from the double curtains to the chair upholstery. The walls, covered with pink embossed paper, were in harmony with the beige woodwork. Small cushions adorned with lace and braids were scattered over the silky quilt. She knew her cousin Pearl envied her, never missing an opportunity to insinuate that her uncle spoiled Lisbeth too much. *Pearl keeps teasing me, calling me the princess of the Dakota Building!*

Lisbeth closed her eyes, her heart aching. The word "princess" was stuck in her head. It was a word she had always known, as it was the same in French and English. Suddenly, a long-forgotten voice resounded in her head.

"I can't take it anymore!" she called out, on the brink of tears.

It wasn't long before Bonnie came knocking on her door.

The servant knew how to handle the fits of hysteria that her beloved girl suffered from. She even went as far as hiding them from Maybel Woolworth, to avoid yet another visit from Dr. John Foster. He was a loyal friend of Mr. Woolworth, who liked to use laudanum as a cure-all.

"There, there, calm down," she said, entering the room. "Only a minute ago you were happy and cheerful."

Lisbeth let Bonnie caress her hair and cheeks. She dried Lisbeth's tears with the corner of her apron.

"Forgive me," whispered the young girl. "I need to get some air. Nothing would make me happier than skating in Central Park or going for a walk."

"Alone? How inappropriate that would be! Sir will accompany you tomorrow, when your cousin Pearl arrives."

"Please let me take a walk outside, Bonnie. My parents won't be coming home for lunch—no one would know. I keep getting told that the city is a very dangerous place, and Central Park is a particularly murderous area. Yet, Pearl is allowed to skate there with friends. It's unfair that I'm not allowed to go out without Mom or Dad!" she exclaimed. "They say my health is too fragile, which is why they've always wanted me to have private tutors. They've never let me attend a real school."

"And you've never complained about it, until now. What's the matter with you today, my little Miss?"

Her employers' behaviour had certainly puzzled Bonnie in the early years after the girl's arrival.

The child had been confined to the apartment and was put to bed at the slightest sign of a cold or fatigue.

She was given English lessons, and later, qualified teachers taught her history, science, mathematics and literature. Lisbeth played the piano and recited poems flawlessly, but the servant often compared her to a hothouse flower, for she was of rare beauty, but deprived of space and freedom.

"You can confide in me—I won't betray you," Bonnie insisted. "Could it be that you're having nightmares again?"

"They're less frequent than before, Bonnie, but there's a recurring one. I see the ocean with its huge, grey waves, and I'm afraid, very afraid. I'm also tiny and convinced I'm about to drown."

Bonnie flinched with embarrassment. Lisbeth had spoken in French.

"Oh, Miss, we agreed to stop it! Mrs. Maybel almost caught us last summer."

"We have nothing to worry about—she isn't here. It's your fault as well, though—you kept talking to me in my first language!"

"But if Sir were to discover our secret, he would fire me!" Bonnie said anxiously.

"I wouldn't let him, dear Bonnie. I don't want you to leave."

"You're a very sweet girl, Lisbeth. I'll come and work for you when you get married."

They winked at each other knowingly. Already, Lisbeth was feeling better. Worried, the maid watched her slip out of her new outfit and put on a pair of culottes, boots and a woollen jacket.

"Bonnie, grab your coat and shoes. We're going for a walk— just a short way, we have time. It'll be my Christmas present!"

Lisbeth's blue eyes sparkled eagerly, and a mischievous smile lit up her lovely features.

"Just a little stroll, then. But not a word to Madam."

"Of course," agreed the girl. "Quick, let's go!"

Maybel and Edward Woolworth knew nothing of these brief outings, nor of their conversations in French. They certainly wouldn't be pleased if they did, and Bonnie was right to fear for her job. Luckily for her, they had been able to keep it a secret— for the time being, at least.

Guerville Castle
3 p.m., the same day

In the space of the last ten years, Hugues Laroche had aged and gained weight. He blamed it on the grief and silent anger that

still plagued him, ostracizing those around him with his unrelenting acrimony. His wife no longer paid any attention to his
ranting. Younger than him and more compassionate, Adela had
devoted herself to good deeds to atone for her wrongdoings
concerning Catherine.

"Our wrongdoings, Hugues," she would say over lunch in
the large, silent dining room. "Thanks to the support I've had
from our priest, I can now see how we pushed our daughter
and Guillaume away, through our contempt and our
intransigence."

Laroche looked up to the ceiling, his lips pursed. Adela would
not drop the subject.

"The generous offer you made to our son-in-law came too
late. You should have thought of it as soon as they got married."

Hugues Laroche had heard this so many times, he had lost
count. Each time he retorted:

"Stop torturing yourself with remorse! Guillaume was an
adventurer who dreamed of conquering the New World. He
seems to have paid a high price for it, that's all."

"Maybe our daughter was calling to him from heaven!"
exclaimed Adela. "They were so in love, their cruel fate might
have reunited them."

"Nonsense!" yelled her husband.

In spite of these verbal duels, tensions had begun to ease
under the centuries-old rooftops of the castle. Laroche had
purchased new land, and the income from his vineyards and his
distillery was growing steadily. Every day he exercised his sturdy
grey stallion, Galant, whom he had schooled himself.

"I'm off to Rouillac," he announced, sitting at the table after
a hearty lunch. "I told Justin this morning in the pantry. He's
probably already saddled Galant. That boy really is an excellent
groom. I can't thank Madeleine enough for recommending him
to me."

"A taciturn young man," remarked Adela. "He appeared out
of nowhere. You've taken him under your wing, knowing nothing about him."

"Justin loves horses and knows how to handle them. The same couldn't be said of Vincent, that lazy oaf."

"Please, don't speak ill of a dead man! Especially since the police still haven't established the circumstances of his death Something tells me he didn't just drown by accident . . ."

"You don't redeem yourself just because you're lying six feet under, my dear," retorted the squire. "Vincent was a scoundrel—he got what he deserved."

Adela shrugged, tired of battling against her husband's insensitivity. However, she was highly suspicious of his frequent visits to Rouillac, the main town in the region.

"Hugues, you haven't fallen for the charms of a young lady, have you?" she asked. "I don't want to be the laughing stock of the county. Be honest! I've noticed you riding off to town several times a week."

Hugues Laroche almost dropped the cup he was lifting to his lips. He let out a forced and bitter laugh. Adela looked at him in annoyance. She was jealous more out of pride than love.

"You have a vivid imagination!" he snapped. "God is my witness, I have been more faithful than most. I may have given in to certain fantasies many years ago, but at my age, I'm no longer tormented by wild desires. You might as well believe me, Adela. The only thing that torments me—torments me permanently—is the loss of our daughter!"

His wife knew at once that he was telling the truth, for she endured the same pain that time had failed to ease.

"So what is it you intend to do in Rouillac, Hugues?"

Her husband sighed. "I kept it from you to avoid reviving your pain or giving you false hope. But it's high time you knew the truth. I've never stopped investigating."

"Investigating what?" Adela asked, somewhat surprised.

Laroche slouched, looking distressed. His craggy features softened. "While I was in New York, I hired a detective to find Elizabeth."

"A detective? You mean like the famous Vidocq?"

"Precisely. I always believed that our granddaughter was

out there somewhere. The man I contacted promised me quick results, but threw in the towel after three years. Still, I just couldn't give up, so I approached another investigator, through a Parisian friend who travels to America twice a year. Elizabeth may be alive, Adela—and if that's the case, I'll bring her home."

"My goodness, I had no idea!" she exclaimed. "Hugues, I must apologize."

The sound of footsteps in the hallway put an end to their conversation.

Justin, the young groom, stood in the doorway. He was dressed in riding boots, a brown corduroy suit, and a tweed cap. He greeted them with a bow.

"Excuse me for disturbing you," he said in a deep, gentle voice. "Galant is getting impatient, Sir. If you're not ready, I can take him up to the park for a quarter of an hour, to warm him up."

"All right, lad. Before I hired you, I never bothered with your famous warm-up that primes the horse's muscles."

Hugues Laroche gave one of his rare smiles. Justin, a cheerful glint in his dark eyes, bowed again and hurried back to the stables.

Madeleine was watching him from the pantry window. Now that the bothersome Vincent had gone, she could weave her web.

Montignac, Charente
4 p.m., the same day

As soon as her husband had gone, Adela Laroche got her docile mare harnessed up to the Tilbury carriage. Wrapped in a heavy foxskin cape and wearing a hat with a veil that concealed her face, she set off for Montignac, taking advantage of her husband's absence.

It was bitterly cold. A fine rain drowned the wintery land-scape, which was dominated by grey stone, bare brown trees, and the dull-silver colour of the river she drove alongside.

I don't care if Hugues chides me again for going out without telling him, she thought. *If I'd listened to him, poor Antoine would never have known how his son died.*

She stopped in the large courtyard of a mill. The paddle wheels shook as they rumbled over the water of an outlet of the Charente river. At once, a figure appeared on the threshold of one of the buildings. It was Jean Duquesne, one of Guillaume's brothers. He hastened to help the visitor out of the carriage.

"I'll take care of your horse, Mrs. Adela," he said with a kind smile. "Father is resting by the hearth; he'll be happy to see you."

"Thank you, Jean. I won't be staying long. It gets dark early at this time of year."

"I can always light your lanterns, if need be."

Adela walked on, avoiding the many puddles on the ground. After the announcement of Catherine's death, she had spent several weeks debating whether to come or not. Then one morning, without telling a soul, she had set out to the Duquesnes' mill.

Seething with regret and remorse, she had been keen to become acquainted with her daughter's in-laws and to see where her daughter had spent her married life.

The miller had welcomed her with open arms.

"We have both lost our children, Madam," he had said, clasping her hand, without care for decorum. "Losing our loved ones is a cruel stroke of fate, yet we must accept that it's God's will, and cherish the memory of these wonderful young people we loved so dearly."

Guillaume's brothers—Jean, the youngest and Pierre, the eldest—were also very friendly and kind to Adela. Weary of her husband's vindictive rhetoric, Catherine's mother had craved benevolence. She had finally discovered a world in which affection and faith were the order of the day.

Without breathing a word to Hugues, she had started to make regular trips to Montignac. Over the course of her visits, which became more and more frequent, she had begun to discover Catherine's true personality.

"Your daughter was a natural beauty," old Antoine had told her, "but more importantly, she had a heart of gold. Down to earth and always cheerful. She loved having us over for a hearty meal every Sunday."

"Cathy often came to help when there was a lot of grain to grind," Pierre had added.

"Once, I fell out of the cherry tree, while trying to pick the best fruits for her," his wife Yvonne had said. "She nursed me, but before doing so, she carried me home on her back. She was brave, kind and big-hearted."

Hearing this had rekindled Adela's grief, but at the same time, it had eased her wounded heart.

I can see why my daughter was happy with the Duquesne family, she had often thought as she journeyed home. *They are wholesome, kind and wise people. Lord, forgive me, for I have been foolish and vain.*

When the squire had found out from Madeleine that his wife made frequent visits to Montignac, he had hollered and screamed, accusing her of betraying him.

"You happily collude with those peasants, Adela—the very ones that robbed us of our daughter! What the hell were you doing there?"

Adela had turned a deaf ear. Nothing in the world would make her renounce her newfound friendship with the miller and his two sons.

For Adela, the Duquesnes' kitchen was a haven of peace and tranquillity. It was a vast room with a low ceiling that was black with smoke, and a monumental fireplace made of local stone. Garlic and onion braids adorned the beams, and today a delicious smell of hot bread rose from a dresser on which three crown loaves with cracked crusts were lined up.

Antoine Duquesne was smoking his pipe, sitting next to his dog in a straw-lined armchair.

"Mrs. Adela, what a pleasant surprise! You don't usually come this late."

"I couldn't help it. I've loved the outdoors ever since I started travelling by myself—thanks to my Tilbury, which I purchased myself. I'm relieved to see you're not ill. Jean worried me—he said you were resting."

"Don't worry, my rheumatism is playing up, due to the wet weather. I suffer less when there's a frost."

"I've brought you a few jars of honey and some aniseed gums, to share with your children and grandchildren," she said, smiling. "They're in the trunk of the Tilbury. Jean will fetch them when I leave. Antoine, my good friend, I learned something today that I wanted to share with you."

The miller's kind face lit up for a moment. Like the dour Hugues Laroche, the pious man also hoped that his granddaughter Elizabeth was still alive.

"Alas, no, I don't have any good news to tell you. I've just learned something disturbing: my husband has not given up trying to find Elizabeth. He keeps in touch with a detective in New York, by telegram."

"A detective, really! Gosh, if your husband has been paying someone for ten years, he must be broke by now!" He nodded, lost in thought. His bright-blue eyes, which he had passed on to Elizabeth, were staring at an invisible point in space.

"Our pretty little girl," he whispered. "It would be a miracle to hear she is safe and sound. Though she has probably forgotten us, if she was lucky enough to be taken in by some kind people."

"Most certainly," sighed Adela.

"I lost sleep over it at the time, imagining her alone in a huge foreign city, abandoned to her fate. She was so adorable. As soon as she could speak, she called me 'Pops Toine'. I've never stopped praying for her."

"I can see she must have liked being here, whereas at the castle she hardly said two words," admitted Adela. "May your prayers be answered!" she said. "Elizabeth would have been sixteen in April, and my Catherine thirty-nine—tonight, at seven o'clock precisely. I light a candle in front of her portrait on this day every year . . . But where are your boys? I was hoping to get the chance to give your grandsons a hug, as school is closed for the holidays."

"Yvonne has spent part of the afternoon at the mill, to grind rye. She sent Gilles and Laurent to their grandmother, who lives on the road to Vouharte."

Pierre entered the room. He looked so much like Guillaume that Adela was overcome with emotion. They had the same build, black hair, tanned complexion and pale eyes.

"Good evening, Madam," he said, greeting her. "Father, I'll take the bread to the grocery store. Do you need any tobacco?"

"No, son, I have enough. Now hurry home to your wife."

The eldest of the Duquesnes packed the crown loaves into a canvas sack. He put on a hooded cape and said goodbye.

"I must leave soon," said Adela. "Antoine, do you really think it's possible to find Elizabeth? I cling to this glimmer of hope—yet some days, I prefer to give up hope and grieve for her. After all, she could be dead, couldn't she?"

Adela was crying. The miller got out of his chair and went up to the bench where she was sitting.

"My dear lady, don't torture yourself unduly. I got through this by telling myself that our fate has already been decided. It was a wrench to say farewell to Guillaume, Cathy and my granddaughter, but I respected their choice and their dreams. I have shed many tears over them and sometimes I still break down. If we ever find out that Elizabeth was spared her parents' fate, I would content myself with that."

Adela looked up and smiled sadly at the elderly man with his gentle-looking face and his white curly hair. His kindness lifted her spirits.

"You must return to the castle," he said, "otherwise I'll worry about you on the roads at nightfall."

"You're right, and I'll have to face my husband's wrath—as always, when he suspects me of having been here. Goodbye, my friend."

Five minutes later, Antoine and his son Jean waved her off, giving her strength for the journey back to the castle. She would much rather have stayed, as the mill was the only place now where she felt free from bitterness and anger.

The Dakota Building, New York
Tuesday, December 23, 1896, in the evening

Maybel Woolworth was leaning over Lisbeth. She never tired of touching her silky dark hair, whose long natural curls fascinated her. Sitting in front of her marquetry dressing table with its three mirrors, the young lady was staring at her own reflection without really seeing it. That evening she was not interested in her little nose, full pink lips or high cheekbones, or even her bright-blue eyes, all of which were undeniably appealing.

"You must look beautiful tonight," whispered Maybel in her ear.

"Why do I need to look beautiful, Mom? What are you both plotting, you and Dad?"

"Nothing, darling! What a vivid imagination you have. Peter Ford has helped us with some very important business, as he's a lawyer, and an excellent one at that. Edward wants to introduce you to him. You must do us proud."

"I feel like an object on show!"

"Don't be silly—a woman owes it to herself to be stylish and attractive."

"Try adding intelligence to that, Mom! A beautiful person without intelligence and education is not necessarily attractive."

"What spirit! Don't worry, Lisbeth—you have such qualities. Now finish getting ready! I'll be in the sitting room."

"Wait a minute, Mom. I want to ask you a question."

"I'm listening, Lisbeth."

"Did anything out of the ordinary happen during my first Christmas here?"

Maybel sat down on the edge of her bed. She seemed puzzled.

"It's strange that you should ask me that, because I was thinking about it just this morning, when I awoke. Ten years ago, around this time, I was decorating the tree and you were excited by the wreaths and the decorations. But that same evening, you ran a high fever, just as you did after the accident. I remember it well—I was terrified. You fell ill and Edward and I thought we were going to lose you."

"What was wrong with me?"

"Meningitis, according to the doctor. He said your life was in danger. I didn't leave your bedside for a whole week—I've never prayed so much in my life. You got better the next morning. Having regained consciousness, you looked at me and . . ."

She stopped, overwhelmed with emotion, before continuing:

"You snuggled into my arms, calling me *maman*—yes, *maman*, in French. That must have been the happiest day of my life."

"Mom, you should have told me this long ago," Elizabeth said, kissing Maybel, who stood up to give her a firm hug.

"I didn't want to unsettle you. The doctor advised me not to talk about your past anymore."

"But I've been thinking about it today, Mom. I even interrogated Bonnie. Something was urging me to piece together the memories of my childhood before I arrived at your home in New York."

Lisbeth's quiet confession left Maybel dispirited. She had gone pale and was biting her lower lip.

"I guess you can't fight that sort of thing. Edward often says that the human mind is an extraordinary machine, but full of mysteries. We'll discuss it with your father. You should put on your sapphire necklace; it looks very becoming on you."

"Okay, Mom. I'll join you soon."

Once she was alone, the girl opened her jewellery box. The prospect of sitting at the table for hours on end, in the presence of a stranger, put a damper on her high spirits after the exhilaration of her morning getaway.

In what way could this man have helped my parents? she wondered, intrigued.

She picked up the sapphire necklace, a gift she had received last year. Just as she opened the silver clasp, she spotted the tin soldier, half hidden under a black velvet ribbon.

Seeing the figurine, its colours faded with time, brought a lump to her throat.

She reached for it.

"A drummer," she whispered. "Bonnie said that I used to hide it under my pillow as a child. It was precious to me. But where is it from?"

She cast her mind back, trying to recall, in vain.

"Never mind," she muttered to herself.

Elizabeth grinned, reflecting on her stroll with Bonnie. They'd gone as far as Central Park. The grass and shrubs were adorned with a thin layer of frost and the icy wind hinted at snow.

"We bought doughnuts near the carousel, and I got to ride on the wooden horses. Oh, how wonderful that was!"

Then she blushed, remembering a stranger who had stared at her in awe as she stepped off the large merry-go-round. A young man whom she guessed was around twenty years old, in a grey suit and a black astrakhan coat, a hat over his ebony hair.

"When he greeted me with a nod, the gaze of his amber eyes sent shivers down my spine," she whispered to herself.

Her young heart had pounded with unexpected emotion, but she didn't know why. She had been unable to conceal her turmoil, and Bonnie had decided they should head back.

"You look too innocent, Miss," the servant had grumbled. "You'd be easy prey for a fortune hunter."

In her room, Elizabeth let out a deep sigh of despair, squeezing the lead soldier in the palm of her hand. She felt jittery.

Suddenly, it was as if a curtain had been ripped open. Slowly and bit by bit, images flashed past her eyes. First white curtains, then a dark room and a colossal wardrobe, whose sculpted doors opened and closed. Breathless, she recalled feeling terrified, but someone had come to reassure her in a low, soft voice:

"Here you are, a tin soldier—my favourite. He plays the drum. He'll protect you during the journey, and if you're still scared, you can tell him to send for me. I shall come and save you."

Trembling, Elizabeth reopened her eyes, almost surprised to be in her beautiful bedroom in the Dakota Building. She'd had a fleeting vision of a small blond boy, who was touching her hand through the bars of her bed.

"Justin, his name was Justin—now I remember! No, that's impossible. Maybe it's just a dream I've recalled. Me and my dreams, my nightmares . . . I've caused Mom and Dad so much worry."

She was sick to her stomach, distraught with disbelief and fear at the sudden resurgence of this memory. She tucked the tin soldier back in the box, amidst the gold, pearl and diamond jewellery.

"I don't want to know anymore," she moaned, as if there was an impending threat lurking in the room. "I'm a Woolworth, Lisbeth Woolworth."

She put on the sapphire necklace and hurried into the hall-way with a stern look on her face, to play the role of the perfect daughter in front of Peter Ford, the lawyer.

Dinner ended on a pleasant note. Edward had talked a lot about his stock-market speculations and Maybel hadn't stopped babbling about the New Year party she would be host-ing. There was hardly a sound from Lisbeth Woolworth, who appeared absentminded, smilingly appropriately at everyone's comments.

"You've been very quiet, Miss," said Peter Ford while they were waiting for dessert. "It's a pity."

"I prefer to keep quiet and listen, Sir," retorted Elizabeth, "even when the conversations are hardly of any interest."

Edward, a little drunk, burst out laughing, sharing his amuse-ment with his wife.

"Did you hear our daughter, Maybel? She adroitly implied that she's bored! Excuse us for being so serious, Lisbeth. You'll have more fun on New Year's Eve with Pearl and her cousins. You'll come won't you, Peter? We'd be delighted to have you."

"With pleasure, Edward. I suppose you'll be celebrating the official adoption of Miss that evening!" he said, his tongue loosened by the excellent Californian wine.

A deafening silence followed. Maybel looked at her husband in panic, who in turn glared at the lawyer.

"Oh, I'm sorry—I've put my foot in it," he said. "Please forgive me, Edward."

"What does this mean?" asked Elizabeth, upset. "Dad, explain it to me."

"Tomorrow, darling—not now."

"On Christmas Eve—just be patient," added Maybel.

"I heard what Mr. Ford said! You still haven't adopted me, have you!" exclaimed the girl. "I don't want to wait to understand. If you've been lying to me all these years, I'd rather know now."

Terribly embarrassed, Peter Ford smoothed his thin, greying moustache.

"It would be better if I left you in private," he said as he got up. "I'm so sorry."

Bonnie approached, proudly carrying a superb pudding drizzled with hot rum. No one congratulated her or even remarked on it. She placed it in the middle of the round table and stepped aside.

"Show the gentleman out, Bonnie," ordered Maybel.

"Yes, Madam."

Elizabeth stared at the pudding without actually seeing it. Mortified, the couple remained silent, not daring to look at her. When the girl heard the front door slam shut, she broke her silence.

"We're alone now. Tell me the truth. Did you or did you not adopt me? Is my name not Woolworth?"

"What does it matter, darling?" protested Maybel feebly. "It's just paperwork. You're our daughter. We love you, from the bottom of our hearts!"

"You bear my name. I love you as though you were my own flesh and blood, Lisbeth," added Edward fervently. "You must believe me! We were going to talk to you at Christmas, before the three of us sign your official adoption deed—a gift I'm impatient to give to you."

"Really? Impatient, Dad? I hardly think so. It has taken you ten years to decide."

"Please, don't be angry, my darling."

"I have good reason. I'm furious and disappointed," said Elizabeth. "I feel betrayed—do you understand? I thought I was a legitimate child—but no, I'm a nobody. I don't even have a name!"

Overwhelmed by grief and anger, she jumped up from the table, hurling her serviette on the floor.

"Lisbeth, come back!" ordered Edward.

"No, leave me alone!"

Elizabeth locked herself in her room. She could feel her pulse beating in her temples and her mouth was dry. Her neat little world had just crumbled. Aware of the Woolworths' fortune and having often heard about the cruel fate of orphans in New York, she tried to reason with herself.

Why did they make me believe they had adopted me? I basically served as their child, but they didn't consider me their daughter.

She stifled a sob. In that moment, she heard a whistling sound outside her window. The north wind was sweeping over the city and the windows were rattling, as if there were monsters howling with rage in the sumptuous building.

It's a storm, she thought. *The first one this winter. It'll snow tonight.*

Elizabeth was perturbed by the fury of the elements. She couldn't think straight. Everything was all mixed up in her troubled mind. The howling sounds of the blizzard rekindled a faint echo of another stormy evening, long ago.

I was afraid, so afraid ... but Mummy comforted me. Mummy Catherine, not Maybel!

She held her pale forehead in one hand and abandoned herself to the crazy series of images and names that was suddenly swirling around in her head.

A dramatic scene came back to her. A man with a stern face was banging the table in the middle of a room with oak-panelled walls, antiquated decor, long velvet curtains and crystal glasses. He was talking angrily, like the wind from the frozen wastelands up north.

"I was utterly terrified. The man was my grandfather, Hugues Laroche," she whispered aloud. "The storm was very violent."

Elizabeth felt her legs give way. Her heart was racing. She lay down, eyes closed, torn between curiosity and fear at having opened the floodgates to her past.

"I remember now," she said quietly. "Yes, and I can finally see them all: Mummy, Daddy, Pops Toine, Uncle Pierre, Aunt Yvonne."

Fleeting visions of the castle appeared before her: the hunting trophies on the stone walls of the grand entrance hall, the mill by the river, her parents' small garden, the rose bushes and lilacs.

"Mummy's hands were so soft, but she's dead. Daddy is so unhappy I can hear him cry at night. I'm scared, and we're both in pain. Oh, those men who are beating him up—they've killed him!"

An anguished cry brought her back to reality. It was Maybel calling her. Edward was knocking at the door, turning the handle in vain.

"Lisbeth, let me explain what happened," he said. "We didn't dare adopt you, for fear of losing you. Someone was looking for you, Lisbeth—a member of your real family."

8

The Past Rears Its Head

The Dakota Building
Tuesday, December 23, 1896, in the evening

"Someone was looking for me...?" muttered Elizabeth, flabbergasted.

She stood up, shouting:

"Who? Tell me, who?"

"Let us in first," begged Maybel. "We're very worried about you, darling!"

The endearment angered her. She didn't want to hear it, thinking she would never be able to call her so-called parents Mom and Dad again.

She defiantly replied in French:

"I don't trust you anymore."

Silence fell on the other side of the door, followed by whispering. In the meantime, Elizabeth started reminiscing.

"Have mercy," insisted Maybel. "Forgive us. Why did you speak in French, Lisbeth?"

Edward was starting to lose his temper. He tried to force the door open with his shoulder, but it merely shuddered.

"At least have the courtesy to hear us out—then you can do as you like!" he shouted angrily.

Elizabeth had to admit she was curious, so she opened the door. The young girl had renewed confidence, now that she could remember meaningful elements of her past. She gave the couple a dignified, almost haughty look.

"So. Who was looking for me?" she asked coldly.

"Darling, don't treat us like we're guilty—we haven't done

anything wrong," protested Maybel. "Come into the sitting room, by the fire. Let's not stand talking in the hallway. Bonnie might hear us, and she doesn't need to know about this."

Hot and bothered, Edward undid his shirt collar. He looked at Elizabeth's exquisite face with suspicion, no longer recognizing his daughter.

It's as if a stranger is standing in front of me, he thought, terrified. *God, we can't let things end like this.*

Never before had Elizabeth's blue eyes looked so clear and ice cold. Her pink lips pouted contemptuously, and her nostrils quivered.

She followed them into the living room.

Maybel and Edward sat down on the sofa, but Elizabeth sat down opposite them. The Christmas tree was glittering, and the flickering of the fire lent a golden glow to the sparkling garlands and coloured glass baubles.

"I understand that you're very angry, Lisbeth," began Edward, "and I don't blame you. But Maybel and I sincerely thought we were acting in your best interests."

He then paused awkwardly. They couldn't reverse the situation now, after years of telling their family and friends that they had adopted her.

"You wanted to know who was looking for you," he resumed. "It was a man, a Frenchman called Hugues Laroche. He had put an ad in several New York newspapers, promising a handsome reward to anyone who could provide him with information about his granddaughter, Elizabeth Duquesne. The ad specified that the child had disappeared on the evening of Sunday, November the 7th, in the wake of a brutal attack on her father, Guillaume Duquesne, member of the Carpenters' Guild. A six-year-old girl, with brown hair and blue eyes."

"Duquesne—yes, of course," Elizabeth said with a lump in her throat.

Yes, that was her real father's name—another missing piece of the jigsaw. Her breathing became jerky on hearing the words, "member of the Carpenters' Guild".

"Everything matched," Maybel added, sobbing. "Once you were able to talk to Bonnie, the day after the accident, you told her that they had hurt your daddy. I was frightened—you were very ill that winter. I begged Edward not to meet this man."

"And after much quarrelling, I gave in to her, Lisbeth."

The trader paused briefly, staring into the flames. Then he continued:

"If only you knew how much I loved you already!"

"Don't blame us, darling," urged Maybel. "I panicked. You got used to us, you smiled, you played, you learned our language. I might as well tell you: I burned those damn newspapers, one after the other."

Edward Woolworth nodded, but to his wife's surprise, he added:

"I did keep one in my safe: a copy of the *New York Times*. If you want to see it, Lisbeth, I can show it to you."

"There's no point now," Elizabeth replied. "I remember my maternal grandfather, Hugues Laroche. I should thank Peter Ford. Due to his blunder, my memory has come back—most likely from the shock! . . . But how *could* you? My grandfather had travelled all the way from France looking for me, and he must have left thinking I was dead!"

Maybel took a sip of the whisky she had poured herself. She was trembling with nerves.

"What if Hugues Laroche had learned what had happened to my father? Maybe he came to New York to help him? I was so young when I witnessed that horrific scene! I had to flee, but my father may have survived and could have been looking for me too!"

"Please, calm down darling," pleaded Edward. "I went to the Chelsea Hotel, in Manhattan, where your grandfather was staying. That was the address he had put in the ad. It was two days after the announcement first appeared. I wanted to glimpse him, without him seeing me. A bellboy pointed him out to me. I didn't like the look of Laroche: he had a hard face and shifty eyes. I couldn't bring myself to hand you over to him—you were so sweet and innocent. I walked away with my mind made up."

Woolworth became silent. He was wringing his hands guiltily. Maybel looked at him with fondness.

"Lisbeth, I'm the one most to blame," she confessed. "I fought Edward for weeks. He eventually agreed to us keeping you here, but was overwrought with guilt. He thought it was the wrong thing to do. I succeeded in reassuring him, saying that we were making you and ourselves happy.

"Even so, we lived in fear of this Frenchman tracing you. For all we knew, he could have stayed on! We only went out in a carriage, and I was careful to hide your hair under a hood in winter and a straw hat in summer. And the years passed by, darling."

Elizabeth finally understood why she had been confined to the Dakota Building all these years. Maybel's confession merely heightened her anger.

"You had no right to do that," she protested. "You should have met my grandfather and told him I was alive. I was afraid of him as a child, but he would have taken me back to France! Over there, I had another grandfather—my 'Grandpa Toine', whom I adored. I can see his sweet face now, and my home by the river. I will never, ever forgive you! Imagine if I found out one day that Papa had been hospitalized after his attack, and that he had come looking for me afterwards? Can you imagine his pain, his grief? I was all he had left!"

"Don't get ahead of yourself, Lisbeth," protested Edward. "I made some enquiries at the time. Your father's body was reportedly recovered from the Hudson River."

Elizabeth let out a short, horrified cry. She now felt closer to her real family; the ten years spent with the Woolworths seemed like a sad masquerade.

"How can I be sure that it really was his body?" she exclaimed bitterly. "You were so desperate to keep me that it must have been convenient for you to believe my father was dead. You have both caused me so much pain this evening. In effect, you took me, hid me and locked me up!"

She was silent for a moment before adding:

"I was just your plaything, nothing else."

"No, no—that's not true!" sobbed Maybel. "What we did may have been wrong, but you were our little girl, and never a plaything!"

"You're being very hard on us," said Edward, grasping his wife's hand to comfort her. "You're right, Lisbeth—in a way, we did take you from your relatives, in defiance of the law. But think about it: would you have been as happy in France, without your parents? We cherished you and protected you, out of love—do you hear, out of love! You are judging us harshly because you can now, as an adult, but would you have reacted in the same way at the age of six?"

It was a well-founded argument and Elizabeth was sensible enough to consider the past with lucidity.

"Would I have thrown myself around my grandfather's neck? I doubt it. I was a child, and Maybel was so affectionate and loving, I would have been very sad to leave her."

Despite her resentment, she had to admit there was a grain of truth in what Edward was saying. He felt her bend and added:

"We were going to tell you everything on Christmas Day. Peter Ford was supposed to give me the official papers after tonight's dinner. I wasn't expecting such a violent reaction from you. You're looking at us as if you've never loved us or called us Mom and Dad! I don't know what to think anymore."

"Neither do I," replied Elizabeth, calmly. "But I do intend to write to my grandparents in France, at Guerville Castle—that name has come back to me too, like numerous other things. My family has the right to know that I'm alive. They will give me news of everyone I loved as a child."

These last words were like a knife through her heart. She thought of the old miller, her Pops Toine—his snowy white hair, his funny limp, the rainy days. Maybe he was dead too.

"Guerville Castle," said Maybel, sniffing, a white handker-chief over her nose. "So Hugues Laroche was rich?"

"Evidently, darling," cut in Edward. "He stayed at the Chelsea, one of the most expensive hotels in Manhattan."

"Yes, of course, and he promised an impressive reward. I am silly—I forgot. Lisbeth, please, give me a smile, or say you forgive me. I'm more to blame than your father. I was desperate at the thought of losing you—you must believe me."

"I do believe you, but I can't forgive you. It will take me a while—that is, if I decide to stay here."

With that, Elizabeth took her leave. They watched her exit the living room with her head held high, looking superb in her blue velvet dress, her long silky brunette hair adorning her shoulders.

"That's it—we've lost her," moaned Maybel.

Bonnie couldn't sleep. The sound of footsteps in the hallway woke her with a start. She lit her bedside lamp and looked at the clock on her mahogany chest of drawers. It was three in the morning.

It's Miss Lisbeth, I'm sure, she thought.

Bonnie stepped into her slippers. Dressed in a long, ample nightgown and wearing a white calico cap trimmed with fine lace, she ventured out of her bedroom. At once, she heard a whisper coming from the kitchen.

And she was not mistaken. Elizabeth was sitting on a stool, holding a glass of water, trembling.

"I see you've been crying, Miss. Another nightmare?"

"No, it's not that. I'm sorry if I woke you up, Bonnie. I couldn't sleep, I was too agitated. My memory came back to me tonight after Peter Ford left."

"There was a lot of commotion. I heard you shout like never before."

"I was furious! You want to know why, Bonnie? Mom said you didn't need to know, but I think you do."

Elizabeth poured her heart out to Bonnie. The servant was outraged when she learnt of her employers' little scheme.

"Good Lord, that's no way to behave!" she snapped. "I did wonder, during the first few months after your arrival at Sir and

Madam's house. For example, I remember raising an eyebrow when they told their family you were a distant cousin they had taken in—on Madam's side, of course. That way, no one could check up."

"How do you mean?"

"Well, Mrs. Maybel lost her parents when she was very young. One of her uncles lived in Arizona, which is where you were supposed to have come from."

"Oh yes, I knew that, Bonnie. They told me at the time that it was better to explain my presence that way. I must have been about seven years old and already spoke English. I didn't particularly care. I felt safe with them, like a bird in a beautiful, comfortable nest. Thinking about it now, it was more like a beautiful golden cage!"

Bonnie breathed a deep, irritated sigh. She arose and started to prepare some hot chocolate.

"This'll comfort us, Miss. I have a lot on my mind now. Had I known about your grandfather's advertisement ten years ago, I would have gone to see him. It's wrong to separate a child from their family, if they have a family willing to raise and love them. You know what I think? This Mr. Laroche, your grandfather, may well have frightened you on the night of the storm at the castle, but he would have pampered and loved you as much as Sir and Madam did. He'd just lost his only daughter—you would have helped to ease his pain."

"Maybe, maybe not," answered Elizabeth. "My grandmother, Adela Laroche, was very strict and highly strung."

Bonnie served her a steaming cup of sweet cocoa.

"You're the only one I trust, Bonnie," admitted the young girl. "I wish you could have met my real parents as I remember them—young and beautiful. Daddy had black hair and greyish-golden eyes. Mummy, whom he nicknamed Cathy, was blonde, with a peachy complexion, and had bluish-green eyes like turquoises. I now also remember how she died during the journey. She gave birth prematurely and lost a lot of blood. I'd been eavesdropping on Colette, our bunk neighbour, who thought I was asleep when I was merely pretending to be. They threw her body in the ocean, and the baby too."

"You've never mentioned Colette before, Miss."

"I'd forgotten about her, but it's all coming back now. I didn't like that woman—she stole my necklace, my mother's baptism medal. Daddy scolded me because he thought I'd lost it. If you only knew how vivid the images are—it's like travelling through time!"

Elizabeth was struggling to hold back tears of frustration, faced with a terrible dilemma.

"There there, don't cry anymore. Tomorrow, you will write a nice letter to your French family, and if you decide to leave, I will go with you. Never mind the pay—I have some money set aside."

"Thank you, Bonnie—you're an angel! But I don't know what I really want. I grew up here in New York, and I like it here. Going out this morning was exhilarating. I would love to go back and visit the whole of Central Park with you. To be perfectly honest, I still love Mom and Dad, even though I can't bring myself to call them that anymore."

The servant pulled Elizabeth to her plump chest, patting her on the back.

The young girl finally calmed down, snuggled up against this kind-hearted woman who would forever have a place in her heart.

The Dakota Building
The next morning, Christmas Eve

Maybel and Edward Woolworth were eating their breakfast in the living room at a pedestal table, without so much as glancing at the big Christmas tree or the open fire. Their day-to-day existence had become meaningless. It had snowed during the night, which would normally have delighted them. They would have stood by the windows with their Lisbeth, marvelling at the snow-covered trees of Central Park and the skaters on the frozen lake.

"What a waste!" lamented Maybel. "The three of us should be choosing the New Year's Eve menu this morning, then going to midnight mass tonight."

"I don't think we'll go to the service at St. Patrick's Cathedral this year, darling."

The Woolworths were Catholic and called themselves good Christians, yet kept Elizabeth away from religious services except on Christmas Eve, when they felt safe amid the congregation.

"What is Lisbeth doing? Is she going to stay locked in her room all day?" complained Maybel again.

"Give her time," urged her husband. "She needs to mull it over. We let her down, and it will take her a while to compose herself. I'm not as worried about it as you are, for I believe she loves us and will come to understand our position. Our actions were clearly wrong—you've got to give her that—but I think the last ten years of happiness we've spent together will weigh in our favour. Ah! There she is!"

They stiffened up, like suspects on trial. Elizabeth's footsteps were gentle, which gave them hope. The couple were disappointed to discover that she was heading straight for the kitchen.

"I'll ring for Bonnie," said Maybel. "It's out of the question that our daughter should prefer the company of our servant!"

"Leave her be, or you'll end up making her hate us," whispered Edward.

"I just wish everything would go back to the way it was," she lamented. "Normally at this time of day, I would be greeting her with kisses and hugs. This is all your lawyer's fault. I forbid you to pay him another dime. His actions are unforgivable."

"Lisbeth's reaction would have been much the same, had we told her tomorrow, Maybel. There's no point beating ourselves up about it—the damage is done."

"No, I'm telling you it would have been different, because we would have broken it to her ourselves, gently. Oh, I'm so terribly sad!"

She went quiet, keeping an ear open. Elizabeth entered the living room holding a sheet of paper.

"Hello, darling," exclaimed Edward.

"Hello," Elizabeth said, keeping herself from adding the word "Dad".

"Lisbeth," called out Maybel, "as much as you hate us, don't be so cold. Give us a smile, at least."

The pitiful state her mother was in weakened Elizabeth's resolve. She avoided the woman's distraught gaze, so as not to waver.

"I've written to my grandfather Hugues," she told them. "I was eager to hear Bonnie's opinion before yours."

"And why?" shouted Maybel.

"Because I trust her and she knows the truth," said the girl. "Bonnie thought you had adopted me long ago, and she disapproves of what you did. If I leave, she'll go with me."

Edward, who was fast losing patience with Elizabeth's insolence, was furious.

"*If you leave,*" he said mockingly. "With what money? Do you think I'm irresponsible enough to let you take the first boat to France? Adopted or not, you're my daughter. Give me that letter—you're not sending anything I haven't read."

"I've written it in French—you won't understand a word!"

"In French!" shouted Maybel at the top of her voice. "You claimed you'd forgotten your mother tongue!"

"I hadn't," replied Elizabeth. "You lied to me for all these years—well, so did I. And I'm glad I did!"

She folded the letter in four and held it tightly. Edward Woolworth didn't dare insist.

"Lord, how did we get to this point?" he cursed. "Do as you please, Lisbeth, but I insist on taking care of you, no matter what. If you want to return to your family, I'll help you. We'll calmly wait for the reply. Promise me you won't do anything stupid in the meantime."

"You have my word, but I refuse to stay locked up here any longer. I want to go out—escorted by Bonnie—and walk around Central Park, and skate and have fun."

"Of course, you're free as a bird now, as long as you're careful," he conceded.

Elizabeth turned her back on him, deeply moved by Maybel's convulsive sobs. She wanted to comfort her, for despite her anger, she was of a gentle and caring disposition.

My letter will arrive at Guerville Castle in two or three weeks' time, she thought. *I shall have an answer by mid February. Oh, my God, that's so far off!*

What if she learned that her father had survived and was back in Montignac? Elizabeth was getting carried away. Nervous and fidgety, she ran to her room and grabbed the tin soldier from her jewellery box, squeezing it tightly.

"Justin could still be living in the castle," she thought out loud. "I must return to France. It's where I belong."

Elizabeth ended up spending more than an hour daydreaming about the journey, which she would make arm in arm with Bonnie. She then got dressed for a long walk in Central Park.

Central Park
The same day, late morning

The immense snow-covered park enchanted Elizabeth, who had just rented a pair of ice skates. Sitting on a bench by the shore of the frozen lake, she breathed in the cold air with delight.

"Be careful, Miss—you're an absolute beginner," said Bonnie, worried.

"There has to be a beginning to everything. Besides, it doesn't look very difficult," replied the young girl with excitement. "And you're wrong—I skated every time Dad took us to the mountains in winter."

Elizabeth bit her lip when she realized she had used the affectionate term "Dad".

"It's only a detail, Miss," pointed out Bonnie. "As long as you're living with Mr. and Mrs. Woolworth, you can continue to call them that—they have indeed been parents to you. I don't condone their lies, but they genuinely love you."

"I know they do!"

Elizabeth brushed a hand over the tweed culottes that revealed her woollen stockings. Maybel had bought her the outfit in early autumn, for a stay in their Appalachian cottage.

"I'm off now, Bonnie. Please don't worry. I'm very happy to be here with you. I think I just saw my cousin Pearl out there on the lake—she'll teach me, I'm sure of it!"

"Pearl? I can't say I see her, Miss."

But Elizabeth had already set off through the passageway lined with wooden fences that led to the rink.

She was eager to start gliding on the ice, intoxicated by the beauty of the scene. The trees around the lake were powdered with snow against the backdrop of a pearly grey sky. Shouts and laughter echoed from one end of the rink to the other, like an ode to youth and freedom.

"Be careful!" Bonnie shouted after her.

The housekeeper remembered vividly Maybel's haggard face when Elizabeth had walked along the corridor of the vast apartment earlier that morning. She was wearing a fur hat on her braided hair, her slender waist accentuated by a fitted corduroy jacket. Mother and daughter had had a brief and painful exchange that had profoundly embarrassed Bonnie.

"Honey, if you happen to bump into your cousin Pearl, please don't tell her," Maybel had pleaded. "Will you be back for lunch?"

"Don't worry, I have no intention of shouting from the rooftops that you deceived and humiliated me," Elizabeth had replied harshly. "Bonnie and I will have lunch by the lake. Pearl has told me about a chalet that sells French fries and sandwiches."

Maybel had retired to her room with a pained look on her face. Diligent as always, Bonnie had been concerned about her mistress.

"Sir has gone to his office, so Madam is all alone, and I haven't prepared her any lunch . . ." she had muttered, feeling guilty.

On the ice at last, Elizabeth was eager to forget the matter. She advanced slowly, arms spread-eagled to maintain her balance. Young skating enthusiasts whizzed past her, squealing quietly. Others dodged her at the last moment, smiling at her.

Elizabeth started to speed up, cheeks reddened by the biting wind. Her efforts came to an abrupt end at the first bend, where she fell flat on the ice. Bonnie gasped, having observed the incident from the shore. Then she recognized Pearl Woolworth, who was skating up to her cousin with extraordinary ease.

Edward's niece was eighteen and wore her copper curls under a green beret, which matched a very elegant, ample ruffle skirt and frock coat.

"I thought it was you, Lisbeth!" she cried as she helped her up. "Have you escaped from Uncle Edward and Aunt Maybel? They can't be far away—they must have come to check up on their princess!"

"Don't call me that, Pearl—you know I hate it! Just so you know, I can go out as much as I like from now on."

"Well, it's about time! Surely Bonnie won't leave your side, though? My governess also escorts me everywhere I go, except for the ice rink. Come on, give me your hand."

Pearl Woolworth was lively, slender and graceful, but nowhere near as beautiful as Lisbeth. Nature might not have graced her with beauty, but she had a bold and dazzling smile that quickly made people overlook her aquiline nose, small forehead and overly square jaw.

"You're going too fast," said Elizabeth, whom Pearl had dragged to the middle of the lake. She was crushing her fingers in an attempt to guide her cousin.

"You fell because you weren't skating fast enough," she explained. "Careful now—we'll turn and then I'll let go of you."

"No, no!"

But Pearl only laughed and let go of her hand. Elizabeth raced forward, laughing too, despite her apprehension.

Suddenly, a skater blocked her path. Elizabeth crashed head-on into him, but the man grabbed her by the waist to prevent her from falling.

"Excuse me, Miss—I'm so sorry," he apologized at once, in a deep, velvety voice.

"It's entirely my fault, Sir—I'm an absolute beginner! You can let go of me now, I should be able to stand up."

He complied, staring at her. When Elizabeth got a better look at him, her heart started to race. It was the young man whose eyes she had met after her carousel ride the day before.

"If you'll allow me," he said, "I'd be happy to guide you without letting go of you, like Miss Pearl Woolworth just did."

"Oh, you know Pearl?" she asked, amazed. "She's my cousin, on my father's side."

"Is she really? How interesting. I don't think I've seen you here before—apart from yesterday morning, that is. But how rude of me—I haven't introduced myself: Richard Stenton. Delighted to meet you."

He reached out his hand to an awestruck Elizabeth. He stared at her with his amber eyes. The young girl found him exceptionally handsome, with his short black hair, pleasing features, and bright white teeth. Only yesterday, she would have thought it inappropriate to follow a stranger on a frozen lake. But today, everything was different. Despite the claims she had just made, she was no longer a Woolworth, but a Duquesne, born in France.

It doesn't matter if it's not appropriate, she thought with a mischievous smile. *I intend to skate every day from now on, so I might as well find myself a teacher.*

"Now, back to the track," joked Richard Stenton. "Trust me."

Elizabeth shuddered. The parents she had loved had betrayed her. For her, trust now felt like a distant memory.

The foreseeable future would only bring her further sorrow, as she would have to choose between the Woolworths and her French family. It would also be hard to maintain her confrontational stance towards Maybel and Edward: their distress saddened her.

"You seem distracted, Miss," said the skater politely. "Sport requires concentration. If I didn't know any better, I'd say something is bothering you. You're young and charming and, being related to Pearl Woolworth, most certainly free from want."

"Some troubles are unrelated to age, appearance and wealth, Sir," Elizabeth answered. "Are you a friend of my cousin?"

"Just a social connection," he replied, tightening his grip on her fingers.

Elizabeth felt a strange emotion, as if she were venturing into a promising new world.

Bonnie was strolling along the lakeside to keep warm, but kept an eye on the young woman. It was freezing, and the icy wind was biting her cheeks and nose.

Who is this gentleman? she wondered from afar. *Now Miss Pearl has joined them. He must be a friend of hers, and he's a good skater. My little Miss is certainly enjoying herself!*

She was determined not to lose sight of Elizabeth, who was speeding along, hand in hand with the stranger. They almost bumped into a group of children, but managed to avoid a collision and embarked on another circuit of the lake at once. Pearl took the opportunity to skate up to Bonnie, her ankles aligned and her arms by her side, looking triumphant.

"Bonnie!" she shouted. "May I invite Lisbeth to lunch with me and my friends? We'll bring her back to you afterwards. They sell fries and doughnuts over there in that adorable wooden cabin."

"Well, why not—providing you tell me the name of this gentleman. He's being slightly too familiar with her, for my taste."

"It's Mr. Stenton! I saw him once or twice leaving my father's house. He's obviously smitten with Lisbeth, but I'll get rid of him. Please, let me entertain Princess Woolworth a little!" laughed Pearl.

"It wouldn't pain me to return home to warmth," said Bonnie, despite her qualms. "But first, tell Miss Lisbeth to come and see me."

A couple of minutes later, Elizabeth stood there clinging to the fence, with a glint of joyful mystery in her eyes. Richard Stenton was standing some distance away.

"I've already made some progress, Bonnie!" she boasted. "But I've got a long way to go. We'll have to come back every morning. Would you mind my having lunch with Pearl, then?"

"Hmm," Bonnie grumbled. "We'll see about that. That young man was holding you very tightly."

"To stop me from falling! Bonnie, I'm so happy—please don't ask me to go home right now."

"Very well, then. After all, you're in Miss Pearl's company, and I'll make sure to tell Madam that. But don't be late."

"I promise," replied Elizabeth, setting off immediately, already gliding with much more confidence.

Bonnie shrugged and turned on her heels.

"Your governess, no doubt," enquired Richard Stenton as soon as Elizabeth was within earshot again.

She was about to lose her balance again, when he caught her. He seemed determined not to let go of her hand. Despite her fine wool mittens and his leather gloves, the touch of his hand troubled her.

"Why yes, Bonnie is my governess," she admitted hesitantly. "She was worried."

"That must be because of me. I see you're a young lady under constant supervision! If you were my sister or daughter, I would certainly do the same, though."

The conversation embarrassed Elizabeth, and she was relieved when Pearl arrived. Used to moving in such circles, she graciously dismissed Stenton.

"I'm sorry, Mr. Stenton, but Lisbeth and I are going for lunch. Our friend Vera is waiting for us."

"I understand. It was delightful to meet you, Lisbeth. And I hope to see you again very soon."

He had emphasized her first name, which irritated Pearl. She pivoted, dragging Elizabeth away by the wrist.

"He likes you—he couldn't make it more obvious!" she snapped. "He's never shown any interest in me, even though I find him very attractive. I've got to say, you're not losing any time, cousin! Be careful, though—I saw you drooling over him!"

"That's not true, Pearl! You're wrong—I was just being myself. I didn't flutter my eyelashes as you did this summer, when Vera's brother complimented you on your swimming skills. Mom said you were flirting."

"Aunt Maybel never squanders an opportunity to criticize me—you're her only yardstick," responded Cousin Pearl. "I would rather be taken for a flirt than a naive fool."

They arrived at the area of the lakeside where the chalet stood. Smoke was billowing out of the chimney and the pleasant smell of fries floated in the air.

"Are you calling me a naive fool?" asked Elizabeth in exasperation.

"Yes—you swoon in front of any pretty boy as soon as you're off the leash. Your parents were right to keep tabs on you."

Vera, a tall blonde girl, waved to them. She was sitting at a small table under the chalet's festooned awning.

"Let go of me, Pearl. I don't want to spend any more time with you—I'm going home!" announced Elizabeth, on the verge of tears.

"Lisbeth, I'm telling you for your own good. Richard Stenton may be a fortune hunter—he must have made enquiries. After all, you are Uncle Edward's sole heiress!"

"I think you're just jealous," retorted Elizabeth. "You always were. Goodbye."

Half an hour later, hungry and upset, Elizabeth locked herself in her room. Bonnie, surprised to see her home so soon, knocked gently on her door.

"I'll prepare you something to eat, Miss. Madam ended up going out. Sir phoned and invited her to lunch at the Delmonico."

"Very well. I'll get changed, Bonnie."

She shed her long culottes onto the oriental rug, together

with her silk bodice and woollen waistcoat. She then removed her stockings. The young woman caught her own eyes in the dressing-table mirror and was surprised to discover how elated she looked.

With her right hand, she touched the roundness of her left shoulder with its pearly skin, then the outline of her breasts, which were already round and firm. She was fully aware of her beauty and felt it awakening something disturbing inside of her. Her thoughts turned to Richard Stenton, and she imagined his amber eyes looking at her naked body. Elizabeth shyly touched her lips, which were flushed from the cold.

"Who will give me my first kiss?" she wondered.

Maybel and Edward Woolworth returned in the middle of the afternoon. Bonnie served them tea in the sitting room at once.

"Miss Lisbeth had a wonderful time skating on the lake with her cousin, Pearl," she said.

"And they had lunch there too, like you said?" enquired Maybel.

"No, Madam. Miss returned shortly after you left for the Delmonico. I believe your niece was making fun of her."

"Pearl is such a nuisance, isn't she Edward?"

"Let's just say that she has a caustic side to her, and has inherited my brother's sense of humour, which can be offensive."

Bonnie left them alone, thinking it better not to mention the seductive Richard Stenton, who seemed very keen on Lisbeth. *Let them take her to Central Park themselves and see what they think of him,* she thought to herself. *I don't think much of him, personally.*

To their great surprise, Elizabeth joined them and sat in her usual place at the marquetry table, which was covered by an embroidered tablecloth. She nibbled on a biscuit, annoyed by the eerie silence that reigned in the room. Maybel poured her some tea, whispering:

"If you like skating, darling, we must buy you some skates. The hire skates aren't necessarily a good fit."

"No, don't spend any more on me," she replied.

"Lisbeth, stop calling everything into question," shouted Edward. "As long as you're under our roof, I want to keep things as they are. We consider you our daughter, and we love you! Even if it means giving up the formal adoption process, now that you know the whole story—though perhaps it's only temporary. Maybel and I discussed that possibility at length this lunchtime. You may no longer have any family in France. If that were the case, why not stay here? Legitimately, of course."

The young woman quietly sipped her bergamot tea. She eventually replied in a soft voice:

"How can I decide? I have never ventured out in New York, never visited any museums or the zoo in Central Park. I don't even know the city. During our carriage rides, I have glimpsed the facades of buildings, and people's windows, horse-drawn carriages, people on the sidewalks, but you have never once taken me into a restaurant or a store. That simple outing to Central Park Lake this morning was an extraordinary experience for me!"

"We can make up for lost time, Lisbeth," insisted Edward. "At least until you leave for France—*if* you leave. Did you post your letter?"

"No, I still have a few lines to add, and a greetings card, as it will arrive after New Year."

Maybel and her husband noticed that Elizabeth was still cold towards them, but this time there was no animosity in her voice. They took it as progress, having decided to prove their good will and not upset her.

"I see. In any case, you can still call us Mom and Dad," added the trader kindly.

"Yes, of course. It's hard for me not to," Elizabeth conceded. "But I have to be honest with you: I'm unable to forgive you quite yet. I might be able to when I have proof that my real father Guillaume is dead."

"We understand, Lisbeth," affirmed Maybel. "As a small compensation for the grief we've caused you, we'd like to invite you for dinner in town tonight, on Broadway. Before that, we could go and buy you some skates."

The offer was very appealing, but Elizabeth's pride wouldn't let her give in.

"No, I don't feel up to that," she said firmly. "I'm going to read in my room. Bonnie can bring me a tray later—don't worry about me."

The couple fell silent in front of this spirited young woman whom they had raised and pampered as though she were their own flesh and blood.

"What a miserable Christmas this will be!" sighed Maybel.

PART TWO

9

The Spiral of Time

The Dakota Building
9 a.m., Saturday, December 26, 1896

Elizabeth closed the sturdy leather bag with shoulder straps that contained her ice skates. Maybel had given them to her on Christmas morning, as well as a velvet jacket with a fur collar. The young girl couldn't stop herself kissing Maybel on the cheek to thank her, as Edward looked on tenderly.

The day had passed calmly, without clashes or quarrels, everyone making commendable efforts to display an appropriate cheerfulness once they'd returned from midnight mass.

"Why shouldn't we go?" asked Elizabeth, surprised when Edward announced they were not going to attend the religious service. "I love the atmosphere of St. Patrick's Cathedral. I feel good there."

The couple immediately changed their minds and the three of them left for the snow-covered streets of Manhattan. The beauty of the cathedral, the Christmas carols sung by a choir, and the golden glow of the candles had undoubtedly lifted their spirits.

Maybel had invited Bonnie to eat with them, which was so exceptional that the poor governess could only pick at her food.

Now, daily life would continue until the New Year's Eve party, to which the Woolworths had invited a great number of friends and family members.

"Well, I'm ready," murmured Elizabeth. "I wonder if I'll see Richard Stenton again . . ."

Her thoughts had frequently turned to him during the past

two days, but she hadn't returned to Central Park until now, mainly to avoid running into Pearl.

Bonnie was waiting for her impatiently in the hallway, wrapped up so warmly that she was suffocating with heat. The apartment was like a furnace.

"Let's hurry, Miss—I'm burning up!"

"Yes, your cheeks are bright red," laughed Elizabeth. "But it suits you—you look like a doll, with your freckles."

"Go on, make fun of me, then!" Bonnie retorted.

They were secretly gleeful about their escapade. Outside, the icy air took their breath away, but they smiled at each other.

"You should shelter from the cold in the chalet—there must be tables inside," advised the young girl. "I must post my letter first. I wish I knew exactly how long it will take for it to reach France. Do you realize it will make the same journey that I made with my parents?"

"But you went the other way!"

The servant had almost said too much—that it would have been quicker to send a telegram to Hugues Laroche. She had even suggested this to her employers, who had pleaded with her not to tell Elizabeth.

"Keeping her with us until February, at least, will give us time to redress our wrongdoings! Please, Bonnie," Maybel had said imploringly.

"Very well," Bonnie had retorted, capitulating at Maybel's tears but feeling guilty.

"Don't walk so fast, Miss—the park is just opposite!" she complained. "Actually, I would like to take this opportunity to share something with you."

"What, Bonnie?" replied Elizabeth absentmindedly.

"I'm single and will remain so. When I was your age, though, I dreamed of having children. So when you came into my life, I loved you from day one, as if you were my own daughter. I would never hurt you—you must know that."

"But I do know that, Bonnie! You even said you would come with me to France."

"I gave you my word, Miss. What would I do without you!"

"I have an idea. Why don't you visit your older sister this morning?" suggested Elizabeth. "By underground train, you would be at Greenwich Street in no time. We can meet up at the station in the early afternoon. I'm allowed to have lunch in town."

"But only when I accompany you, Miss! I can't leave you alone for hours on end. Sir and Madam would be angry, and . . ."

"But they won't know, Bonnie! You hardly ever get time off. Only last night you said you were sorry you hadn't seen your sister in two months."

Bonnie gazed into Elizabeth's blue eyes. Though tempted, the governess wouldn't give in straight away.

"I'm not fooled, Elizabeth—you just want me out of the way in case Mr. Stenton turns up at the ice rink!"

"You know his name?"

"Yes, I asked your cousin Pearl."

"Who is not really my cousin at all, in fact. And you, Bonnie—you called me by my Christian name: that's a first. Please, if you love me, then do this for me. I need some space, to do as I please without being watched over."

Bonnie tried to remember herself at sixteen. Born into poverty, she had trekked across the city to find work, without her big sister chaperoning her on her travels.

"If you weren't a wealthy young lady, I wouldn't mind," she lamented. "There are thousands of girls your age who do not have a chaperone—but you, you're different. And you're so naive."

Disappointed, Elizabeth thought back to Pearl's venomous remark, calling her a naive fool.

"I'm not exactly likely to learn anything if I'm not let off the leash, am I?" she said indignantly. "I promise to be very careful and if I meet Mr. Stenton. I will behave appropriately."

"Jesus, I should hope so!" said Bonnie, alarmed. "All right, but be on time, or I'll inform the police."

Elizabeth laughed, as her governess winked at her at the same time. They said goodbye in front of Central Park's tall gates.

Central Park
The same day, half an hour later

Richard Stenton sighed with relief when he finally spotted Lisbeth Woolworth among the many skaters. Sitting on the covered terrace of the chalet, he was now sipping a glass of beer, having spent quite some time observing the young ladies skating across the lake.

He watched her for a moment with interest before taking to the ice. The girl was skating at a steady speed, though he could see from her tense expression that she lacked confidence.

"Luckily, her cousin Pearl is not here," he muttered under his breath.

Elizabeth noticed him straight away, but pretended not to see him, eyes focused on the bend she was entering. As soon as he approached, her young heart started to pound heavily.

"Hello, Lisbeth," he exclaimed. "I waited for you yesterday, but you didn't turn up."

"It was a festive day, Sir," she replied, feigning indifference.

"Indeed, but I came anyway, hoping to bump into you. Did you have a nice Christmas?"

"It was nothing exceptional. I stayed in my room reading the novel I was given: *Washington Square*, by Henry James."

"Gee, that's a sad story," remarked Stenton.

"Have you read it too, then?"

"Of course, back when I was your age."

"You don't know how old I am," she said, laughing.

"I would put you at twenty—no, eighteen."

"Wrong. I'll soon be seventeen, I think."

Her answer intrigued Stenton. He frowned in amusement. Then he grabbed her right hand with an authoritative air.

"Don't be afraid—I'm taking you to the other side of the lake. You need to improve your style, to honour your beautiful new skates."

"I got them for Christmas," she admitted. "Please don't go too fast—the wind is so cold, I can't breathe."

Richard Stenton obeyed immediately. He was a natural skater and moved with grace and ease, despite being very tall.

"Don't make this more difficult than it is, Lisbeth," he chuckled. "For starters, you could tell me when your birthday is."

"For starters, Mom says that a woman should never reveal her age. And secondly, I find you too inquisitive. Never mind when my birthday is—they spoil me every day of the year!"

Elizabeth was playing hard to get, but only half-heartedly. The young woman would gladly have told him everything about her broken childhood, but was too proud. She preferred him to think she was a rich heiress, rather than some orphan taken in by a wealthy couple who had taken custody of her by illegitimate means.

"You're right, I have this failing whereby I want to know everything about people who fascinate me," he admitted. "But your aura of mystery just adds to your beauty."

Elizabeth couldn't help feeling happy and exhilarated. They did a full circuit of the frozen lake in silence. Light flakes were fluttering in the air, and children around them were shrieking with excitement.

"Can I buy you a hot chocolate?" suggested Stenton, pointing to the chalet, whose tiny windows were lit up. "I have a hunch that your governess isn't on duty at the lakeside today!"

"I suggested she visit her sister," confessed Elizabeth with a smile. "My parents don't know, though."

"How bold! I sense a rebellious streak in you."

Lost in thought, Elizabeth got caught up in the spiral of time. In her mind's eye she could see her mother Catherine, the evening they had dinner at the castle. She couldn't remember the details of the heated, angry discussions, but she certainly remembered the rebellious character of the beautiful young blonde woman who'd stood up to Hugues and Adela Laroche.

"Dad says I have a strong personality," she said quietly. "And now let's talk about you!"

Richard Stenton stiffened. He helped her get seated at an outdoor table, and she sensed his unease as he squeezed her fingers even tighter.

"Let's just say that I'm trying to blend into a milieu that is not really mine," he muttered.

"What do you mean?"

"I spend time with friends of your cousin Pearl and Vera, her faithful sidekick, but I remain a bit of a mystery to these young people. If they knew where I was from, they'd turn their backs on me."

Elizabeth nearly replied that she could well find herself in the same situation. Maybel and Edward Woolworth had begged her not to say anything, so she made no comment.

"Do you despise me now? Will you agree to see me again?"

"Of course I will. I'm not like Pearl and her friends."

"You're adorable, Lisbeth," he sighed.

They sipped their hot chocolate and nibbled on biscuits. Troubled by Stenton's ardent stare, Elizabeth gazed at the landscape, and watched the pirouettes performed by a scruffily dressed ten-year-old boy.

"He's a natural," she said admiringly.

"Fortunately, Central Park is accessible to all social classes," said Richard seriously. "Did you know that this beautiful place, with its many attractions, was once a vast expanse of swamps and wastelands interspersed with large boulders? The destitute lived here, raising goats and pigs."

"No, I didn't."

"Once these poor people had been driven out and their slums had been torn down, the heavy work could commence. It took twelve years and cost millions of dollars. The result is certainly impressive: a beautiful park containing several species of trees, not to mention a museum, a zoo, a vantage point and a carousel."

"I would dearly like to visit the zoo. My parents would never take me there."

"Then I promise to take you there tomorrow, Lisbeth. But you should know that some animals sleep all day long during this season, especially bears."

Elizabeth nodded and suddenly turned very pale. She had a flashback of a vivid scene that had taken place here in Central Park.

There was a bear trainer with a wide-brimmed hat and a gravelly accent—and I can still see the frantic look in the animal's eyes. If I could only remember its name ... she thought. *They were on the boat, too. I had given them a coin that Daddy had slipped into my hand. Now I remember—Garro was his name! His master wanted to keep me, so I could dance with the bear and make money for him. I had a narrow escape.*

"Lisbeth? Please, Lisbeth—what's the matter?" asked Richard Stenton, surprised by her tense face and blank expression.

The young girl was staring right through him. She was reliving her mad scramble through the lawns of the park to escape the bear handler.

I wasn't paying attention—I was terrified—just like the day before, when Daddy was urging me to run away between blood-curdling screams. Edward couldn't have avoided knocking me down.

Elizabeth put her hand on her neck, deeply disturbed by this flashback. Stenton was talking to her, but she could hardly hear him.

"It's nothing," she stammered.

"You feel faint? Do you get this often?" he enquired.

"Yes. Our family doctor blames it on my nerves. I must go now, Sir."

"Let me walk you back part of the way, or I'll worry about you."

"Very well, but I'm supposed to meet Bonnie in the early afternoon. If I go home without her, my parents will know I concocted a plan to be alone."

"Meaning we couldn't go to the zoo tomorrow?"

"That's right."

"Well, in that case, we are doomed to go on skating and eating French fries and grilled bacon here—providing you feel up to it."

"I don't really have a choice, do I!"

They smiled at each other, surprised and delighted to feel so close.

The Central Park ice rink
Wednesday, December 30, 1896

Elizabeth had had the most wonderful time with Richard Stenton over the last few days. They would meet by the ice rink at ten o'clock in the morning and have lunch together under the chalet awning. Edward and Maybel knew about these meetings but were careful not to interfere.

As for Bonnie, she had been excused from chaperoning Elizabeth, especially since they needed her to prepare the residence for the New Year's Eve reception.

Her new-found freedom both surprised and exhilarated Elizabeth. She was correct to attribute the Woolworths' sudden generosity of spirit to their remorse. Stenton, who had become "Richard" to her, had been just as surprised.

He told her so again that morning, as they were skating in the middle of the lake, holding hands.

"Do your parents really allow you to go out by yourself to meet me? It's extremely unusual for a wealthy young lady of your age to be able to do as she pleases!"

"What's bothering you, Richard? Are you afraid of getting into trouble because of me? I have no reason to lie to you. My mother has even invited you for New Year's Eve—she would like to meet you. Pearl will be there, with her parents and her friend Vera. There will be a lot of people."

Richard Stenton had stopped near the shore, pensive.

"I'm afraid I won't be able to come, Lisbeth," he whispered. "I'm busy that evening."

"What a shame . . . In that case, try to drop by for a quarter of an hour at least, at the start of the evening?" she begged with her sapphire eyes and a slight pout. He turned away in embarrassment, ashamed to have to deny her this happiness.

"I can't, Lisbeth. And I have to leave early today. We won't be able to have lunch together. I've been neglecting my work, and I'm accountable. Please don't be angry."

Very disappointed, Elizabeth mastered her emotions, trying to look cheerful. She tried to think of the wonderful moments they had shared, such as the zoo visit last Sunday, and their excursion to Vista Rock on Monday, from where they'd had a panoramic view of the park.

The young man had proved to be a charming and competent guide, whose knowledge had fascinated her. Secretly, though, she preferred their skating sessions on the lake, as that was the only time Richard held her hand tightly, something he wouldn't do when they were walking together.

"I'll see you next year then," she joked.

"I sincerely hope so," he said with an air of sadness.

"What's wrong, Richard?"

"I wish I knew more about you," he confessed suddenly. "We have seen each other every day since Friday, but I still don't know anything about you. You almost fainted again at the zoo near the bears' compound, for no apparent reason. I'm worried about your health and I have a strange feeling you are hiding something important from me."

Elizabeth was torn. She guessed that he was either very intuitive, or that she had actively confused him herself, by not answering his questions.

"If I intrigued you that much, you would attend my mother's party," she replied with malice.

"I'd love to meet your parents at a later time, Lisbeth. I'm sorry, I have to go."

He stroked her cheek and politely waved goodbye before he left, flashing her a big smile that filled her with joy.

Not knowing what to do with herself and peeved at suddenly being abandoned by Richard, Elizabeth decided to attempt a few pirouettes at the lakeside. She didn't get further than her third attempt. Cheeky laughter echoed her fall. Elizabeth looked around angrily to see who was mocking her.

A ten-year-old little rascal was skating near her, performing a series of remarkable jumps.

"It's bad manners to laugh at the young lady," scolded a tiny dark-haired woman sitting on a nearby bench.

Elizabeth did a double take: the woman had spoken in French. Still laughing, the child came to Elizabeth's aid.

"You didn't hurt yourself too much, did you, Mademoiselle?" he asked, also in French.

She recognized him as the young skater she and Richard had been watching with admiration. She was about to thank him when she had a flashback of last night's dream.

I've already seen this scene ... I was alone, I fell, and this boy skated towards me, at full speed. And that lady on the bench with her little girl was there, too!

"Are you hurt, Miss?" repeated the child, in English this time. "I'm sorry—I couldn't stop myself laughing, Miss."

"I understand French," she answered, feeling disorientated and confused.

"Ah, did you learn it at school? As for me, my father was born in France. I speak English, French and some Italian."

"Tony, stop bothering this young lady," shouted out the woman as she got up from the bench.

"He's not bothering me, Madam! Is he your son? He's better on the ice than me."

Elizabeth had spoken in her mother tongue, so fluently that the other woman answered in French.

"Yes, he's my son. I bring him here every year as soon as the lake freezes over. He's taught himself, and a neighbour lends him some skates."

Tony had already skated off again, hands gracefully wrapped behind his back. Elizabeth made it to the lakeside, under the fearful gaze of the little girl, who had black hair and grey-green eyes.

"Would you like to skate too, when you're a little older?" Elizabeth asked her.

The child immediately hid in her mother's skirt. The latter cheerfully answered for her:

"Oh no, Miranda's far too delicate for that!"

"How old is she, Madam?"

"Five years old, and terribly shy! She would rather stay at home in this cold weather, but I don't want Tony to walk back on his own. My husband works on a construction site, and I no longer have anyone to babysit her. My mother died this fall."

The woman's explanation left Elizabeth even more confused, for her dream was still haunting her.

"My condolences, Madam," she said, about to leave.

"Would you be French by any chance, Mademoiselle?" inquired the lady kindly. "Excuse me if I'm being nosy, but as Tony told you, his father is from Picardy in France."

"Uh, yes," said Elizabeth hesitantly. Her heart was pounding with emotion.

She had just spotted something that deeply unsettled her: little Miranda was wearing a gold medal on her thick woollen jumper. It was nothing extraordinary, yet the shape of the medal and the embossed design were oddly familiar to her. Elizabeth's mouth went dry.

This profile of the Virgin Mary holding baby Jesus looks precisely like the one on my mother's baptism medal! she thought. *But I must be going crazy. It must be just a very popular design.*

The child's mother stared at her, with not an inkling of what was going on in her mind.

"Are you looking at her medal?" she finally asked.

"Yes—it's so pretty! Excuse me, I lost one very similar to it."

"We didn't find it or steal it, Miss!" replied the woman vociferously, with an anxious frown.

"I'm not accusing you of anything, Madam," stammered Elizabeth. "I'd better go now."

But she couldn't move. Her legs were shaking, and tears were stinging her eyes. Her skates unsteady on the thin layer of snow that lay on the ground, she hesitantly made it to the bench.

"Are you all right, Miss?" the woman asked, looking concerned.

"I don't feel very well," Elizabeth said, gasping. "Mummy had the same medal, that's why I'm so sad."

A deep silence followed. Miranda started to cry, which made Elizabeth look up. Her mother had taken the medal off her and was holding it in the palm of her hand.

"My daughter insists on wearing this piece of jewellery every day, even though it's far too precious for her. My husband and I are very attached to it. Baptiste is afraid that she will break the chain. But I think I did the right thing in letting her wear it this morning. Mademoiselle, what was your mother's name?"

"Catherine Duquesne—why?"

"Good God!" exclaimed the woman. "Here, take it!"

She placed the medal in the palm of Elizabeth's gloved hand, its reverse side showing. Elizabeth cried out in surprise upon seeing the meticulously engraved inscription:

Catherine Laroche, December 23, 1857

"And your daddy was Guillaume Duquesne. I am Lea, the wife of his friend Baptiste Rambert. I was supposed to meet you ten years ago, one evening in November. We waited for you in vain—for you and your father."

"Lea and Baptiste Rambert?" repeated Elizabeth, aghast. "That doesn't ring a bell—I'm sorry. I was so young—about your daughter's age."

"Indeed, and Tony was a beautiful baby of six months. I searched for you, Elizabeth. I went to the Sisters of Charity and to the children's aid office. I even attended the departure of several Orphan Trains, hoping I could give your grandfather good news."

"What? You were in touch with him?"

"He came to see us in the Bronx, about a month after your disappearance. He'd made the journey because your dad hadn't replied to his letters," explained Lea. "Goodness, you do look pale. I have shaken you up, telling you all this without prior warning. That's me—I don't beat about the bush. Baptiste keeps telling me off for it."

"Don't reproach yourself, Madam. I'm so grateful to have met you, and for being able to hold Mummy's medal."

"Hold it! But you can keep it—it's yours!"

"I wouldn't want to upset Miranda. Let me give her another medal, at the very least. Madam, would you mind if I gave you a hug? I would have done so ten years ago, if tragedy hadn't struck Daddy."

"Come here—let's have a hug! And please call me Lea, okay?"

Trembling with joy, Elizabeth kissed the woman's cool cheek. All of a sudden, Tony's skates screeched to a halt in front of them.

"*Maman!*" he shouted in French. "I'm hungry—can we go now? Why are you crying?"

"I'll tell you later, little rascal," replied Lea, between sobs of joy. "Here, put your shoes on."

Elizabeth took the opportunity to admire the gold medal, turning it over in her hands. She remembered how it used to shine on her mother's neck and felt as if she were reconnecting with her, after their abrupt separation on board *La Champagne*.

But Elizabeth was about to make a new, promising connection with Lea and her children. She felt close to all of them and had a strong urge to go one step further.

"I have to meet your husband, Lea," she said. "He worked with Daddy for one week. I'm certain he'll be able to talk to me about him."

"And you will tell us what happened to you! God is my witness, during the past ten years, I've not been able to stop myself from going up to dark-haired girls with bright-blue eyes. Guillaume had described you to Baptiste, bragging about your ringlets."

"You spent all that time looking for me?" exclaimed an ecstatic Elizabeth.

"I had to find out if you were still alive. I had promised Mr. Laroche, the day before he left."

"But how did you get hold of Mummy's medal? An unscrupulous neighbour stole it from me in the Bronx."

"That Colette, who called herself Coco, without doubt," snapped Lea, nodding her head.

"Yes, that's her. How come you know her?"

"I'll tell you everything I know later, Miss Duquesne, but I have to leave now—the children are hungry and the wind is picking up. Come and see us tonight, or tomorrow morning. My husband will be there, he's on leave."

"What if I came with you now? I was planning on having lunch with a friend at the chalet, but he had to leave early."

"The handsome fellow who accompanied you earlier? He was looking for you too—he visited us twice, in spring and summer. I can see he's found you."

"Richard Stenton? You must be mistaken!"

"That's not the name he gave me, but I'm sure it's him. He works for his father, who runs a private detective agency near Longacre Square."

Elizabeth felt numb on hearing this. She was torn between anger and disappointment, and wondered how many more times she would be lied to, manipulated, or betrayed. The attraction she felt for the handsome Stenton and her growing feelings towards him disappeared in one fell swoop.

"I will return to France as soon as possible," she said to Lea, in a quaky voice. "There is nothing to keep me here anymore."

"The young gentleman doesn't know who you are, does he?" asked Lea. "I should have held my tongue—I'm sorry. I can see I've hurt your feelings."

"Don't worry—I'd rather know the truth. I can't take any more lies. It's clear to me now why he was so interested in me."

"Hugues Laroche has certainly paid out a lot. He's tried many other investigators, never giving up hope of finding you alive and well."

It comforted Elizabeth to hear how her grandfather, whom she had been so afraid of as a child, had not given up trying to find her. She complained about the slow pace of transatlantic mail.

"I posted a letter to my grandparents on Saturday, but they won't receive it for weeks. Crossings are more perilous in wintertime."

"You could have sent a telegram, if you have their address," offered Lea.

"But of course! Why did no one suggest this to me earlier? You should know that I was taken in by some very wealthy people . . . It's a long story."

Tony and Miranda listened to their conversation, without interrupting or asking for anything. Lea Rambert praised them with a smile.

"We're going home," she announced. "We need to hurry."

"I'll come with you," insisted Elizabeth.

Lea and Baptiste Rambert's home
The same day

Elizabeth was about to discover another side to the gigantic city of New York. She had been living in an elegant fortress, never seeing the crowds, or the poverty. The Rambert family lived on the south-eastern boundary of the Bronx and Manhattan. After a trip in an omnibus drawn by four horses, Lea took her down a long street, then up to the fourth floor of a dilapidated building.

In the stairwell, foul smells mingled with the stale odour of fat. The young girl discreetly covered her nose with a corner of her scarf. She looked in horror at the chipped plaster, the dirty paintwork and the graffiti on the walls.

Elizabeth's surprise hadn't gone unnoticed. "You get used to it. The important thing is that the inside is clean," said Lea. "You've clearly been living in the lap of luxury."

"Luxury, luxury!" chanted Tony as his mother led the visitor into their apartment.

"We have four rooms—it's wonderful!" said Lea, smiling.

"You must be very comfortable here," nodded Elizabeth.

The four rooms in question would have fitted into the Woolworths' sitting room, but the apartment was very tidy, with meticulous attention paid to details such as a bouquet of holly on the sideboard, framed prints, and macramé curtains. They brightened up the modest furnishings.

"Sit down, Miss Luxury," joked Tony, looking at her cheekily from under his dark fringe.

"Tony, will you shut up!" said Lea. "What a way to behave!"

"But you said she leads a pampered life, Mom."

"Don't be silly—you know very well what I meant."

"Don't scold him," begged Elizabeth. "The people that took me in live in the Dakota Building, and the man that I call Dad made his fortune in the cotton trade, so . . ."

"You live in the big castle near Central Park?" marvelled the boy.

"Yes, Tony. But I could have grown up here, for your father had found us a room in this neighbourhood, ten years ago. You were a baby and I was supposed to help out your mom."

"You remember all that?" cried Lea in astonishment.

"My memory came back only a few days ago. I think it was just lying dormant in my mind for the past ten years."

Lea took a better look at Elizabeth, whose impeccable elocution, elegance and expensive clothes had turned her into an accomplished young lady.

"I feel much more at home with you, though, Madam," Elizabeth confessed.

Miranda started to cry again. Her mother pushed her towards one of the bedrooms.

"Go and play a little, Miranda! Tony, look after your sister— Miss and I want to talk in peace."

Elizabeth was moved by the shy, raven-haired little girl. She took off her gold bracelet, set with fine turquoise patterns, and handed it to the child.

"Please, take it. I want you to have it, in exchange for your necklace," she said sweetly.

"No, it's too much for a little girl of her age," interrupted Lea, dismayed. "What if she loses it!"

"Please, it'll make me happy. I'm just so glad to have Mummy's baptism medal back. Take it, Miranda."

Tony whistled in awe, before taking his sister, who was speechless with joy, into the adjacent room. Lea shrugged.

"Baptiste won't let her keep such a precious piece of jewellery," she sighed. "Though I'll try and persuade him to."

This exuberant and hot-headed woman in her forties bore a wilful expression that amused Elizabeth. She had no doubt that her husband would yield.

"I have something else to give you," said Lea. "Baptiste found it near where your father was attacked. We got it back from the police after they closed the investigation."

She opened a drawer at the bottom of a cupboard and retrieved an envelope, from which she pulled out a copper button.

"It's engraved with the Carpenters' Guild insignia."

Elizabeth took it from her and examined it at length, with tears in her eyes. She tried in vain to remember her father's velvet jacket.

"Are you certain he died that night?" she asked feebly. "I was hoping for a miracle."

"A body was recovered from the Hudson River a few days later, and this button matches then ones on its jacket, my poor darling."

"Yes, I'd heard. Lea, I must tell you my story now."

"I'm listening, but let me feed the kids first."

Guerville Castle
6 p.m., the same day

As young Elizabeth Duquesne sat drinking coffee in Lea Rambert's home on the other side of the Atlantic, it was already evening in Charente.

Adela Laroche was sitting by the fireplace in the drawing room, leafing through *L'Illustration*, a high-end magazine that her husband subscribed her to.

"Should I draw the double curtains, Madam?" asked Madeleine, after filling the large wicker basket with logs.

"Yes, please. And you can serve me a glass of port—I'm feeling morose tonight."

The maid contained a grin, as her mistress was never very cheerful, and poured her a little too much port.

Brisk footsteps suddenly resounded in the hall. Hugues Laroche appeared and gestured at Madeleine to leave the room. She slowly walked towards the door that led to the pantry staircase.

"You're back!" shouted Adela as soon as they were alone. "So, is it her?"

She had been living on a faint glimmer of hope the whole week.

"Fred Johnson has promised me a definite answer in the next few days. He replied mid-afternoon to the telegram I sent yesterday. He thinks he's found our granddaughter, who seems to go by the name of Lisbeth Woolworth."

Laroche leaned over his wife's chair and kissed her on the forehead, which was framed by grey-blonde curls. She didn't dare rejoice yet.

"What makes this detective think it's her? Hugues, if this is a red herring, I'll lose heart completely. It will end up making me ill."

The whole problem had made Adela sensitive to the slightest thing. She clasped his hands. Laroche couldn't bear seeing his wife distressed and sought to reassure her.

"I'm sure we'll soon see Elizabeth again—trust me."

Madeleine was up to her usual tricks, lurking behind the door. She pulled a face, fists clenched. Justin saw her enter the kitchen briskly and guessed that she was annoyed.

"What are you upset about, Madam?" he asked coldly.

"It's not funny. Apparently, they've found Elizabeth."

The young groom stared at her. He had thought he would never set eyes on Elizabeth again, the little girl he had comforted one November evening, many moons ago. After several years spent hiding under the eaves in a tiny room, he had been hired by Laroche as a stable boy, a job he was passionate about.

He'd been introduced to Laroche as a distant relative of one of Madeleine's cousins, and had been living in the stables ever since, which suited him perfectly. The only drawback was that Madeleine kept a strict eye on him.

The housekeeper claimed to be his aunt, but forbade him to disclose this to their employers. Henceforth, he was to address her formally and to cease being on first-name terms with her.

This woman thrives on lies, bitterness, and hatred, he thought, sitting at the table, a bowl of soup in front of him. *If Elizabeth ever returns, I must warn her.*

He finished his scanty supper and dressed to go out again. It was raining, and the north wind was gusting.

"Where are you off to now?" asked Madeleine.

"One of the mares keeps licking her flank. She might have a colic—I'd better watch over her tonight," he replied. "I'm happy to sleep on the hay."

"Do as you think fit," she said between her teeth. "Send me Alcide—I need to talk to him."

Justin nodded. Alcide was the new gardener, a thirty-five-year-old man trained by rheumatism-plagued Leandre.

Alcide had become Madeleine's lover, now that she no longer had Vincent. The latter had suffered a violent and still inexplicable death.

Lea and Baptiste Rambert's home
The same day, the same time

Lea was all ears as Elizabeth told her story—from the accident in Central Park when she was six years old, to the Woolworths' latest revelations. She also briefly mentioned her encounter with the so-called Richard Stenton.

"I'm in a very difficult predicament," concluded the girl. "I still love Maybel and Edward, who cared for me, and cherished and over-indulged me. But I blame them for lying to me, letting me believe they'd adopted me long ago."

Lea's Italian blood had given her a fiery character. She was frank and didn't usually spare anyone. Elizabeth and her story were no exception.

"I think there are many people in far harder situations than you, Elizabeth. What is it you find so difficult? At worst, you will return to France, live in a castle, and be lovingly cared for by your grandparents. Or you could decide to stay in New York, in a very wealthy family, with people who treat you as their own child. The Woolworths are a well-known family—I never imagined you'd grow up in such circles. They were at fault, I agree, but at the same time, I can sympathize with them. They loved you so much, they didn't want to risk losing you."

"I'd already figured that out on my own," replied Elizabeth, a little hurt by the lecture. "I concede that I was very fortunate. I could have ended up wasting away in an orphanage. Yet, I didn't have the life I'd dreamt of, which was to live here with Mummy and Daddy, and the baby which would have been born in America. We wouldn't have been rich, but the four of us would have been happy."

Her voice was quavering, as she tried to hold back her tears. Lea took her hand.

"I can well imagine, my poor darling! My husband and me were sick to our stomachs, imagining your terrible fate. That's why I carried on searching for you, hoping you would at least be able to return to France. Excuse me for being so frank. I'm unable to pretend."

"Please don't apologize—you were right to give me a little jolt. I suppose that many orphaned girls are victims of abuse, and fall into both moral and physical destitution. I'm very grateful that I was spared that, Lea."

"My poor little one," she murmured in Italian. "It's getting late. Your parents must be worrying, and I still haven't told you how I recovered your Mom's medal."

"I'll take a carriage back. Do tell me quickly. I'm so glad to have this piece of jewellery back, and to be able to touch it."

"It's a rather unusual story," began Lea. "It was before Miranda was born. My mother used to look after Tony, and I took any work I could, even though Baptiste earned good money on the site. At that time, I was working in a big launderette for two months, just a tram station away from here. There were about ten of us running the machines that washed, rinsed and spun stacks of bed linen and tea towels from the nearby hotels. One of the employees there was called Colette and I recognized her straight away. I had gone to see her the day after you and your father disappeared. But when I told her I knew her, she denied it, screaming that she'd never set eyes on me before."

Lea paused to drink some water and check on the children. She then eagerly resumed her story.

"Colette was French—I was the only one she could talk to. That woman spent her days moaning! Her husband had left her for an Irish girl, and her eldest son Leonard had turned into a shoplifter."

Elizabeth closed her eyes for a minute. Hearing the name Leonard jolted her memory.

"I remember him!" she shouted in surprise. "The evening we were coming to see you, with our only piece of luggage in tow, Leonard threw an apple at Daddy, saying it was for me. He had a younger brother called Paul."

"Colette entrusted him to a neighbour in the block, but she complained about her too, saying she didn't give him enough to eat," Lea resumed. "At first I sympathized with her, of course. But before long, I came to understand that Coco was spending her pay on drink and had gone off the rails. She often cried, saying she wanted to return to France."

"Colette stole my medal while styling my hair!" Elizabeth exclaimed. "I was too shy to ask for it back. When Daddy enquired about it, she replied that I must have lost it while playing."

"Maybe she was feeling guilty, because she still had it and was even wearing it," suggested Lea. "One morning I said to her, 'That's a fine medal!' She replied with a twinkle in her eye, saying, 'If I ever need money, I'll sell it!' But she didn't get the chance. A week or so later, there was a serious accident in the launderette. One of the spin dryers became detached—no one knew why or how. The steel roller killed a woman, and left Colette with serious injuries to her head and spine."

"Oh, my God—how awful!"

"The poor, unfortunate woman spent countless hours in agony in hospital. I felt sorry for her and visited several times. Thanks to the laudanum which eased her pain a bit, she was able to talk to me. It was then that she told me to take the gold medal, sell it and give the money to her boys. I agreed, promising her I would take care of her boys, as far as possible. But as she held out the gold medal, my eyes fell on the inscription. Can you imagine my distress upon seeing the name *Catherine Duquesne*? It didn't take me long to get the truth out of her, and she admitted to having stolen the medal off you."

"And then what happened?" asked Elizabeth. "What became of her boys?"

"When I told the story to Baptiste, he decided to hold on to the piece of jewellery. Colette died shortly afterwards. My husband gave a small sum of money to Leonard, who took off with it immediately, and Paul was taken to an orphanage. He must have left on one of the trains that takes young boys out West."

"That's so sad," said Elizabeth gloomily. "It seems that immigrants rarely have the dream life they imagined during the crossing. Lea, I must go now, but may I come back to see you?"

"I'll make sure you do," joked the kind-hearted Italian. "Baptiste will definitely want to meet you! Join us for lunch the day after tomorrow, on January 1st—it's a holiday here."

"I will. But let me ask one final question. You received my grandfather, Hugues Laroche. What was your impression of him? He used to put the fear of God into me when I was small."

"At first, he made quite an impression on me," replied Lea. "He was a very distinguished gentleman, although rather arrogant. But it didn't take long to see how unhappy he was. He'd lost his only daughter, and when he arrived at our house, he learned that his son-in-law was most likely dead, and that his granddaughter had disappeared. He blew his top at first, but quickly calmed down. The man was very upset, I could feel it. He's been looking for you ever since."

Deeply moved, Elizabeth stood up and put on her coat and gloves. The anger she felt towards the Woolworths, which had softened for a while, now returned with full force.

"When I think that my grandfather was standing right here in this room, Lea, I have no desire to go home. Even the word 'home' rings hollow now, just like calling Maybel and Edward Mom and Dad! No matter the circumstances, they should have taken me to the Chelsea, to comfort the poor man who was grieving and who needed his granddaughter. I hate them!"

Lea said nothing. She went up to Elizabeth, who hugged her.

"Be brave," Lea whispered in her ear.

The Tide of Scandal

The Dakota Building
Thursday, December 31, 1896

The Woolworths' party was a hit. Maybel gracefully moved from one guest to another, wearing a magnificent green velvet dress adorned with beige lace. Her husband gazed at her with melancholy.

No expense had been spared. French champagne flowed, alongside a buffet of the finest foods including caviar, smoked salmon, lobsters and poultry aspic. A waiter was assisting Bonnie, who ensured that everything went like clockwork.

The vast sitting room sparkled under the crystal chandeliers, just like the ladies' diamonds, rubies and fine pearls. They were chatting cheerfully, competing with each other for elegance.

"Are you sad, Uncle Edward?" whispered Pearl, perched on the armrest of the trader's chair.

"No, my dear niece. I just have a lot on my mind and am a little tired these days."

"I think Elizabeth does too," she remarked maliciously. "How can she sulk when she's that pretty and dressed in such a beautiful gown?"

Pearl looked jealously at her cousin's ravishing figure. Elizabeth was wearing an exquisite dress that evening. Maybel had given it to her that very morning, but didn't get the slightest smile in return—just a mumbled "Thank you."

"A one-off I ordered in London," said Edward Woolworth.

Elizabeth looked over at them, sensing they were talking about her. The silky, pale-pink fabric shaped her bust and accentuated her slender waist. Both bodice and skirt were embroidered with sparkling sequins. The V-shaped neckline revealed her round, pearlescent shoulders and cleavage. Her dark hair contrasted with her milky complexion.

"The Princess of the Dakota Building," scoffed Pearl, disappointed with her flat chest and straight hair.

"You look just as delightful, and you at least seem to be enjoying yourself," replied her uncle in a disenchanted tone.

"Oh, I am, Uncle—and I'd love to dance with you once the pianist starts playing."

Pearl walked off, smiling at everyone she encountered, whether male or female. Edward in turn got up and joined Maybel, who was standing by a window.

"Lisbeth could make an effort," he whispered.

"She's deliberately being cold, to punish us. I had the impression she was starting to forgive us—if only she hadn't met that woman, Lea Rambert. Did you hear her last night, when she returned alone after dark? According to her, we are responsible for her grandfather's grief. She says she would have preferred to live with him in his castle, and other such nonsense."

Maybel trembled nervously. "Sometimes I want to slap her, she's so ungrateful and insolent, but I don't because she's not my daughter," she admitted.

"Yet you would have every right to. You love her deeply and took care of her for all these years. We both did."

"No, Edward—we'd lose her for good then!"

"I wonder about that. Perhaps we should behave like real parents, with the firmness that goes with it."

"I don't know," Maybel whimpered. "Tomorrow, she's going to have lunch with those people, the Ramberts—there's no stopping her."

"Maybe, but I intend to accompany her and explain why we acted in this way," retorted Edward. "Lisbeth is fantasizing over a grandfather whom she imagines is kind and loving. I could paint a different picture. That Laroche gave me the creeps. He had a cruel face—I remember it well."

Elizabeth, a glass of champagne in hand, was watching them both, certain she was their topic of conversation. The arrival of one last guest had gone unnoticed by her; yet the newcomer headed straight for her, an expression of longing and joy on his face. Dressed in a fashionable tuxedo, he was taller than most of the other guests.

"Lisbeth," he said softly, once he'd got to her, "I was able to get away—I was dying to see you again. And no regrets—you look absolutely stunning!"

Richard Stenton was gazing at her, convinced he'd never seen such bright, blue eyes and delicate features.

"Oh, Mr. Stenton, what a surprise!" cried Pearl, who had run up and recognized him. "Only yesterday my father was talking about you and your plans to become an architect!"

"Mr. Stenton," repeated Elizabeth scornfully, nevertheless excited to be near him.

He was very attractive; his amber eyes sparkled when he smiled. Elizabeth knew she would have been happy and proud to introduce him to Maybel and Edward, had she not met Lea Rambert. But the time had come: the game was over now.

"Excuse me, I think there's been a mistake," she said out loud. "It's Mr. Fred Johnson we have here with us, isn't it? I can't bear any more lies, so I might as well reveal your true identity and profession here and now!"

He turned white as a sheet, while the entire Woolworth family—Edward and his brother, Maybel, and his sister-in-law—drew nearer, intrigued by the altercation.

"What's that supposed to mean?" asked Pearl, who thought Elizabeth was joking.

The indignation, the helpless fury that Elizabeth had been harbouring for a whole week overrode her etiquette, good manners and the hypocrisy that was expected at high-society gatherings. Thoughts were rushing through her head.

She saw flashbacks from her nightmares—of her dead mother being tossed into the ocean, of her father assaulted by thugs. Instinctively, she touched Catherine Duquesne's baptismal medal, the only piece of jewellery she had put on for this reception.

"Sometimes, one can't get around the truth," she added, confidently. "Mr. Fred Johnson works for a detective agency, so I very much doubt that he is an architect! I'm also sceptical as to his intentions towards me. He wanted to teach me to skate, he hoped to see me as much as possible, but it was just to find out who I really am!"

"Lisbeth, I beg you, please stop!" implored the young man.

"Why would I? I have nothing to lose, since I will be returning to France, to my country, to my real family! I'm not related to Maybel. No—I'm not a poor grand-niece of an uncle from Arizona!"

"Darling, please, stop!" protested Maybel. "Not tonight! Please!"

"Whether tonight or tomorrow, all these people should know where I come from! Do you see this gold medal? It belonged to my mother, Catherine Duquesne, born a Laroche in France. My parents were immigrants. Mummy died during the crossing and Daddy a week later, here in New York, ten years ago."

Edward grabbed her by the wrist, mad with rage. Elizabeth had never seen him so angry.

"I advise you to shut up!" he ordered. "You're making a spectacle of yourself."

"Making a spectacle of myself by revealing *your* charade, Dad?" Elizabeth spat out.

Pearl stepped back, horribly embarrassed. This was serious—she could feel it.

"For the past ten years, I've been told my name is Woolworth, that I was adopted out of love—me, the poor lost orphan from Central Park! It was all lies. Those whom I loved and cherished just a few days ago, those whom I called Mom and Dad in good faith—they brought me back here injured, nursed me, and decided to keep me. They hid me away from the outside world through an elaborate web of lies, while my grandfather was out there looking for me. He came to America because he loved me! I would have grown up in Guerville Castle in France, surrounded by my real family . . ."

Fred Johnson, aka Richard Stenton, froze, his face pallid. Panting, Elizabeth regained her breath and was about to burst into tears of frustration. The trader let her go, at the behest of his brother Matthew, who asked him outright:

"Is this true, Edward? Have you and Maybel had the temerity to take a little girl away from her own family? You lied to us!"

The other guests were watching the scene but keeping a respectful distance. As for Bonnie, who stood in a corner of the sitting room, she was in complete disarray.

"Lord, have mercy on us," she whispered. "She shouldn't have done that—no, she shouldn't!"

"I wanted to meet Hugues Laroche, her grandfather, while he was in New York," Edward replied. "He didn't exactly strike me as trustworthy. You want the truth, Lisbeth? Well, you should know that ten years ago, I sincerely thought you'd be happier with us! Did you even stop to think before embarrassing us in front of our friends and family? What sort of man was Laroche, letting his own daughter and granddaughter leave the country in search of a better life, while he was very wealthy? Where was his compassion in all this?"

"It was my parents' choice—I remember it very well," Elizabeth replied, sobbing. "It was their dream and, try as he might, my grandfather wasn't able to stop them! But he never forgot me, and Fred Johnson is proof of that. Go on, tell them that Hugues Laroche sends you large sums of money from France to find Elizabeth Duquesne, a brunette with blue eyes, of French origin!"

Singled out in front of all the guests, he had no choice but to confess, which he did with ease and disdain:

"Yes, our agency has been working for Mr. Laroche for three years now. He was convinced, and quite rightly so, that his granddaughter was still alive. I would like to point out that he had previously employed other private investigators—to no avail."

Maybel was so embarrassed and ashamed, she couldn't stop crying. Hysterical, she ran towards the hallway but, blinded by tears, she knocked over a pedestal table supporting a very valuable Chinese porcelain vase. It shattered at her feet, into a thousand pieces.

"My poor aunt, your evening is ruined!" exclaimed Pearl.

The remark was so inappropriate that an embarrassed Matthew glared at his daughter furiously:

"And a lot more than that has been ruined!" he yelled. "Doris, we are leaving!" he called out to his wife. "I'm truly sorry for you, Lisbeth. Don't hesitate to turn to me for help, if you need it."

"Thank you," Elizabeth sighed, aware that she had caused a terrible scandal.

Fred Johnson hadn't moved an iota. He was glowering at Elizabeth, who scowled back at him, head held high.

As Edward took the sobbing Maybel to their bedroom, the detective whispered to the girl:

"Are you satisfied with yourself now?"

"And you?" she replied bitterly. "I'm fed up with you. You only came up to me at the ice rink to find out if I was the girl you were searching for, and when I didn't tell you, you pursued me. Now go and tell my grandfather, although my letter informing him will arrive before yours."

"Whatever. He will receive a telegram from me the day after tomorrow."

"How could you, without coming to me first!"

"It's a requirement of my job, Lisbeth."

Pearl, about to leave with her parents, reappeared in a hurry. She looked daggers at Elizabeth.

"Have a good trip, little brat," she mumbled. "I was fond of you because they told me you were my cousin. Now I'm relieved

I'll never have to see you again. And if ever you are worried about Uncle Edward and Aunt Maybel, rest assured that I'll be there to console them when you've gone. I say 'if ever', since you ooze selfishness and ingratitude. They gave you absolutely everything you would never even have dreamed of, had you stayed in the streets where you belong, without a cent in your pocket!"

"Your snide remarks are cruel and uncalled for, Pearl," replied Fred Johnson.

"Who do you think you are?! I can see your game clearly now. You didn't hesitate to enter my parents' home, pretending to be something you're not. In fact, you two go well together."

With this, she stormed off into the hallway, where Bonnie stood waiting, arms swamped by a heavy silver fox-fur jacket.

With burning cheeks, Elizabeth had to contend with dozens of curious, disconcerted glances. No compassion could be read in them.

"No doubt all these wealthy people also think I'm ungrateful and selfish," she said.

"In certain New York circles, scandals are hushed up, Lisbeth," whispered the detective. "Please, I'd like to talk to you, alone."

"I prefer not to, Sir."

"Very well, but then I won't see you again before you leave for France—and I owe you an explanation."

She turned away to hide her eyes, which were misty with tears. Bonnie came running, anxious to attend to her precious Lisbeth, and above all to spurn the intruder.

"Mr. Johnson, I think it is—unless you prefer to go by yet another surname," she said, quietly handing him his hat and coat. "It's hardly proper to play with the feelings of a young lady!"

"Bonnie, don't get involved!" reprimanded Elizabeth. "I'm old enough to stand up for myself."

The governess was speechless. She took a step back, while Fred Johnson got dressed to leave. He said goodbye with a quick nod of his head.

"Don't take the trouble to show me out, Ma'am," he said graciously to Bonnie, who still couldn't find her tongue.

Maybel and Edward had deserted the large sitting room, the scene of their humiliation. Elizabeth grabbed her woollen shawl from the back of an armchair and followed briskly in the footsteps of the young detective. He pretended not to notice her, but they were soon alone on the landing of one of the four storeys. A lift shaft opened in front of them, the grid revealing intricate gilded bronze designs. A young operator stood there at their service.

Johnson slipped him a banknote, implying that his services were not needed. Elizabeth was relieved.

"I await your explanations, Sir," she said, exasperated by his feigned indifference. "Don't make me come down with you into the yard."

He spun round and stared at her, his amber eyes gleaming.

"My explanations will be brief, Lisbeth. I just wanted you to know that I was sincere during those wonderful hours I spent with you. I work for my father, a demanding and tough businessman. For a whole year now, I've been in charge of investigating any young girl who might be Elizabeth Duquesne. You matched the portrait we'd sketched, based on a photograph your grandfather sent us of you on your fifth birthday."

"In that case, why were you so cautious? Why didn't you ask me outright if I was the person you were looking for?"

"Such an approach would have been too brutal. And I was supposed to take things gently. You could have been suffering from amnesia or concealed your identity. And you did avoid answering my questions! Why was that?"

Elizabeth shrugged, distraught. She hadn't had the time to bare her soul to him when they were together.

"The lift is going up, someone must have called it from the top floor," she noted, talking over the noise it made when halting at their level.

"Don't change the subject!" he protested. "Have you forgotten what I said the day before yesterday? I told you I wanted to learn more about you, Lisbeth. I hoped to God that you were not the granddaughter of Hugues Laroche. I prayed that I would have proof to the contrary. That's why I came tonight, despite the opposition from my parents and my sisters."

"I still don't understand," she stammered.

"Quit playing games, Lisbeth! I fell in love with you and couldn't bear the thought of you on the ocean, sailing far away from me to live in your grandparents' castle!"

Elizabeth was moved. Fred Johnson's voice resonated with fervour and frankness. He was scared of losing her; nothing else mattered at that moment.

"How can I trust you? I can no longer call Maybel and Edward Woolworth Mom and Dad, and I only know you as Richard, not Fred. Why did you use a false name?"

"Mr. Laroche insisted on it, so my father made enquiries into New York's high net-worth families. His choice fell on the Stentons, for they were once among the city's most illustrious and wealthy families. Their few surviving members are now based in Chicago. I first approached Matthew Woolworth, to get invited to social gatherings. I do have a degree in architecture, by the way, but I haven't been able to obtain any interesting contracts so far."

"One lie after another," she moaned. "Even if what you say is true, I couldn't make my anger and disappointment go away."

"One thing intrigues me. How did you find out who I really was?"

"Fate took me to Lea Rambert, who was sitting at the edge of the ice rink. Her little Miranda was wearing my mother's baptism medal. It was Lea who recognized you."

"I see," he murmured. "It was meant to be. Lisbeth, come to Central Park tomorrow morning, I beg you. I would like to make it up to you and get to know you more, even if it means I'll suffer more when you go."

"Tomorrow? No, that's impossible, Lea has invited me to lunch," she replied. "I'm going to meet her husband, a friend of my father's, and that's very important to me. I'm going to leave for France as soon as I'm able, so I'd rather say goodbye now."

Elizabeth sighed and lowered her head, exhausted from meeting Fred Johnson's gaze. She could read desire in his eyes. Then, in a masterful fashion, he pulled her against him. His lips were burning with passion as he kissed the young girl for the first time.

"I have no better proof than this to show you how I feel," he whispered in her ear, breathless.

He was waiting for the sting of a slap, a fierce lecture, or for her to frantically escape his embrace. The rebellious spirit and sensual nature she'd inherited from her beautiful mother took him by surprise.

"Nothing more?" she enquired, audaciously.

Her mouth slightly open, her throat pulsating, she took him on, intoxicated by the exhilaration she felt from his big hands around her waist and his arousing kiss.

"What do you want, Lisbeth?"

He was staggered by her brazenness and her beauty. He was certain she would grow into an unbelievably attractive and irresistible woman with unique appeal. Yet, he was taken aback when she threw herself at him, kissing him passionately.

"I will think about you a lot, Richard. In my mind you will remain Richard Stenton, my skating teacher. But once I'm on the other side of the Atlantic, I will manage to forget you. Good evening."

Elizabeth left him dumbstruck, and even more in love with her. He followed her with his gaze, cursing fate for putting such an enchantress his way, only to take her away again.

Back in the apartment, she had to face a pouting and offended Bonnie. Elizabeth went straight to her room, but her governess followed her.

"I need to be alone, Bonnie! Please take care of the guests."

"Sir is doing a better job of it than I am, little Madam," she replied. "I talked him out of going after you when you stormed out of the room with that man, Stenton or Johnson, or whatever he's called. He has no manners—you must be heartbroken."

"Not because of him, Bonnie," sighed Elizabeth, closing the door behind them. "Right—I suppose I'm in for a lecture now?"

"Madam put herself to bed—she was hysterical. I disapproved of how she and Sir behaved back then, but I don't see why you had to expose them in front of their family and friends."

"I was utterly furious with them all! When I saw Richard there, or rather the detective, all that pent-up anger inside me came out, Bonnie. Last night, I told you about my visit to Lea Rambert's house and what she taught me about my grandfather. It was just too much to bear. I'm sorry I was rude to you earlier—please forgive me."

"I will always forgive you, Lisbeth, but your parents will be less forgiving. You have caused them a lot of pain."

"They've caused me pain too. I suppose I wanted to get back at them."

"That's an ugly thing to want, my poor child! You really aren't the same person anymore. As a young girl, you were nothing but sweet, obedient and loving. Your only struggle was these nightmares, from which you woke up screaming and in tears. My cuddles and singing used to console you."

"You sang softly and in French," admitted Elizabeth. "It never failed to have a soothing effect on me."

Bonnie had started to relax and sat down on the edge of the bed. Her plump fingers were fiddling with the seam of her white apron.

"And then you began to have violent outbursts—maybe not as violent as tonight, but your anger was real. It started when you were thirteen years old. The first time, you broke a plate, because I forbade you to taste the custard while it was still hot. And it went on like that."

"I must have inherited my grandfather Hugues' temper. I remember him bellowing while a storm was brewing outside.

My memories are so vivid all of a sudden, Bonnie. It has been this way ever since December 23rd, which is unlikely to be a coincidence."

Elizabeth reversed her mother's gold medal and read out loud: "*Catherine Laroche, December 23 1857.*"

"It's the day she was born," she stammered, in shock. "Good Lord, please tell me I'm right about this. I'm certain that Mummy helped me recover my memory, from up there. She wants me to return to my roots, to both my mother's and my father's family. I've been praying to see my dear Pops Toine, Guillaume's father, who absolutely adored me. Bonnie, will you come with me?"

"I gave you my word, Miss," replied the governess. "No matter where you go, you'll need a chaperone."

The girl sat down beside her and gave her a crushing hug. There was a sharp knock on the door. Without waiting for an answer, Edward entered, surprised to see Bonnie there.

"Please leave—our guests are departing. You must see them out," he said.

"Yes, Sir."

As she rushed out of the room, Elizabeth was forced to face the trader's cold gaze. All tenderness and closeness had vanished from his face and he eyed her as if she were a stranger.

"Maybel is extremely upset by the scandal you've caused," he began. "As for me, I'm bitterly disappointed. I can understand your resentment, your anger, but to accuse us like that was the lowest of the low. Some of my biggest clients were there, and after the stunt you pulled tonight, I may well have lost them."

"That hadn't crossed my mind," she admitted, embarrassed.

"Of course not—you were thinking about yourself, as always. Without a doubt, this is our own fault, as our world has always revolved around you, our little Lisbeth. That's over now. Think about it: if one of the guests wanted to ruin me, they'd only have to go to the press. As a result, we could be subject to a judicial enquiry and may well be prosecuted for 'kidnapping' you. I've tried to smooth things out with our guests, putting the fit you threw down to your nervous troubles. I specified that we had planned to tell you on Christmas Eve, giving you the choice of staying with us or leaving."

"Are you sure you would have done that?" said Elizabeth.

"It was certainly very naive of us. We were going to adopt you, having had no news from your French family, and we were convinced you would be delighted. But we would have offered you the opportunity of reuniting with Hugues Laroche, if that was what you wanted."

"I wish I could believe you, but I can't. It hurts so much to be betrayed. Fred Johnson lied to me, just like Maybel and you did. But he did it for his job, whereas the two of you selfishly locked me in a golden cage."

Edward Woolworth raised his arms up in the air and started pacing up and down the room. His gaze wandered bitterly over the ornaments, the jewellery in its precious wooden box, and the fine undergarments laid out on the back of a chair.

"It's easy for you to talk about a golden cage, Lisbeth. You didn't seem to mind living in clover over the last ten years! Even tonight you were happy to wear this outrageously expensive dress, before hiding in your room to play the offended little princess."

"But . . . Dad!"

"Please don't call me that anymore. Let's get things straight, shall we, to avoid causing ourselves more pain. We were so happy, the three of us, but you've destroyed everything. I have therefore decided that you will return to France on the first boat. Of course, I intend to pay for your trip. You are free to take your clothes, personal effects and books with you. The sailing conditions may be tough at this time of year, so I will book you a first-class cabin."

Surprised by the icy tone of the man whom she had grown to love as a father, Elizabeth became tense. The long-awaited departure was now looming, and her throat tightened with apprehension.

"It might be better to wait for my grandfather's response," she suggested hesitantly.

"Mr. Johnson will inform him promptly that you are alive and ready to return to him. There are faster ways of contacting him, telegrams being one of them. What are you afraid of? Hugues Laroche has spent vast amounts of money trying to find you; he will be delighted to have you back."

The irony in his voice hadn't gone unnoticed by Elizabeth. She retaliated immediately.

"That's not the problem. In fact, I was thinking that my grandfather would be happy to pay the travel expenses. What is more, we need two tickets: Bonnie will accompany me."

"What did you say?!" yelled the trader. "Talk about adding insult to injury! Bonnie has been working for us for fifteen years now—I hired her when we lived near Wall Street. How could she have the heart to abandon Maybel, who is so generous to her? What other schemes have you been cooking up, Lisbeth?"

"As far as scheming is concerned, I'm lagging way behind both of you," Elizabeth retorted. "Bonnie doesn't want to be parted from me. She'll follow me wherever I go. After all, she's not a slave!"

Edward was close to slapping her. He pointed his index finger at the girl, eyes bulging with impotent rage.

"She can get the hell out of here, but be sure to tell her that she can pay for her crossing out of her own pocket!"

He left, slamming the door behind him.

New York
Friday, January 1, 1897

Elizabeth went to the Ramberts' house by herself. Light snow-flakes were falling on her hat and on the icy pavement. A cold wind was blowing, but the girl breathed it in deeply, grateful to be free and to walk where she wanted in the gigantic city she barely knew.

The smile on her lips was nevertheless tinged with sadness.

Everything is happening both too fast and too slowly, she thought. *I said goodbye to Richard and am still feeling light-headed from the kissing. I wanted to leave, but thought I had weeks ahead of me, and now I'm supposed to take the next boat.*

She was so distracted by her jumbled-up thoughts that she took a wrong turn. A carriage came out of nowhere and would have knocked her down, if a firm hand hadn't held her back.

"You should pay attention," said the detective in his deep voice.

She turned towards him. He was looking at her sternly.

"Where are you going?" he demanded. "Why have your parents let you out without your governess?"

"Were you following me? Am I not allowed any independence?"

"It's reckless at your age."

"I've seen girls younger than me out on their own, without a chaperone. Please don't bother me again, Mr. Johnson."

"My boss, who is also my father, as you know, has asked me to keep a close watch on you, now that we've found you alive. What would Mr. Hugues Laroche have to say if there had been an accident today?"

His remark made an impression on Elizabeth. She stared defiantly at Johnson with her bright-blue eyes.

"Well, if these horses had run me over or trampled me, my short life would have gone full circle. Edward and Maybel Woolworth were riding in a horse-drawn carriage when they knocked me down in the driveway of the park. I was unconscious and they took me home with them. You know the rest of the story."

"Lisbeth, I want to know everything about you," he pleaded.

"I'm sorry, we won't be seeing each other again. The Woolworths have had enough of me—I'll embark on the next boat. Don't hold me up any longer, I'm going for lunch at the Ramberts' and I plan to buy some sweets for the children first. I still have my allowance."

The detective could sense her distress, in spite of her efforts to conceal it.

"I'll take you there, with or without your consent," he announced. "The neighbourhood you're heading for is not suitable for a young lady as beautiful and elegant as you. I would never forgive myself if you were attacked."

Elizabeth did not protest and was secretly ecstatic. From time to time she glanced at him, sideways, and her heart skipped a beat.

"I want go skating tomorrow morning," she said all of a sudden.

"I'll try to be there as well, then, Lisbeth. You don't look very happy to me. Is it the thought of leaving New York?"

"I'm afraid so—I truly enjoyed living here. It was a privilege to receive piano lessons and private tuition, and the women who taught me were always lovely. I used to have tea with them after every lesson. Bonnie would serve delicious cakes, and Maybel took an interest in my progress. It was certainly a very cooped-up existence, but the apartment was suitable for it—it's huge, isn't it? When I was eight years old, Edward's mother visited us and gave me a beautifully crafted toy. She was already a widow and died six months later."

"One thing worries me, Lisbeth. How will you communicate with your family and friends once you're in France? You must have forgotten your native language."

"Don't worry, I'll be just fine," she answered in French.

"Come again? I didn't catch that."

"I was just teasing you. I still speak it but have kept it a secret. Bonnie's mother was from Normandy, a province by the sea. During the first months, Maybel asked Bonnie to translate what I was saying. After that she was asked to switch to English, but she didn't heed their instructions. We continued to converse in French in secret. But I have a question for you, too: Why did your father insist on you using a false identity?"

"I've already told you, Lisbeth: to increase my chances of getting into wealthy circles. My father started at the bottom, as they say.

Our agency is not much to look at, and my studies in architecture cost him an arm and a leg. I owe him, so I respect his wishes. But as it happens, Richard is my middle name. I even prefer it to Frederic, which always gets shortened to Fred, or worse still, Freddy."

"Then I shall continue to call you Richard, given how little time we have left together," Elizabeth said excitedly.

Richard didn't have the courage to answer her. He was happy just to hold her little velvet-gloved hand.

"I was planning on taking the tram, but we've missed the station," she complained.

"A carriage is approaching—let's hop in."

They found themselves sitting tightly together on a bench. The heavy vehicle rapidly gained speed thanks to the four draught horses pulling it. Elizabeth couldn't resist the temptation of laying her head against Richard's shoulder. The contact with his male body troubled and intrigued her, arousing emotions she didn't know she had.

She dreamt of kissing him again, fully aware that the setting wasn't appropriate. Richard did end up kissing her at the bottom of the Ramberts' building, but just a peck on her forehead, much like an older brother's.

"I don't want to suffer," he admitted. "I'll therefore have to avoid seeing you again, Lisbeth. Don't wait for me tomorrow at the ice rink."

"Are you going to send a telegram to my grandfather?"

"Only by necessity. It would be dishonest to withhold news from him that he's been hoping to hear for the past ten years. Unfortunately, I can't stop you from leaving New York."

Elizabeth watched him walk away, her mind in complete turmoil.

Lea and Baptiste Rambert's home
The same day

As soon as she knocked on the Ramberts' door, Elizabeth stopped thinking of Richard's amber eyes and enchanting smile. The past had come to the forefront of her mind.

"Daddy and my grandfather must have climbed this stairwell at least once," she mused.

The carpenter opened the door with a radiant smile, a glint of joy in his eyes. He was a burly man of medium height, with short, grey hair.

"Hello, Elizabeth!" he exclaimed in French. "Come in quickly—it's cold out there on the landing. I'm so happy to meet you!"

He took her by the shoulders and kissed her on both cheeks. Lea, who was standing a bit further away, nodded happily. The children, dressed in their Sunday best, were dancing from one foot to the other.

"I hope this New Year will be a good one for you in every way," added Baptiste.

"Thank you, Sir—I . . ."

Elizabeth was choked with tears. Lea rushed to hug her anxiously.

"Don't cry, dear," she said as she cuddled their visitor. "Sit down, please. There you go, my husband is shedding a tear now, too."

"I'm sorry, Lea—I'm making a show of myself," whimpered the girl. "It's truly wonderful to be able to converse more in French again—maybe that's why the past is coming back to me, and with such clarity. You should know, Sir, that we were on our way to your house the night Daddy was attacked and beaten to death. I found out recently."

"I know," he said. "And I still blame myself for not having looked for you both earlier in the nearby alleys. I could have saved my friend. Guillaume and I came face to face with some pretty rough brutes in the Rhone Valley, and we used to send them packing with our Carpenters' Guild canes."

"Please tell me about Daddy, back in the days when you knew him. I really miss him . . ."

Baptiste sat down at the table opposite Elizabeth. He was trembling with joy as he looked at her.

"If only he were here to see his daughter, his beloved

princess," he replied. "God is my witness, after your mother's death, you were all he had to live for."

The table was already set and Lea cut short the conversation, anxious to serve up.

"First, let's eat. The little ones are hungry—it's a holiday, and they're impatient to tuck into the feast. I've made you a dish from my country, Elizabeth: lasagne. It's flat pasta, with layers of meat and vegetables, covered in Parmesan cheese."

"I've never tried it Lea, but it smells very good."

"And I've bought a bottle of Chianti in your honour," added Baptiste. "I suppose it's also for my wife, who is partial to Italian wine. Whether we like it or not, we can't get away from our roots!"

"You can talk later—I'm going to serve now," his wife chipped in. "Miranda, Tony, lunch is ready!"

Elizabeth had rarely tasted such a special dish, and she'd never before eaten in such a cheerful, unpretentious family atmosphere. For dessert, there was chocolate cheesecake. Elizabeth then took a pack of aniseed gums with a red ribbon out of her handbag.

"I bought them for the children at the grocery store opposite your building. I don't know the area, or I would have bought them something more special."

"That's very kind of you, Elizabeth," replied Lea. "They rarely have sweets at home. Would you like some coffee?"

"I'm afraid I can't—I'm of a very nervous disposition, according to the doctor who checks on me regularly. He also forbade me to drink tea, but of course I didn't listen to him."

"How funny!" laughed the carpenter. "Lea is a real live wire, with or without coffee!"

The couple were laughing, which aroused a painful longing for the past in the young girl's heart.

"Mummy and Daddy would have been just the same," she said quietly. "We would have lived in a similar dwelling, and spent Sundays and holidays together. Why did such bad luck befall us? My parents were cursed. Lea must have told you, Sir, that most of my childhood memories were a total blank to me, until they suddenly returned on the evening of my mother's birthday."

"Fate dealt all three of you a hard blow," admitted Baptiste. "Starting with your trunks that disappeared, the storm—and then the rest, which I won't go into now. Go on, have a small glass of wine, Elizabeth."

The girl sipped a little Chianti, while the carpenter reminisced about his friend Guillaume Duquesne.

"We both left on the same day to tour France with the Carpenters' Guild. I was from Picardy and your father from Charente. We got along very well, both at work and in the evenings when we studied. He did a fine job and was more talented than a lot of others. Together, we restored the roof structure of a church near Limoges and carried out repairs to a town hall roof in the Jura region."

Baptiste spent more than an hour churning out a panorama of memories. The children were playing in their room and Lea was washing the dishes. She came back to the table as her husband was about to conclude his story:

"When Guillaume returned to Montignac, I settled in Paris. He used to write to me and told me he had got married. He described Catherine as if he were reciting poetry: she was the love of his life. Your parents were deeply in love, Elizabeth."

The girl agreed, overcome by a profound sense of peace.

"But Baptiste, you still have Guillaume's letters!" exclaimed Lea. "You must hand them over to his daughter. I think you'd be happy to read them, my poor child!"

"Oh yes, very happy!" affirmed Elizabeth. "Except they were not written for me—they belong to your husband, Lea. But I'd love to borrow and return them before I leave."

"You're leaving?" enquired Baptiste, brows furrowed. "To go back to France?"

"I am, and very soon. Lea must have explained my situation, and what I discovered. I can't bear the thought of living so far away from my family."

The carpenter scratched his beard, puzzled.

"Hmm," he murmured.

"Is something bothering you, Sir?"

"Perhaps it is nothing to worry about, but those people, the Woolworths, they acted without thinking. I must admit though, at that time I may well have done the same, in their position. I know things, since Guillaume used to confide in me a lot during the week when we were both working on the same site. On her death bed, your mother Catherine had made him promise never to hand you over to her parents."

"Are you quite certain of this, Sir?"

"Oh, yes! She claimed you wouldn't be happy with them. I found it hard to believe, on hearing his description of Guerville Castle, the stables, the vineyards. Still, when your grandfather came to visit us, when he was sitting at this very table, I understood where your mother was coming from."

Lea sighed with annoyance. She pointed a finger threateningly at her husband, who shrugged his shoulders wearily.

"You shouldn't have told her that, Baptiste! Mr. Laroche was grief-stricken when he came to see us, that's all."

"But I will never forget that moment, Lea! I informed him of his son-in-law's disappearance, pointing out that we had every reason to believe he was dead—and he didn't respond. Nothing! Not a quiver in his face, not a word of sympathy. He was only interested in what had become of you, Elizabeth."

"Yes, I'm aware of that," the girl replied. "I mean no offence, Sir, but a few years have gone by since then. Mummy was a free spirit—she longed for adventure and upset her parents by marrying Daddy. In fact, my grandfather's attitude that day is consistent with the memory I have of him: a hard, cold and angry man. It's entirely possible that I have inherited some of his personality traits. If Mummy made my father promise this, it was probably because I was a very sensitive little girl at the time."

Overcome by affection, Baptiste cupped her hands in his.

"Elizabeth, if you think you have the courage to reclaim your place at Guerville Castle, the place your mother couldn't wait to leave, then go," he said solemnly.

"I will pray for you, my pretty girl," sighed Lea.

"Thank you both for being so kind and honest with me," replied Elizabeth. "I will never forget you."

II

Back in France

On board La Touraine
Tuesday, January 12, 1897

The wind dried Elizabeth's tears as she watched the Statue of Liberty and New York's myriad buildings shrink in the distance, resembling a long piece of stone lace with whimsical outlines. Despite the icy wind, she lingered there stubbornly, clutching the handrail tightly.

The vast liner *La Touraine* carried her away like a steel giant, its flanks streaming from the strong swell and the huge waves that crashed onto the hull. She was fascinated by the swirling backwash of grey water around the ship. Fleeting green reflections disappeared and resurfaced in its depths.

God, what a horrible departure! she thought, taking deep breaths to calm her nerves. The final few days with the Woolworths had left a bitter-sweet taste in her mouth. *I made Maybel so ill, she could hardly get out of bed. But even so, she wanted to accompany Edward to the quayside to see me off.*

She couldn't stop thinking about the elegant yet frail-looking woman, who had been trembling and choking on her sobs as the crew pulled the anchor. Before she got on board, Maybel had held her tightly, caressing her cheeks and cupping her face in her hands.

"You will always be my daughter, Lisbeth," she hiccupped. "You made me so happy, my darling. Please, just call me Mom once more—one last time."

"I'm sorry, Mom!" cried Elizabeth as she hugged her. "I forgive you. I forgive you both. I do love you both . . .!"

"If you are unhappy in France, if you miss your life here, write to us and come back, darling," whispered the distraught trader. "You are our daughter and we will think of you every day."

Edward Woolworth said this with one hand on his heart. His anger had been a flash in the pan, overridden by feelings of remorse and genuine grief at losing their precious Lisbeth. When he purchased the first-class ticket at the headquarters of the French Line, he paid for Bonnie's trip too, leaving the envelope containing part of her savings untouched.

"Ultimately, it reassures me to know she is with Bonnie," he explained to Maybel. "She needed someone to travel with, someone dependable to look after her."

They were good parents, thought Elizabeth, numb with cold, recalling how generous the trader had been. *Thank God none of the New Year's Eve guests told the press about their shenanigans. It was just a minor "in-house scandal", as Dad put it!*

Now that she was on her way to Le Havre, she regretted spurning the love and affection her parents had tried to show her since Christmas.

"Mom, Dad, you loved me, and for love's sake, I forgive you. I shall miss you," she whispered.

Seagulls were circling over the ocean, emitting raucous cries that made her shudder. She wasn't alone on the upper deck, which was reserved for first-class passengers.

She noticed a couple laughing and chatting. There were also a few distinguished-looking gentlemen wandering around, one of them using a telescope that he was pointing at the coast.

Several people had discreetly greeted her since boarding, and she replied reservedly, shielded by her wealthy exterior.

"Ah, Miss, here you are!" said Bonnie, tapping her on the shoulder, trying not to look at the ocean. The poor woman was white as a sheet.

"I have unpacked your trunk and toiletries," she stammered. "But my stomach is turning—I'm going to have to lie down. You might want to have a look at your cabin—you'll see how luxurious it is. Sir has spared no expense. There's a lounge area, a private bathroom, and my own bed is in a corner."

"I shall stay out a little longer, Bonnie. But you're ill—go and lie down. Once we get offshore, *La Touraine* is liable to pitch a lot more."

"Oh, God, I feel worse!" she moaned. "Please come to the cabin at once if you get any unwanted attention!"

Elizabeth replied with a smile. "Don't worry, these people are well bred. I can handle the smooth talkers."

"You say that now . . ." grumbled Bonnie, before staggering towards the corridor.

Relieved to be alone again, the young girl adjusted the Chinese silk scarf that held her hat in place. She turned her back on America, which could scarcely be seen now, and looked up at the vastness of the pearly-grey sky.

Why am I so sad? she asked herself. *I would have loved to see Richard again, but he kept his word. I waited for him at the rink for three mornings in a row, but he didn't show up.*

The detective had indeed finished his mission for Hugues Laroche. On January 2 at ten o'clock, a telegram arrived at Guerville Castle. A reply had followed, delivered to the Woolworths' address two days later. She knew the text by heart:

> *God finally heeded our call. We look forward to your prompt return to France. Your grandparents who love you dearly.*

On the banks of the Charente river
The same day

Adela Laroche whipped her mare to go faster. A heavy rain was falling on the grey countryside. The swollen river was heaving between its banks, which were dotted with reeds and willows. The road to the castle had never seemed so long and arduous. She was almost standing upright, flapping the reins, her face transfixed with an incredulous smile.

The wheels of her carriage splashed through muddy puddles. Its hood was being shaken by the wind, making an annoying rattling sound, but Adela was unstoppable.

Looking out of a window, Pierre Duquesne saw the carriage hurtle into the courtyard at breakneck speed. He sent his brother Jean to greet the visitor.

"First of all, put the mare in the barn. She's sweating and could catch cold," he advised. "I wonder what's going on—look, Mrs. Laroche is running towards the house."

Jean made the sign of the cross, fearing bad news. Then he rushed outside, grabbing the mare by her bridle.

"I'm sorry your mistress has been giving you a hard time," he whispered to the animal.

Meanwhile, Adela barged into the main room of the house. Antoine Duquesne was sitting by the fire, as usual.

"Antoine!" she cried. "There has been a miracle! I would have come earlier if I could have. Elizabeth is alive, and today she boarded a ship bound for Le Havre! Our little girl is coming back!"

Out of breath, she helped the old man get up. First, he stared at her in bewilderment; then a look of wonder came over his face.

"The Lord has answered our prayers, my dear friend," Adela continued. "The postman delivered the telegram on Saturday at noon. The message is longer than usual. I've brought it for you to see. Go on, read it!"

She brandished a rectangular piece of paper.

"I need my spectacles! Read it out, Adela. Gosh, my heart is leaping like a hare. I'm going to see my granddaughter again—my little girl!"

"Yes, she'll be here in about ten days' time! Listen closely:

"*Have found Elizabeth living in a wealthy New York family. It is definitely her. She wants to return to France.*

"The detective has followed up with further messages, and Elizabeth herself has confirmed that she's coming. I brought her telegram along too:

"*My dearest grandparents. I have written to you. I will board* La Touraine *on Tuesday the 12th of the month. With much love, Elizabeth.*"

Antoine Duquesne was staggering on his aching legs. He cursed his rheumatism, which prevented him from dancing on the spot. His bright-blue eyes were misty with tears. He hugged Adela, giving his joy free rein.

On hearing the news, Pierre and Jean stood motionless in the doorway, flabbergasted.

"Lads, this is a beautiful day—one of the most beautiful of my whole life!" cried their father, still clutching Adela's arm. "It's taken my breath away! Elizabeth is alive, and she's coming home to us!"

The two brothers looked at each other, dazed. They vaguely remembered a pretty little dark-haired girl who was affectionate, giggly and loved to cuddle.

"Are you absolutely certain of this?" said Pierre, who rarely showed any enthusiasm.

Adela handed him the telegrams, which he read, nodding his head, before passing them on to Jean. Adela was bursting with joy.

"She might arrive before her letter does. The mail travels by sea too," she said.

"I must thank you for coming to inform me, my dear. I never really lost hope, but America seemed so far away, and it's such a huge place. I didn't think this detective would ever find the slightest trace of our granddaughter."

"Yet he surprised us all! My husband is all of a fluster. Of course, he'll pick up Elizabeth at Le Havre. I prefer to stay and get the castle ready for her return. We must throw her a ball, a huge party!"

"Will we be invited? After all, we're her family too," said Jean, even though he was already certain of her reply.

"If the decision was mine and mine alone, then of course. But Hugues will refuse."

"You shouldn't ask questions that put Mrs. Laroche on the spot, Jean," said his father indignantly. "Elizabeth has survived.

I will be able to hold her again, before I die, and I ask for nothing more. Besides, she's not a child anymore—she'll certainly come and visit us."

"Of course, and I'll accompany her," said Adela. "I understand how hurtful my husband's animosity towards you must be, but remind yourselves that the real party in Elizabeth's honour will surely take place here at the mill."

Her own sob cut her off. The old miller patted her shoulder sympathetically.

"Don't you worry, Adela," he said kindly. "Pierre, get the cider out of the sideboard. I propose a toast!"

On board La Touraine
The same day

Bonnie was lying on her bed, her face pallid, her eyes closed and a handkerchief on her mouth. She had already been sick twice. Renowned for its speed, the ship was now navigating offshore, ploughing through the ocean's mighty waves.

"I wish there was something I could do," said Elizabeth sympathetically, unaffected by the sway.

The young girl had finally reached her luxurious cabin with its high-quality furniture. She strolled from the lounge area to the bathroom, dressed only in her undergarments and an ivory satin corset.

"Heavens above, get dressed Miss, it's January!" begged her governess weakly.

"But it's hot in here, Bonnie! I just had to get out of my tweed suit, stockings and coat. This evening we shall dine in the first-class dining area, and I will wear one of my best gowns."

"I couldn't possibly eat a thing!"

"If you did, you would probably feel better!"

"That's what my mother used to say," sighed Bonnie.

They had decided to converse in French during the crossing, to familiarize themselves with the language again before they reached Charente.

"You don't regret accompanying me?" enquired Elizabeth, as she pulled the pins out of her bun.

"No, Miss. If I wasn't so ill, I'd brush your beautiful hair for you."

"I can do it myself, Bonnie. You're my friend, even if I have to introduce you as my governess. Which reminds me: you should start using my first name!"

"I couldn't possibly do that, Miss."

She nearly gagged on her last word and rushed to the sink. Elizabeth hurried to her aid.

"You haven't eaten anything, Bonnie—you're only vomiting water. Come on, let's have a nice cup of tea and some cakes."

"I'm better off lying down, Miss. I'll join in tomorrow, when I feel better."

It took another two days for Bonnie to start feeling better. The liner was making good progress. The Atlantic Ocean was calm now, and many passengers were strolling on deck, under a pale-blue sky.

Elizabeth had become accustomed to watching the sailors work, from the covered terrace on the upper deck. Having left her governess in the cabin, she breathed in the icy morning wind, her beautiful face turned towards the endless ocean. She tried not to think of her arrival in France: it would have brought too many daunting questions with it.

The young girl was afraid of finding the mill abandoned, her Pops Toine laid to rest in the cemetery and her uncles living far away from Montignac.

"Miss Duquesne?"

It was the Captain himself—a man in his fifties with silver hair. He looked most dignified in his navy-blue uniform, bearing the emblem of the French Line.

"Sir?"

"Apologies for disturbing you, but I must talk to you about a rather delicate matter," he said, lowering his voice. "Mr. Woolworth, who introduced himself as your guardian, asked to meet me the day before we set sail. I received him in our company's New York offices. He entrusted me with a mission that I am committed to carrying out. It concerns your mother, Miss."

"My mother?" repeated Elizabeth, perplexed.

"Indeed. Mr. Woolworth told me about the tragedy that befell your family during your first crossing on *La Champagne*, ten years ago. He thought you might like to throw a wreath overboard at the spot where the funeral took place. We received a large bouquet of white roses on the morning of our departure."

"I had no idea, Captain."

"It was my duty to inform you. We will soon be in the waters where your mother is resting—that is to say, tomorrow evening, if sailing conditions remain stable."

"But my mother died halfway through the journey, Sir, and we haven't travelled far enough yet!"

"*La Touraine* is faster than *La Champagne*, Miss. Much faster, in fact. In July 1892, I crossed the Atlantic in six days and just a few hours—a record that earned the ship the prestigious Blue Ribbon Award."

"Congratulations, Captain," Elizabeth murmured, overcome with emotion and surprise. "I'm very touched by this gesture from my . . . guardian, Mr. Woolworth. I have also been wanting to find the location and bought a small pearl wreath. You must let me know when we're in the right spot."

"Alas, the location we've been given is only approximate, but the soul is immortal, isn't it? Those whom we have cherished and mourned are watching over us, whether laid to rest or entrusted to the depths of the ocean. I had to witness my younger brother, as well as a good friend of mine, disappearing under the waves."

"My condolences, Sir. And thank you for your kindness. You should know that I share your faith and convictions."

"I'm delighted to hear that, Miss Duquesne. I won't disturb you any further, but if you wish, you're welcome to join me at my table tonight."

It was a tradition reserved for the wealthiest of passengers, and Maybel had mentioned it on the quayside. Elizabeth agreed that she would think about it.

I can't leave Bonnie alone while she's so sick, she thought shortly afterwards. *It's a shame she still isn't feeling good enough to join me outside. Only yesterday, one of the sailors reported the sighting of large numbers of whales.*

She was still thinking of the huge mammals that had followed the ship when suddenly, Bonnie emerged at the other end of the deck. The sun had brought the colour back into her cheeks, and she was looking cheerful as she walked towards Elizabeth.

"I finally feel a little better!" she announced proudly. "I just had one of these nice milky coffees in the dining room, and some buns."

"Thank God! I was getting terribly bored without you."

"I doubt you'll have time to get bored in the coming days. Guess who knocked on our cabin door?"

"Bonnie, how could I possibly know? Was it one of the bell-boys? Or the steward?"

"I'm afraid it's someone you know!"

"Why do you say, 'I'm afraid'? Pearl Woolworth? *Dad?*"

"It was your Richard Stenton or Johnson, the private investigator. Mr. Laroche, your grandfather, supposedly instructed him to keep an eye on you during the crossing."

Elizabeth was flabbergasted. Her eyes scanned her immediate surroundings and the lower deck, but Richard was nowhere to be seen.

"You shouldn't tease me like that, Bonnie. If Mr. Johnson were on board the ship, I would have seen him by now, for he would have made his presence known right from the start."

"I'm telling you, I saw him! We talked on the cabin threshold. He asked me to inform you that he's on board *La Touraine*. Like me, he was suffering from seasickness, but the ship's doctor managed to get him up on his feet again."

The news plunged Elizabeth into a state of disarray. The girl had hoped to see Richard before boarding, but he had tried to avoid her. Only two days ago she'd thought she was in love with him, but right now, she had no desire to see the man.

"I'm entering a whole new chapter of my life, with my family, and there's no place in it for him," she said. "Moreover, I'm sure he's lying. My grandfather would never have asked him to look out for my safety."

"What do you intend to do, Miss?" asked Bonnie, while observing the movement of the waves.

"We've been invited to dinner at the Captain's table tonight. Please come—I'll lend you one of my dresses."

"But I wouldn't fit into one of your dresses, Miss—you're so slim! And I've got no place amongst all those rich people."

Elizabeth kissed Bonnie on the cheek. The offshore wind was loosening strands of hair from Elizabeth's low bun. She contemplated her own brown velvet suit, slim-fitted jacket, and carefully polished leather boots.

"Don't say that, Bonnie. People shouldn't judge each other so harshly. I know we've been enjoying the Woolworths' generosity. They raised me in total luxury. But even so, I still have childhood memories as the daughter of a loving couple living in a modest dwelling, and I'm grateful for that. What matters most is generosity and moral values, whatever your background."

Bonnie shot her an ironic side glance.

"All the same, Miss—you did tell me about travelling in steerage as a small child, about the stench in the dormitories and the insanitary conditions. I'm sure you're much more comfortable in the luxury of our cabin, not to mention the excellent food and impeccable service. I'm not making anything up—those were your words last night."

"I know, Bonnie, and deep down I'm a little ashamed of it. It'll be different in France, though. I shall help my grandfather run his vineyards and do his accounts for him. I . . ."

"While living in a castle," added Bonnie. "But we'll discuss it later—your guardian angel is here."

Richard was walking towards them, looking drawn and pale. He had a blue scarf around his neck, and the dark circles under his eyes brought out their amber hue. Elizabeth trembled with delight at seeing him; all her good intentions had gone with the wind.

Guerville Castle's stables
Thursday, January 14, 1897

After a week of relentless downpour, the rain had finally subsided. A ray of sunlight peeped through the tiny window, adorning Mariette's bare shoulder with a halo of gold. Justin kissed her warm silky skin.

"Stay a little longer," he begged.

The young laundry maid, who worked at the castle three days a week, arched her back, looking dishevelled but cheerful. Pulling back the sheet, she sat up and placed her hands on her pointed breasts and rosy nipples.

"I can't. If I get home late, my father will go spare," she protested.

"But I want you again, Mariette," insisted Justin, who was wearing nothing but a nightshirt.

She pulled him to her breasts, which he covered in kisses. There were on the vast hay deck of the stables, where two basic rooms had been created using partitions. Hugues Laroche lodged his grooms there, as had his father before him.

"We're safe in this place. No one will ever come up here," said Justin, breathing heavily as he stroked her thighs. "Just tell your father you had to do the ironing as well as the laundry. He won't come to check."

"Oh, that's for sure," she said, cheekily. "You're right—we might as well make the most of it."

Mariette hugged him tightly, intoxicated by his soft skin and tanned, muscular body. He took her once more, with a hard pelvic thrust, causing her to moan with pleasure.

This long, drawn-out embrace culminated in the delightful state of ecstasy they were both hungry for.

"This time, I really am going," she laughed.

Justin rolled over next to her, kissing the nape of her neck.

"You're sweet," she sighed, while hastily picking up her undergarments that she'd cast aside. "And handsome, too."

"Thank you, darling—I don't get many compliments."

"You say that, but I heard you're in the boss's good books. Old Leandre was telling my mother about it in the wash-house."

"Mr. Laroche thinks I'm good with horses, but that requires no effort from me, as I love the beasts."

He stretched out, content. Mariette looked at him tenderly.

"If I get in the family way, will you be angry?" she asked worriedly. "We do it often, so it could happen."

"I would do the honourable thing and marry you," he answered at once.

She stood up to put on her faded green dress. Her blonde, wavy hair reached right the way down her back.

"Even so, I like Bertrand better," she muttered. "I lost my innocence to him, and when his father dies he'll get some wheat fields and the house—meaning I won't have to do Adela's laundry anymore."

"In that case, why don't you just go to Bertrand and not come up here again!" snapped Justin, his pride wounded.

"Don't get upset," Mariette pleaded. "I like you too, even though you have nothing—just your bare hands to earn a living with. Bertrand was unlucky—his number came up for the army."

Wistful, Mariette laced up her worn-out, dusty shoes.

"In less than two years, it will be my turn to register and get called up for military service," he said morosely. "Madeleine won't be able to lie to Mr. Laroche any longer, as I'll need identification papers."

"Oh, what a nasty piece of work that woman is! I can't believe she's your aunt. Don't worry, your secret's safe with me. Besides, I'm sure that if your number comes up, the boss will send someone else in your place. He won't want to lose his groom."

She winked at him, plaiting her hair and donning her white cap. She then whispered:

"Is it true, what they're saying in the village—that the Laroche heiress is coming home? Was she in America?"

Justin nodded, fastening his belt before adding:

"Yes, Sir has confirmed that Elizabeth Duquesne was living with a wealthy New York family. Her boat is due to reach Le Havre on Monday. He'll take the train on Sunday to welcome her."

"Jesus, she must be a pretty young lady, with beautiful dresses!" enthused Mariette.

"I wouldn't know, I've never seen her," lied Justin.

"Of course not, smart arse—you haven't been here long. Well, I'm off!"

"Hurry up—the back yard is still deserted at this hour," he said, kissing her on her lips.

Once alone, Justin opened the small window which looked out onto the slate rooftops of the castle. He had been living secretly in the attic until Madeleine had decided to pack him off to a farm in south Charente, to work as a stable hand.

"I was eleven years old and had lost hope of Elizabeth returning," he said to himself. "She'll have forgotten me anyway. She's probably lost the tin soldier I gave her. What the hell am I doing, reminiscing about this?"

A series of whinnies brought him back to reality. It was time to distribute the grain and hay. He jumped up immediately and hurtled down the staircase, nearly tripping.

The horses became agitated upon seeing him. They were stretching their heads over the stable doors, shaking their manes.

"All right, all right, I'm coming!" he cried cheerfully.

Hugues Laroche found him busily handing out the oat rations. He whistled to him.

"Do you need me, Sir?" enquired Justin, surprised. The castle's owner rarely came to the stables at this time of day.

"You will accompany me to Rouillac tomorrow morning," Laroche told him. "I want your opinion on a mare I intend to buy for my granddaughter. I don't know if she can ride, but we'll soon teach her if she can't."

"In that case, Sir, we should get a docile, well-trained animal with a supple gait," replied Justin dutifully.

"I actually think I've found a little gem!" bragged Laroche. "But I could be mistaken, so I prefer to have your opinion."

He gave Justin a friendly pat on the back. The beaming young groom bowed his head with respect, then returned to his work.

On board La Touraine
The same day

Richard walked gingerly up to Elizabeth. Though she smiled at him, he noticed a strange glint in her eyes.

"Leave us alone a while, can you, Bonnie? Mr. Johnson won't hurt me, as he's supposed to be here to protect me."

"Are you quite certain, Miss?"

"I am. I'll meet you for lunch."

Bonnie retreated, glancing behind her at the couple before disappearing from view.

"Your governess wasn't very friendly to me earlier on," Richard complained.

"I can see why," replied Elizabeth coldly. "Can you explain to me what you are doing on board this ship? First you decide you no longer want to see me in New York, then suddenly you show up here in the middle of the ocean."

"I embarked at the last minute, at your grandfather's request. This is, above all, a business trip. Mr. Laroche has agreed to pay me my fee when we get to Le Havre. It was my father who agreed to the arrangement—I merely obeyed his instructions."

Despite her joy at seeing him again, Elizabeth did her utmost to appear hostile—but she couldn't help being curious.

"All you ever do is obey, Richard! A man as docile as you would hardly make me a good husband—not that I'm interested in marriage."

"Stop your silly games, or I'll have to kiss you, and your reputation will be in tatters," he whispered, taking her by the waist.

Filled with conflicting emotions, she nimbly escaped his grip. She desperately wanted Richard to kiss her, but was terrified it would awaken her desire for him. He had too much power over her.

"You wouldn't dare, for I would be forced to tell my grandfather that you are an incorrigible seducer and not worthy of being paid. As for your mission, perform your duties, but stay well away from me. Better still, become ill again—then I won't have to see you!"

At first, Elizabeth had been feigning contempt, but now she was genuinely livid.

"You heard me! Don't speak to me again and stay away!" she exclaimed.

"But, Lisbeth, what's the matter? Is this a joke?"

He tried to take her hand, but she pushed him away brusquely, attracting the attention of a steward, who ran up to her.

"Miss, is this gentleman bothering you?" he asked in French, about to usher Johnson away.

"Yes, he is—thank you very much."

Distressed, Elizabeth fled the deck. She felt more at ease back in the cabin, where Bonnie rushed to greet her.

"What am I doing?!" the girl exclaimed. "It must be my nerves—I'm so uptight!"

"Come on, Miss—breathe deeply and sit down," Bonnie advised. "You're different to other young ladies. You have spirit, which only adds to your charm."

"What do you mean? I wasn't like this before, that's for sure. I now get angry at the drop of a hat, and end up pushing away people I care about."

She suppressed a panic-stricken sob, huddled up in a comfortable leather armchair.

"My poor mother referred to it as being 'shaken up'," said the governess with a smile. "Personally, I think you're in love with this man."

"No, Bonnie. He infuriates me with his smooth voice, glances and smirks. But I'm not proud of what I did. I told the steward that he was bothering me. Fortunately, Richard couldn't have understood a word—we spoke in French. How could I be so foolish? Now I can no longer speak to him, and everyone thinks he's a cad."

"This only confirms that I'm not mistaken, Miss. You *are* in love with him!" triumphed Bonnie. "The first time she falls in love can send a young lady out of her mind. I may be single, but I did fall in love once, when I was your age. It was the grocer's son, a neighbour. He was such a handsome boy!"

"What was his name?"

"Harrison. I made a point of running into him when he had finished his deliveries. I couldn't sleep and felt like laughing and crying at the same time. My mother used to make fun of me."

"And why didn't you get married?"

"Harrison preferred a little brunette called Nora who worked in her parents' flower shop. He married her, and shortly afterwards I joined the Woolworth household."

"I'm sorry, Bonnie—that's so sad! But who knows, you may find a new sweetheart in France!" exclaimed Elizabeth boldly.

"God forbid—I have enough on my hands with you. Oh, don't pull that face, I'm just teasing."

They went on discussing Richard Johnson and the handsome Harrison, before joining the other passengers in the dining room, where a waiter hastened to present them with the day's menu.

It had become gloomy outside, and the sky was now a leaden grey colour. Torrential rain was beating against the windows. The inclement weather had diminished Elizabeth's appetite.

"Bonnie, it looks like a storm is brewing," she moaned. "I remember very well how the weather turned like this, ten years ago. And according to the Captain, we're heading for the waters where Mummy is resting."

"A storm? That's all we need now! Try not to think about it, Miss."

But it was too late. Elizabeth was already reliving the violent tremors that had shaken and battered the steerage of *La Champagne*. Although a big vessel, it had been blown about like a small raft.

"You wouldn't believe how afraid I was, Bonnie. People were screaming and falling out of their bunks. Objects were rolling everywhere as the ship rose and then tilted on its side. I wanted to be near Mummy, but I slipped, crashing into things, so she got up to help me. She was thrown to the floor and died shortly afterwards. It was my fault—do you understand?!"

The young girl had been whispering, but her last words had come out as a shout. The passengers sitting at a nearby table looked at her, intrigued.

"I didn't really understand this until today," she added, distraught.

She was choking. Bonnie watched her jump out of her seat and dash towards the corridor leading to the covered terrace.

"Is there a problem, Madam?" asked the waiter.

"We'll eat later—please excuse us," Bonnie said, embarrassed.

Huge waves were raging against the ship as it continued its course at high speed. The roll knocked Bonnie off balance as soon as she got outside, where she got caught in the downpour at once. The governess scoured the upper deck, but Elizabeth was nowhere to be seen.

Utterly confused, Elizabeth had rushed to the lower deck that the steerage passengers had deserted because of the weather. She longed to get closer to the broken waves and confront the raging ocean that had deprived her of her mother and childhood. She was wearing neither coat nor hat, and the rain immediately drenched her from head to toe.

Clinging to the iron railing, she contemplated the furious ocean, with its greenish reflections, as though it were her worst foe. Her brown locks were stuck to her bodice, and the icy, wet fabric chilled her to the bone.

Her grief had been plaguing her ever since her memory had returned. It was driving her crazy. A sailor in black oilskins called out to her from the top of a metal ladder. Deaf to his cries, she could only hear the rumblings of the raging ocean.

"Lisbeth—no!"

Richard emerged behind her. He grabbed her by the waist and pulled her backwards with all his might. She struggled in vain.

"What were you about to do, Lisbeth?"

The detective could feel her trembling with cold in his arms, her words muffled. He had to almost carry her by force to his second-class cabin. Elizabeth stopped struggling. She was pale and her eyes were tightly shut. Richard laid her down on his bunk and wrapped her in a blanket.

"We have to dry you and change you out of these clothes quickly," he said, busy rubbing his own black hair with a big soft towel. "If you promise to stay here without running away, I'll go and fetch your governess. Promise me that if I leave, you won't go and throw yourself into the sea, will you?"

"I don't know," she replied weakly.

"In that case, I have to stay with you, to avoid a disaster."

He sat down at her bedside. Elizabeth looked extremely fragile, almost like a child.

"What's going on in that pretty head of yours?"

"Chaos, Richard," Elizabeth whispered. "And despair and anger, but there is also this burning desire to live by my own rules and be free. I so wish I could never go to sleep again, and never dream again."

"That would be a shame, Lisbeth—dreams are often fabulous and exciting. If you would just tell me the whole truth about yourself!"

But the young girl just shook her head and stared at him defiantly. Once again, Richard was struck by her extraordinary beauty—her plump, deep-pink lips, her vivid blue eyes and her tangle of dark hair—which aroused in him a physical response he couldn't control. He bent down and kissed her gently, before taking possession of her mouth, hungry for her, and carried away by his desire. She could hear his jerky breathing and feel the febrile playing of his hard tongue, his hands roughly fondling her breasts and lower back.

"Don't, Richard—no, please," Elizabeth begged, managing to turn her head. "Not this—not you!"

She stiffened in disgust. Once again, she could see herself in the middle of the night, her heart pounding furiously, awakened by a new nightmare. As always, she struggled to remember the exact details, but the overall picture made her want to scream.

"When we get to France, I'll marry you. I won't return to New York, because I can't live without you, Lisbeth," he whispered in her ear as he slid his hand under her skirt, touching the top of her thigh.

His experienced hands danced and probed as he quivered with lust. Elizabeth was utterly bewildered. At the mercy of her innocence and newly roused passion, she almost gave in when a new bout of panic overcame her.

"No—I told you, no!" she shouted, slapping him in the face.

Elizabeth refused to let Richard take her. The scene was unfolding exactly as in her nightmare, in which she had struggled to fight off a stranger who had hungered for her in the same way. All she had been able to see in the darkness was the man's profile, a face veiled in black. She had jerked in agony as he had violated her lower body, inflicting excruciating pain on her.

Elizabeth cried louder and louder, hitting Richard repeatedly, so that he pulled away from her and straightened up. He was horrified.

"You have no right," she sobbed.

Richard stepped away from the berth and stood at the end of his cabin, staring at her.

"I apologize, Lisbeth. I behaved like a brute, but I thought you wanted this too."

"Certainly not—and especially not under these circumstances! You took advantage of my confusion and my grief!"

"It certainly wasn't my intention. It was the way you looked at me—I couldn't resist what I saw in your eyes. You were driving me crazy!"

Trembling with rage and exasperation, Elizabeth sat at the edge of the bunk. Richard seemed sincere, though his words had a strange ring to them.

"I thought I had feelings for you," she declared, "but I no longer do. You disgust me."

"Please forgive me!" he begged. "I did save your life, Lisbeth!"

"You didn't save anything at all—I had no intention of jumping. Tomorrow, the ship will be navigating in the waters that swallowed my mother's body ten years ago. She died following a premature birth, which was my fault. I will cast a bouquet of white roses and a crown of pearls into the sea, and pray with all my heart. I wouldn't have missed this for the world, nor my return to Charente, where my family awaits me."

Suddenly, voices could be heard outside. Someone said Elizabeth's name.

"They must think I've joined Mummy at the bottom of the ocean," she said with irony. "I must go and reassure everyone that I'm all right. I'm warning you—don't come near me again, or I'll have to tell the Captain."

She threw back the cover and left the cabin. Richard staggered, then crashed into a chair. He was crushed. No one would see him again, whether on deck or in the gangways, until *La Touraine* entered the port of Le Havre.

12

Back to Her Roots

Le Havre, on board La Touraine
Monday, January 18, 1897

Before returning to his cabin, the Captain accompanied Elizabeth and Bonnie to the ship's bow. Moved by the tragedy that had befallen his young passenger, he had strived to show her kindness and compassion.

"So, this is where my family is from!" exclaimed Bonnie, as her gaze wandered over the nearby Normandy coast. She shouted to make herself heard above the seagulls' shrieks and the noise of the engines. Small boats were dancing on the waves near their ship, which was turning.

"Yes, we shall soon be in France," said Elizabeth. "I must admit, I'm feeling rather nervous about it. After all this time, I might not even recognize my grandfather anymore—I was so young the last time I saw him."

"Don't worry, Miss. I'm sure you will," Bonnie said reassuringly. "He must be on the quayside, watching out for the ship to arrive. I hope you told him about me?"

"I let him know that I would be accompanied by my governess and former nanny."

"Indeed," said Bonnie. "And I'm still taking care of you. I had the fright of my life on Thursday and still haven't got over it! I thought you had drowned when I saw a sailor lower a boat into the water—I almost went hysterical. But thank God, you turned up just then, soaked from head to toe. And that very evening, there you were again, dressed in your finery for dinner with the Captain!"

"He invited me—I couldn't refuse. He's a charming gentleman who has some fascinating tales to tell. I'm sorry I caused you so much worry, Bonnie. Once we arrive at the castle, things will get better—you'll see."

"Let's hope so. It frightened me to see you faint after throwing the roses overboard."

"I told you what happened, Bonnie," sighed Elizabeth. "I must have been hallucinating, for I glimpsed Mummy's face between the waves. She was smiling back at me, looking *so* beautiful . . ."

"When we get to the countryside, I'll give you something for your nerves. I know some very effective herbal remedies from when I used to go to an apothecary in New York for Mrs. Maybel, when she was trying to get in the family way. They recommended she drink herbal tea, and I think you would benefit from an infusion of valerian, chamomile and sage."

Elizabeth was barely listening to her. The ship was moving slowly, as it was being towed along the quayside by two tugboats. Gleaming in the faint sun, the city's rooftops could be seen in the distance, throwing shimmery patterns on the water's surface.

Thank God Bonnie doesn't know what happened in Richard's cabin, she thought. *She thinks he saved my life.*

The episode was haunting her in more ways than one. From time to time, she shuddered with excitement as she recalled his kisses, the touch of his hands, and his passionate words. But whenever she was reminded of the distasteful and violent scene of her last nightmare, his shameful behaviour revolted her.

"I wonder if your grandfather will spot you right away among the crowd Miss Elizabeth," whispered Bonnie excitedly.

"Oh Bonnie, you said it! It sounded so nice. Oh, please, say my first name again!"

"You really are fickle, Elizabeth," Bonnie laughed. "One minute you're down in the dumps, and the next you're all sweetness and smiles."

As Elizabeth kissed Bonnie on the cheek, the ship's siren sounded. Lively cheers burst out from the fishing boats, *La Touraine* and the tugboats.

"Have you noticed how mild the air is?" Elizabeth asked. "Winters are less harsh here than in New York."

"You're right," nodded Bonnie. "I think I'm going to like it here. What about Richard Johnson—where is he? I guess he's keeping a low profile."

"I imagine he'll return to New York on the next boat, provided he gets his money right away."

Elizabeth could now clearly see the faces of the people waiting on the vast quayside.

"They've dropped anchor," she added quickly. "Look, Bonnie—the sailors are putting up the gangways. I know it sounds silly, but I'm scared."

"Calm down, my dear," replied Bonnie, "you're very pale. You must come along now—people are starting to get off."

Hugues Laroche struggled to contain his impatience. He was every bit as nervous as Elizabeth, unable to believe that he would finally see his granddaughter again. Mingling with the crowd, he scanned every female on the deck of the liner.

Where is she? he thought. *What if she's already ashore and looking for me?*

Dressed in a black coat with a fur collar and fawn leather boots, the squire jostled some people who were trying to get to the first-class passenger gangway. Further up, staff were rushing to transport the many pieces of luggage on trolleys to the railway station or warehouses.

A pretty woman in a fitted grey tweed coat smiled at him hesitantly, but she was too old. He paced up and down looking for Elizabeth, turning around in rage whenever someone bumped into him.

Suddenly he spotted her. A radiant young girl with bright-blue eyes and Catherine's gait was walking towards him. She wore a pink woollen shawl and her hair was braided. A small hat that matched her velvet dress completed the outfit.

"Grandpa?" she called out, waving.

A small, plump, auburn-haired lady holding a tapestry bag was trotting behind her. He had no doubts: it was Elizabeth and her governess.

"Grandpa—it's you, isn't it?"

"Elizabeth," he said, choking with emotion. "You look just like your mother, my dear child!"

Hugues Laroche stepped back to get a better look at her, not even looking at Bonnie, who discreetly scrutinized his face. With his short brown hair, moustache and silvery sideburns, he reminded her of a hawk.

"Was the crossing smooth? You didn't get sick, Elizabeth?" he asked, to make polite conversation.

"I didn't. Aren't you going to kiss me, Grandpa?"

The question somewhat surprised Laroche. He had been brought up not to express affection, which his parents regarded as something that only "common" people did. Adela had to pretend to take offence at any sign of affection he gave her, even though she was secretly delighted.

"I was so nervous about seeing you again," added the girl. "I used to be afraid of you when I was little."

At that, she stood on tiptoe and kissed him on the cheek. He hesitated for a moment before giving her an awkward hug.

"Our train leaves in less than an hour, so let's not linger any longer," he said as he let go of her. "I'm glad you speak French, my dear child, even if you do have a slight accent."

He finally decided to acknowledge Bonnie, who bowed her head.

"Good day, Sir. I'm delighted to be in France, and to make your acquaintance."

"Likewise, Madam. I wish to thank you for looking after my granddaughter. But now let's go—I have reserved a compartment away from all the noise. I can't stand crowds."

He pointed in the direction of the railway line. Elizabeth felt neither disappointment nor joy. Her mind was blank, but she was determined to let herself go with the flow all the way to Charente.

"What about Mr. Johnson?" whispered Bonnie in her ear.

They looked around them in vain. "Grandpa, aren't you waiting for Mr. Johnson? Didn't you mean to pay him here in Le Havre?"

"What are you talking about, Elizabeth?" protested Laroche, genuinely stupefied. "Are you telling me he was on the boat, too?"

"He was indeed—Bonnie will confirm that. He claimed to be there to protect me, upon your instructions. You shouldn't have gone to such expense, Grandpa."

The squire's already stern features hardened. He flared his nostrils.

"The man was lying to you, Elizabeth. I can assure you that I have no outstanding debts with the Johnson agency. I cleared my account two weeks ago and no longer owe them a single penny. To hell with him! He must have sneaked onto the boat for some arcane reason that has nothing to do with us, thank goodness!"

Bonnie had to stop herself from giggling, intrigued by the term "arcane", which was not part of her French vocabulary.

Elizabeth didn't laugh; she felt uncomfortable. The expression "to hell with someone", though frequently used, rekindled painful memories.

The day before we left, during dinner at the castle, I thought I saw the devil, but it turned out to be my grandfather, she thought. *His eyes were burning, and he was gesticulating while he shouted and hollered.*

She forced herself to push the thought out of her mind, persuading herself that she was being oversensitive. All these events had taken place a long time ago, and things were different now. As she walked beside Bonnie, she thought of Richard Johnson's terrible lies and the despicable way he had behaved towards her. She shuddered, wondering why he had fabricated such stories and what he was doing in France.

Maybe he still hasn't given up on me, she thought. *What if he takes the same train as us?*

Bonnie noticed that Elizabeth kept looking around anxiously. "Don't be afraid, Miss—I'm here," she muttered.

On the train to Charente
Monday, January 18, 1897

Hugues Laroche relaxed slightly when they were settled in their first-class compartment. Still somewhat ill at ease, he spoke softly and avoided his granddaughter's gaze.

"Was the lunch to your liking, Elizabeth?" he asked, as they were returning from the dining car.

"It was delicious, Grandpa," Elizabeth replied, "though I would have eaten anything with gusto upon learning that all is well at the mill. I was afraid you would announce that my grandfather Toine was dead, or that my uncles had moved away."

"Good heavens, you are impetuous!" he remarked. "I was going to brief you later, but you beat me to it. The way you've been raised leaves a lot to be desired—this is not New York!"

"And yet Maybel and Edward Woolworth were sticklers for social etiquette and decorum, Grandpa," she replied, piqued.

"Maybe in the American way," Laroche mumbled.

He sat down in front of her and opened a newspaper. Elizabeth did not dare respond. She observed him surreptitiously, studying his unappealing features with trepidation.

During the meal, Laroche had been going on about his vineyards and wine selection. He offered figures and names of different grape varieties, as if she were going to help him run the estate.

All this bores me to tears, she thought, *but maybe I should take an interest in it. After all, I am his heiress.*

It was two o'clock in the afternoon. The steam train was travelling at a comfortable speed, amidst lowland chequered with ploughed fields bordered by hedges.

Bonnie was enchanted by the French countryside. She smiled to herself whenever they went past meadows and herds of rust-coloured cattle and horses. The future with her beloved Lisbeth looked bright.

"How long before we get to Charente, Sir?" she enquired.

"It will be very late, Madam," he replied, folding his newspaper. "We have to change trains in Orléans and take the line that serves Angoulême, where we will spend the night. Tomorrow morning, a carriage will pick us up and take us to Guerville Castle."

"I never imagined that one day I would be living in a French castle!" enthused the governess.

"Our castle is in fact a medieval fortress," said Hugues Laroche, having mellowed slightly. "There was no point teaching you its history when you were a child—you wouldn't have understood," he explained, looking at Elizabeth.

"No time like the present, Grandpa. And Bonnie is as interested as me."

Laroche hesitated for a moment before deciding to tell his story.

"The foundations are very old, for the fortress was built on a citadel dating from the time of the Goths, a German tribe. When my great-uncle was carrying out excavations, he spoke of an underground tunnel, and even an aqueduct."

The vocabulary used by the squire was getting too convoluted for the governess, who resolved to keep nodding with approval, a serious look on her face.

"Our castle was at the centre of a remarkable estate that dates back to the 12th century," he continued. "It thus witnessed a number of battles between the French and the English, before Richard the Lionheart seized it in 1178."

"Richard the Lionheart!" exclaimed Elizabeth. "I have read about the crusades, in which he was portrayed as the bravest of the brave."

"Of course, over time the fortress got damaged and underwent renovation work too," Laroche added hastily, delighted that his granddaughter was finally showing an interest. "Do you remember the drawbridge, my dear child?"

"Vaguely, Grandpa. But I do remember the trees in the park, the pointed slate rooftops, and the small half-moon tower."

"You will have plenty of time to explore the castle, and your grandmother will be happy to show you around. Unfortunately, we have no idea in which room King Henry IV would have slept. One thing I do know, though, is that Louis XIV set foot on our grounds during his travels."

"Who was Louis XIV?" Bonnie had the misfortune to ask.

"Only our Sun King!" snapped Laroche. "Are all Americans as uninformed as you, Madam?"

"Grandpa! Don't be unkind. Bonnie couldn't have known. New York's schools only teach American history!"

The squire shrugged his shoulders, muttering something to himself. He decided it would be better to reserve the history of Guerville for another occasion.

"What about Grandma? How did she take the news of my return? Was she pleased?" asked Elizabeth, unaware of the impropriety of her question.

"*Pleased?* That's something of an understatement! Adela is a changed woman, and it's a pleasure to see her so happy. Elizabeth, you should know that the death of your mother Catherine had an absolutely devastating effect on your grandmother. But thanks to her faith, she has started to recover her strength. My determination to find you kept us going, and the good Lord rewarded my efforts."

"I'm very grateful to you, Grandpa. When I heard you were looking for me, I was overwhelmed."

"Another understatement," added Bonnie. "Miss Elizabeth was deeply shaken."

Laroche frowned, irritated by the governess's intervention, but decided to disregard it. He put the newspaper down beside him.

"Tell me everything you went through, dear child, after losing your mother and father. Don't be afraid to go into details—we have the whole afternoon ahead of us."

"Very well," Elizabeth said. "I did outline it all in my letter, though. Did you not receive it? I even enclosed a photograph of myself."

"Not yet. We will reach the castle before your letter does," he said with a smile.

Hugues Laroche was on the verge of another rant when they had to change at Orléans station. By the time Elizabeth had finished relating her story, he was in a blind rage, cursing the Woolworths. He shouted out his orders rudely to the baggage handler and complained about the smell of coal and scrap metal.

"You shouldn't have told him that Mr. Edward went to the Chelsea ten years ago," muttered Bonnie reproachfully.

They were walking a safe distance behind the squire. Elizabeth looked resigned.

"I had to tell them—I'd already put it in my letter. For what it's worth, I understand his reaction. Mine wasn't any different."

"Still—your grandfather is a cold, uncompromising man. I didn't like his remark about your poor upbringing."

"Keep your voice down, Bonnie," Elizabeth hissed. Then her tone softened: "I can never thank you enough for coming with me. If you hadn't been with me during the crossing and today, I would have felt terribly lonely and forlorn."

They looked at each other knowingly. Laroche was climbing into a carriage, waving at them to hurry up.

"Quick, Bonnie!"

Elizabeth stepped onto the footboard, then reached out to the less agile Bonnie to help her up. Suddenly, a male figure caught her eye at the end of the platform.

"It's Richard!" she said to herself with dismay. "He was on our train. What does he want from me?"

Elizabeth had been careful to mention neither their meetings at Central Park ice rink, nor the New Year's Eve scandal.

The girl had no intention of relating how they had kissed, or how scary the episode on the boat had been. She was determined to keep all this a secret—even Bonnie wouldn't be told. Not yet, anyway.

"Come and sit down, Elizabeth," said Hugues Laroche impatiently as he entered the corridor alongside the compartments.

"Go ahead, Bonnie," she whispered. "I'm watching Richard Johnson. I want to make sure he doesn't get on our train."

"My goodness, he's following you—there's no doubt about it. You must tell your grandfather, Elizabeth," Bonnie urged. "Johnson knows the Laroches' address. Whether he gets on the train or not, he can easily trace you."

A rail worker approached to close the door and they should have stepped back, but Elizabeth lingered. As soon as he'd left, she jumped up to look out of the oval window. The train had set off. It was travelling so slowly that you could easily see the platform moving past, but Richard Johnson had disappeared.

The Three Pillars Hotel, Angoulême
Same day, nightfall

Elizabeth and Bonnie had dozed off during the latter part of the journey. The silence, the constant rocking of the wagons and the rain beating on the windows once they were past Orléans, had made them drowsy.

Hugues Laroche didn't say another word about the Woolworths. His anger had not disappeared; it was merely on hold.

He continued to read his newspaper in silence, regularly opening his thick black notebook to jot down a few lines. At Angoulême station, he hailed a cab, which took them to a luxurious hotel called The Three Pillars. It was already nightfall.

"And our trunks, Grandpa?" wondered Elizabeth, when she saw the pretty room that she was to share with Bonnie.

"The trunks," he repeated. "Don't worry, I've made the necessary arrangements. They will be delivered here after dinner. Now, let's go downstairs—I'm starving. It's the country air, the best in the world."

"It's also much milder here than in New York," remarked Elizabeth.

"And the people are more honest here, generally speaking," he added. "Do me a favour, Elizabeth—don't mention that devilish place again. It's like hell on earth to me."

"I'll try. I'm sorry I upset you, Grandpa."

Laroche glanced at her with relief. He liked his granddaughter's modest attitude and humble apologies.

"You seem less rebellious and undisciplined than your mother," he said. "However, you have certain ways that are a little too free for your age, which we'll have to change."

Bonnie coughed, catching Elizabeth's attention. She was pulling faces at Laroche behind his back. Elizabeth made a wide-eyed face at him, trying not to laugh. For the two women, tensions had eased after their days of preparation for the journey to France.

Bonnie was thoroughly impressed by the meal. She was tucking into a meat pie and sliced duck breast garnished with mushrooms. The taste of garlic took her by surprise, as she never used it in her cooking.

"It's delicious, Grandpa," said Elizabeth. "I can't wait to see the castle again and hug Grandma. And then hopefully, I can go to Montignac tomorrow afternoon? Pops Toine and my uncles will be dying to see me, too."

"We'll see about that, my dear," Laroche replied cautiously. "You're a young lady now, and you shouldn't call Antoine Duquesne that anymore. It sounds ridiculous at your age."

Elizabeth nodded politely but she was seething inside, exasperated by Laroche's constant chiding. At that very moment, her thoughts turned to the small blond boy, Justin.

"May I ask another question, Grandpa?" she asked, with a hint of sarcasm.

"Go ahead."

"Do you still have a servant named Madeleine working for you?"

"Good heavens—you remember her? She keeps a good tight rein on all our staff."

"She had a nephew, didn't she?"

He had the same look of disbelief on his face as Adela had had, ten years ago.

"Madeleine, a nephew? Where did you get such nonsense from? She was an orphan of the State and has neither brother nor sister, or we would know about it. No lineage was found in the Public Assistance file apart from three distant cousins."

Elizabeth was both disconcerted and suspicious. Could it be that she had misunderstood, or that Justin had lied to her? But in that case, what had he been doing in the nursery on the evening of the storm?

A waiter in a black suit and white shirt appeared with their desserts. The squire diverted his gaze to the ramekins topped with vanilla cream, then gave a quick run-down of his staff.

"The old gardener Leandre is still there, assisted by Alcide—a wretched fool, that one. Madeleine employs two maids: one helps out in the kitchen, the other with the cleaning. The butler, Jerome, handed in his notice after the death of Vincent, the groom who oversaw the stables. I have taken on a young man to replace him—he's very reliable and very efficient. I even asked his opinion in the choice of your mare. He reassured me that it was a good buy."

"My mare?"

"Indeed. You will ride a superb six-year-old chestnut bay, an Anglo-Arab."

"But I don't ride!" Elizabeth protested. "I've been scared of horses since the accident I told you about."

This was a white lie. Edward Woolworth had often taken her to give stale bread and sugar to the black gelding that pulled his carriage—the horse that had knocked Elizabeth down that fateful day. She had always been happy to stroke him affectionately, knowing it wasn't his fault.

"My granddaughter, afraid of horses!" cried Laroche indignantly. "What nonsense! You'll soon get used to it—you'll have to. Your mother was an experienced rider. You should have seen her galloping along the paths, jumping over tree trunks—and side saddle, too. Maybe you don't know what side saddle is?"

"I do! From my bedroom window, I could see ladies riding in that fashion in Central Park. I've also seen pictures of the saddles they use."

"Then I'll show you the one your mother used, tomorrow. I take very good care of it."

"Mummy never told me she used to ride horses. In fact, she never talked much about her childhood."

"Your grandmother will be happy to tell you about the wonderful life Catherine led before she got married," murmured Laroche. "With all due respect to your late father, Elizabeth, he didn't have much to offer her."

Except love—true love, Elizabeth thought, too shocked by his words to respond. *Bonnie is right: my grandfather is a cold, insensitive and rude man.*

Without touching her dessert, she feigned exhaustion in order to be able to slip back up to her room. Her governess quickly followed, muttering profuse apologies to Hugues Laroche.

"Miss, I can see you're at breaking point," she said sternly as soon as she entered the room.

Elizabeth was sitting on the edge of her bed, crying. She was dabbing her eyes with a lace-tipped handkerchief.

"I thought I would be able to cope with this, Bonnie," she confessed, sobbing. "Nothing is going the way I thought it would. His horse-riding comments were infuriating, not to mention his other remarks. If I have to listen to him bad-mouthing Daddy every day, I'll go and live at the mill with the Duquesnes."

"Come on, Miss—it'll all work out. We knew it wouldn't be easy to reconnect after ten years, especially in the light of the tragedies that struck your family. Tell me, is Madeleine's nephew the little boy who gave you the tin soldier?"

"I thought so, but maybe it was all just a dream, Bonnie? It was so long ago, I might have just found and kept the toy."

"That's highly unlikely, given how often you've talked about that boy."

"Maybe, but I'd better not mention it to Grandpa again. It'll just make him angry."

"You're exhausted. Let me help you undress."

Bonnie had a gentle, maternal way with her, and her voice soothed the young girl's hurt feelings.

"As the days go by, you'll feel better. I'm sure that your

grandmother is more affectionate and easier going than Mr. Laroche. And don't forget you have a second grandfather, plus your Duquesne uncles! They will be over the moon when they see you again."

"You're right," Elizabeth sighed. "What would I do without you, Bonnie?"

"I will always be here for you, dear. Now, try and get a decent night's sleep and you'll feel better in the morning."

Even so, Elizabeth couldn't stop crying. She lay down and pulled the sheets right up to her nose. She was unhappy, extremely anxious and homesick for her life in New York. It wasn't the luxurious Dakota Building apartment she missed, nor the lifestyle, but Maybel and Edward.

Mom, Dad, you were *my parents,* she thought. *You gave me so much love and you were right—adoption isn't just a piece of paper, it's a commitment, and you gave your whole lives to me.*

She recalled their farewell on the docks: Maybel's devastated face, her thin hands trembling on Elizabeth's cheeks.

And how thoughtful it was of Dad to send a bouquet of white roses on board, in remembrance of Mummy.

The Woolworths' boundless generosity sprang to mind yet again, since the trader had also taken care to slip her an envelope containing a large wad of French bank notes.

"In the event you have any pressing needs, you won't have to depend on the Laroches," he had told her.

Elizabeth couldn't hold back any longer and started to howl. Bonnie got up and came over to stroke her forehead.

"Don't be sad, Miss," she whispered.

"I fear I made a terrible mistake leaving New York so hastily. In fact, there was no rush, and I made poor Mom suffer so much. She was desperately upset the day I left."

"You'll have to write her nice letters to comfort her. And later on, there won't be anything stopping you from visiting them both."

Bonnie held her hand and rocked her, until Elizabeth eventually fell asleep. The governess returned to her bed, worrying about the future. Elizabeth's return to France clearly wasn't going as planned.

Hugues Laroche, who had been suffering from insomnia since he had lost his only daughter, managed to fall asleep quite quickly that night. However, he was awoken at one o'clock in the morning by a shrill scream coming from Elizabeth's room. Concerned, he put on his dressing gown and went to knock on her door. His ear to the door, he could just about hear the governess's voice.

"What's going on? Is Elizabeth ill?" he called out.

A dazed Bonnie opened the door but prevented him from entering. She was wearing her nightcap.

"Miss had a nightmare, Sir. I've given her some water—there's nothing to worry about, your granddaughter just isn't a good sleeper."

"Ah, she must take after me," he said. "Try to stop her from screaming her head off, though—it's keeping everyone awake. This is a hotel, after all."

"I'll do my best, Sir," Bonnie replied curtly.

Elizabeth was listening to them, sat up in bed, her arms wrapped around her knees, trembling.

What does all this mean? she wondered. *I can't go on living like this, for pity's sake.*

As usual, she put the nightmare down to her nervous condition. She had started having them when her parents were preparing to leave for America. This was when the terrifying scenes from her nightmares had first become reality.

"I didn't let your grandfather in, Miss," whispered Bonnie as she returned to her bedside.

"Thank you, Bonnie. He would most certainly have scolded me. It was a dreadful nightmare! If it is meant to come true, like the one with Mummy and Daddy, then I'd better run away right now."

"Shh, don't talk nonsense! Why won't you tell me what you saw?"

"That would be too complicated—it's all so confusing. To be perfectly honest, I can't bring myself to tell you."

"And yet, you told me you saw Lea Rambert's son skating in your dreams."

"I didn't mind telling you about that one, because it was a nice dream. Without it, I would never have recovered Mummy's baptism medal and met Baptiste Rambert. Forgive me, Bonnie— go and get some sleep. I could be panicking for nothing."

The governess complied, sad not to be able to help. She might not be educated, but she had a good dose of common sense.

My little Miss is different to other people, she thought. *I realized this as soon as she was put in my care. She's always been extremely sensitive and highly strung, and sees things in her sleep that come true. We'll make sure we go to church more frequently here in the village, to light candles and pray for her. I've got more time now.*

The prospect of no longer having to work from dawn till dusk soothed Bonnie. Before long, she was snoring gently. Elizabeth suddenly had an idea.

"Why haven't I thought of this before?!" she muttered to herself, leaping out of bed to rummage in her bag. "I shall write it all down."

She lit a small yellow lamp after taking a fresh notebook and an ink pen from her bag. Then, as if in a trance, she put on paper each detail of the violent and depraved scenes she had seen in her sleep.

The Three Pillars Hotel
The next morning

"You look very pretty in that outfit, my dear child," said Hugues Laroche to Elizabeth over breakfast. Bonnie felt smug, as she had chosen Elizabeth's outfit the previous evening.

"Thank you, Grandpa," the girl replied, though having to call him that was starting to annoy her.

She smoothed the fabric of her embroidered bodice, which had a round neck made of beige cotton. A straight, fashionable brown woollen skirt adorned with leather accentuated her hips. Her matching slim-fitting jacket rested on the back of her chair.

"Do you drink coffee or tea?" asked Laroche. "I recommend hot milk, if you're a bad sleeper. You'll see, living in the countryside and horse riding will soon improve your health!"

Elizabeth hesitated over whether to reply, then decided against it, still troubled by what she had seen in her nightmare.

"According to Dr. Foster, the Woolworths' doctor, I am of a nervous disposition," was all she said. "Apart from that, I'm in good health."

Hugues Laroche frowned. He looked at his pocket watch, a masterpiece of gold craftsmanship set with rubies. Bonnie stifled a cry of admiration.

"Justin should be here soon," Laroche said. "I asked him to be here at eight o'clock sharp."

"Justin," repeated Elizabeth softly.

"Yes, of course," her grandfather retorted, annoyed. "I told you about him yesterday on the train. He's the new groom and will be hitching my two cobs to the carriage. Hopefully, your trunks will fit in the back. You'll have to keep your suitcase at your feet, Madam," he added, looking at Bonnie.

The governess only nodded, her mouth full of delicious butter croissant.

Elizabeth concealed her excitement at the prospect that it could be the same Justin she had seen in the nursery ten years ago.

I'll soon find out, the girl thought. She knew better than to question her grandfather, and contented herself with drinking her milk distractedly.

"In fact, we could have got off the train in Vars," he announced suddenly. "But it can be dangerous to drive a horse-drawn carriage in the middle of the night. Besides, I wouldn't sleep in the only inn in that town, for all the tea in China."

"That's right," commented Bonnie, "the train stopped at Vars station—I saw the sign on the wall."

"I wanted the best hotel for your homecoming, dear child," added Laroche, ignoring Bonnie's remark.

"That's very kind, Grandpa. I've finished, and would like to take a walk outside, if you don't mind."

"But you haven't touched your croissants or the bread," he protested. "In any case, there's no way I'm going to let you go outside alone. Please stay seated. I have yet to broach a very important subject, and it seems opportune to do so now. You should know that you are henceforth under my guardianship until you reach the age of majority. My solicitor has drawn up the relevant papers."

Stupefied and utterly displeased, the young girl folded up her napkin. She felt as if a trap were closing around her, and made no effort to hide her anger.

"I managed to gain a little independence in New York, after being hidden away, as I told you. If I'm not free to do as I please here in France, I have no reason to celebrate my return."

Indignation emanated from her beautiful blue eyes. Laroche turned away to hide his discontent. He was reminded of his daughter's protests when she demanded to marry Guillaume Duquesne. His lips pursed as he repressed this bitter memory.

"No reason, you say?" he repeated hotly, emphasizing each word. "I suppose your grandmother's happiness doesn't matter to you at all! You couldn't care less about learning to run some of the most famous vineyards in Europe, could you? You will inherit the whole estate upon my death—the castle, the farms! Do you really want to renounce this inheritance in the name of a freedom that could be your downfall?"

Hugues Laroche kept his voice down, so as not to attract the attention of the other guests.

"The subject is closed," he decided after a moment's hesitation. "But don't worry—I don't intend to deny you any of the distractions that are appropriate for a young lady of your age and status. Adela will be delighted to accompany you to Angoulême, and this Saturday evening, she is throwing a ball to welcome you home. I would also like to mention that horse riding on our land would be a great way of asserting your independence."

"Well, in that case, I'd better learn to ride as soon as possible," she said provocatively. "You really have thought of everything, dear Grandpa. Thanks to the horse you bought me, I will be able to visit my other family, the Duquesnes."

Laroche looked at her grimly. Just when Bonnie thought war was about to break out, Justin appeared at the hotel reception desk. The young man had taken care of his appearance, and his first wages had allowed him to buy riding breeches in thick twill cloth, gaiters, and a fur-lined leather jacket. He wore a grey flannel shirt under a green sweater.

Despite his efforts, the receptionist wrinkled her nose in disdain.

"Mr. Laroche is waiting for me," explained Justin.

"We will let him know, young man."

Having spotted his groom, the squire burst in. He gave Justin a friendly pat and smiled.

"You're exactly on time—a virtue I truly appreciate, Justin. Elizabeth's trunks are in the hallway—a hotel employee will help you load them."

"I left the carriage on the fairground, as you requested, Sir. I brought Colas with me so that he could watch over the horses."

"Perfect! I'll pay the bill. The ladies are coming."

Elizabeth joined her grandfather as Justin was about to leave. When their eyes met, the ten-year interval between now and their last encounter evaporated at once. He bowed his head respectfully and she quietly said hello to him.

Laroche felt the pockets of his coat before shouting: "How stupid of me! I've left my wallet in the bedroom. I'm going up to get it."

With a morose look, the receptionist gave him his key back while checking the bill again. Elizabeth rushed up to Justin.

"Is it really you?" she asked. "The nephew of the housekeeper, Madeleine?"

Elizabeth recognized his blond hair, even features and dark eyes, but above all, his kind nature. The girl reached into her bag and there it was—the tin soldier that he had given her. She hastily put it back.

"Yes, it's me," he confessed, whispering. "But please don't tell Mr. Laroche about my aunt, or that I was already at the castle at that time, or I will lose my job."

He gave her an embarrassed smile, enchanted by her beauty. She reminded him of a fine porcelain statue of exquisite colours—pink, bright blue and snow white.

"I'm so happy to see you again! I hoped for ages that you would return," he said. "Excuse me—I must take care of your trunks."

He nodded towards a porter dressed in brown livery, who came running up to them.

"I won't say a word, I promise," Elizabeth whispered.

Suddenly, a firm hand landed on Justin's shoulder. Hugues Laroche scrutinized his face, intrigued.

"What did you promise Justin?" he asked Elizabeth, without taking his eyes of the groom.

"I told him about my fear of horses, and he reassured me, so I promised to be sensible about it," Elizabeth replied.

"We've already discussed this, Elizabeth. You will indeed have to be sensible about it, as you put it. But I have an idea: why not let Justin give you riding lessons? He's likely to be more patient than me."

The groom and the porter crossed the paved street, each holding a handle of the heaviest trunk.

"I would like to try it, Grandpa," replied Elizabeth, whose eyes followed Justin's slim, supple body. "Yes, I'll do my best. Won't I, Bonnie?"

"Yes, Miss—I have no doubt about that," replied the governess, amused.

13

From the Castle to the Mill

En route to Guerville Castle
Tuesday, January 19, 1897

The horses were trotting at a steady pace. Their russet-coloured manes fluttered in the wind, and their shod hooves threw up greyish splatters as they trampled through puddles. After two weeks of rain, the air was very mild, and the meadows were dotted with yellow dandelions, the first of the season.

For several miles, they followed the River Charente, which was just visible between the ash trees and willows. Elizabeth's spirits lifted as she recognized the landscape. She was sitting next to her grandfather, while Bonnie was on the front bench, her suitcase at her feet.

The carriage was a comfortable and stable ride, with good suspension. "What a fine way to travel," enthused Bonnie.

She was about to compare it to the New York omnibuses, which were also drawn by sturdy horses, but refrained just in time, to avoid annoying Hugues Laroche.

"It doesn't feel like winter at all," said Elizabeth.

"Spring arrives earlier here than in other parts of Europe," replied her grandfather. "The castle gardens will soon be an enchanting sight. Crocuses, daffodils and jonquils will rear their heads before March, and the roses will follow in May. Catherine loved roses."

"Yes, I remember," said Elizabeth dreamily. "We had yellow rosebushes in our garden in Montignac. Do you know what happened to our house, Grandpa?"

"Old Duquesne didn't sell it—he rented it to a schoolteacher for three years."

His remark annoyed Elizabeth. She looked angrily at the squire's wizened face.

"*Old Duquesne!* How dare you call my grandfather that, in front of me! Your lack of respect makes me question your upbringing, too."

"I will not take lessons off you!" he roared. "You are extremely ill-mannered."

"Well then, so are you!" Elizabeth retorted furiously.

Perched up front in the driver's seat, Justin was stupefied.

He had never witnessed anyone answer his employer back. Sitting next to him was Colas, an eleven-year-old village boy. Justin stooped, as if to take the blame for the girl's insolence.

"I suppose we're quits then, my dear child," said Laroche with a smirk.

Elizabeth looked at him blankly. Her grandfather seemed suddenly delighted with their heated exchange.

"I loathe weaklings, cowards and those who run away scared. But you stand up to me, which proves that you should be capable of running the estate when I'm gone. Justin, give the beasts a jolt, will you—we're going too slowly."

The two cobs hastened their pace. Elizabeth remained silent, lost in thought. *This afternoon I will go and visit Grandpa Toine and ask him for the keys to our little house—my home. If life in the castle turns out to be unbearable, I'll move to Montignac.*

Justin turned around for a second and caught sight of her tense face, her cheeks rosy from the cold. Her rare beauty troubled him. In his eyes, she was still the frightened little girl he had discovered in the nursery, eyes glistening with tears. He remembered how happy he had been to hold her warm hand through the bars of her cot. She would grow into a very beautiful young lady—but also very rich, alas!

He turned to face the road again, unaware that Elizabeth, too, was gazing at his shoulders and his mass of blond hair that protruded from his velvet cap. She knew already that Justin would be her friend and ally.

Bonnie gave a gentle cry of admiration upon seeing the castle, whose towers stood against a backdrop of blue sky. The château was surrounded by gigantic oaks and cedars with bluish branches. Elizabeth trembled.

"I remember!" she shouted out. "It feels like only yesterday. What about the huge fir tree, Grandpa? I can recall it being struck by lightning on the evening when we were at the castle. There was a terrible storm."

"What a good memory you have!" Laroche exclaimed in surprise. "I haven't forgotten, of course—I was devastated when that tree fell. I planted a larch in its place, which is already a good size. How foolish I was to wallow in self-pity about that tree, unaware that a fate a thousand times worse was awaiting me! I still don't know how I survived Catherine's death. It must have been the thought of finding you that kept me going. But let's not talk about it any more—Adela must be in a frenzy."

The carriage climbed up a wide gravel path that led straight to the castle's inner courtyard. Elizabeth saw a group of people gathered outside, most of whom were dressed in black and white.

"Our servants," said her grandfather.

"Where is Grandma?" Elizabeth asked. "I can't see her."

"Adela is standing further back, on the porch step. Keep calm, please."

"I suppose well-brought-up people don't show their emotions."

"That's right."

The carriage came to a halt. Justin leapt down from his seat to open the doors. Bonnie accepted his help and grabbed his hand, but Hugues Laroche rushed to steady Elizabeth.

The girl smiled at all the servants who were politely waiting to greet her. Madeleine barely tilted her head, lips pursed. She was wearing a black dress with an immaculate white apron. A thin cap covered her chestnut hair. Old Leandre and Alcide, the gardeners, gave a slight bow.

Mariette was there too. The blonde girl was dressed in a grey skirt and a white blouse, with an apron tied around her waist.

Adela was waiting, her slight body stiff in her purple satin outfit, and her greyish blonde hair carefully styled. Despite her nerves, she didn't falter in her role as mistress of the castle.

"Grandma!" called out Elizabeth, although she was struggling to recognize her.

In her memory, Adela was an attractive woman with a stern face and cold eyes. Her distressed face showed the ravages of time caused by immense grief.

"My child, at last! Come here!" cried Adela. "You have grown into such a beautiful young woman. I praise the Lord for reuniting me with you."

Elizabeth's throat was in knots. She ran towards her and hugged her, kissing her grandmother on each cheek.

"Oh, my darling child," Adela moaned. "How happy I am!"

"Let's go inside," suggested Laroche, feeling both relieved and embarrassed.

Elizabeth followed her grandparents into the grand entrance hall, where she was reunited with the hunting trophies: deer, wild boar and roebucks with their glass eyes and stiff hair seemingly frozen in time.

Outside, Bonnie was patiently waiting with the luggage. Justin took the horses and the carriage back to the stables. The governess looked at each of the staff in turn.

"Who is that gingerhead?" grumbled Madeleine with a wry grin. "A wretched American, I assume!"

"I'm not going to take orders from her, that's for sure," added Alcide.

"Hello everyone!" cried Bonnie. "I am Miss Elizabeth's maid. And yes, I do speak French."

Leandre took off his beret and muttered hello. Annoyed, Madeleine did an about-turn and entered the castle.

"I will show you to your room, Madam," said the young maid who had been hired to assist Madeleine, who delighted in giving her all the housework to do. "Germaine, at your service."

Bonnie liked her sweet face, bright smile and greyish-blue eyes. A small white bonnet adorned her straw-coloured hair.

"Thank you, Germaine. You will have to ask them to bring Miss's trunks upstairs. I will unpack them myself."

"We'll do it when Justin comes back from the stable," retorted Alcide, whose pale face had a gormless look about it.

"Very well," said Bonnie. "I'll follow you, Germaine."

Elizabeth crossed the dining room, where the table was set for just three people. She scrutinized every detail, surprised to discover that nothing had been moved or changed. Adela was overjoyed as she followed her granddaughter, admiring her long dark hair and delicate profile, mesmerized by her sweet voice.

"I remember the paintings, the big green velvet curtains and the silver candlesticks, Grandma," Elizabeth said. "And the butler, Jerome. He used to bring me dessert. Daddy was sitting here and Mummy there."

Adela let out a shriek of horror, almost choking. "You're right! How can you remember it so precisely?"

"Let's talk about it later, Grandma. It *is* rather peculiar. There's one room in which I never ventured as a child: the large sitting room."

"Then let's go there now!" said the mistress of the castle enthusiastically. "But you should know that it's a mess, as I'm throwing a ball there on Saturday. Germaine still has to polish the parquet, and I have asked for the furniture to be moved against the wall and the carpet to be rolled up."

"If you don't mind, we'll visit it another time," replied Elizabeth hesitantly.

"Not at all, my dear! In any case, you will pass through it on the way to see your grandfather and I—the large sitting room is adjacent to our suites now. Hugues had the bright idea of setting up living quarters for us in the Duchess of Guerville's chambers. The castle belonged to her in the 17th century, and she was very keen to restore and embellish it. Thanks to her, we have the two windows in the drawbridge tower and these two superb rooms that give access to the keep."

Adela took her arm affectionately, laughing gaily. With one hand, she opened the light-grey double door to the drawing room.

Hugues Laroche, who was sitting near the large marble fireplace in the dining room, was playing the piano with his index finger. Suddenly, he grabbed his leather wallet and took out a yellowed, worn photograph.

"The day of your twentieth birthday, Catherine," he whispered. "I took you to Angoulême, to have your portrait done. The photographer complimented you on your beauty and you smiled at him. Then a year later, to my misfortune, you met Guillaume Duquesne."

He closed his eyes for a few seconds, breathing jerkily. Then he put the photo away, his face strained. Laughter was coming from the drawing room. He arose and rang for Madeleine, who came running.

"Sir?" she asked humbly.

"Add a place setting for Miss's governess."

"But I thought she'd be eating in the kitchen, like the rest of us?"

"You thought?" he flared up. "I pay you to obey my instructions, not to think. I demand that you show her respect, Madeleine—do you hear?"

"Yes, Sir."

Adela and Elizabeth, alerted by the squire's shouts, left the drawing room.

They watched Madeleine as she laid a fourth place setting on the dining-room table.

"Your governess is having luncheon with us," said Laroche to his granddaughter. "The missing place setting was a pure oversight that has since been rectified."

"But it wasn't an oversight, Hugues," said his wife, surprised. "You didn't tell me this lady was coming."

"Without Bonnie, the crossing would have been an even bigger struggle for me," confessed Elizabeth. "She looks after me and knows how to console me."

"If Bonnie means that much to you, then she is certainly welcome," said Adela, smiling.

Touched by the warmth and spontaneity of her grandmother, Elizabeth felt a surge of relief. The woman she remembered from her childhood had changed. She wasn't aware yet just how big the transformation was.

Guerville Castle
Two hours later

After a hearty lunch, Bonnie longed to take a nap, but she insisted on hanging Elizabeth's many outfits in the large wardrobe first.

"Your grandmother is charming, Miss," she told the girl, sitting on the edge of the four-poster bed. "I can tell she truly loves you."

"That's all I care about, Bonnie. She's a changed woman—maybe I misjudged her as a child. I used to think she was cold and cranky—I hardly ever saw her."

"What's bothering you then, Miss?" said the governess, looking worried. "I can see that something is troubling you."

"My head is spinning with thoughts. First, what was Richard Johnson doing on board *La Touraine*? And why is my grandfather being so cold, sanctimonious and malicious? And then there's Justin . . ."

"The groom," sighed Bonnie, as she smoothed out the creases in a silk summer dress. "I saw you speak to him in the hotel lobby."

"It turns out he really is the small boy in the nursery I told you about, but he begged me not to tell anyone. Apparently, Madeleine is hiding the fact that he is her nephew from my grandparents. I hope to meet him alone to find out more."

"In that case, you should start these riding lessons as soon as possible!"

"You're right. It seems that lies are rife everywhere, not just in New York. Maybel and Edward lied to me, so did Richard, and now I have to lie for Justin."

"Saying nothing isn't lying, Miss. Apart from all that, how are you settling in?"

"They have, naturally, given me Mummy's room—the one she had as a girl. I peeked into the drawers of her dresser, and there are still some of her belongings in it. How strange—she left without taking anything, or hardly anything."

Bonnie bent down and pulled a box out from the wardrobe. She half opened it, eager to show the contents to Elizabeth.

"Miss, look—it's your mother's riding outfit. It's hand-stitched, in a superb woollen fabric. And look at the colour—such a lovely light green! Not a typical colour for a riding outfit. And it's been wrapped in tissue paper and looks brand new."

The governess turned the box around. A date was inscribed: *December 23 1877.*

"Mummy's eyes were this green colour, and sometimes a bit bluish, like the ocean," whispered Elizabeth. "And that's the date of her twentieth birthday. It's odd—I only arrived in France yesterday but I've already learnt a lot about her. I still have sweet memories of her from my childhood, but now I'm discovering her life in the castle—riding horses, dancing at balls . . ."

"Your grandmother will be delighted to tell you about your mother, I'm sure. But you must get changed now."

"There's no point, I'm comfortable. We're setting off soon, I must gather the gifts I bought. I can't wait to see my other grandfather, the mill and my uncles."

After the meal, Adela announced that they would both visit Antoine Duquesne.

"Justin will harness the carriage and I'll accompany dear Elizabeth."

Hugues Laroche made no comment but looked daggers at his wife. The friendship she had formed with the old miller had been the cause of many heated quarrels, on which Madeleine loved to eavesdrop.

"But you haven't even given your grandparents here their presents yet!" exclaimed the governess.

"I'll make sure to do it tonight. Are you sure you won't be bored alone here, Bonnie?"

"I don't think so! I'll carry on sorting out your clothes, and then I'll write a letter to my uncle in Queens. It all seems so far away now! I used to live there when I was young."

"But you're still young!" laughed Elizabeth.

"I wish I were. At thirty-two I'm an old maid."

A loud whinny attracted their attention. Through a window, they could see Hugues Laroche astride a tall grey horse that was prancing about, pawing the ground and bucking. Between shouts, the squire whipped it repeatedly. Suddenly, the animal bolted down the pathway.

"Well, your grandfather is an experienced rider," sighed Bonnie.

"Maybe—but above all, he's cruel," huffed Elizabeth.

She trembled nervously at the thought of Edward Woolworth, who had always been kind to his black gelding.

"Oh look, there's Justin!" she exclaimed.

Unaware of the eyes on him, the groom was watching his master disappear on horseback. Elizabeth noticed how worried he looked.

"I'm going down," she called out. "I want to see my horse."

"Your grandfather would probably prefer to present it to you himself."

"Too bad—he must have forgotten to mention it!"

Elizabeth caught up with Justin as he headed towards the stables, a large building separate from the castle. He heard her footsteps on the gravel and turned around anxiously.

"What are you doing here?" he demanded. "The carriage isn't ready."

"I saw my grandfather leave, so I decided to come. I thought we could chat, just the two of us."

Their encounter ten years ago in the nursery seemed so recent to her. Justin had known exactly how to console her that evening, fanning the flames in the hearth to dispel the darkness.

"You haven't changed much," she said warmly.

"I've grown up, like you, but our features haven't changed. Please Miss, keep away from me."

He looked suspiciously at the building adjacent to the fortress, which housed the pantry on its ground floor.

"My aunt is probably spying on us from the kitchen," he said.

"What if she is? I'm dying to see the mare my grandfather bought, upon your recommendation."

"All right. Follow me, please."

Justin seemed more at ease in the stables. Elizabeth wandered over to a series of stalls on either side of a paved alley. Some of the horses had their heads over the half-doors, their necks stretched towards the visitors and their ears pricked up.

"How many horses are there?" she asked.

"Twelve, plus your mare—that makes thirteen."

Old Leandre, who was standing nearby, crossed himself upon hearing the number thirteen.

"Oh, misfortune doesn't need *that* to strike," she exclaimed bitterly.

"I heard about your parents," Justin muttered. "I'm very sorry. I used to hide behind the big chest in the kitchen and listen to my aunt, who loved spouting the news—especially if it was bad."

"Justin, why won't she introduce you as her nephew? My grandfather really likes you—he told me how satisfied he is with you. And Madeleine has worked here a long time."

"I've asked myself the same thing, Elizabeth. Even as a small boy, I was confined to the attic. My aunt used to say that Mrs. and Mr. Laroche would throw her out if they found out that I lived in the castle. I was so terrified of making the slightest noise! I lived under the rafters, but as soon as it got dark, I couldn't resist exploring the hallways on the first floor. I used to go into the nursery, as it was full of toys."

"And that night, you must have been hiding in the wardrobe when Madeleine put me to bed?"

"You haven't forgotten, have you?"

"I'd forgotten much of my childhood, but one day when I touched the toy soldier, it all came back."

Justin's face lit up on hearing this. Embarrassed, Elizabeth averted her gaze.

"Come here—your mare is in this stall on the left. She has a very pretty name: Pearl."

"Oh no!" Elizabeth shrieked. "That was my cousin's name in New York."

Justin burst out laughing. He led her to a fine-looking dark bay horse, whose coat had a velvety sheen.

"I've already ridden her—you have nothing to worry about," he explained. "She's well schooled and docile."

"You'll help me, though, won't you? Can I change her name?"

The groom shrugged, accustomed to doing as he was told. Elizabeth plucked up courage and stroked the mare's white blaze.

"You should really return to the castle now," advised Justin. "Mr. Laroche could be back at any minute. He's always furious when Mrs. Adela goes to the Montignac mill."

"Does she go there often?"

"You could say that! Now I must prepare the carriage."

"Can't I stay with you?"

The young groom gave a resigned look. Elizabeth followed him into the room where the coaches and harnesses were stored. She recognized the carriage and brushed its top with her finger. Then her gaze fell on another, black-and-yellow vehicle.

"Your mother's Tilbury," said Justin quietly.

Elizabeth felt a bit faint. In the space of one day, she was discovering her mother's past and having to adapt to a new life in France. On top of that, she missed Maybel and Edward, who were now an ocean away.

"Justin, I thought I would be so happy back here, but I admit I've been finding it quite hard. A random couple took me in when I was a hungry, distraught and terrified six-year-old roaming the streets of New York. I thought it would be easy to leave them, with no regrets—but I was so wrong. Please—will you be my friend?"

Justin was moving leather straps and tack around, looking stern. He hesitated, then said in a soft, humble voice: "During your riding lessons, we can chat. Elizabeth, I was eleven years old when my aunt sent me to Aubeterre, to work as a stable hand. Luckily, the master of the estate taught me to read and write. I studied as much as I could, trained the horses and looked after them."

"So why did you come back?"

"Three months ago, my aunt came to see me. She told me that Mr. Laroche was looking for a groom and that I would be a perfect fit. Deep down, I was delighted at the prospect of returning to the castle. But there was one condition: I had to pretend to be a newcomer to the county. Madeleine pretended she had run into me in the village. Upon my arrival, I recited what she'd told me to say—that I was an orphan looking for work, both of which were true."

"Just like me," said Elizabeth, touched.

Justin could hear a faint gallop in the distance, and panicked.

"Mr. Laroche is on his way back! Leave, quickly, through this door. Pretend to be strolling in the park!" he said urgently, pointing to a vaulted door. "I don't want to lose my job, now that you're back!"

She obeyed, invigorated by his dark, seductive stare, and by what she read between the lines. Richard Johnson had vanished from her mind, replaced by Justin and his tanned complexion, golden hair and kind eyes.

On the banks of the River Charente
The same day, one hour later

"Spring will soon be here, my dear, and it will be the sweetest spring I've had in years," said Adela cheerfully. She was driving the horse-drawn carriage. "I despaired of ever seeing you again, and now you're here. What more could I want!"

The girl was touched by these loving words, and leaned affectionately against her grandmother.

"You're not the person you used to be, Grandma. Please don't be offended, but when my memory came back, I recalled a stern and cold lady."

"But I was indeed! I was trapped in the preconceptions my parents had instilled in me. And that evening, during Catherine's last dinner at the castle, I was in such torment, paralyzed at the thought of losing you all. I'm terribly sorry for that today. You must forget about the past, my darling, and enjoy the present, while forging your future."

The word "darling" was balm for Elizabeth's soul.

She looked up to admire the pale-blue sky, dotted with snowy white clouds. The route skirted the Charente river, which was swollen by the winter rains. The waters glittered in the sun, and the landscape radiated a profound sense of tranquillity.

"I owe a lot to Mr. Duquesne," pursued Adela. "Believe me, I was a sad soul in the wake of the tragedy. I can't remember how or why I had the idea, one day, to venture to the mill in secret. Maybe I needed to share my grief with Guillaume's family. Antoine welcomed me with open arms, not blaming me for anything. Hugues had built an impenetrable barrier between us and the Duquesnes, out of contempt and hatred."

"Hatred—really?" enquired Elizabeth. "And you call my Grandpa Duquesne by his first name?"

"After all these years, we've become good friends. He taught me humility, and thanks to him, I rediscovered my faith—and I don't mean just occupying a seat in church on a Sunday. The Lord must have forgiven my wrongdoings, as he's helped me find you again. I won't allow you to come to harm, ever again."

If Elizabeth hadn't been distracted by the rooftops of the mill and its large square porch, she would have asked her Grandma what she meant by "come to harm". But her thoughts were elsewhere, and her heart was racing with joy as the carriage entered the mill's vast muddy courtyard.

"My God, I can't believe it!" she shrieked. "Nothing has changed."

The sight of the castle had failed to make an impression on her. But here, in front of the large grey stone walls and the burnt-wood shutters, her whole body trembled with emotion. This was where she had spent her childhood—in these old buildings, and the small dwelling she used to occupy with her parents.

Antoine Duquesne appeared on the doorstep of the lodge. He was waving frantically, his wrinkled face beaming with happiness and his blue eyes brimming with tears.

"Pops Toine!" shouted out the young girl, jumping down from the carriage. "Pops Toine!"

She ran towards him, her arms outstretched, indifferent to the many puddles that soiled the bottom of her skirt. Having heard her voice, Pierre and Jean rushed outside, too.

"My little one, my beautiful little girl!" sobbed the old man as he held her tightly.

Then his voice failed, but they were content to just hug each other, struggling to believe they weren't dreaming.

"Is it really Elizabeth?" said Jean, who had seized the mare's reins. "Mrs. Adela, I wouldn't have recognized her!"

"I assure you, it's her, Jean. But she's a young lady now."

Pierre, too, was stunned and scratched his beard with a puzzled look. He was rooted to the spot.

"We're in a fine state to welcome our niece," snorted Jean, covered from head to toe in flour. "We were filling sacks for the Vouharte bakery."

"You don't need to be embarrassed, gentlemen," said Adela cheerfully. "You have a noble profession, providing bread for your fellow countrymen."

Without letting go of her, Antoine Duquesne moved a step away from his granddaughter.

"Let me look at you, little one!" he said breathlessly. "I thank the Lord Almighty for his unbridled mercy! We are finally reunited with you, after all these years of mourning, doubts and faint glimmers of hope."

The miller signalled to his sons, who were still standing by the carriage. Helped by Jean, Adela got down from her seat.

"Uncle Pierre, Uncle Jean!" shouted Elizabeth, turning to run towards them. She used to call to them like that whenever she fell, or wanted to be pushed on the garden swing.

"My goodness, a miracle!" cried Pierre as he kissed her.

"Holy mackerel, you're pretty!" laughed Jean.

Elizabeth stared at them in turn. They looked so much like her father that she started to weep.

"Come on inside, children!" exclaimed Antoine Duquesne. "Woe betide my poor legs that are floundering! I had forgotten what happiness is."

He chuckled when Jean rushed to his side to lend him a hand.

"I'll go and find Yvonne," announced Pierre. "She should be around, and our sons too. Their teacher has agreed to let them go early so they can celebrate with us. I have two handsome little boys, Elizabeth—Gilles and Laurent—your first cousins!"

"Grandma told me on the way. I can't wait to meet them!"

"It's incredible how good your French still is, after ten years in America!" exclaimed Jean admiringly.

"My governess's mother came from Normandy. We spoke French in secret, without telling my parents—I mean, the people who took me in. I thought of them as my parents. But I'll give you the whole story later."

Montignac village
The same day, the same time

Frederic Richard Johnson couldn't take his eyes off the medieval castle that overlooked the narrow streets of Montignac. He stood at the bottom of a stone staircase that was flanked by two round towers. It was the former fortress's walled access to its large square keep, a stronghold passed from one lord to another over the centuries.

The detective had never seen such a building before, which to him looked like something out of a fairytale. Mesmerized, he promised himself that he would sketch it the next day. France bewitched him in the same way Elizabeth Laroche did.

"Yes, bewitched," he said quietly, fully aware of his dreadful American accent when speaking French.

His arrival had caused a stir that very morning. He had booked the most beautiful room in the Pont-Neuf Inn, his accent arousing widespread curiosity. He had lied to Elizabeth about not speaking French, too, having learned the language in junior and high school. It was a little rusty, though, so he'd bought a small bilingual dictionary.

Some of the elderly village women, with their black dresses and white caps, were eyeing him suspiciously. Richard greeted them, lifting his beige felt hat.

His height and his elegantly cut suit—in fact, everything about him—caused him to stand out from the locals of Montignac.

Lisbeth will soon hear that I'm in the area, he thought. *At first, she'll be furious, but I'm sure she'll want to see me. And if by any chance she were to tell her dreadful grandfather, I would explain everything to him. I'm not doing anything wrong, just earning a crust.*

Pleased with himself, Richard was tempted to climb the steps of the castle. He rubbed the stones of one of the towers, which were linked by a section of wall, oblivious to the fact that hundreds of years ago, an iron harrow had served to close off access.

"I will try and find someone who can tell me the history of the castle," he muttered, as he entered the compound.

Shortly afterwards, after climbing countless steps, Richard stood in front of the ruins of the huge keep. He sat down there in the sun on a block of limestone, marvelling at his discovery.

Charente's mild climate was a blessing to him. His thoughts turned back to Elizabeth. He remembered the intoxicating moment when he had seized her icy lips with his mouth and kissed her wildly, in the throes of lustful frenzy, his hands on her breasts, her hips, and her satin thighs. He could see the expression on her face, as she lay on the bunk in his cabin, looking infinitely enticing, like a washed-up mermaid.

Comparing her to a mermaid relieved his conscience, since old legends told of the irresistible charm of these sea creatures, whose singing attracted sailors.

"And the boats would smash onto the reefs ..." he mused. "I'd better be wary, should Lisbeth entice me again." He would never have behaved like a wild buck if she had not given him that look.

Still feeling the sting of disappointment, he stretched out his long, athletic legs. About to get up, he took a photograph of Elizabeth out of his jacket pocket. He sighed and laughed at himself:

"If I get to marry her, I'll be the happiest man in the world, not to mention that I'll also be very rich."

The old photograph portrayed a smiling, wistful Elizabeth, who was wearing a sapphire necklace on her lace dress. Before embarking on *La Touraine*, she had given in to Maybel Woolworth's pleas and had her photo taken, for it to be framed and placed in the living room. Richard Johnson would never part with it.

The Duquesnes' mill
The same day, two hours later

"I'm sorry, Elizabeth, but we'll have to be on our way soon," said Adela regretfully. "The evenings are drawing out, but we must be home before nightfall. We can come back next week."

Antoine Duquesne grabbed his granddaughter's hand and kissed it. He couldn't get enough of her laughter and the spontaneous affection she showered on him.

"Why wait so long, Grandma! Why not the day after tomorrow?" exclaimed Elizabeth. "Bonnie can accompany us."

"I'm counting on that," added the old miller. "I must thank her for taking such good care of you."

"We'll let you know—it all depends on my husband's mood," sighed the mistress of the castle. "Hugues wants to spend some time with our granddaughter, too, but he finds it hard to express his feelings."

Her statement was followed by a dubious silence. Pierre's wife tried to save the situation.

"In any case, we'll see a lot more of each other," she said cheerfully. "It's simply wonderful to have you back with us, Elizabeth. Think of the happy times we'll spend together this spring and summer!"

Yvonne was kind-natured and devoted, and Elizabeth hadn't hesitated for a second before kissing her on her rosy cheeks. Her chestnut hair was neatly tucked under a small hat she had sewn for herself, and she was wearing a brown twill dress, which was just how Elizabeth remembered her.

"I often talked about you to my boys," she added. "Gilles and Laurent used to pray for your return, every evening before going to bed."

"My cousins!" enthused the young girl. "I had no idea you existed, until recently. Uncle Jean, where did I put my tapestry bag?"

"On the edge of the sideboard. Let me fetch it."

Shyness had given way to familiarity. Elizabeth imagined staying at the mill, sleeping and living there. In comparison, the castle suddenly seemed unwelcoming, despite her grandmother's kindness.

She shelved the idea for the time being, determined to split her days and maybe even her nights between Guerville and Montignac.

"I picked out a few small gifts, not knowing whether I would see you all again. Yvonne is right—we must be grateful for the opportunity to be together again. Pops Toine, I don't know if you still smoke a pipe, but I brought you one made of elm, and some English tobacco."

"Thank you, my little one—it'll make a change from the grey stuff that I use very sparingly."

"My dear uncles, for you, I brought two pocket-knives. The blades are made of steel and the handles are carved ivory. Dad advised me—pardon me, I meant Mr. Woolworth."

"Don't apologize, my child," said Adela. "Regardless of the decisions they made, these people acted as parents to you and probably saved you from a terrible fate."

Elizabeth quickly recounted what had happened to her after the attack on her father in an alleyway in the Bronx.

Antoine, Pierre and Jean tensed up, their faces stern, as they imagined Guillaume being beaten to death.

Adela had told them about this tragic event many years before, and was touched to see that they were still affected by it.

"I didn't forget you either, Yvonne," resumed Elizabeth, handing her a velvet pouch that contained a turquoise necklace.

"Oh, it's beautiful!" Yvonne cried. "Dear Lord, I would hardly dare to wear it—maybe just on a Sunday for mass. Look, Pierre!"

"And I have caramels, known as 'toffees', for my two cousins!"

"Toffees," mumbled Laurent, the youngest, in his French accent.

"They're delicious! Have one right away, Gilles."

She helped them open a round box made of coloured cardboard, which contained the sweets, wrapped in gold paper.

"I will keep the paper too," Gilles said seriously. "It shines so brightly . . ."

Elizabeth regretted that she didn't have any toys for them. Even so, they threw themselves around her neck, covering her with kisses.

"Thank you! You're beautiful, like a princess," whispered Laurent.

"You are adorable," Elizabeth replied faintly.

Suddenly the words "my princess" were swirling round in her head, and she was sure she could hear her parents' voices.

Deeply perturbed, she quickly closed her eyes.

If only we could go back in time, she thought. *I would only be five years old, like Laurent, and Mummy and Daddy would be here, so happy and in love.*

"Elizabeth, what's the matter?" asked Adela.

"My head is spinning. It's the cider we drank, that's all. I'll feel better after a glass of water."

Pierre handed her one at once, smiling at her with a fatherly look. But Yvonne was probably the most affectionate of them all. She had always been devoted to Elizabeth, right from the time when she was a cheeky little girl with a doll's face, taking her first steps in the mill yard.

Adela took a worried look at the clock on the wall. She got up and put on her coat and gloves.

"We must go now, Elizabeth," she insisted.

"I'm coming. Can we take the way past my parents' house, as planned?"

"That really wouldn't be convenient in a horse-drawn carriage, Elizabeth—and we no longer have time to walk there. Next time we'll come early so you can visit it."

"Don't worry, little one," added Antoine Duquesne. "My daughter-in-law takes great care of it. She airs it and cleans it, and everything is in its place."

"Thank you, Yvonne! Thank you, Pops Toine! I'll see it soon in any case, won't I? I've probably had enough emotion for today, anyway."

Their goodbyes delayed them even further, so that the day was coming to an end when Adela finally set off, forcing the mare to trot faster.

"Are you happy, Elizabeth?" she asked, raising her voice over the sound of hooves, the rattling of harnesses and the squealing of iron-rimmed wheels.

"No, Grandma, I'm not just happy—I'm *very* happy. But I really must learn to ride. That way, you won't have to drive me to Montignac each time I visit my family."

"I am always delighted to see Antoine and his sons, and I'm afraid you won't be allowed to travel all that distance on your own. You won't master horse riding in a couple of days, my dear."

"You mean Grandpa will forbid me to ride beyond the boundaries of the estate? But why? Because he never forgave Daddy for marrying Mummy? What does it matter now? It's not my uncles' fault or Pops Toine's."

"Hugues hopes to turn you into an accomplished young lady, who will run his estate as his heiress. He had the same hopes for Catherine, but Guillaume broke his dreams. If I had given him a son, everything would have been different. But let's talk about the ball now, shall we? It's a much more cheerful subject! Do you have a suitable gown?"

"Yes—the one I wore on New Year's Eve in New York. It's truly beautiful," said Elizabeth in a flat voice.

No one will succeed in keeping me locked up, she thought. *Least of all the man who hated my father.*

14

A Spider in Its Web

Guerville Castle
Friday, March 12, 1897

Hugues Laroche had set up an enclosure behind the stables to train his horses, trotting and galloping them on a sandy oval track.

Elizabeth had been taking lessons from Justin for almost two months now. He was careful not to push her too hard, but taught her almost every day, which meant that they spent a lot of time in each other's company.

That morning a warm wind was blowing, and birdsong could be heard in the forest. Daffodils splashed golden yellow dots over the park's lawns, and the ornamental shrubs were garbed in a faint pink bloom under the sunlight.

"Good, well done!" shouted Justin. "I can tell you have more control over each gait now, Miss. One more lap at a gallop, and we'll call it a day."

Elizabeth had to get used to the side saddle with its two pommels, which required a very special way of sitting. Her grandmother had taken her to Angoulême to buy her a suitable brown twill outfit with a top hat, a white scarf and leather boots.

"I would rather sit astride, like you and Grandpa," she replied. "It's more practical."

"Only men do that," answered Justin.

"Meaning I have to conform to social convention yet again! Why don't we go for a proper ride this afternoon? I'm bored with going round in this pen and trotting along the edge of the estate."

"Mr. Laroche doesn't think you're ready."

In truth, Justin thought otherwise, but was careful to keep it to himself. He was worried that the precious time they shared could come to an end. They had grown very close, laughing crazily at the slightest thing, their youth breaking down barriers and social differences.

Elizabeth saw her grandparents arriving and pushed her horse into a gentle trot.

Adela was holding her husband's arm while shielding herself with a pink silk parasol.

"We have come to watch your exploits!" exclaimed the squire.

Justin straightened up, head held high and a distant look on his face. He greeted the couple with a bow.

"Miss has finished her lesson, Sir," he said boldly. "Pearl is starting to sweat."

They hadn't changed the horse's name, which was now a source of amusement between Elizabeth and Justin. They giggled at the thought of the American cousin being on the receiving end of the commands given to the animal.

"Do another lap at a gallop, my dear child, and don't forget to hold your whip properly!" ordered Laroche.

"If you're satisfied with my progress, will you let me go for a ride after lunch?" ventured Elizabeth. "Justin would accompany me, of course."

"Certainly not!" snapped her grandfather. "And when you're ready to go out into the countryside, I'll be the one accompanying you. Don't start to think of yourself as an experienced rider—you're not a patch on your mother."

"Hugues, why are you so unpleasant?" said Adela angrily. "Our granddaughter is trying really hard to please you, and you rebuff her each time."

Fed up with witnessing yet another quarrel between his master and mistress, Justin hastily made his way to the stables. Elizabeth's indignant tone stopped him in his tracks.

"You are bitter, unfair and always in a bad mood, Grandpa!" she shouted. "But I know what makes you so cranky: Grandma and I go to the Montignac mill too often for your liking. Don't forget I have family there too! Yet, I do everything to please you. I had to attend three tiresome balls, where I was a laughing-stock, as I didn't know how to dance the waltz properly. I visited all your vineyards with you, listening to your lengthy explana-tions, and now I'm doing my utmost to stay on a horse! What's the point of these lessons, if I'm only allowed to trot monoto-nously around the park!"

In her anger, Elizabeth pulled sharply on the reins. Taken by surprise, Pearl bucked.

"Get down from that animal immediately!" roared Hugues Laroche.

Justin came running. Looking pale, Adela tried to reason with her husband, who had rushed inside the enclosure.

"Calm down, Hugues!" she begged.

"I will calm down when I'm shown some respect!" he shouted. "Elizabeth, I order you to get off! Do as I say!"

"No!" Elizabeth cried, backing up her mare.

Neither Adela nor Justin could intervene. Laroche ripped the whip out of his granddaughter's hands and he gave her left calf a lashing. The blow, slightly cushioned by the thickness of her long skirt and boots, merely heightened Elizabeth's anger.

The squire stared at her, blind with rage, but it wasn't Elizabeth he saw in the beautiful young woman who sat perched on her horse. The blue eyes that stared back at him had taken on a green reflection, and the tied-up brown hair suddenly seemed blonde. He remembered his daughter Catherine stand-ing up to him like that years before, and he had lost his temper then, too.

"Hugues, no!" pleaded Adela. "Please, not again—come to your senses!"

But he struck her with his whip again. Justin shouted in outrage, echoing Elizabeth's cry of pain.

"Sir, stop it!" he said frantically.

He couldn't bear the scene before his eyes and threw caution to the wind, jumping over the fence and placing himself between

Laroche and the frightened mare who was trampling the sand as she pranced on the spot.

"You stay out of it!" scolded the squire, lashing him in the face.

"No, Grandpa, stop!" screamed Elizabeth.

In a flash, she was back on the ground, not knowing how she had dismounted so quickly. Justin usually helped her, and she relished the feel of his hands around her waist.

"I hope you are happy now—I *did* get off my horse!" she exclaimed. "But I will never forgive you for what you just did."

She looked desperately at Justin, whose right cheek and mouth were streaked with blood. Adela was petrified, an expression of utter despair on her stark white face.

"I'm returning to the castle, Grandma," said Elizabeth.

"Wait for me, my darling! I don't feel very well."

"No wonder," Elizabeth said, distressed. "Come here, let me take your arm."

They walked away, leaving Hugues Laroche and Justin face to face, under the spring sun.

"I suppose I am dismissed, Sir?" Justin enquired boldly.

"Just leave me be. I need to be alone," replied the squire.

He was holding Pearl's reins. Suddenly, he pressed his forehead against the mare's neck, eyes half closed. Justin walked to the stone water trough, which was filled by a spring. He splashed cold water over his face to relieve the burning sensation.

Elizabeth looked at the castle in anger, feeling sorry for her grandmother. In the early days, she and Bonnie had admired the beauty of the old fortress, with its drawbridge that was hardly used anymore, a second entrance having been built at the end of the last century. The imposing edifice, with its high towers crowned by pointed slate roofs, and impressive walls, now looked like a prison to her.

"I have to know, Grandma—why did you say to him, 'Please, not again'? Does Grandpa often hit people who don't obey him? Mummy, for instance, when she was young?"

"What are you talking about, child? I was so shocked by your grandfather's attitude that I started yelling nonsense at him. I can't deny he has a short temper, and I've seen him treat dogs or horses with malice, but certainly not Catherine . . ."

Elizabeth was highly intuitive, and sensed at once that she was lying. Her heart bled for Justin, who had rushed to her defence and whom she had deliberately abandoned, hoping he wouldn't be thrown off the estate if she was convincing enough in feigning indifference to him.

"Grandma, you can speak to me openly—I'm no longer a child," she insisted. "Did they get into some serious arguments when Mummy wanted to marry Daddy?"

Adela was shaking, leaning heavily on her granddaughter's arm. She had repressed so much grief and fear in the past that she couldn't cope with reviving the pain.

"In all families—rich or poor, happy or unhappy—disagreements, disputes and misunderstandings happen," the elderly woman said, gasping. "Hugues didn't want to lose his only daughter, which is understandable. He had hoped that she would marry a local nobleman, and that she and her husband would live in the castle and manage the vineyards."

"Daddy wasn't interested in that kind of life, was he?"

"I don't know anymore, Elizabeth. It was so long ago. I don't know if you remember, but the day before you left for Le Havre, during that unfortunate dinner, Hugues made your father an offer, a golden opportunity for Guillaume—but he turned it down!"

"I haven't forgotten, Grandma. Not Grandpa's shouting, nor my parents' unwavering resolve, nor even how spiteful and unkind Madeleine was to me that evening."

Adela stopped in her tracks, staggered by these words. She looked incredulously at the kitchen windows.

"Madeleine? What do you mean? She's a model employee and invaluable to me, in more ways than one."

"Maybe—but she terrorized me that night. As soon as we got into the nursery, she scolded me and shook me, complaining about the inconvenience I was causing her, threatening me with the most terrible things if I told Mummy how she was treating me."

"I find that hard to believe," replied Adela. "You were probably afraid to sleep alone up there, and since it was a housekeeper and not your mother who put you to bed, the situation made an impression on you. Memories have a habit of distorting facts, my darling."

"Not mine, Grandma," asserted Elizabeth. "I told you about the flashbacks I have of some very specific scenes, with vivid detail. This ability of mine used to surprise the Woolworths, and it often worried Bonnie, just like my nightmares and dreams."

"Yes, you told me, Elizabeth. I think you are suffering from extreme anxiety, and heightened sensitivity."

"You are refusing to see how serious this is, Grandma!"

"Not at all— but I put it down to your childhood trauma. Admittedly, those people in New York raised you as well as they could, but they were unable to erase the deeper wounds from your heart and soul. Be honest—you told me you've slept soundly ever since you returned to the castle."

"That's true."

They remained silent for a moment. Elizabeth could hardly keep herself from telling her grandmother about the appearance of little Justin in the nursery. But that would have meant breaking the promise she had made to the young groom, who inspired tender feelings in her, although not sensual desire like Richard did.

"Getting back to Madeleine," said Adela. "She might be devoted to me, but she is strict and confrontational with the other servants. You know she wasn't lucky enough to be a mother, or even to have a family. It's hardly surprising she couldn't handle you. But come on, let's go inside now—I'm exhausted."

Elizabeth decided not to persist, in order to spare her grandmother, who was clearly very distressed by it all. Even so, she was furious, and her mind was made up. *I will do as I see fit from now on, even if it means lying and disobeying. I don't care if I get punished,* she resolved.

Sitting in a blue velvet wing chair, Bonnie was eagerly awaiting her return. Her room was adjacent to Elizabeth's, but she flitted between the two at her whim. Elizabeth rushed in, slamming the door behind her.

"Ah, Miss, you're here at last! Don't make so much noise— I've got a headache."

"I'm sorry, Bonnie. My goodness, you're injured!"

"It's nothing, just a bad fall. I have a nice bump and a small cut. Madeleine treated me with Arnica balm after cleaning the wound."

Elizabeth leaned over and examined her bruised forehead.

"It's not pretty," she sighed. "What on earth happened to you?"

"Madeleine invited me to have coffee with her in the kitchens during your riding lesson today. I feel more comfortable downstairs in the pantry than on the *étage noble*, as your grandmother calls it."

"Bonnie, please get to the point!" Elizabeth snapped impatiently.

"There's nothing to tell, really. I fell, that's all. I'm still going to help you change out of your riding clothes, of course."

"That won't be necessary. I shall go riding again after lunch."

The governess held back her tears, struggling to hide her annoyance and sorrow.

"You remind me of your grandfather when you use that tone," she complained. "And you're going off yet again. I've only been to the mill with you once, because Mrs. Adela claims the carriage isn't suitable for three people. I'm bored, Miss, and you're always angry these days."

Confused and ashamed, Elizabeth drew a quilted pouffe over and sat on it. She took Bonnie's hand.

"Forgive me—I would hate to become like my grandfather. I realize I have neglected you, but I thought you were busy sewing during the day and taking the time to read and improve your knowledge. Grandma monopolizes me with things that hardly interest me. Let's not fall out, please, Bonnie! Come, I have time now. Tell me what happened."

"I didn't trust Madeleine at first. Then little by little, I got to know her. She hasn't had much luck in life, you know."

"Yes, my grandparents told me, but I still don't understand why she lies to them about Justin."

"I didn't dare tell her that I know about her nephew. Finally, this morning, she insisted on showing me the pond where old Leandre found Vincent's body, the former groom who drowned. I went just to stretch my legs in the park. She told me all the intimate details! She and Vincent were lovers. He was found with blows to the head, so the police were suspicious about the cause of death."

"What a strange idea, to take you there!"

"Miss, I've seen it all in the streets of New York, and there wasn't even a body this time. Nothing but dark water, and hundreds of tadpoles. She went on to ask me into the guard-room. My goodness, she piles up empty bottles there and hides new ones in between them. She said that we could try a Bordeaux one evening."

"So she steals from my grandmother!" said Elizabeth indignantly.

"I said the same to her, Miss. Madeleine replied that your grandparents are very rich and don't even notice."

"Of course they don't notice; she is the one who takes care of the purchasing and deliveries!"

"I'll get to the point, as I can see you're yawning. It's a creepy place, this guardroom: a large, dark vault with rubble on the ground. Apparently, the debris there dates back centuries. We started to climb down a steep stone staircase. I was following her closely, and suddenly, she tripped. We both screamed, as she was trying to hold on to my skirt, to no avail—she fell flat on the steps, and I lost my balance, toppling over to the side. My poor head struck one of the boulders that are down there."

"Bonnie, you could have been killed!"

Elizabeth held her governess's hands even tighter. She was petrified, imagining what could have happened.

"What would I do without you, Bonnie?"

"Oh, you wouldn't miss me for long—in fact, no one would miss me," wailed Bonnie. "Madeleine is quite right—if you're not married at my age, you're doomed to face your old age alone. When you have a husband of your rank and children, you'll replace me with a qualified nanny who didn't grow up in America. I still don't read French particularly well, so . . ."

With that, Bonnie burst into tears. Elizabeth stood up and hugged her.

"No wonder you have a migraine, if Madeleine's been filling your head with such nonsense—not to mention the fall. Bonnie, you will stay by my side—I don't want to lose you! A husband of my 'rank'—whatever next!" she snorted. "Social status, manners, etiquette—I don't care for any of that, Bonnie. And if I have children, you'll be their nursemaid—I'd never want anyone else."

Elizabeth continued to comfort her dear friend. She could see how upset Bonnie was, and decided not to mention her own woes.

"Grandma is in her room; she has told Germaine to bring her a tray. We will have lunch here."

"Please, Miss, don't be angry with Madeleine. She was truly sorry, and I promised to keep her secret about the wine bottles."

"Secrets and more secrets!" said the girl, enraged. "Don't worry, I won't say anything for the moment. Let me ring for Germaine."

In the castle stables
Two hours later

Justin was saddling up Galant, the squire's grey stallion, when Mariette ventured down the pathway leading to the stables. A basket full of laundry on her left hip, she stopped in front of the stall.

"Hello," she said, softly. "I thought I'd come and find you, seeing that you no longer bother seeking me out."

"You're off work today, so what are you doing sneaking around here with that basket?"

"You never used to complain when I dropped by!"

"The boss will be here soon—you'd better leave, Mariette. It's been a lousy day. If he finds you here and his horse isn't ready, we could both be dismissed."

"Mr. Laroche is still in there, talking to old Leandre, so stop fretting. It seems more likely that you don't want to see me anymore! I'm not blind—I see you only have eyes for the young lady!"

Justin's irritation was apparent in the rough manner in which he saddled up Galant. The stallion became agitated and tried to bite him.

"I still have lots of work to do, but as soon as I have time, I'll come and see you. I don't want to take any risks. I've been thinking: if you got pregnant, I don't earn enough for us to get married."

He turned to face her.

"But what's that! Somebody has hit you—you have a bruise on your face!" she said, alarmed. "Who was it? The boss?"

"No, I caught a branch while galloping down a trail earlier. Please, just go." He pointed to the back door of the building.

The girl nodded, smirking.

"You're a dumb fool, Justin," she whispered. "I'm sure you're in love with the beautiful Elizabeth. Firstly, she's not that beautiful, and secondly, she's no better than any other girl. I'm the one who scrubs your princess's rags! She's no different to anyone else."

Justin glared at her. He was embarrassed and angry. Mariette pretended to be frightened and then vanished. Shortly afterwards, Laroche entered through the double door. Justin was relieved that he hadn't seen the young laundry maid.

"Galant is ready, Sir."

"Very good, my boy. I'm leaving for Aigre and I'll be back

during the night. I'm in need of exercise and some space. I had lunch alone for the first time in years, my wife and granddaughter having taken refuge in their rooms. Why should I deny myself a little distraction?"

He was surprised that his groom didn't answer.

"Have you lost your tongue Justin?"

"No Sir, but my opinion is irrelevant."

Astonished, the squire observed him as he led Galant outside. Laroche followed, while checking the contents of his jacket pockets. He had everything he needed—a full wallet, his pocket watch, and his cigars.

"Justin!" he called out. "I was wrong to lose my temper with you this morning. You didn't deserve to be hit. I have never had a groom as capable as you taking care of my horses."

He grabbed the stallion's reins and slipped a golden Louis d'Or coin into the young man's hand.

"I can't accept it, Sir," he said, shaking his head. "My wages suffice."

"And proud with it, too! You're a dark horse, aren't you? I heard from Madeleine that you're sleeping with young Mariette. Put this coin aside for your wedding."

Smirking, Hugues Laroche winked at him pointedly, then jumped into the saddle, eager to gallop off to the inn where he would play cards before joining a voluptuous young servant girl upstairs.

Justin watched him take off down the pathway. He then studied the golden coin, his dark eyes glowing with contempt.

A quarter of an hour later, Elizabeth entered the stables. She found Justin sitting on a crate, still busy examining the coin he was rotating between his fingers. He recognized her light footsteps and jumped up.

"I was afraid you wouldn't be here!" Elizabeth said quietly.

He flinched, confused by her informal manner. She put a comforting hand on his wrist.

"When we're alone, we don't need to behave like servant and

lady of the castle," she grinned. "My grandfather has gone; I saw him galloping down the path. Justin, I'm sorry he hit you! I should have obeyed him right away."

She caressed the red swollen mark on his face, but he seized her hand and pushed her away.

"Don't do that, please. I had to stand up for you—I couldn't just stand by and watch. But let's leave it at that—each of us sticking to our respective role. Mr. Laroche humiliated me in giving me this coin; it was as if he were paying me off for taking his wrath out on me."

"So he didn't dismiss you, then? Thank God—I feared the worst. Please, Justin, keep the money—you might need it."

"Stop being so familiar with me—it's very patronizing, bosses talking to their servants like that. You used to show me a bit more respect."

He fell silent, gasping. Elizabeth was lost for words. Then she said softly:

"I do respect you, Justin—I was just trying to get closer to you, flouting social conventions. If my parents hadn't died ten years ago, I would be a mere immigrant girl, working in a New York shop."

The young man smiled sweetly. He put the coin in his jacket pocket.

"Forgive me—you're neither proud nor snobbish, I noticed that as soon as you arrived. Tell me, does it hurt? Your grandfather was very brutal, the second time he lashed you."

"Oh, it's stinging a bit, but I didn't get changed. Justin, can you help me saddle up Pearl? I want to go to Montignac. I must be quick—if my grandfather returns, he'll forbid me to leave the castle grounds."

Justin made her sit on the large wooden storage box which he used as a bench.

"Don't worry, Mr. Laroche is riding to Aigre, which is much further than Rouillac. He'll be spending the afternoon there. Now, let me see your leg."

"There really is no need," she protested lamely.

"Horses play up when I try to tend to them, so I expect you to be more sensible than that, Elizabeth."

Overruled, she slowly raised her skirt, revealing a calf clad in a beige wool stocking. Justin knelt down and examined it.

"What a vicious brute!" he said between his teeth. "You're cut—it's been bleeding. I have a very good ointment, but you'll have to take your stocking down. I'll bandage it up afterwards."

"Then turn around or close your eyes," she demanded.

He obeyed, and she stared at his regular features, well-defined mouth and high cheekbones.

"You can look now," she said, troubled at having to reveal part of her body.

Justin had a closer look at the open wound. It was starting to heal, but the skin was inflamed all around. He was about to go and get the ointment, when he realized he had Elizabeth's pearly white knee in his hand. Without thinking, he gave it a gentle kiss.

"I'm so sorry—I shouldn't have done that!"

"It was nice, don't apologize."

She moved closer to him, hoping for another kiss, on her lips this time. But he had already jumped up and was scouring the cupboard.

"I think it would be better if you put the ointment on yourself," he said. "Here's a strip of gauze, for the bandage."

Elizabeth was succumbing to her female instinct, which had been awakened by Richard. She longed to feel his touch and his kisses.

"What are you so afraid of?" she asked, in a changed voice. "I'd rather *you* did it, Justin. I even go to bed early so I can meet you here at dawn. We get on so well together."

He backed away, shaking his head. She sighed and spread the herbal balm on top of the cut.

"Don't be angry with me, Miss. I promised myself I wouldn't come near you, or at least not in this way. It's hard enough having to cope with my aunt's lies. If I fell in love with you, I would be so unhappy that I would have to leave."

"Are you not calling me Elizabeth anymore?"

"That was a mistake. Young ladies like you should be shown respect. If I had you in my arms, I would want to carry you up into my room."

"And do to me what you're doing with Mariette?"

"Jesus! Who told you that?"

Elizabeth wrapped the bandage around her calf. She skilfully secured it and pulled up her stocking.

"Madeleine has been going to great lengths to win over my governess. I had lunch with Bonnie, and she mentioned that Mariette had gained your affections. Apparently you proposed to her, if what your aunt says is true."

Panic-stricken, Justin seized the opportunity to put up an impenetrable barrier between Elizabeth and himself.

"Yes, it's true. I have a sense of duty. I would of course do the honourable thing and marry Mariette, should she be expecting my child. Of course, the wedding might have to take place after my five-year term of national service, as my number might come up next year. But anyway, let me saddle up Pearl. Don't forget what I taught you: if she gallops, give her some rein so she doesn't lean on the bit."

"Five years," repeated Elizabeth, following closely behind him. "A lot can happen in five years."

"Be that as it may, have you told your grandmother you're going off riding?" Justin said in a stern voice. He did his best to avoid getting too close to her.

"Only Bonnie, and she won't say anything. Don't worry, if my grandfather notices I'm gone, I'll say you tried to prevent me from leaving, and that I lied to you. I will do whatever it takes to stop him from ousting you."

Elizabeth touched Justin's shoulders, then stood on tiptoe and tried to kiss him on the mouth. He turned away sharply.

"I asked you not to provoke me," he said.

"You sound like Richard Johnson," she muttered.

"Who's that?"

"A New York detective hired by my grandfather. He spent

years trying to find me. When he first approached me, I naturally assumed he liked me. But he lied to me too, like the Woolworths."

"And you provoked him?" asked Justin suspiciously.

"Apparently, just by looking at him!" replied the young girl with amusement and a touch of pride. "On New Year's Eve he kissed me."

"Is that all?"

"He also followed me on board the ship, where he kissed me again . . . but more eagerly. And I spotted him again on the platform at Orléans station."

Justin cursed under his breath. Enraged, he grabbed the side saddle and a bridle, and harnessed the mare, teeth still clenched.

"What's the matter?" asked Elizabeth. "Justin, you look upset! Bonnie kept saying I was in love with Richard, but she was mistaken. I was a little afraid of him—I feel more at ease with you."

"I don't want to hear any more! I understand now. In fact, you've been laughing at my expense—me, the poor stable hand!" he said sharply. "News travels fast in the countryside. An American has taken a room at the Pont-Neuf Inn—a handsome man, according to Mariette, who ran into him at the fair. Come clean: I suppose it's the famous Richard Johnson, and you're on your way to join him right now. You probably meet up with him in Montignac every time you go there with Mrs. Adela. She's probably in on your little secret, too."

Elizabeth was dumbstruck and astonished by Justin's accusations and reaction.

"I didn't know that Richard Johnson was staying here in Charente!" she said in amazement. "And it's completely absurd! I will inform my grandfather at once, and I forbid you to accuse my grandmother of anything. We spend a lot of time at the mill visiting my Grandpa Toine, my uncles, my little cousins and my aunt Yvonne. I don't believe you, and I'm so very disappointed. What would that detective be doing in this area? If he was hoping to see me again, I would have bumped into him already. He would surely have made his presence known."

Elizabeth's vociferous reaction raised doubts in Justin's mind. He took Pearl out of her stall and led her behind the building.

"At least you're no longer being too familiar with me," he said in one breath. "I only have to annoy you, and you immediately address me with more respect."

"Heavens above, you're so stupid!" she cried, on the verge of tears. "Help me up! I can't wait to get away from this place, and you!"

Justin grabbed her by the waist with a fierce sweep of his arm, pulling her against him for a moment, breathing in the sweet smell of verbena from her silky hair.

"Pardon me, I was wrong to accuse you," he muttered. "I can see you're telling the truth, Elizabeth. Just be careful."

He lifted her up a little and hoisted her into the saddle before checking the girth and the stirrups.

"I'll be waiting for you tonight at the crossroads between Vouharte and Guerville," he said quietly. "Talion needs exercising—Mr. Laroche hardly ever takes him out these days. The journey will seem shorter on horseback than in a carriage, so do keep an eye on the time."

"Thank you, Justin. You should know I don't hold it against you. I can see now that you're jealous."

She had read enough novels to recognize the signs. Despite her grandfather's violent outburst that morning and her argument with Justin, she felt light-headed and a touch exhilarated. The springtime wind smelled of freedom.

From the kitchen window that overlooked the inner courtyard, Madeleine saw Elizabeth disappear. She gave a sly grin. Over the years, hatred had been consuming her devious mind, whetting her thirst for power.

"You want power!" Vincent used to say when she told him what she was stealing. "Poor old Madeleine—you'll only ever be a servant, grovelling at your boss's boots! You can say what you like, but no one will believe your nonsense."

Reminiscing about her former lover, she nodded with satisfaction.

At least I won't have to listen to that stupid layabout anymore, she thought to herself. *Damn it, I tried to get him away from here. He didn't want to leave, but that's too bad for him. And that stuck-up little Madam—she'd better not get in my way!*

Madeleine relished the thought of the harm she would cause Elizabeth. She had just concocted a wicked plan.

Germaine, who lived in fear of Madeleine, entered and called out faintly:

"Madam rang the bell—didn't you hear?"

The young girl agreed to all of Madeleine's whims, which included addressing her formally, in keeping with her role as housekeeper.

"So? Go upstairs and find out what she wants!" she barked. "Can't you see I'm busy!"

Just fourteen years old, good-natured and willing to please, Germaine was easy to exploit. She smoothed her little white apron with the flat of her hand and dashed off. However, she soon found out it was Madeleine whom Adela had rung for.

That old hag! thought Germaine. *If I were to tell Madam about all the things that disappear and end up in the guardroom …*

But she knew perfectly well that she wouldn't—she was terrified of what the dreadful harridan would do to her. Madeleine had threatened the young chambermaid, telling her that curses would befall her entire family. Germaine was superstitious and didn't dare step out of line.

Montignac
The same day, one hour later

The village of Montignac was bustling early in the afternoon. Since her return to France, Elizabeth had only been there once before, accompanied by her grandmother, her aunt Yvonne and Bonnie.

We had a fun time at the fair and almost bought some turtledoves for the castle's aviary, she recalled. *Maybe Richard was there too, spying on us.*

She guided her mare among the passers-by and carts, most of which were drawn by mules. By chance, she ran into her uncle Jean, who was pushing a wheelbarrow full of sacks of flour.

"Well, look who it is! I hadn't expected to see you today," he exclaimed. "Are you on your own? I didn't know you could ride!"

He seemed displeased and forced a smile. Elizabeth was quick to reply:

"This is my first outing by myself, Uncle Jean. I have a letter to post, then I'll stop by at the mill to say hello to Pops Toine."

"I'll be back after you, then. You'd be better off on foot—your horse could get spooked."

"Don't worry, my mare is very docile—nothing scares her. I'll see you later, Uncle Jean!"

He continued on his way after mumbling a hesitant "Yes." Elizabeth finally saw the sign of the Pont-Neuf Inn, on the banks of the river, where a porch led into a paved courtyard. A stable hand rushed to grab Pearl's reins.

"I'll take care of her, Miss," he said attentively.

"I wish to take some refreshment here. Can I enter the building without going through the street?"

"Certainly, Miss. There's a passageway for guests who leave their carriages in the barn."

"In fact, you might be able to give me some information. I would like to pay a visit to the American gentleman who is staying here. I'm from New York myself."

"Ah, I would never have believed it," stammered the boy, aged about fifteen. "I don't have a clue where America is. The gentleman is in room 4, on the right on the landing. He wanted a river view."

"Thank you," Elizabeth said kindly, relieved she had brought some change with her. She left the young valet a good tip. The boy repeated "At your service" three times, while leading the mare away.

When Elizabeth finally stood in front of room number 4, she started having second thoughts, but plucked up her courage and gave two quick knocks. She thrived on adventure and the unexpected—a dimension of her personality the Woolworths had tried to suppress by wrapping her in cotton wool.

Richard Johnson opened, not bothering to ask who was there. When he recognized her, he was so stunned, she had to contain her delight.

"Lisbeth! You came! God, I was right to hope! Come in, please."

"I'm only here to ask a few questions, so don't start rejoicing. What are you doing in France—or rather, in Montignac?"

Richard closed the door behind them. Elizabeth felt jittery at seeing him again. She turned her back to him, pretending to look at the room's decor.

He's so tall, and his eyes are pure amber. I'd forgotten just how attractive he is, she admitted to herself. *And he looks even better in that white shirt, with an open collar and no tie.*

"Lisbeth, in all sincerity, I was convinced that when the weather got better, you would come."

"But . . . but you speak French! With a frightful American accent, certainly, but it is French!" she shouted furiously. "I didn't even realize at first. One more thing you lied to me about!"

"I only speak a little. I'm practising my French here, Lisbeth—I learnt it at school and am trying to improve my skills. It's not easy—the locals have an odd way of talking, 'odd' being the operative word."

"I suppose you mean the local *patois*," she grinned. "That way, they're confident you won't understand a word."

"*Patois*? What's that?"

"The local dialect of this region. Richard, I'm asking you again: what are you doing here? And why were you on the ship? My grandfather said he didn't owe you any money and didn't even want to meet you. I also saw you at Orléans station, and now you've taken a room in the village where I was born!"

Richard walked to the window overlooking the river. Leaning over the wrought-iron railing, he stared at a barge that was moored in the shade of a willow tree.

Elizabeth walked around a table strewn with paper and books. She was hot, and unbuttoned her jacket. Richard did an about-turn.

"Would you like a cup of tea? I ordered some ten minutes ago, as the coffee in France tastes quite disgusting."

"Gladly," she muttered. "But you still haven't answered my question."

Johnson raised his arms in the air, clearly embarrassed. He then reverted to English, to express himself with greater conviction.

"What if I told you I was working, Lisbeth? No, I didn't come to Charente for your beautiful blue eyes, even if they do haunt me—like your smile and your kisses."

She sat down, feeling nostalgic upon hearing the language of New York City, which conjured up Maybel's soft, melodious voice.

"Who do you work for?" she asked. "And don't say my grandfather—I wouldn't believe you."

"I'm in a very awkward position, Lisbeth. I feel like a ball thrown back and forth by the rich. The only positive thing is that I'm only a few miles away from you now."

He served her some tea that was over-brewed for her liking. Elizabeth was annoyed at herself for being so pleased to see him. It was proof that he still had power over her. She tried to appear cold, hostile and suspicious, but her body told her otherwise, as she quivered at the thought of his hands caressing her in the cabin of the liner.

"I agreed to keep an eye on you and was well paid by Edward Woolworth in return," he admitted. "He came to see me at the agency a few days before you left for France. The man absolutely adores you, Lisbeth. He didn't trust Mr. Laroche. Mrs. Woolworth agreed with him—she was worried sick."

"Dad did that?" she murmured, shocked at first, then touched that they thought so much of her. "And may I ask how, exactly, are you keeping an eye on me, locked up in this inn?"

Richard sipped his cup of tea with a mischievous smile on his face. He replied in French:

"I've already sent them three letters, telling them about your various occupations. I haven't even had to set foot on the castle grounds. There's no need, as there are enough people here to keep me informed."

"Like who? I hope you haven't asked my father's family, the Duquesnes?"

"I'm under strict orders not to bother either the Laroches or the Duquesnes, and it goes without saying that I must keep a low profile. The blacksmith who shoes your grandfather's horses lives on the other side of the bridge. He told me that you were learning to ride, and that you were 'not stuck up' and 'very pretty'. I sometimes see your grandmother's carriage on its way to the mill or in the village, and you snuggled up beside her. Then I spotted you and Bonnie on the day of the fair last month. The Woolworths reply to me by telegram after receiving my letters."

Taken aback by his gabbling, Elizabeth told him to stop. But he carried on, looking worried all of a sudden:

"How did you know where to find me, Lisbeth? You weren't supposed to know that I'm in Charente."

"News travels from one village to another," she retorted. "People inform me too! My friend Justin told me that you were staying at this inn. He found out through my grandmother's laundry maid, Mariette. I had planned to visit my Pops Toine, but instead I used the opportunity to find out if this rumour was true."

"Your 'Pops Toine'?" he repeated, looking puzzled.

"Yes, that's what I called him as a child, and it still pleases him. Richard, you're wasting your time here. I advise you to return to New York. I don't want to be a financial burden on Dad—I mean, Mr. Woolworth. I've written to them too, saying I'm not in any danger. There's no need for you to be here."

Elizabeth stood up and buttoned up her jacket. Her pretty face had lost some of its sparkle and she glanced anxiously out the window.

"What's the matter, Lisbeth, darling?"

"Nothing—and I forbid you to call me 'darling'! It's inappropriate."

"Can I call you 'my dear Lisbeth', then?"

"No, you can't. In France, I'm known as 'Elizabeth'. Goodbye—I won't be coming back. Your mission makes my skin crawl. I loathe the idea of being watched and spied on."

But Richard quickly took her by the waist with one hand, cupping her chin with the other.

"You're different, even more beautiful, more irresistible," he whispered in English.

The young girl's heart was pounding. When Richard pressed his mouth on hers, she closed her eyes and abandoned herself to the kisses her body hungered for. Their lips joined together in subtle and intoxicating harmony.

Elizabeth burned with desire that confused her. Voluptuous waves of pleasure swept over her as he stroked her breasts and hips with rough movements. Her submission, her gasps, her intense sensuality were driving Johnson wild with desire.

Despite the shame he felt at what had happened in his cabin on board *La Touraine*, he was unable to contain himself. He lifted her up and carried her onto his bed. She didn't react and closed her eyes, knowing with trepidation that this was it: Richard was undoubtedly going to make her a woman.

"Darling, my darling," he whispered in English. "I love you—don't you know? I love you!"

On opening her eyes, Elizabeth saw him undo his belt and drop his trousers. He then crashed down beside her, pushing up her skirt and thrusting his hand between her thighs.

"Lisbeth, my beauty, my precious love," he moaned in her ear.

His breathing got harder and harder as his fingers ripped off the tiny mother-of-pearl buttons of her calico undergarments. He let out a hoarse cry upon feeling her warm, moist flesh.

Once again, Elizabeth tried to resist Johnson and gain control of her submissive body. This wasn't love—she was simply unable to resist the power he had over her body.

"No, get off me!" she cried. "I don't want to!"

"Why?" he asked, surprised. "I love you so much, Lisbeth."

"Well, I don't love you!"

In her mind's eye, she could see Justin's blond hair, as he shyly kissed her on the knee. The young woman quickly got up and ran to the other side of the room.

"I don't want to, and I can't!" she shrieked.

Richard was breathing heavily in the middle of the bed, resting on one elbow.

"You won't, because wealthy young ladies don't do such things, but one day you'll be mine, and all mine. You won't escape me, Lisbeth—I *will* marry you."

Richard was frustrated at being within seconds of such all-consuming pleasure. Elizabeth opened the door. She wanted to punish him for the hold he had over her.

"Don't tell anyone what just happened between us when you report to Edward Woolworth, Mr. Johnson. If you do, you risk losing a lot of money. Goodbye."

He was incapable of answering or detaining her.

15

Heartache

The Duquesnes' mill
The same day, Friday, March 12, 1897

Elizabeth contemplated the still waters of the river before entering the mill yard. She listened fondly to the sound of the run-off from the big paddle wheel, as it plunged into the current with a dull moaning sound.

Her words to Richard, "I am not in any danger", were haunting her. Extremely intuitive, she sensed that they didn't ring true. Something she couldn't put her finger on did pose a danger.

Worried, she headed for the barn, where she tied up her horse, not bothering to unsaddle it. The place seemed deserted, which only added to her disquiet. And yet, she found her grandfather sitting by the fireplace, as usual.

It was the first time she had visited without Adela, and he looked up in surprise.

"Hey! Hello, my little one! Are you on your own? Have you learned to drive the carriage?"

Elizabeth kissed him affectionately before replying.

"Pierre has gone to Angoulême, so he's not here to help you with the carriage. And Jean is out delivering flour," he said, looking concerned.

"Don't worry, I managed just fine, Pops Toine. I came on horseback, and I even galloped Pearl down the path that runs along the river."

"They let you come all this way by yourself?"

The miller's bright-blue eyes gave away his concern, but Elizabeth didn't notice, as she was scanning the decor around her, delighted to be reunited with the unassuming dark wooden furniture, the charred beams and the onion and garlic plaits hanging from nails.

"I would love to live here with you," she sighed. "Or in my parents' little house."

"*Your* house," he corrected her. "It's all yours—I've made the necessary arrangements with the solicitor. Tell me, little one, are you unhappy at the castle? And how come they let you travel about eight miles without a chaperone?"

She sat on a stool near the hearth, where a large oak log and a stump of ash were burning. Her grandfather always prepared soups and stews on the embers, using four iron tripods of different sizes and many cast-iron pots.

"It would be a lot easier for you if you had a wood-burning stove, Pops Toine," she commented. "That way, you wouldn't have to bend over all the time, which doesn't do your legs and back any good."

"Yvonne calls in every day to cook for me," he replied. "But you still haven't answered me, little one!"

"There's nothing particularly wrong at the castle. Grandma is extremely loving and tender towards me, and Bonnie keeps me company in the evening. I don't want for anything, but I still think I would be happier here."

"Why?" he insisted, taking her hands.

"I recapture my childhood when I'm here with all of you. It makes me feel safe."

She immediately regretted her words upon seeing her grandfather's gentle face tense up.

"How silly of me to tell you all this, Pops Toine," she quickly added, trying to sound cheery. But she couldn't help herself and began to weep like a frightened little girl. The old miller took her hands in his.

"Tell me what's wrong, my little one."

"My grandfather Laroche scares me sometimes," she confessed, sniffing. "He hasn't changed a bit, whereas Grandma is a new woman, thanks to you. She even said it herself."

"Hugues Laroche has always terrorized everyone around him," replied Antoine Duquesne quietly. "Good heavens, it's nothing new—he was the same before he got married. Elizabeth, I hope he's not being heavy-handed with you?"

The girl was reluctant to tell him about the incident that morning. She knew she sometimes flew into rages herself, and thought she had inflamed the situation by refusing to obey Laroche.

"He's my legal guardian, therefore I'm supposed to respect him and behave appropriately," she said quietly.

"But to what extent, little one?"

Elizabeth didn't answer, and the old man remained silent. They then looked at each other in alarm, realizing they were afraid to speak the truth.

"He whipped me this morning, on my leg! I've never seen him so angry. Grandma was there, yet she didn't say anything. Justin intervened, so Grandpa struck him on the face too. It was all so violent and unexpected! He set out for a long ride this afternoon, so I seized the opportunity to go out riding after lunch, despite being forbidden to."

"Good God—I hope it doesn't start up again!" worried the miller.

Adela had had the same reaction earlier that day. Elizabeth was fraught. Shaking with nervousness, she started walking around the table.

"Grandma said the same thing when I told her Grandfather had gone out, but she lied when I asked her what she meant by it. You must tell me the truth: what mustn't start up again?"

"God forgive me for breaking a promise made twenty years ago! But you have a right to know the truth, Elizabeth, my little one. I could die at any moment, and then there would be no one to warn you anymore. Your uncles don't know about it."

"Know what?" she pleaded.

"Come and sit down—I'll feel braver if I'm holding your hand. I hope Catherine up in heaven will know that I had no choice."

Antoine Duquesne was very pale. He looked embarrassed and kept sighing, as if he was carrying a heavy burden.

"Your mother frequently resisted her father, from the time she left boarding school, when she was your age. It was the year in which she turned eighteen—that December, to be precise—but they gave her her present in the summer: a superb bay mare, a thoroughbred. Catherine was a natural rider and was absolutely thrilled to have her own horse. She used to gallop across the tracks and fields in all weathers. I'm not going to talk about her political views—you must have gathered that she just wanted to lead a simple life, based on moral values such as sharing, humility and kindness."

"I guess so—otherwise she wouldn't have married Daddy, and they wouldn't have travelled to America as humble immigrants," she replied.

"I learned all this when your mother and father were living in Montignac, little one. Guillaume was so in awe of Catherine that he shared some secrets with me about what she had endured at the castle. Later, your mother told me about it herself, and I promised her I would never tell anyone, especially not you."

"But why?"

"She wanted to protect her father's reputation. He had apologized for his violence and begged for forgiveness."

Elizabeth hesitated, suddenly afraid to hear about her mother's dark past.

Antoine Duquesne had always been a devout and kind man of a calm disposition. He considered acts of anger or brutality as offensive and blasphemous.

"I suspect that my other grandfather used to hit Mummy when she didn't do as he ordered?" she said.

"If only it were merely that, my little one! As I told you, Hugues Laroche couldn't bear to be opposed. But above all, he feared losing Catherine, should she get married. He got it into his head to accompany her when she went out on horseback. If there was a ball, he would insist on having every dance with her, no suitor being to his liking. And then Adela had the idea of buying her daughter a riding outfit in green velvet for her eighteenth birthday. Your mother only wore it once, in the spring. According to her, the colour matched her eyes and marked a new start."

"Yes, Bonnie and I found it at the bottom of her wardrobe in a box. It still looks like new."

"Alas, she had the wild idea of setting out alone on horse-back, to visit a boarding-school friend who lived in Rouillac," continued the miller in a hoarse voice. "And all hell broke loose when she returned. Her father was lying in wait for her. He grabbed her horse by its reins, then knocked Catherine to the ground. The groom at that time, a certain Macaire, approached with Laroche's shotgun in his hand. He shot the poor innocent beast before your mother's very eyes. Catherine was speechless with horror, but a few seconds later, her father struck her savagely with his whip."

Elizabeth started to feel dizzy. She dried her forehead, which was covered in beads of sweat.

"This is just abominable, Pops Toine! Now I understand Mummy's fears better! Do you remember me telling you that I met Daddy's friend in New York, Baptiste Rambert? As I announced my plan to return to France, he told me something peculiar which I didn't give much thought to at the time. On her death bed, Mummy apparently made my father promise never to hand me over to my grandparents Laroche. She said I would be very unhappy at the castle."

"And she was right, little one! You don't seem happy, despite all your efforts to make us believe you are. Old fool that I am, I thought that Hugues Laroche would mellow with age and would no longer suffer the same torments as before."

"What torments?" she asked impatiently. "Explain it to me, Pops Toine! Jean will be back any minute, and we won't be able to discuss it then. I also have to return—Justin will be waiting for me at the crossroads between Vouharte and Guerville."

Antoine Duquesne raised his arms up in the air. He glanced at his granddaughter, whose beauty and innocence wrenched his heart.

"Hugues Laroche loved his daughter too much, little one—in a way that you shouldn't love your own flesh and blood. That's it—I said it! And I hope to God that he won't start loving you in this way, and depriving you of your freedom, by abusing his guardianship rights, consumed by jealousy.

"He could have killed your mother when she announced she was marrying Guillaume. But she was of age, and he couldn't stop her. Don't forget that Catherine fled the castle a week before the wedding, and we took her in. Laroche came here with Macaire and threatened us with the most dreadful things, but I didn't give in to his intimidation. After that, he never set foot in Montignac again.

"You must have been about three years old when the situation was resolved. They made up, and your mother forgave him. It came as no surprise to me that my son wanted them to go and live in America."

"Or that Mummy was determined to travel across the ocean to finally be free—really free," added Elizabeth, shocked. "Pops Toine, what should I do now?"

"Be wary of this man until you reach the age of majority, little one. Keep your distance, don't defy him, and spend most of your time with your grandmother. Adela suffered bitterly with all this in the past, so she will protect you."

"I'm not so sure about that. This morning, she didn't say anything in my defence—but Bonnie and Justin will look out for me."

"Justin, yes, he's a good person, but . . ."

He stopped talking when Jean arrived, holding up a fine brioche with a golden crust.

"A present from the baker," he laughed. "Elizabeth, taste this for me! It's made with butter and duck eggs. I've brought you some milk too, Dad."

Jean's big smile, his bright grey eyes and the black lock of hair on his forehead, made the young girl want to cry. Out of her two uncles, he was the one who looked most like Guillaume.

"I'm not hungry, but I'll have some to please you, Uncle Jean," she said, her throat in knots. "You should have some too, Pops Toine—it looks delicious."

Elizabeth learned nothing more that day. She got back to the castle before Hugues Laroche, and was aloof and uncommunicative with Justin, though she did meet him, as agreed. She let him take care of Pearl, pretending she had a terrible migraine. When Madeleine sneaked up on her on the first-floor landing, she brushed her aside with annoyance.

A little later, she locked herself in her room, instructing Bonnie to tell Adela that she would not be having dinner.

"Get some rest, Miss," advised her governess, bringing her tea and biscuits. "You've put me in a tricky position, you know. I told them you were here all afternoon, and then you waltz in through the main hall dressed in your riding outfit! Your grandfather will know you disobeyed him."

"I don't care, Bonnie," replied Elizabeth, propped against her pillows with a soft quilt pulled up to her chest. "I'm not scared of him."

Her voice was trembling. She suddenly burst into tears, throwing herself into Bonnie's arms.

Guerville Castle
The same day, evening

Madeleine was waiting impatiently behind the kitchen window for Hugues Laroche to return. She didn't want to miss the return of her "master", as she referred to him in front of the other servants, but whom she secretly called "the devil" when thinking of his heavy-handedness and brutality.

Until Justin comes in for his supper, I know the devil isn't back yet! she thought. *Of course, Sir's groom must stand to attention waiting for him, whatever the weather. But it's going to change—yes, it's all going to change!*

She finally heard the sound of hooves in the courtyard. Lurking behind the curtain, she peered at the rider. His back was straight and his head was held high. The park had a dark bluish tinge to it in the dusk, and Justin was walking to meet Hugues Laroche, a lantern in his hand.

"The boss isn't going to be happy!" she sniggered, exhilarated at the thought of causing harm to Elizabeth.

Germaine—busy cleaning radishes and lettuces—glanced, worried, at old Leandre, who was already at the table. The gardener was stuffing his pipe, exhausted by his day and indifferent to the rest of the world.

Alcide was stacking logs near the colossal wood stove.

"Don't move, any of you!" ordered Madeleine. "I have some business to attend to. Germaine, plate up for us."

Laroche entered the former Romanesque hall, which had been converted into a grand entrance hall. He took off his felt hat, adorned with a pheasant feather, and removed his jacket. The squire felt relaxed, after a few glasses of cognac, a game of cards he had won, and an hour in good company. He winced with annoyance when he saw Madeleine emerging through a narrow door leading from the pantry.

"What do you want?" he barked.

"I need to talk to you, Sir."

"If it's about household or domestic concerns, speak to Madam."

"Poor Madam hasn't left her room, thank goodness," whined Madeleine.

"Why 'thank goodness'?" asked Laroche, frowning.

"Well, some things are best not seen, given Madam's fragile state! But I feel duty-bound to tell you, Sir."

Irritated, he gave up the nice prospect of a last drink in his leather armchair by the fireplace in the drawing room. Madeleine couldn't wait to inject her venom.

"It's about Miss Elizabeth, Sir. You were barely gone when she sneaked off on her horse. She came back just under an hour ago, and in a right state."

Hugues Laroche did not shout or display any anger. He felt his whole body tense up.

"I assume Justin helped or accompanied her, then?" he said quietly.

"Oh no, Sir—your groom was here the whole time, as Mariette was hanging around, you see."

"All right—thank you, Madeleine. Now get out of my sight! I loathe snitchers."

"But, Sir . . . I was trying to help."

He gestured to her to move back, as he couldn't bear to look at her; she disgusted him. As soon as he was alone, he grabbed a wicker stick from the bottom of the coat rack.

Elizabeth was pretending to read a fashion magazine, sitting on her bed, while Bonnie feigned embroidering a place mat. One was thinking about what had happened in the inn, blushing slightly under her serious demeanour; the other was thinking of Jean Duquesne, who had given her a guided tour of the mill earlier that day.

Violent knocking on the door startled them both. The ornate copper handle was turning in vain.

"Elizabeth, open up immediately!" shouted Hugues Laroche. "I forbid you to lock yourself in!"

Bonnie looked alarmed, and Elizabeth nodded to her to open the door.

"Miss, your grandfather seems furious, probably because you went out!"

"If so, then I'll explain to him why I left."

Trembling, Bonnie opened the door. As she stood in the doorway, the squire grabbed her by the elbow and pushed her into the hallway.

"We don't need you!" he spouted viciously. "Damn Americans!"

He closed the door behind him and turned the key again, to Bonnie's great despair, as she had noticed the wicker stick.

"Good evening, Grandpa," said Elizabeth, appearing very calm. "I would ask you in future not to push Bonnie, who is first and foremost my friend and does not deserve to be insulted.

What do you intend to do with this stick? Punish me for having gone to seek a little affection from my Grandpa Antoine, a pious and gentle man?"

Dumbfounded, Laroche lost his composure. It was not so much his granddaughter's tongue-in-cheek tone that bothered him, but the scene in front of him. He had never seen her hair loose before, hanging down like a silky brown curtain of soft waves. She was dressed in her pink nightgown with a very fine woollen shawl draped over her small shoulders, revealing her adolescent breasts.

He could feel his old demons stirring in the pit of his stomach, and his mouth turned dry. He wanted to smash the two large oil lamps arranged on the bedside tables, to shield his eyes from his granddaughter's beauty.

"You had every right, after all," he muttered. "I'm sorry I hit you this morning. You were angry with me, so you decided to disobey me. It's fair game."

She looked at him attentively, feeling helpless. Then she thought of Justin.

"I may not be as good a rider as my mother, but I saddled my horse myself and I really enjoyed the ride. Pearl gallops beautifully."

He turned his back to her without answering. Still suspicious, she added: "Who told you I went out riding? Probably that harridan Madeleine? I ran into her when I got back."

"Your grandmother and I trust her implicitly."

Elizabeth chuckled derisively. Laroche threw her a quick glance.

"What's amusing you?"

"Your misplaced trust, that's all."

"Discuss such topics with my wife. I don't get involved with the servants—not if I can avoid it. And in future, please ask me first, if you envisage riding to Montignac. The paths are not safe. Justin will go with you, providing you don't have a penchant for commoners. That said, I can't imagine my groom would betray me."

"A penchant for commoners!" repeated Elizabeth. "You mean, like my mother? She loved Daddy more than anything. She was right to run away, to marry him."

Things probably wouldn't have escalated if Hugues Laroche hadn't discredited Guillaume Duquesne. He'd already been regretting it when Elizabeth hurled her scathing reply at him.

"Catherine did not run away!" he protested. "Who told you such nonsense?"

"It doesn't matter!" she said angrily. "But I won't allow you to do that to me, I warn you. I'll marry whomever I want."

Her grandfather's fingers tightened around the wicker stick, with which he trained his hunting dogs. He wished he were face to face with old Duquesne, to give him a few lashings in the face, as it was obviously he who had told Elizabeth what had happened between him and Catherine.

"I have been lenient with you," he whispered between his teeth. "You are very ungrateful. Let's leave it there for tonight."

He was determined not to look at her. She saw him turn the key and leave the room.

He's running away from me, like a scared little dog! she thought.

As soon as he got into the hallway, Hugues Laroche encountered Adela and Bonnie, both looking extremely anxious. His wife was holding a copper oil lamp, its flame barely diffusing any light.

"So you're spying on me now?!" he shouted. "I didn't do anything, damn it—I didn't hit her! By golly, she's feisty, that one! For a second, I could have sworn I was looking at Catherine again."

"And that's what terrifies me, Hugues," murmured Adela before walking away on faltering legs.

As for Bonnie, she rushed into the room and sat on the edge of Elizabeth's bed.

"What happened?!" she exclaimed. "I alerted your grandmother and she was ready to intervene."

"You shouldn't have troubled Grandma," Elizabeth retorted. "I need to be able to stand up for myself for another four years, until I become an adult. I certainly would have preferred to have one of my uncles, or Grandpa Toine, as my guardian ... Just *why* do I have to depend on Grandpa?"

"I don't know, Miss."

"He must have gone to see his solicitor as soon as he learned of my return, and paid him a hefty fee. He thinks he can buy his way to anything, Bonnie," Elizabeth sighed.

Bonnie took her hand. She was struggling to recognize her little Lisbeth from New York.

"Don't be sad. We're here to make your life easier," she pleaded. "Your grandmother Adela, your family at Montignac, and me! After all, I did follow you to France."

"I know that, Bonnie. In the meantime, I'm going to tell you a secret—you will know who I'm alluding to."

In hushed tones, Elizabeth told her that Richard Johnson was staying at the Pont-Neuf Inn, relating in detail what the seductive American's new job involved. Of course, she was careful not to disclose that they had kissed and what had nearly happened afterwards.

Bonnie was stunned and her heartfelt thoughts went to Maybel and Edward Woolworth, before she announced rather abruptly:

"You won't be meeting Mr. Johnson again without a chaperone, Miss. If you need to speak to him, I'll come with you."

"Gladly, Bonnie—I would like Grandma to come along, too. We will go on Monday. Justin will hitch up the carriage, and we can have tea at the mill."

Elizabeth kissed her governess on the cheek, smiling. For no specific reason, she suddenly felt a surge of confidence.

The Dakota Building, New York
Five months later: Wednesday, August 18, 1897

That evening, Maybel Woolworth rushed to greet her husband as soon as he got in the door. She was wearing just a purple silk negligee because it was so hot. The sunset's orange glow filtered through the muslin curtains of the living room's windows.

"You look gorgeous," exclaimed Edward, holding his jacket. "It's a real furnace out there. Why are you so cheery, darling? Would it be a letter from Lisbeth?"

"Yes, it is! It arrived this morning, but I wanted to wait for you before opening it."

Maybel had shed many tears after Elizabeth left, and the more time went by, the sadder she became, until finally slipping into a depression. Dr. Foster was worried and had prescribed his usual remedy: laudanum. Edward would get home to find his wife in a drowsy state, and more often than not lying down in Elizabeth's room.

Saddened by this, the trader had endeavoured to spend more time with his wife. Her zest for life had been slowly returning ever since she began receiving letters from France.

"The bond is not severed, darling," she had sighed. "Lisbeth is thinking about us."

They had become accustomed to reading Elizabeth's long letters together. It was a moment of shared joy, which left them in awe, imagining the places and events she wrote about in her expressive and lively manner.

"She hasn't written for the last month and that has made you ill," said the trader sadly. "It's a thick envelope—maybe she has sent us photos."

He removed his tie and unbuttoned his shirt collar. Restless and excited, Maybel served him a glass of lemonade.

"I told Norma to take the evening off—I wanted to be alone with you," she said, in a coaxing tone.

"I don't think you like her, do you?" laughed her husband.

Since Bonnie's departure, the couple had changed maids three times. Maybel had been using the service offered to Dakota Building residents, which provided qualified maids and cooks.

Edward had nevertheless insisted they hire a new live-in maid. He knew how lonely his wife felt when he was away. Before Norma, there was a tall blonde girl from Kansas, and before her Dorothy, and before her Shirley. None of them were to Maybel's liking.

"Hurry up and sit down," she begged, her auburn hair in a soft bun, her bathrobe showing off her shapely figure. "I can't wait much longer—I'm opening the envelope."

He watched her as she opened it, using a vermeil letter opener with an engraved ivory handle.

As soon as she took out the folded sheets of paper, some prints appeared.

"You were right, Lisbeth has sent us pictures!" she cried. "I'll set them aside, we'll look at them later."

"Do as you like, Maybel," the trader replied, stroking her thigh.

"Behave yourself!" she protested, though her eyes were saying the opposite. "Oh! Edward, Lisbeth is calling us Mom and Dad! I was always worried she would become more and more distant with us . . ."

"Read it, honey—cut the suspense."

Maybel took a deep breath, a bedazzled expression on her face, and finally read out aloud:

Dear Mom and Dad

I'm sorry it has taken me so long to write to you, but I was worried about Grandma Adela's health. I spent days and nights at her bedside. Bonnie and I were very frightened, as my dear grandmother became ill so suddenly at the end of June that the doctor said she had been poisoned. This was a distinct possibility, since mushrooms had been on the menu several times. It rained a lot in June, so Leandre, the gardener, was able to gather wild mushrooms. Strangely enough, Grandpa, Bonnie and I were not ill.

Maybel became silent for a moment. She was pale and looked at Edward in shock.

"How stupid of them to eat mushrooms! Lisbeth could have been poisoned too."

"The French do have odd tastes, darling."

"Oh yes, they eat snails too!" she exclaimed. "I'll continue."

Unfortunately, Grandma got weaker and weaker and had to stay in bed. She has lost a lot of weight and is a pitiful sight. I realized how much I loved her when I understood I could lose her. I cared for her as best I could, with the help of our dear Bonnie, an expert in herbal remedies.

Those sad days when we feared we would lose her erased the joy I had felt at the celebratory ball given for my seventeenth birthday on April 22. I am enclosing some pictures taken on this occasion by a photographer from Rouillac. I have noted the first names of the people on the back, most of whom I have already written to you about.

Grandpa was deeply affected by his wife's illness. In a letter I wrote to you in the spring, I told you about a serious argument we'd had. Everything was later resolved, thanks to Richard Johnson's advice. I am taking great delight in writing to you again, though I had to threaten Grandpa with changing my legal guardian, to get more freedom and not have to obey his every instruction.

Maybel's lips curled with a slight smile. She placed the letter on the pedestal table. Edward pulled her to him.

"You were right to send that detective there," she said. "He's proved to be both smart and very effective."

"And I believe I was right to. Laroche is violent and a bully," said the trader with anger. "I'm convinced that Lisbeth hasn't told us the whole truth about him."

The couple exchanged a kiss. Elizabeth's departure had brought them closer together and rekindled their passion.

Maybel took a sip of lemonade before continuing to read:

I am dividing my time between the castle and the mill, due to Grandma's ill state of health.

My Grandpa Toine is also very worried about Adela and I am eager to give him some news.

Thanks to Justin, the young man I keep telling you about, I am now an experienced rider and know how to drive the carriage.

On a lighter note, you still haven't told me what your niece said about my horse bearing her name. Please, if you haven't yet done so, tell her and let me know how she reacts.

"I remember it well—Pearl was outraged!" recalled Maybel, laughing. "Your brother too. I'll reply to Lisbeth tomorrow, and this time I'll tell her how indignant her cousin was. Edward darling, I would so love to see our daughter again! She's been living apart from us for almost eight months now."

"I'd take you to France right away if we were invited, Maybel. But Laroche is furious at us. Have you forgotten the accusations he put in his letter we received in February, and how he threatened to sue us?"

"We could stay with the Duquesnes, or in a guest house," she begged. "Please, I miss Lisbeth."

"One day we will—just be patient!" he sighed.

Reassured, Maybel read a little faster, in her haste to look at the photographs:

What else can I tell you? The castle grounds are is an enchanting sight in summer. Bonnie and I go for strolls, and I pick flowers to brighten my grandmother's room. I have a little secret for you: Bonnie and my youngest uncle Jean, who is the spitting image of my father, have become very good friends, and I have a hunch they are quite fond of each other. I dare not ask her about this because deep down, I'm afraid of losing her, should she decide to get married.

That's selfish of me, as she would become part of my family, and I feel ashamed for even contemplating coming between her and her happiness.

Everything would be different if I were an adult: I could live in my parents' house and be near the mill. Alas! I must wait another four years or get married myself.

*These last few lines are going to cause you concern, for
which I apologize. Do not pay too much attention to them; I
have written candidly, according to my state of mind.*

*Before I sign off, Richard Johnson has asked me to inform
you of his plans. He wishes to spend the rest of the year in
Charente but refuses to do so at your expense. He really is a
character. I don't see him very often, but he was proud to
inform me that he had been hired by someone at the* prefecture *in the city of Angoulême. This is an ancient city built on
a rocky promontory. You would find it very picturesque.
Grandma has taken me there twice and we visited the Saint
Pierre cathedral and did a tour of the* remparts. *Someone's
calling me now—most likely Bonnie. Unfortunately, I will
have to close now.*

With much love to you both. I promise to write again soon.
Your Lisbeth

Edward took a look at the page, a little surprised at the abrupt
ending. Maybel looked disappointed.

"She hastened to finish—there's even a crossing out! We
don't know the exact date she wrote the letter, either—she didn't
put it in. I hope nothing serious has happened. Edward, you'll
have to explain some of these words to me, the ones she didn't
translate: *prefecture* and *remparts*!"

"I promise to give you a definition later, darling, but what
about the pictures?"

"Of course—the anecdote about Johnson made me forget
about them! I'm sure he's in love with Lisbeth, or he would
already have returned to New York."

"Or he may have fallen for the charms of a pretty French
maiden . . ."

"I'm disappointed, Edward. Everything in this letter
shocks me. Bonnie and Uncle Jean, Mrs. Laroche's illness,
and that Lisbeth thinks about getting married just to live
independently."

"They're just words. Calm down."

He reached for the photographs. On the first, Elizabeth was dressed in her riding outfit, sitting side saddle on her horse. She was holding herself very upright, looking proud.

"Good God, I barely recognize her," lamented Maybel.

Edward agreed. He studied the full-length portrait that followed with relief. Elizabeth, dressed in a splendid ball gown, was posing in the castle's large drawing room. A pretty twist of hair rested on her right shoulder, exposed by the bold neckline of a pearl-embroidered bodice. It accentuated her small waist, from which several muslin veils streamed out like a plant's corolla.

"What a beautiful outfit!" sighed Maybel. "It looks very French. Shame we don't know the colour. Could it be blue, or pink?"

"Ask her when you reply to her."

They spent a while studying this photograph in fascination. Although he didn't dare say so to his wife, Edward noticed an eerie anguish in Elizabeth's smiling eyes.

"My God, she's growing more beautiful every day . . ." mused Maybel.

The couple held each other tightly, then studied the third and final shot. It was a picture of Adela, Elizabeth and Bonnie. Justin, standing back from them, was holding the reins of a grey horse.

"If that's the groom, he's quite handsome," commented Edward. "You should double check he isn't a neighbour."

"No, that's definitely Justin—it says so on the back. Mrs. Laroche still looks quite young, though rather gaunt—especially compared to Bonnie, who seems to have gained weight. But Lisbeth looks happy in this one."

Maybel put the letter and photographs back into the envelope and placed it on the pedestal table. Overcome with emotion, she took refuge in her husband's arms.

"We won't ever see her again," she moaned. "I feel it, deep down. And Scarlett read it in my cards. Tarot cards reveal the future."

Scarlett Turner, a wealthy heiress and a friend of Maybel's sister-in-law Doris, was their new neighbour, who had bought an apartment on the top floor of the Dakota Building.

"I'm glad you enjoy Scarlett's company, but I wish you weren't so into tarot cards. I'm a strong advocate of logic, and there will most certainly be a way of seeing Lisbeth again. Stop torturing yourself. Our dear neighbour is having quite an influence on you with her cock-and-bull stories."

"Scarlett hasn't made anything up. She saw a figure in the third-floor hall—our hall. A fuzzy shape that passed through the wall. And she hears noises at night."

"Sheer nonsense—ghosts don't exist, honey."

He stopped talking, giving her a kiss and then another, more passionate one. Maybel was delighted and hurried to slip out of her negligee. Aroused by her nakedness, Edward stroked her breasts and the small of her back. The luxurious apartment was plunged in semi-darkness, emphasizing his wife's pearly body. He then removed his own clothes.

"I don't want to think any more," she breathed before kissing him.

"You must, Maybel. Think of us, just us!" urged Edward.

During one hour of crazy kissing and lovemaking, they forgot all about France, Guerville Castle and even their beloved child who had returned to her roots.

Guerville Castle
Thursday, August 19, 1897

It was six o'clock in the morning. Since Adela's illness, Madeleine made sure she was the only one who served her breakfast, not letting anyone else near her mistress at that time.

Hugues Laroche had moved back into their old room, to avoid disturbing his wife who slept a lot. Elizabeth and Bonnie were thus able to take turns at her bedside, making sure she ate her lunch and dinner.

A doctor from Angoulême, Dr. Trousset, was unable to give

a diagnosis from the symptoms described to him. He left saying she should get plenty of rest, drink chamomile infusions and eat a light diet.

Laroche was so distraught by his wife's state that everyone felt genuinely sorry for him.

"Grandma will recover, Grandpa," said Elizabeth reassuringly when they went for a short ride together. His granddaughter's words comforted him, and he thanked her with a faint smile.

Madeleine repeated much the same thing while pulling back the heavy red velvet curtains to brighten up the room.

"You'll recover in no time, Madam. I've prepared you a nice milky coffee, buttered toast and a boiled egg."

"How thoughtful you are, Madeleine!" sighed Adela. "The fresh eggs will do me good, I'm sure. I would so love to get up and enjoy the last of the summer."

The maid helped her to sit up, wedging two large pillows at her back. She then placed the tray, equipped with small removable feet, in front of her mistress. Emaciated and listless, Adela thanked her with a nod.

"It's my pleasure, Madam. It's about time you reclaimed your place at the castle," replied Madeleine. "Everything is much harder without you. I didn't want to say anything, but Sir even called me a snitch once. If you ask me, he doesn't see what's going on, right under his eyes."

"My husband? But you know him—he doesn't miss a thing!" Adela took two sips of coffee. It was far too sweet for her, so she put it back down.

"It's easy to say he doesn't miss a thing, but he has given free rein to Miss Elizabeth, and she's taking advantage of it. It shakes me up, to see what I see."

"Come out with it!" said Adela impatiently, ill at ease. "You don't usually hold back when you have something to say."

Madeleine turned away to hide her emotions. Reassured by her carefully worked-out plan, she made her first move.

"Your granddaughter is behaving badly with poor Justin, a

decent boy—everyone here agrees with me. She's chasing after him—you can ask old Leandre. The other night, I saw them kissing."

"What are you talking about? Elizabeth spends most of her time with me—she hasn't even been to Montignac in recent weeks. With Justin, did you say?"

"Sir must have noticed something, but he has nothing but praise for his groom."

"I'm not interested in gossip, Madeleine. Be a dear, and leave me alone to eat my egg."

But the maid dragged a chair up to the bed. She sat down, arms crossed, an arrogant look on her face.

"What are you doing, Madeleine? I told you to leave me alone."

"I can't, Madam, I have to say my piece!" replied the woman, suddenly turning green with rage. "The only reason I'm telling you about Justin and Elizabeth is because it would be very wrong for those two to . . . but the damage is probably done. It's about time you knew where he came from, that handsome blond boy . . . You should know, he is Sir's son. That's right—I know it must come as a shock, such news, especially in your state!"

Adela turned white. She gazed at the hardly recognizable Madeleine, whose coarse features were now deformed by rage.

"Heavens above, you must have been drinking! How else would you dare to reel off such nonsense?"

"I haven't had a single drop. And, wait for it—I am his mother! Do you remember how, right before Catherine's wedding, you had a miscarriage? We had a lot of work, me and Margot—Mariette's mother—cleaning your sheets. What can I say? We're all made the same, us girls."

"Madeleine, I asked you to leave! I hate crudeness. I'm really disappointed in you. Get out!"

"But I haven't finished yet, Madam. When you were gushing blood, Sir wasn't getting his pleasure! At that time, he wasn't getting it from harlots either, and was very frustrated. Damn it, he had to come to me, didn't he? I didn't even know him at that time, Madam—I was new—but that didn't stop your husband. He climbed up to the attic and forced himself on me. At first I was disgusted, then I started to get a liking for it . . ."

Adela's heart was racing as she said a silent prayer. She could no longer stand the voice, nor the sight of Madeleine— her gruesome stare and ugly facial expressions. Madeleine was shrewd enough to speak softly, so as not to attract the attention of the squire or Elizabeth, who was asleep in the next room.

Adela was aware of this. She wanted to ring for Germaine, but her left arm was causing her excruciating pain, and her right arm felt like it was paralyzed.

"It's not true," she stammered lamely. "You're lying—you just want to hurt me."

"Oh no. It's my turn now," whispered Madeleine, exhilarated at the thought of getting the revenge she had been dreaming of for years. "I was very ashamed when Sir got me in the family way. I confessed, and the priest lectured me."

"You were never pregnant, Madeleine," stuttered Adela. "You cannot hide a pregnancy!"

"Oh yes you can, Madam, except at the very end. Don't you remember—I left the castle for two months, to go and stay with my aunt? The nipper was born there, in a hamlet near Rouillac. I called him Justin, as there is no justice in the world for us servants."

Adela's mind was fuzzy, but she could vaguely remember Madeleine being absent at a time when chaos reigned in the castle.

"Yes," she whispered, "Catherine had met Guillaume, she was in love with him, but Hugues opposed their engagement, and one night, he tried to . . . But no, I must be mistaken."

Her eyelids were half closed, and she couldn't breathe.

Madeleine laughed silently. "Ah, it seems your memory is

coming back, Madam. I brought my boy back here when he was two years old. I didn't love him—in fact, I hated him. He grew up in the attic, locked up there, and if he dared to make any noise, I would punish him. I promised myself I'd tell Sir everything when the time was right. We all know round here that Mr. Laroche always dreamed of a son, an heir. Well, it turns out he's got one right here. The estate will be his—the land, the vineyards . . . It won't go to your stuck-up little madam."

"Shut up!" moaned Adela. "Have mercy, shut up and get out of my room! I don't want to hear you anymore. Be quiet!"

Adela's thoughts started to become more lucid. Deep inside, she knew Madeleine was telling the truth. When Justin had arrived in Guerville, she hadn't paid any attention to him, but had slowly begun to appreciate him.

A handsome boy and very kind, very talented, she thought. *And he resembles Hugues, of course—I should have noticed. Oh, dear Lord—he's Catherine's half-brother! Good grief, what is wrong with me?!*

Adela was suffocating; her chest felt as if it were in a vice, and her pale face tensed up. A spasm shook her entire body, causing her tray to topple over. Madeleine got up and put her chair back in its place, without taking her eyes off the dying woman. As soon as she saw that Adela was unconscious, her mouth agape, she rushed into the hallway screaming:

"Help! Oh, my God! It's Madam—please help me!"

Hugues Laroche came running. He was in the midst of getting dressed and was only wearing riding breeches and an undershirt. Bonnie, who was emerging from bed, put on her flannel bathrobe, forgetting to take off her nightcap.

Elizabeth had already rushed to her grandmother's bedside through the inner door that joined her room to Adela's. She screamed in horror at the grim scene she had already seen in her nightmare just one month ago: "The tray on the carpet, the broken cup, the spilt coffee, and Grandma knocked back on her pillows as if dead," she whispered. "Oh God—no, please!"

She lifted Adela's inert head and covered her with desperate kisses as her grandfather burst in, closely followed by Bonnie.

"I think she's dead, Grandpa!" cried Elizabeth, sobbing. "Lord, forgive me—I could have saved her."

16

A Year of Penance

After filling the hay racks, Justin fed the horses. He was surprised to see Elizabeth stagger into the stables, dishevelled, dressed only in her nightgown. When she called his name, reaching out to him, he dropped the bucket of grain and rushed to her side. She could barely stand up.

"What's happened?" he inquired in alarm.

"Oh Justin—Grandma is dead, and it's all my fault! I wish I were dead too. I had a nightmare last month in which I saw the event unfold, but refusing to believe it, I kept quiet. I should have known better: eventually my nightmares always come true!"

Elizabeth had spoken so rapidly, she was gasping for breath. Justin struggled to catch everything.

"Please, tell me again, and slower this time. Are you quite certain Mrs. Laroche is dead?"

"I am. I saw her, Justin—lying there on her bed, her eyes rolled back. It was ghastly!"

"I see now why you're so upset, Elizabeth. Your grandmother was getting weaker every day—it didn't bode well. There, there, calm down!" he said affectionately.

The young man hugged and cradled her. He was about to bend over to kiss her, but Elizabeth pushed him away brusquely.

"It's over, Justin—no more kissing or putting your arms around me, though it breaks my heart. Thank God that's all we did!"

He stepped back in astonishment. As the days and weeks had gone by, they had grown very close, keeping their romance under wraps—or at least, they thought they had.

They enjoyed play acting in front of others, in which he would call her "Miss" and treat her like a lady, while she spoke to him like a servant. Hugues Laroche had been fooled by this and had let Justin accompany his granddaughter riding. This gave them the opportunity to stop by the river and chat for hours, which usually culminated in kisses and fondling.

"What do you mean, Elizabeth?" exclaimed Justin. "Have you changed your mind? If it's because of your American, be straight with me. You said you have no feelings for him, and told me repeatedly you were no longer seeing him."

Elizabeth leaned against the door of a stall, clasping her hands. Disclosing what she had learned struck her as an almost impossible task.

"Richard is not the problem, Justin. You are Mummy's brother! Half-brother, I mean. We can never get married."

"Elizabeth, why are you making up such hogwash?"

"Hogwash, you say? This morning, I overheard a discussion in Grandma's bedroom. Madeleine and Grandma were talking; Madeleine has been bringing her breakfast in bed since she fell ill. I decided to go in to greet my grandmother, so I quickly got up. But when I turned the handle, I heard fragments of sentences that stopped me in my tracks. I put my ear to the door and heard Madeleine say that you were her and my grandfather's son, and therefore the real heir to the estate. She called me a stuck-up little madam, and suddenly there was a noise, probably the tray falling to the floor, followed by a moan. The next thing I knew, that witch Madeleine was screaming for help in the hallway. I ran to Grandma's bedside at once, but she was already dead!"

Elizabeth's whole body was trembling. She looked like a lost child, in her long white nightgown.

"I give you my word that my aunt had been drinking!" said

Justin, enraged. "If I were her son, she would never have ill-treated me like that. She used to insult me and lash me with a belt, whenever she wasn't making me eat mouldy bread. No, I don't know what got into her to invent that story, but don't believe a word of it, I beg you."

"Yet she was adamant. Apparently, you were born in a hamlet near Rouillac. Even if it wasn't the truth, Grandma's heart couldn't take it. I hate Madeleine, Justin! I'll have to see that she is removed from the premises, whether she's your mother or not! And I am going to tell my grandfather—he owes me the truth!"

The horses began to neigh impatiently, waiting for their grain, pawing the cobblestones with their hooves. Justin quickly finished feeding them in front of Elizabeth, whose bright-blue eyes were full of tears.

The groom then started to wonder. Hugues Laroche had indeed been very friendly to him, often praising him and patting his shoulder.

"Perhaps he already knows who I really am?" he asked anxiously. "He put my wages up and gave me a Louis d'Or gold coin."

"How inappropriate of him!" she said, outraged.

"Still, he should remember whether he slept with Madeleine or not."

Elizabeth silently agreed. She walked slowly away, turning her back on Justin. She had been waiting for the day when they would be married—now, her hopes of finding happiness with him were dashed. The young woman was nauseated by this latest cruel stroke of fate, which separated them in such a painful and irreversible way.

"If it turns out I am Mr. Laroche's son, I will leave tonight," Justin shouted after her. "I'm not interested in the money, the land, or the castle. If you'll never become my wife and we'll never live in your parents' house, I'll have lost you forever, so it'll be best if I go. That's how much I love you, Elizabeth."

She didn't have the courage to reply. He watched her walk up the paved alley, out into the morning mist, and stared at her helplessly, hoping to retain her image forever. His mind was made up: he was going to join the army.

The Duquesnes' mill, Montignac
Saturday, August 21, 1897

The old miller nodded sadly, stroking his granddaughter's hair as she snuggled up to him. Elizabeth had arrived on horseback shortly after sunrise. As soon as he heard the sound of hooves in the courtyard, he crossed himself. He knew at once that something bad had happened.

Elizabeth went straight into the lodge, her cheeks rosy from the exhilarating gallop in the dawn wind. Antoine Duquesne was standing by the window, braced for bad news.

"Has my friend Adela died?" he exclaimed. "My poor little girl, we must pray for her."

"No, Pops Toine—Bonnie saved her! If she had died, I would have come the same day to tell you. But Grandma survived, thanks to Bonnie."

Elizabeth led her grandfather to his chair and sat down next to him. She tried to collect herself enough to recount the drama that had taken place at the castle.

"I was convinced Grandma was dead and couldn't bear to see her like that. I had seen the same scenario in a nightmare, so I ran away. I needed Justin, the only person who could comfort me! And then Germaine told me Grandma was still breathing and had regained consciousness. Bonnie made her swallow some brandy, rubbing some of it on her chest. But even so, Grandma is still very ill. Yesterday, Dr. Trousset came back and was unable to say how much longer she has to live. He says there is something wrong with her heart."

The miller listened without interrupting, but his gnarled and wrinkled fingers reached for her hand. The prospect of never seeing Adela again hit him hard. But he had to focus on soothing Elizabeth, whose nervous state of mind concerned him.

"Life hasn't been very kind to you, little one," he muttered. "You lost your parents when you were just an innocent child, and now you may soon lose your grandmother's support, too."

"It's not just that, Pops Toine—I feel guilty. Justin has already left the castle—I'll have no one left to confide in."

"But there's Bonnie, she's your friend!"

"She wants to stay at Grandma's bedside, and there are things I didn't want to tell her. That's why I've come to talk to you, and you alone. Where is Uncle Jean?"

"Probably fishing, with Pierre. They go every Saturday, setting their lines at dawn. And Yvonne won't bother us—she took the cart to sell her eggs at the fair. You just said Justin had left. Why?"

Elizabeth stifled a sob. Then she told him all her secrets: her childhood nightmares; her other dreams; Madeleine's revelations; and the reason behind Justin's departure.

"He left without saying goodbye," she choked. "And I still haven't told my grandfather about that woman's abominable behaviour. He's so devastated. Yesterday he cried as he knelt beside Grandma's bed. In fact, it would be inappropriate to burden him with the details—I'm sure Madeleine is lying."

"Do you really think so?" asked the old man quietly.

"So you think it's true, then?"

"Nothing would surprise me about Laroche, but the strangest thing in all this, little one, is your nightmares. They bring you sad messages about the impending or distant future. Did you know that my wife Ambroisie also suffered from them? You never knew her—she died before you were born. Ambroisie feared God and went as far as to tell the priest about it. He said her dreams were prophetic."

"Yes, that's the term. I read an article on this phenomenon shortly after I arrived in Guerville. I began writing down what I saw on the night we spent at the Three Pillars Hotel. It was the only way to prove I wasn't insane."

"You're not insane, my little one. On the contrary, you have inherited this gift from Ambroisie, an utterly devout person."

"Then I should be grateful and use it wisely. As a child, I used to forget some of the terrifying images I saw, but if I had told Daddy that I had foreseen his attack, he would have been on his guard."

"This is all in the past, Elizabeth. In my humble opinion, each man's fate is already written in the stars. You are shown images of the future, but that doesn't mean that you can change the course of events. Only God can do that."

His words reassured the young woman. She dried her tears and hugged her grandfather affectionately.

"I'll drink a cup of chicory with you, then head back to the castle," she said, feeling more confident. "I'll try to drop by once a week, to give you news."

They enjoyed a peaceful moment together, sipping the hot chicory and gazing at each other fondly.

"I have inherited your clear blue eyes, Pops Toine," said Elizabeth. "Are mine really that clear?"

"Yours are beautifully clear, little one, as you are very young—and you have wonderful long eyelashes too."

Elizabeth's thoughts turned to Justin. She missed him terribly.

"We had planned to get married when I was twenty-one," she sighed. "I wanted to move into my parents' house with him."

The miller gathered that she was referring to Justin, and stroked her cheek.

"It's been a terrible shock for you both, learning that you're related," said Antoine Duquesne. "But nothing stops you from being friends—no one will find anything wrong with that."

"If he ever comes back," Elizabeth replied, with a lump in her throat. "But you're right, Pops Toine. Justin would be a wonderful friend, and since he is Mummy's half-brother, I would feel that a little bit of her lived on. I had deep, genuine feelings for him, but no desire to rush things. I'd wanted to do everything properly."

"Thank God for that, little one—incest is one of the most terrible sins on earth. Now hurry home quickly to Adela, and if she can hear you, tell her that I am praying for her with all my soul. Make sure you're careful: Madeleine has a bad reputation."

Elizabeth promised to do so, and left the mill feeling reassured. However, she still had one more battle to fight.

"Madeleine has to go," she repeated to herself. "Bonnie will help me get rid of her, and I know how we'll unmask her."

She galloped along the river path. Wisps of mist were floating on the surface of the green water, which was iridescent from the sunlight.

"I can't swear to anything," Bonnie had whispered the day before, at Adela's bedside. "But I have a pretty good knowledge of plants, and know that if your grandmother had ingested foxglove, it could have caused her heart to fail. It's a miracle she didn't die on the spot."

These words stuck in the young rider's mind.

Guerville Castle
The same day, evening

It was the first time the squire had eaten in the dining room since nearly losing his wife. Elizabeth had suggested it, and he was quick to accept, relieved to get a sense of normality back into his life.

Of course, he was in the dark about the plot that his granddaughter and Bonnie had cooked up to get Madeleine away from Adela's room and confine her to the kitchen. That evening, Germaine would prepare the tray for Adela.

Elizabeth asked Madeleine for a dish of summer truffles and duck fillets, Madeleine's most closely guarded recipe. Both of them were equally suspicious of each other.

Has the stuck-up little Madam been listening at the door? wondered the housekeeper. *I hardly think so—otherwise she would have told Sir . . .*

Is she really a murderer? wondered the young girl. *Maybe she was simply seeking justice for her son, if Justin is indeed her child—but then, why would she want to kill Grandma?*

Elizabeth's pretty face showed no signs of her inner turmoil. She was wearing a lovely mauve silk summer dress, the cut of which emphasized her cleavage and small waist.

"You look delightful, my child!" complimented Laroche.

They sat at the oval table, which was draped in a white damask tablecloth.

The silverware and crystal glasses gleamed in the candlelight, and a fragrant breeze entered through the open windows, lifting the netting of the curtains.

"Justin's sudden, unexplained departure really has shaken me. I had faith in him," Laroche said in a sombre voice. "To top it all, he fled like a villain on the very day when I thought I was going to lose my wife. You can imagine my disappointment."

"Yes, Grandfather."

"Did he say anything to you? After all, you did spend time together."

"Indeed—something forced him to leave," Elizabeth replied.

Madeleine had already served them a cucumber salad and aspic eggs. She was on her way back to clear the plates. Elizabeth gave her an ironic side glance, sending a shiver down the servant's spine. Hugues Laroche didn't notice; he was busy observing the soft sheen of the pearls on the young girl's cleavage.

"Hurry up, can you, Madeleine!" she ordered.

"Yes, Miss."

"Don't be so hard on her," muttered the squire. "I know her—Madeleine is affected by your grandmother's condition. To tell the truth, I fear that Adela may not be able to leave her bed for weeks, possibly months."

"Bonnie and I will take good care of her, don't worry. I would particularly like to oversee what food she is given, and what food you are given too. I made sure to oversee the preparation of the salad and eggs, even the aspic jelly."

"Heavens above, what for? Is there something you're not telling me?"

"I'm just being prudent—you'll soon find out why. Especially if you ask Madeleine to eat with us when she returns."

"Are you out of your mind? I have enough to worry about as it is, Elizabeth, and have no desire to eat in the company of one of my servants. I must urgently find a new groom, but it will be difficult to replace Justin. What an idiot to sneak off like that!"

Elizabeth's heart was racing. She began to doubt whether she should have devised such a risky plan. It would have been easier to simply disclose everything to her grandfather, who would then have questioned the servant. But she had to verify a few things herself that were of the utmost importance.

"Ah, the main course is on its way—I can hear footsteps!" she shouted. "I ordered your favourite, Grandpa: truffles and duck."

Intrigued, Laroche shrugged his shoulders. The air was warm and smelt strongly of roses, and his granddaughter looked radiant in the golden candlelight. Yet, he sensed a looming threat amidst this harmony. The memory of this strange moment would haunt him for years.

Madeleine, whose pale face was drawn, abruptly placed the dish in front of Elizabeth, serving her first. As soon as Elizabeth's plate was filled, she looked at it, bewildered.

"I don't like the smell," she said. "Either the truffles are undercooked, or the meat is not fresh."

"I prepared it as usual, Miss!"

"I'm not so sure about that, Madeleine. Try the sauce yourself and tell me what you think."

"Me, I don't eat all that stuff!" she protested.

"Yes, what are you playing at, Elizabeth?" asked her grandfather, exasperated. "Serve me, Madeleine, and be done with her whims."

Elizabeth's face hardened, and she jumped up. The young woman no longer had any doubts. She grabbed the housekeeper by the elbow and forced her to sit in her place.

"I'm asking you once again to taste the sauce, or a piece of duck, or even a slice of truffle," she insisted. "Don't make such a fuss. Did you know, Grandfather, that in this season, our beautiful countryside is full of flowers, including foxgloves, with their pretty red or pink bells?"

"Thank you, I do know what a foxglove is!" he thundered. "Just what is your little game, Elizabeth? Never mind—do as she says, Madeleine. At least it'll make a change from your potato stew."

Being ordered to taste the food, Madeleine went bright red before turning very pale again. Once more, she tried to dodge the trap the young girl had set for her.

"I cannot, Sir. It's not right that Miss should mock poor people like me."

"Don't be silly, you're not going to collapse if you swallow some of our fare!" laughed Laroche, intrigued by her reluctance. "Get on with it, or I'll force you to swallow it."

Elizabeth stepped back a little, embarrassed and even horrified upon seeing master and servant together. She could easily imagine them in a more off-colour scene. Nineteen years ago, the frustrated squire would join Madeleine in the attic to have his wicked way with her, not caring about the consequences.

"She would rather run away than swallow a morsel off my plate, Grandpa!" Elizabeth cried. "You told me a few weeks ago that you trusted this woman implicitly, and I laughed. Madeleine has been lying to you for years. She steals wine and other goods from you, which she hides in the guardroom. But that's just petty theft compared to . . ."

"What?!" roared Laroche.

"I suspect her of trying to slowly poison Grandma, and most probably me too. I have had a lot of stomach aches this last month, and foxglove is a poison that causes heart failure. I don't know what mixture she was concocting for me tonight, but it's certainly easy for her to determine which portion of the food to give me, without putting you in danger. It all started with the mushroom dish in June. Remember, I didn't touch it because there was too much garlic for me, and you barely took a spoonful."

Hugues Laroche noted that the housekeeper was trembling. He jumped out of his seat and stood behind her, grabbing her by the shoulders to prevent her from getting up.

"Well, say something, Madeleine! Elizabeth wouldn't make such accusations if she didn't have proof!" he shouted.

"I didn't do any of that, Sir! Nor have I stolen wine, or tried to kill Madam, who is so good to me! Miss is mad, yes. She has it in for me—I don't know why, but she does!"

"I'm not mad!" raged Elizabeth. "I heard you, Madeleine, when you were tormenting my grandmother with your despicable revelations, in that hateful voice of yours. And I was not mad at six years old either, when I told my parents that a little boy had come to comfort me in the nursery, claiming to be your nephew. Yes, he really existed, that kind, dark-eyed child. He even told me his name: Justin . . ."

Laroche stiffened. He looked around him frantically, without releasing his firm grip on the housekeeper's shoulders. The feel of her rough skin through the fabric and the sweaty smell emanating from her armpits repulsed him.

"I didn't want to burden you with this yesterday or the day before," continued the young girl. "You were so distressed. Like me, you thought for a moment that Grandma was dead."

Laroche dismissed this with a hand gesture, without releasing his grip on Madeleine.

"Justin! You're saying he was at the castle ten years ago, on the night of the storm—the night before you left?" he cried out, dumbfounded. "How is this possible? Adela and I would have known if a small child were living under our roof."

He fought against the temptation to wrap his fingers around the servant's neck and strangle her. Elizabeth could sense it.

"Let her speak, Grandpa! If you try to silence her, then you're just as guilty. Do you understand now what made Justin leave and abandon his beloved horses? He isn't Madeleine's nephew, like she led him to believe for years, ill-treating, starving and beating him. He's your son!"

"My son!" exclaimed the squire, looking bewildered. "What proof is there of such an accusation!"

Laroche stared at Elizabeth, dazed. Her contained anger and dignified posture only enhanced her beauty.

"Are you denying that you may be Justin's father?" she asked quietly.

"And how would I be?!" he roared. "I would never have lowered myself to sleep with a woman who reeks of manure and grease!"

Neither Laroche nor Elizabeth saw Madeleine seize the meat knife lying near the plate. She dealt a blow across the back of the squire's right hand. He yelled and let her go. Immediately, the servant jumped up, a look of pure madness on her hideous face, which had taken on a greenish tinge.

"If we're washing our dirty laundry in public now, I'll refresh your memory, Sir! You came up to see me, every day for a whole month, to get your pleasure. And then I fell pregnant. Yes, Miss—I told Madam all about it, just to make her swallow her foolish pride. I'm not as stupid as I look—I'm well aware that she just uses me to serve her port all day.

"Your heir, Sir, is not this goody two-shoes, but our son Justin. When he was born, I hated him. I hated you both and vowed that one day I would get my revenge, and make you pay for all you did. And then it hit me that your brat is entitled to his share, meaning I'll be able to take it easy one day."

Hugues Laroche wrapped his bloody hand in a napkin, staggering and dazed. Like his wife two days earlier, he recalled the affinity he felt for the young groom, appreciating his love of horses and excellent riding skills. One thing bothered him, however. *How could Justin, an educated and good-looking young man, possibly be the son of this harridan?!* he thought to himself. *Ultimately, I suppose he could be my child.*

He rapidly calculated how long ago it was that his tyrannical sexual urges had led him to Madeleine's straw mattress. *It was*

twenty years ago. Adela had had a miscarriage, just when we were
hoping to have a little boy. I was losing Catherine to Guillaume and
was drinking rather a lot at the time, and didn't have a choice. It was
either her, or ...

"Grandpa?" cried out Elizabeth all of a sudden. "Stop her!"

Madeleine was trying to escape, to get to the door that led
to the pantry. Disorientated, she had dropped the knife on
the floor. Laroche swiftly grabbed her by her arm, twisting it
backwards. Overwhelmed by the pain, Madeleine struggled
in vain.

"Go and get Alcide so he can help me control this shrew!" he
shouted to Elizabeth. "And send old Leandre to the village to
get the police."

Guerville Castle
Three days later: Tuesday, August 24, 1897

Elizabeth and Bonnie sat opposite Laroche in the large drawing
room, which smelt strongly of varnish. Bouquets of roses and
dahlias brightened up the dark furniture. Germaine had chosen
the most beautiful flowers to grace the grand piano, hoping to
please Adela, who loved playing it while admiring the yellow
roses in their Bohemian crystal vase.

The squire smoked a cigar, his face marred by bitterness and
anger. He had just returned from Rouillac bearing very serious
news that was eating away at him.

"Madeleine admitted everything," he said after a long silence.
"She will be transferred to Angoulême prison tomorrow morning. I have been harbouring an evil creature under my roof for
more than twenty-five years. Thank God Adela didn't die as a
result of this filthy woman's shenanigans, or I wouldn't have
handed her over to the police but strangled her with my bare
hands."

"What exactly did she admit to, Grandpa?"

"Part of what you had already suspected, Elizabeth. First, in
June, the poisoned mushroom dish. She knew the dish wouldn't

be to my liking, and I had to be spared, so as to appoint my so-called son as sole heir to my estate. But she wanted to get rid of you, my dear child, and get revenge on Adela. Then, 'bitterly annoyed that she'd missed her chance', as she said in her statement, she made Adela swallow other mixtures she'd concocted, and then foxglove on Thursday morning."

A big, frightened sigh inflated Bonnie's chest. She was glad that she had always had an interest in plants, which could both cure and kill you.

"I was puzzled by your wife's heart condition," she explained. "Dr. Trousset couldn't detect anything in the heart when he examined Madam. I then told Miss Elizabeth about my suspicions, especially after seeing a strange residue at the bottom of the cup from which she drank her *café au lait*."

"Thank you for having such insight, Bonnie," acknowledged Hugues Laroche. "If you could henceforth keep an eye on my wife's health, I will reward you significantly."

"No need, Sir—I'll gladly do it, at no additional cost."

He nodded. Elizabeth didn't take her eyes off him, hoping to learn more.

"Grandfather, has Madeleine committed other crimes? I believe she deliberately made Bonnie fall down the stairs of the guardroom. I don't know why, as my governess was no threat to her in any way."

"You never can tell what's going on in a sick mind," professed the squire. "The officer who questioned her told me a lot. He said Madeleine had demonstrated intelligence and cunning, bragging about causing the death of Vincent, her lover and my former groom."

"But why?" asked Elizabeth.

"He'd got in the way of her plan. She had to free up the position of groom to introduce me to Justin, who had lived hidden away in the attic from the age of two to eleven, and whom she had recommended to me that winter, telling me he was an orphan from south of the Charente river. The poor boy grew up in appalling conditions."

"One thing astonishes me. Madeleine had no reason to make him believe she was his aunt. More recently, she forbade him to speak of it, but luckily, he confided in me."

With a heavy heart, Laroche fell silent, diverting his gaze from his bandaged hand. He had described an evil monster of a woman but had failed to mention that he had raped her when she was young, stealing her innocence. Blood rushed to his face as he recalled it with precision:

I liked it, because she was frightened and tried to resist me as I took away her virginity like a madman. I did what I wanted with her afterwards. As I was having my way with her, I was thinking of . . . yes, I imagined it was Catherine, that I was getting my fill of my own daughter, which excited me even more. So, who is the true monster—Madeleine or I?

"Insanity and its consequences still remain a mystery to medicine and science," he said. "The human soul is unfathomable, but hatred and resentment often lead to crime."

Bonnie made the sign of the cross, then quietly stood up. She was shocked by everything she had heard. That Justin was probably Laroche's son made her sad for Elizabeth, who had confessed her feelings for him to her.

"If you no longer need me, Miss, I'd rather go back to your grandmother's bedside," she said softly. "I've entrusted Mrs. Adela to Germaine, who is very dedicated, but she has a heavier workload now."

"I'll be with you soon, Bonnie," replied Elizabeth. "I do hope that Grandma will get well again. Now that she's no longer being fed poison, she should recover, shouldn't she?"

"May the Almighty Lord hear you, my child!" sighed Laroche.

They were alone now, just the two of them, both haunted by the image of Justin.

"What do you intend to do, Grandpa?" asked the young girl. "I'll be very sad if Justin doesn't return. I'm worried that he joined the army, before he was due to be called up."

"That fool!" exclaimed the squire, seething. "And did you really need to spout all that twaddle to him, telling him his aunt was in fact his own mother? You should have discussed it with me first, and we would have decided together."

"Twaddle?!" Elizabeth shouted, horrified. "In that case, prove it, Grandpa! Swear on the Bible that you never had intimate relations with Madeleine! Why would she accuse you of it?"

"How would I know! The woman is deranged and is trying to lay the paternity of her bastard on me."

His use of such an offensive term angered Elizabeth. She stared at Hugues Laroche, her clear blue eyes sparkling with indignation.

"There's nothing like frankness!" she retorted. "I hope with all my heart it isn't true, because I have strong feelings for Justin, and it's mutual. In fact, we were planning to get married, once we've reached our coming of age. But if he's Mummy's brother, I know that we will never be joined in matrimony!"

"In short, you were plotting all this behind my back, not even knowing where the boy came from!" Laroche roared. "You intended to marry a groom? Damn it, you're just like your mother, with no pride or consideration for your social status, attracted to the first handsome boy who crosses your path!"

Though hurt by her grandfather's contemptuous words, Elizabeth held back.

"Do you, or do you not think Justin is your son?" she persisted. "If he is, then we must find him and bring him back here, to his home!"

Laroche's mind couldn't think straight. He was fuming, convinced that his granddaughter had offered herself to the young groom.

"Are you pregnant by him?" he growled in muffled tones.

"No! How dare you ask me such a thing?"

"Well, I recall you interrogating me too!" he shouted.

He jumped out of his chair, overcome with fury. The crystal vase filled with yellow roses served as an outlet: he seized it and threw it hard against the wood panelling, where it shattered into a thousand pieces. A shower of petals littered the waxed parquet floor.

"There'll never be any proof of paternity except that stupid bitch's ranting and raving!" he hollered. "But fine, I suppose Justin could be my son. There are certain things about him that appear familiar to me—facial expressions, certain movements. And he is blond, the same golden blonde as Catherine."

"I hadn't thought about that," moaned Elizabeth. "Now that you say it, maybe the reason I felt so at ease with him was our blood ties. Grandpa, please, can you make enquiries at the army? He ran away to protect me, not wanting to deprive me of my status as sole heiress to your estate. But I'm willing to love Justin as I would a family member. I miss him, and so do you!"

Hugues Laroche agreed with a confused mumble. He seemed very upset. Out of pity, and anxious to guide him in the right direction, Elizabeth went up to him and put her hand on his shoulder.

"My dear girl, I'm so glad I have you," he said meekly. Turning towards her, he embraced her fiercely. He held her very tightly, burying his rough face in her loose hair, which was held back by just a ribbon above her forehead.

"You're all I have left," he whispered in her ear. "You smell nice, you're sweet."

"Let go of me, Grandpa, please!"

But he didn't let go, continuing to hold her tightly, caressing her back, her waist, trembling and panting. When he kissed the nape of her neck, Elizabeth panicked, picturing the terrible scenes from the nightmare that had terrorized her on board *La Touraine*. The man in black, his face veiled in gloomy shadows. Recognizing his musky smell and blunt manner, she suddenly realized who he was.

"Let go of me—you're insane!" she shouted at the top of her voice, succeeding in pushing him away. "I couldn't breathe— don't ever do that to me again!" she exclaimed. "I'm warning you—if you do it again, I will leave. I have enough funds to pay for a trip back to America."

Laroche took several steps backwards, not daring to look at her. Elizabeth stormed out of the living room, cursing her grandfather and the old castle where so much depravity, hatred and grief were festering.

The Pont-Neuf Inn, Montignac
Saturday, July 16, 1898

Richard Johnson had managed to get the same room he had booked a year ago. The heat was stifling, and a thunderstorm was brewing, so he preferred to stay near the open window that looked onto the river. The detective was fascinated by the movement of the leaden clouds that were being propelled by a gale-force wind, and the swallows' acrobatic flight along the riverbank.

Richard jumped when he heard two light knocks on his door. His "Yes, come in" didn't sound very confident. He felt nervous at the thought of seeing Elizabeth again after three months.

But there she was, and he found himself gazing at her with the same passion as before. Dressed all in black with a veil obscuring her beauty, she was holding an embroidered velvet rosary in her left hand.

"Hello, Lisbeth—sit down. I've sent for a cold meal for us both, since it's past noon."

"That's very kind of you, Richard," Elizabeth replied quietly. "But I'm not hungry."

"Would you like a glass of wine then, or some tea?" he urged.

"Later maybe, when I've calmed down. I'd much rather you told me about yourself, about your life in Angoulême, and your work," she begged. "I have spent months cooped up, oblivious to the rest of the world, the countryside, the city, the ocean, New York."

She took off her hat, revealing her soul-stirring pale face, which had lost its childlike roundness. Elizabeth had lost weight.

"Take the chair over there—it's the most comfortable one," he suggested, moving the seat forward and sitting down on the edge of the bed. "What would you like to know about my life in France?"

"Well, you have clearly made considerable progress in terms of language," she remarked. "Although you still have an accent."

"The young ladies love it! No, on a more serious note, Lisbeth—forgive me for calling you that, but it sounds softer and more English—my new job, which you scoffed at last year, remember, actually takes up a great deal of my time."

"Yes, I was surprised and a little amused to hear that you were appointed English teacher at the local secondary school! If you're still there, the headmaster must be pleased with you."

"We've become the best of friends," replied the American. "I often dine at his house—his wife and children are very fond of me. They even found me a really nice place to stay, with a fantastic view of the countryside and the cathedral."

Richard took a bite out of an apple, and Elizabeth held back a sigh.

"Something saddens you," he said quietly. "It must have taken a tragedy for you to want to come and see me."

"Unfortunately," Elizabeth whispered, with tears in her voice, "my grandmother passed away last week, and we buried her the day before yesterday. Her death released her from all her suffering of the past few months. She was bedridden in the end, a terrible ordeal for such an active and proud person. Without Bonnie by my side, I don't know how I'd have coped. It's not easy to watch someone you love languishing in bed, reduced to a vegetative state."

For the sake of modesty, Elizabeth didn't go into further detail and only thought to herself: *Poor Grandma—her back was covered in bedsores. We had to change the sheets often, give her the bedpan and wash her. In the beginning, she was still able to talk to us, but her words were meaningless and barely audible.*

"What about the investigation I commissioned you to carry out?" she asked instead, changing the subject.

"Your Justin is nowhere to be found, Lisbeth!" the detective sighed.

"He's not my Justin. He's my uncle, my mother's half-brother. And Grandpa wants him back at the castle as much as I do."

"I did my best," Richard argued. "Without a family name, it's very difficult to trace someone. For all we know, he could be using any name, except his mother's."

"Quintard," Elizabeth retorted assertively. "I was relieved to hear that she escaped the guillotine, and will spend the rest of her life in prison."

The American got up and started pacing around Elizabeth. A cold meal consisting of a tomato salad, cooked roast pork and fresh bread had been served on the round table.

"How cold you are, Lisbeth," he said. "And hard. Where have your lovely smile, dimples and rosy cheeks gone? From your letters, I know that you do a lot of horse riding and that you never miss a service at the church of Guerville, but you're so young—you need to start living again . . ."

"I'm surviving, Richard, although I don't feel like I turned eighteen in April—it's more as if I turned thirty. At least the worst is behind me now. My grandmother is resting in peace, after all this pain and suffering. I am convinced that her mind was intact right until the end, trapped in an inert body that had given up. I could see in her eyes how much she was suffering, and how much she loved me."

"Who wouldn't love you?" Richard exclaimed. "My offer still stands, Lisbeth. I'll marry you as soon as you consent to it."

"That would require my grandfather's permission, Richard," she replied wryly. "I doubt he'd agree to an American running his wonderful estate."

Richard could hear genuine pain in her voice, tinged with fear. At the risk of being sent packing, he knelt down before her.

"Elizabeth, I am determined to cherish you for as long as I live. I must meet Mr. Laroche and prove to him that I am of good faith, good character and well educated. I could help him run his vineyards and manage his accounts. We would be happy, my love. I know you're afraid of marriage—I've come to accept that—but once you've experienced sensual pleasure, you will love me."

She cast an intriguing glance at him, grabbing a slice of bread. He took it from her hands and made her take off her jacket.

"It's too hot to wear this sort of clothing," he said.

A thunderclap shook the sky, and a strong gust of warm wind blew into the room, causing the curtains to flap. Richard unbuttoned the high collar of the girl's grey silk bodice.

"Thank you, I feel more comfortable now," she admitted. "On second thoughts, I will have a glass of wine."

He leapt to his feet and served her. Elizabeth took a sip and closed her eyes for a moment. She opened them again with a gentle but desperate smile.

"There are certain things I didn't tell you in my letter, Richard. Last autumn, my Uncle Jean took over from Justin at the stables. He wasn't much use anymore at the mill, which is in decline, due to the modern flour mills they have around Angoulême now. My uncle Pierre and his wife Yvonne had financial difficulties, and I was able to help them, thanks to Edward Woolworth's generosity. I write to them regularly, and Maybel's letters raise my spirits when I feel down."

"And your Uncle Jean knows how to take care of horses?"

"Yes—he wasn't very interested in running the mill. The flour made him cough. And then he started to grow fond of Bonnie—you know what I mean? I think they're in love ... I envy them."

Suddenly Richard leaned over and kissed Elizabeth on the lips. She didn't resist. A thought crossed her mind:

Let it be him ... the young and handsome one.

17

Love's Trials and Tribulations

Richard Johnson was still kissing Elizabeth, who was nestled up against him, when the storm broke out. A succession of thunder rolls and heavy rain battered the village, and a refreshing wind carried the sweet fragrance of wet grass through the open window.

"I can't leave yet—I must wait until it stops raining," Elizabeth said, secretly ecstatic at being so close to him. The touch of his strong masculine body comforted her.

"Yes, it would be dangerous," Richard replied, stroking her back through the silk of her bodice. "We're nice and safe here with the door closed and bolted. Lisbeth, I never stopped thinking about you during all these long months spent in Angoulême."

She moved away from him to watch the water cascading down the river. It was true, the room was a refuge from the outside world, a safe haven in the midst of the downpour. He wrapped his arms around her from behind and laid his chin on her shoulder, whispering:

"I'm sick of being parted from you. I gathered from your letters that you were unhappy. Please marry me—then you'll be free, and I'll look after you."

"It's not up to me, Richard—I haven't yet reached the age of majority, and my grandfather would refuse. He . . . he behaves rather strangely at times. I've already told Bonnie about it, as we're very close."

The American forced her to look at him. He shuddered when he saw her frightened expression and the profound anguish in her bright-blue eyes.

"What exactly do you mean?"

He had ceased to address her with the customary formality appropriate for a young lady, for deep down, he considered her his. This pleased Elizabeth, as it reminded her of the familiarity she'd had with Justin.

"My grandfather is very fond of me, to put it mildly," she confessed. "He hugs me and puts his hands around my waist, whenever he's not holding me tightly in his arms. I was too afraid to go to the stables alone, so Bonnie told my Uncle Jean, who said he would protect me."

"And he thinks that's enough—looking out for you?" shouted Richard. "If I were your Uncle Jean, I'd tell Laroche what I thought about his vile antics."

"Maybe I'm imagining things!" Elizabeth said, exasperated. "He may have become more affectionate and attentive because of Grandma's long illness."

Richard glared at her anxiously as he stroked her cheek. She lowered her head.

"Lisbeth, you're deluding yourself."

"I know. Deep down I know that his behaviour isn't normal. You should know that he did the same to Mummy when she was my age—Pops Toine told me that was why she fled the castle."

The young woman sobbed nervously. Richard saw a flash of lightning streak across the dark sky above the ash trees lining the river. A huge cannon shot of thunder rolled out.

"Let's move away from the window—it's dangerous," he advised. "Come, you're shaking. I think you must flee too, my darling. Perhaps you could get married with the consent of one of your uncles or your other grandfather?"

"But why are you so intent on marrying me?" she asked in surprise.

"To rescue you, but above all because I adore you. Yes, I'm madly in love with you. And I want you like I've never wanted

any woman before. I guess you're one of those who give themselves only once married."

"What would you know about it, Richard?" Elizabeth replied
sternly.

She stared at him boldly, and once again he saw that beckoning look in her bright-blue eyes, the look that had made him lose
his mind on board the ship.

"Stop playing games with me, Lisbeth," he murmured. "I'm
not going to lose you again."

Without taking her eyes off him, the young girl began to unbut-
ton her bodice, revealing a beige satin corset. She removed the
bodice seductively as he admired the outlines of her round arms
and young breasts. Her brazenness astonished him. She then
unfastened her skirt and petticoat, which spilled down around her
legs that were wrapped in fine black stockings held up by garters.

"Lisbeth," Richard moaned.

Elizabeth wasn't smiling. The girl stared at him, fascinated by
his masculine face, large forehead, straight nose, golden amber
eyes and shiny thick black hair. She imagined his satin-skinned
body under his shirt, the shape of his muscles, and his engorged
penis beneath his white linen trousers.

As for Richard, he looked with admiration at Elizabeth's body,
sculpted by her embroidered lingerie. The glimpses of bare flesh
it offered reminded him of those naughty photographs gentlemen viewed with delight, eager for hidden pleasures.

He broke the spell that had set him ablaze by lifting her up
and carrying her to the bed.

"You might want to take my shoes off," Elizabeth hinted
sweetly.

"I'll take off everything that prevents me from seeing your
naked body, my beauty."

Elizabeth would have gladly closed her eyes, but she endeavoured to keep them open, to watch the look of elation and pure
joy on Richard's face as he was finally about to conquer her. He
unlaced her boots and carefully removed them, massaging her
small, slim feet in his large, warm hands for a few moments.

The sound of the rain, that had eased off by now, stoked her excitement. When he undid her corset, he gave a brief, delighted cry at the sight of her unrestrained white breasts and brown nipples. He hastened to cover them with greedy kisses, biting the hardened tips and skimming them with light caresses of his tongue.

"This time you want to," he stammered. "How beautiful you are, my beloved!"

In a lustful trance, his firm lips roamed the pearly skin of her docile, languid body. His movements were clumsy as he pulled down the gossamer silk undergarment that shielded the dark fleece below her slender belly. He had to restrain himself to avoid tearing the silk.

"What about you—aren't you going to undress?" asked Elizabeth, her voice weak with fear and impatience.

She was not going to retreat now. Her desire to discover carnal pleasures with Richard was overwhelming. The man knew exactly how to arouse the deepest recesses of her young body.

Just the day before, in the large drawing room darkened by the drawn curtains, her grandfather had once again squeezed her tightly against him. The room was filled with the fragrance of boxwood branches in vases, the exquisite scent of Madonna's lilies, and the fleeting smell of wax.

The oak casket in which Adela's body had been displayed was placed there, so that the inhabitants of Guerville and the local area could pay their last respects to the mistress of the castle.

Little Germaine was crying, Bonnie was sniffing, clutching a wet handkerchief, and even old Leandre was there, dressed in his Sunday best, devastated by Madam's death.

Last night, Grandpa took me in his arms, a wild look in his eyes, telling me over and over again that I was the only one he had left to love and cherish, and his mouth brushed against mine, she recalled. *Then, he caressed my lower back.*

Disgusted and frightened, Elizabeth had felt extremely vulnerable, especially as her Uncle Jean was not allowed in the castle. He was confined to the stable quarters where Justin had lived.

"You look frightened, darling, but there's no need!" whispered Richard.

He had taken off his shirt and was pulling down his trousers. Fascinated, she concentrated on the sight of his sturdy shoulders and his smooth, hairless chest. He was a most handsome man, athletic and muscular.

Stop thinking! she ordered herself. *I must enjoy the present moment, forget my nightmares and cease thinking about these terrible events.*

Then came the inevitable moment when Richard stood next to her completely naked, displaying his manhood, the size of which took her by surprise.

"Are you sure it's not going to hurt?" she asked quietly.

"Of course not," he breathed.

Elizabeth glanced at the window. The storm was still rumbling, and it was raining hard again. Suddenly he sank down beside her. This time it was no longer Richard Johnson, but some wild buck eager to possess her and satisfy his desire.

He began by gently stroking her between her legs, then he rolled down her stockings. He was in love with her, but was also thrilled by her suggestive garments and black stockings.

"You are beautiful from head to toe, my darling," he panted, before leaning over her lower abdomen. "Don't be nervous—there's no reason to be afraid."

With the kiss of a hungry ogre that caught her by surprise and made her blush, he kissed her most private place. When he flicked his tongue on this very sensitive part of her, Elizabeth's breathing got quicker and quicker as her body responded in a state of rampant excitement. Her innocent young body was engulfed in passion. She arched and twisted, gasping for breath, traversed by exquisite waves of pleasure.

Soon, she was at the mercy of the insane pleasure derived from his kiss, confidently stroking her lover's back, shoulders and hair. But Richard, driven by his own sexual frenzy, guided her hand to his erect penis. He forced her to apply regular movements that made him grunt with satisfaction.

A little embarrassed, she yielded to his will, unsettled by the feel of that hot rod pulsating beneath her fingers. The anger of the weather outside echoed the sexual turmoil that gripped her. She let out muffled protests and incredulous moans.

Richard did not let up, stroking her from her breasts to her buttocks, between her thighs, along her back, rolling her from one side of the bed to the other, so as not to miss any part of her exquisite naked body. He covered her satiny white skin with rough kisses. She was almost ready to receive him, tormented by an instinctive urge to feel him inside her, to be consumed, to discover male–female union.

An experienced and gallant lover adept at paying compliments and making promises, Richard Johnson knew how to keep his mistresses in a state of excitement right up to the end. But the moment to yield to his domineering nature had come: he had done his duty, and could now focus on his own needs and pleasure.

Richard finally set about forcing the fragile hymen that symbolized her virginity. Enthused and proud at being the first, he didn't spare her. Experience had taught him to be persistent and not heed protests or complaints. Elizabeth screamed in pain at first, but quickly bit her forearm when she remembered that they were in an inn. The burning sensation she felt frightened her and shattered her desire and pleasure.

"At last, you're mine, all mine!" panted Richard.

He thrust deep inside her, using brute loin force. She begged him for mercy as he smiled at her, his amber eyes shining with triumphant joy.

"Wait, please!" she implored.

But he could barely hear her in his ecstasy. By taking her with such ardour, he could release himself from months of pent-up frustration and obsessive thoughts, in which he had undressed and penetrated her a hundred times. Convinced that she would become his slave, now that he had marked her with his seal, he waited for her to surrender and abandon herself to pleasure.

Elizabeth was suffocating under his weight. She could no longer hold him in her arms and just lie there, torn apart, subjected to his insatiable fury, which he interspersed with words she didn't understand. Yet she could tell that his language was raw, reserved for sexual encounters devoid of feelings.

"Please, that's enough!" she whimpered. "I can't take it anymore."

Astonished, he paused for a few seconds, before resuming his spasmodic thrusting so forcefully that she began to cry. Her tears relaxed her, and little by little, she succumbed to a coy acceptance of the male organ that was probing her without respite. She placed her hands on her lover's back and dug her nails into his flesh. Her body reawakened, sending warm and delicious waves through her belly and breasts.

"Yes, yes," he gasped, as he felt her submission.

Elizabeth suddenly experienced a strange but intensely pleasurable sensation. She wanted to scream out, to hug Richard, to feel his mouth on hers. He forced her to wrap her legs around his loin; in this way, she offered her whole being to him, and he stifled a sensual moan.

"Oh, oh, oh, yes . . ." she cried in turn, burning up and confused.

The room's decor, the pounding sound of the rain, the rumble of thunder—Elizabeth was no longer aware of anything around her. She surrendered, swept away from reality and consumed by a senseless, unimaginable sensual pleasure. Her body gave way to infinite ecstasy and mad lust. Richard found himself trapped by the young woman's intimate flesh and released himself inside her, with a sudden cry from the depths of his being.

He lay on top of her, fulfilled. Elizabeth fought him off wearily.

"I couldn't breathe, you're heavy," she panted.

Her heart was pounding as she lay there, bedazzled and disoriented.

She'd never imagined such sensations could exist.

"My sweet darling!" he whispered, pulling her to him. "I love you even more now. How about you?"

Elizabeth had closed her eyes, exhausted, almost drowsy. He asked her again, kissing her on the forehead.

"I don't know—a little, perhaps," she replied.

Richard looked at her in surprise.

She snuggled into the hollow of his shoulder.

"You did hurt me, you know!" she said reproachfully.

"It won't hurt the next time. Lisbeth, don't fall asleep. You need to go to the bathroom. There's a bidet—wash yourself well, please. There's no need for you to get pregnant right away."

Elizabeth remembered something she'd read in a New York magazine. When she got up, she glanced at him derisively.

"A journalist claimed that the French are great romantics and Americans much less so. It looks like they were right!"

"You're making me sound like a cad, now ... I'm simply being *pragmatique*. That's a French word I found in the dictionary."

"I'm familiar with the term, thank you."

She turned her back to him and entered the bathroom. He sighed happily as he watched her round buttocks disappear. Leaning on one elbow, he grabbed his cigarettes, then noticed a stain of fresh blood on the embroidered yellow satin quilt.

I'll reimburse them for the linen, he thought. *My beautiful little Lisbeth, made for pleasure. A gift from heaven.*

Elizabeth washed herself, then gathered up her clothes, corset and petticoat. Richard laughed as he jumped out of bed. He pointed to the window.

"It's still raining, even though the storm is over," he said. "You can't leave yet!"

"I have to—I really must visit my Grandpa Toine. He wasn't able to attend Grandma's funeral, which was very hard for him. They had become very close these last few years."

Richard grabbed her clothes and threw them on the floor. They were both naked and she saw that he still wanted her. She would have liked to take offence at this, but the sight of his erect penis troubled her, as she remembered the extraordinary pleasure it had given her.

Richard saw her hesitate. He bit into a strawberry and passed her one. A long, fruit-infused kiss followed. Then, lying diagonally across the bed, Elizabeth succumbed to her lover's will. He had taken care to remove the quilt and blankets. This time he was much gentler, and she discovered different aspects of pleasure.

"I love you—oh yes, I love you!" she cried out afterwards.

She stroked his face and touched his lips with her fingers, spellbound by his seductive face and wild gaze.

"You will love me more each day," he promised. "Remember one thing, Lisbeth darling: your grandfather will no longer be able to oppose our marriage. Tomorrow I shall ask him for your hand, saying that we have gone too far, that I am a man of honour and that I must atone for my sins."

Elizabeth was seized by terror. Her thoughts turned to the squire's anger: this was a man who'd got his own daughter's mare shot to punish her for disobeying him.

"That would end in a tragedy," she said, shaking her head. "The hunting rifle is loaded and stored within easy reach in the grand entrance hall, and the gardener, Alcide, would do anything to keep his job. You could be wounded or killed, Richard. No, we'll have to be intelligent about it. Be patient. I'm willing to marry you, but only in a few weeks' time. You'll have to take me far away from here as soon as we're married—I've got money, don't worry."

Richard, who wasn't the hero type, agreed to the arrangement. He helped her get dressed, sad at the thought of her leaving.

"Come back tomorrow!" he insisted. "It's Sunday, I'll keep the room. Monday, I have to be at school around 7 a.m. Say that you're going to church here in Montignac—please, Lisbeth."

"I'll try, but don't get your hopes up."

They kissed again. When Elizabeth walked down the deserted corridor into the courtyard, her legs barely held her up. Her inner thighs were sore, and she longed to sit down in the carriage. The stable hand greeted her.

"I looked after your horse, Miss."

Elizabeth gave him a generous tip. He thanked her with a lewd wink that displeased her.

He knows what we've been doing, she thought. *So much for my reputation—at least my worst nightmare can no longer come true now.*

Elizabeth drove Adela's carriage back to the mill. The young woman was gleeful, now that she had successfully freed herself from the worst of her visions. She knew now that the man in black, whom she had seen steal her virginity and whose face she hadn't been able to make out at first, was indeed Hugues Laroche.

"At least it can't happen now!" she said to herself.

Guerville cemetery
The same day, two hours later

Antoine Duquesne, in his Sunday best, stood in front of the tomb in which Adela Laroche had been laid to rest. The steps of the memorial, closed off by a wrought-iron gate, were hidden under sheaves of natural flowers and wreaths of coloured glass. The late-afternoon light lent a golden tinge to the centuries-old stones of the surrounding tombs, and a warm wind stirred the roses, lilies and anemones.

Elizabeth held the arm of her grandfather, whom she insisted on taking to the cemetery. The old miller hadn't been comfortable with the idea.

"What if Laroche sees me there, in the village?" he had said doubtfully.

"The village of Guerville and its seven hundred inhabitants don't belong to Grandfather!" Elizabeth had retorted. "We needn't worry. I'm sure he's gone to Rouillac, like every Saturday."

She struggled to call the squire "Grandfather". Even though she said it out of habit, it seemed inappropriate and repugnant.

"I greatly valued Mrs. Adela's friendship," declared Antoine Duquesne. "During the last ten years that I spent grieving for

Catherine, Guillaume and you, she was a great support to me. Even though I was grieving, it made me happy to see her mellow, reverting to the compassionate and caring person she must have been in her youth. Life with Laroche had made her bitter."

"And yet she loved him, Pops Toine—she told me as much."

"It's a hard fall when you love someone and then discover their despicable nature. Adela adopted a stern and uncaring attitude, shutting out all feelings. But she trusted me, and I soon learnt why she sent Catherine to boarding school at the age of ten. She had to get her away from Laroche, who had an unhealthy fondness for her. But come, let's not talk of these things anymore."

Deeply upset, Elizabeth could hardly contain her anxiety. She helped the old miller into the carriage and pointed to the square bell tower of Notre-Dame de Guerville Church, a Romanesque building stripped of its Gothic features.

"Did you want to go and pray in church?" she asked.

"No, little one, take me home. I pray day and night, anywhere under the heavens; God is all around."

Elizabeth climbed onto the footboard and sat down beside him, holding the reins. The chestnut mare trotted off as soon as Elizabeth clicked her tongue.

"Pops Toine, you know how much I love you and how much I have dreamt of living in Montignac, in my parents' house. Unfortunately, I must wait another three years, in fear of this depraved individual. Would you be very sad if I left? Richard Johnson, the American I told you about in May, wants to marry me. He genuinely loves me, and I've told him how frightened I am of my despicable grandfather."

An expression of intense disgust came over Antoine's face. He grasped his granddaughter's forearm.

"So, the monster is up to his tricks again?" he exclaimed. "Why didn't you tell me, little one? Or even your uncles? There are laws against this sort of thing. You have enough money to consult a lawyer and demand to be removed from his guardianship. For Christ's sake! What has he done to you? Has he touched you? From tonight onwards, you must live at the mill. If Laroche turns up, I'll greet him with my shotgun. I defended your mother and will protect you too. We can rely on Pierre. If Laroche tries anything whatsoever, you'll have nothing to fear."

Grandpa Toine's sudden and unusual anger comforted, but also troubled Elizabeth. She hesitated in exposing Hugues Laroche outright, as he hadn't yet transgressed certain boundaries.

"Please, we're not at that point yet!" she cried. "Bonnie is looking out for me. She hasn't left my side since Grandma died—don't worry about it too much. Maybe I'm imagining things and my grandfather is just being affectionate with me, or let's say *very* affectionate. I promise I'll come to the mill if I feel threatened. Until then, I'll simply be more careful and keep a packed suitcase, in case I need to flee all of a sudden."

The old man heaved a deep, sad sigh.

"To answer your question," he said, "yes, I would be very distressed if you left. I would miss you very much, for you are my ray of sunshine, my little joy. But if your happiness and freedom are at stake, then you must go. Besides, I'm not alone—I have Pierre, Yvonne, that treasure, and my grandsons. Married or not, you'll come back to us, and I'll wait for you as I did before. After all, I'm not yet seventy-five."

"You're still a young man, in fact!" Elizabeth joked. "Oh, Pops Toine, if you knew how much I love you!"

Elizabeth made the horse trot and before long, they were following the path along the Charente river. The miller showed his granddaughter a kingfisher with a turquoise-and-orange coat, and a couple of herons. The leaves of willows and tall ashes rustled in the wind, and the grass on the embankments glistened, beaded by the rain.

"The thunderstorm that broke early in the afternoon did some good," said Antoine Duquesne. "It's cooled the air down, and the earth was in need of irrigation."

"I couldn't agree more . . . it was a nice storm that calmed me down," Elizabeth replied dreamily, breathing in the crisp air.

She had become a woman to the rhythm of the thunderclaps, rocked by the melody of the rain, and felt a sensuous warm wave pass through her, as she visualized Richard's muscular naked body. The young woman longed for his kisses and the smell of his body.

Oh, I do love him! she marvelled. *I love him truly, and he wants to marry me.*

For the first time since Justin had left a year ago, Elizabeth felt light-hearted.

The Guerville estate
Friday, August 26, 1898

Hugues Laroche urged his big white stallion to gallop and the animal pounded the ground with its iron hooves. Elizabeth's mare, Pearl, was quickly left behind. Although slender and racy, she couldn't match Galant's performance.

The squire had taken his granddaughter to inspect his vineyards, as the grape harvest was approaching. Since she had pushed him away, terrified by his embrace and kiss on the nape of her neck, Laroche had kept his distance.

The ever-faithful Bonnie kept a watchful eye on him from dawn till dusk, and her menacing glances ensured he kept a safe distance from his granddaughter at the castle. In the stables, he had to confront a scowling Jean Duquesne.

Guillaume's younger brother was a very good stable hand, though he remained taciturn and hostile. The squire considered him a good worker and had no intention of dismissing him.

They had reached an agreement: Duquesne would lodge in Justin's old room and eat there, never venturing beyond the outbuildings that included the barn, stables and various wood and tool sheds.

"Very well, Sir!" Jean had declared, proudly. "For all it's worth, I have no desire to cross the boundary onto your estate."

Bonnie and Elizabeth often joined him for lunch, and the young lady enjoyed spending time in the small chamber where

Justin had lived. He had left behind several items, such as the Post Office calendar, a painting of the harvest, a cheap round mirror, and his riding gaiters.

After slowing down his stallion to a fast trot, Hugues Laroche entered an alley lined with linden trees, which led to some large buildings. It was then that Elizabeth was finally able to catch up with him.

"My mare had to work really hard to keep up, Grandpa," she shouted, annoyed. "Look how she's sweating!"

"If Pearl is incapable of galloping such a short distance, I'll get you another horse," he retorted.

"You call that a short distance?" she cried, taking exception. "It was at least three miles!"

The squire made a point of not looking at his granddaughter, who was dressed in her mother's pale-green velvet riding outfit. He wondered whether she had chosen to wear it on purpose, to embarrass him.

"Don't you dare—I want to keep Pearl!" exclaimed Elizabeth. "I have grown very fond of her. We simply shouldn't push her so hard—she seemed to have more energy in the spring."

Her grandfather gave her a quick sideways glance. Then in an obnoxious voice, he explained:

"Galant covered your mare, who was on heat. I put them both in the meadow. She is approximately five months gone."

Elizabeth couldn't help but blush, because of Laroche's sneering tone and the way he emphasized the words "covered" and "on heat". To hide her embarrassment, she said:

"You should have let me know. I wouldn't have taken her out this morning, especially such a long way."

"Don't worry, she can work for a few more weeks."

He dismounted in front of the large double door of one of the buildings. Immediately, a man ran up and grabbed the stallion's reins.

"Hello Colin, I have come to show the wine cellars to Miss Elizabeth, who will take over the running of the estate, in a few years' time. Take care of her mare—rub her down and don't let her drink straight away."

"Yes, Mr. Laroche," mumbled the cellar employee.

He lowered his head, but discreetly admired Elizabeth, who looked stunning in her spring outfit. She dismounted from her horse, refusing her grandfather's help. The squire, too, couldn't help but find her strikingly beautiful, with her brunette hair braided at the back, and her hat of the same green as the tight-fitting clothes that accentuated her figure.

Once again, the squire saw his daughter Catherine in her, and he had to take a quick step back to avoid touching her and breathing in her fragrance.

The young woman followed him into the darkened cellars, where oak barrels and copper vats were lined up.

"We are in the Fins Bois region," he said. "I mainly produce cognac, but also an excellent Pineau."

Elizabeth's sense of smell was besieged by strange odours of alcohol, dry stones and tannin. Despite the comings and goings of the workmen preparing the harvest equipment, they suddenly found themselves alone, in an office swamped with registers and books, and paintings adorning the walls.

"I come here often, my dear child," stated Laroche. "But this is the office of my manager, Damien Signac. He can't be far away. He'll teach you how the business works, should anything happen to me."

"I'd rather go back outside, Grandpa," Elizabeth replied uneasily. "It's very hot and there's no air in here."

"Catherine liked this place, in particular this office," Laroche continued, without listening to her. "She was also passionate about horse breeding. If I had listened to her, we would have had to build more stables at the castle."

Hugues Laroche walked around the heavy cherry-wood table and sat down in the leather armchair, then lit a cigar.

"Elizabeth, you have no idea who Catherine was before she met Guillaume Duquesne. She used to assist me and was keen to run the estate one day. Sometimes, against my wishes, she would help with the harvest, never afraid of getting her hands dirty, nor of climbing on the tip-cart to empty her sack of the best grapes. As I watched her, I thought I could have done with marrying a woman of her calibre. I loved Adela with all my heart, but she was only interested in dancing, chatting with friends, and decorating the castle. Catherine was a raw diamond. When I had to consider finding a husband for her, all her suitors seemed pathetic and unworthy of her. I was foolish enough to hope that she would never leave me."

Ill at ease, Elizabeth shook the whip she had kept in her hand.

"That's your daughter you're talking of," she told him sternly. "You speak of her as if she had existed for your convenience."

"Of course, I was wrong. She fell in love . . . with a carpenter, a miller's son. I had to accept it. You cannot rewrite the past—it's better to prepare for the future."

Elizabeth sensed danger in those last words. Her intuition was getting sharper and helped her think at breakneck speed. Hugues Laroche had taken her to visit the wine cellars, providing her with a wealth of information on running the estate. He wanted her to give him what he hadn't been able to obtain from his daughter.

"Mummy was free to love a man of her choice!" she cried. "I have an excellent memory. On the evening of our departure for Le Havre, she was very attentive and kind to you. I don't know how she managed to forgive you, after what you put her through! You shot her horse on the day when she was wearing this very outfit. But killing an innocent animal was nothing compared to your bullying and desire for possession, at any cost. I am warning you, I will not be a substitute for Mummy in your delirious, sordid schemes!"

Elizabeth was overwrought. She was afraid of her grandfather and had reacted with defiance. Laroche suddenly stood up, an unhealthy glint in his brown eyes. The nostrils of his hooked nose were trembling with fury.

"Little bitch!" he muttered between his teeth. "I spent a fortune trying to find you in America, showering you with gifts.

I let you run around the county as you please. I hired your uncle, that yokel, just to please you. I feed and house your governess, who is getting fatter every day—and this is how you treat me? I expected more gratitude from you!"

"And I thought I would get affection, tenderness and respect! That's what one expects from a grandfather, and that's what I get from Grandpa Toine," she answered back.

Laroche approached Elizabeth, his fists clenched.

"You deserve a beating, but I mustn't make that mistake, or you'll slip through my fingers, too."

"Whether you beat me or not, I'm going to leave. You might be my legal guardian, but if I tell the solicitor who signed the deed how you treat me, he will certainly help me so that I can go and live at the mill."

Hugues Laroche crushed his cigar in the crystal ashtray on the desk, laughing quietly.

"How I treat you!" he repeated with a theatrical gesture. "When my wife died, I held you close to me to console you and ease my pain. On the spur of the moment, I kissed you on the neck when your head was down—there is nothing unwholesome about that. What will you tell my old friend and attorney, Mr. Rigaud? I gave you a pedigree mare, a set of pearls, a wardrobe of dresses, and I'm not keeping you locked up in a tower, am I? Come now, Elizabeth, stop behaving like a silly child. I have several matters to attend to here. You'd better get back to the castle or visit old Duquesne. Rumour has it he won't last much longer."

"You really are despicable!" she cried, as she hurried out of the room.

Ten minutes later, Elizabeth took a straight, grassy path through the vineyards. Her eyes wandered over the bunches of grapes, which were nearly ripe, thanks to the sultry August heat. Pearl trotted at a steady pace, shaking her pretty silken head.

"There, my beauty. *I* won't make you gallop," she sighed.

To dispel her dark thoughts, she imagined the tiny new life growing inside her mare. She calculated that the foal would be born in February. Her heart ached, as she recalled the painful memory of the baby her mother was carrying on board *La Champagne* twelve years ago.

I could have had a brother that age, she thought to herself. *He'd be playing on the Bronx's infamous sidewalks, or Daddy would have made enough money for us to live somewhere tranquil.*

She was frantic and felt a nagging desire to see Richard and take refuge in his arms. They had met on Saturday and Sunday afternoon at the Pont-Neuf Inn. Her frequent visits had already aroused the curiosity of the Montignac locals, and rumours pertaining to her reputation soon got back to the Duquesne family.

Pierre had been outraged by his niece's behaviour, but his wife Yvonne had talked him round. As for Antoine, as the eldest member of the family, he said that the young folk were not doing any wrong.

"The man Elizabeth has been meeting is American—they love to be able to converse in English about New York and the Woolworths, whom Elizabeth still writes to," he said. "What's more, they will be getting married soon, which will prevent Laroche from causing any more harm."

Pierre Duquesne then proposed a solution that would stop the gossip:

"If it's serious, Father, then let her meet with her American in her own home. Yvonne keeps it clean and aired, and it's some distance from the village."

During a visit to the mill, Jean suggested the arrangement to Elizabeth. The young woman decided to write to Richard at once, delighted by the idea of showing him the humble home where she had spent her early childhood.

Guerville Castle
The same day, one hour later

The stables seemed deserted when Elizabeth entered, holding Pearl by the reins. She put the mare back in her stall and removed her saddle and bridle. Her Uncle Jean's absence puzzled her, but she assumed he was with Bonnie. The governess never missed an opportunity to walk in the park in the hope of running into her "lover", as she referred to him now.

"Uncle Jean?" she called out, just in case.

"Your uncle's not here!" replied a shrill voice, in a pronounced Charente accent.

Mariette appeared, a malicious glint in her eyes. She leaned against the stable door, chewing a blade of grass. The young laundry maid still worked at the castle, where she assisted her mother, Margot.

"Hello," said Elizabeth kindly. "What are you doing here? It's not laundry day."

"I was hoping for news of Justin, my intended. I'm sure he writes to you!"

"No, I'm sorry, Mariette—he hasn't been in touch. I wish he had, as I'm very worried about him."

Mariette seldom spoke to Elizabeth, and her appearance today aroused the young woman's suspicion. She could see the laundry maid was thrilled about something, and her instincts were on edge.

"Say, Miss, is it true what they say? Justin is the boss's son?"

"We have no proof. Who told you about this?"

"Alcide. Madeleine taught him to eavesdrop, just as she used to. They should've cut that witch's head off—she can put evil spells on us from her prison."

"I doubt it—she was meant to be transferred to Bordeaux."

"Well, tell that to Germaine! Poor thing, her mother broke her leg the other day when she went down to the cellar. That Madeleine constantly threatened her, saying terrible things would happen to her and her family."

Elizabeth held back an irritated sigh. She signalled to Mariette to step back, so she could lock Pearl up. The rack was already full of hay and the mare had clean water. Carrying the heavy side saddle, she went to the tack room. The young laundry maid followed her in.

"I wanted news from Justin because I'm four months with child. He'll have to come back and marry me, won't he?"

"What did you just say?" said Elizabeth angrily. "But that's impossible. Justin's been out of the county for a year now. If you're pregnant, it certainly isn't by him."

Outraged, the young woman scrutinized Mariette from head to toe. She was a rather pretty young girl with blonde hair, pink skin and an overbearing chest, but her sly expression and thin lips spoiled her. The bottom of her blue canvas skirt was frayed, and her yellow linen camisole was worn thin.

"I saw him again, my intended, not so long ago," she boasted, looking smug as she waddled. "We slept together in my father's barn. Justin couldn't get enough of me, because I don't make him jump through hoops, like you do!"

Puzzled, Elizabeth's thoughts were racing, her mind on high alert. Not only did she have the gift of seeing the future in her dreams, but she was also adept at detecting untruths.

"You're lying," she snapped. "You're telling me you're pregnant because you hope to marry the possible heir to the estate— is that it? I can easily unmask you too, just as I did with Madeleine. She exuded vice and crime, and my governess wasn't mistaken when she said that my poor, unfortunate grandmother had been poisoned with foxglove."

Mariette looked a little worried, but insisted impertinently: "I know who I'm sleeping with, don't I? I'm a well-brought-up girl, you know!"

"Alas, I'm sorry, but I know, from a reliable source, where Justin is. He joined the navy and is sailing towards Toulon. I paid a detective to find out."

Elizabeth had lied brazenly, to force the laundry maid to retract her words.

"And I also know from Justin that you intended to marry a certain Bertrand, the man who took your virginity and who will inherit some property when his father dies—a house, and plots of wheat. You said you preferred him to Justin, and that Bertrand's military service would be over in less than four years. But would you believe it, your mother Margot and old Leandre tell me he's already returned! Bertrand was discharged exactly five months ago. You should publish the banns quickly— I'll give you a new dress and a silver bracelet with turquoise stones for the wedding."

"Oh, Miss, really?!" murmured Mariette, flabbergasted. "Are you quite serious about the dress and the bracelet?"

"I am, for I always keep my promises. And I'll offer you two gold Louis d'Or coins on top of it."

"Oh my, thank you, Miss!" exclaimed the laundry maid. "Thank you so much."

Then she hurried off whistling. Elizabeth leaned against the nearest wall. She would have given anything to see Justin walk in and giggle with her about Mariette's little ploy, but it was her Uncle Jean who joined her in the tack room. It smelled strongly of leather and the bay-laurel ointment used for greasing the horses' hooves.

"Ah! You're back!" he called out in amazement.

But for once, he wasn't smiling. Reminded of her father, Elizabeth would have liked to seek refuge in his arms. The two brothers had the same black curls, the same grey eyes, and the same face shape—only Jean's smaller frame put them apart.

"Grandpa advised me to go home—he had a lot to do in the winery. Are you in trouble, Uncle Jean?"

"Am I just! Talion, the grey gelding, was suffering from violent colic. I took Leandre's advice and walked him a bit, but after a quarter of an hour the poor beast collapsed and couldn't get up again. I'm afraid we lost him."

"Oh no! Grandpa loved him. He'd left him in pasture this summer, as he needed a rest. Besides, he prefers riding Galant."

"I'll surely be dismissed before nightfall," lamented Jean. "And then I won't see Bonnie anymore. That is, unless you . . ."

"What—what do you mean?"

"I agreed to work for Laroche mainly to be near Bonnie, and to keep an eye on you too, of course, even if I'm not allowed to set foot in that damn castle. It could be quite simple, really. You marry your American, I'll marry Bonnie, and we'll all leave the county together."

"But, Jean, you're deluding yourself. Documents have to be drawn up for a marriage to be lawful—a church blessing is no longer sufficient—and no registrar will agree to it without my guardian's consent."

"What about Father? Antoine Duquesne is your grandfather, too—he can give his consent. Why do you insist on staying here, for goodness' sake?"

"I don't know. Something is keeping me here that I have yet to discover," replied Elizabeth firmly.

The discussion was getting heated, but then Bonnie arrived, just in time to cut short the quarrel that was about to begin.

"Miss, Richard Johnson arrived at the castle and Germaine has taken him into the large drawing room. Come quickly—he's demanding to see Mr. Laroche."

Elizabeth took off her hat and handed it to Bonnie before running outside, torn between panic and joy.

18

From Catherine to Elizabeth

Guerville Castle
The same day

Richard Johnson was admiring the paintings in the large drawing room when Elizabeth entered the room, hesitantly, not sure
if her attire was appropriate. She was wearing her mother's
velvet outfit.

As for Richard, he looked every inch the rich foreigner and
even addressed Germaine in English.

"Ah, Miss! At last," cried the maid. "I feel so embarrassed, I
didn't understand what the gentleman was saying, but he kept
repeating your name, so I let him in."

"You did the right thing, Germaine. You can leave us now,
but bring us some coffee and tea, please."

"Yes, Miss."

Once she was alone with Richard, Elizabeth threw herself at
him. He'd expected her to be angry, and he kissed her back,
somewhat surprised.

"I was dying to see you," she whispered in his ear. "By a
stroke of luck, my grandfather won't be back before noon.
But Richard, what were you thinking of, coming all the way
here?"

"Mr. Laroche hasn't seen me before, so I intend to pass
myself off as a wealthy American wishing to purchase some
cognac and discover this splendid chateau from top to bottom.
It looks like a medieval fortress. There's even a drawbridge and
high towers. We have nothing like this in New York!"

"The Dakota Building is very stylish, though," Elizabeth

replied dreamily. "If you lived here, you would soon notice how heavy the atmosphere is. Having memories of my mother here helps me cope. I even moved into her room, which still contains all her belongings from when she was a young girl. I can still sense her presence."

Richard glanced at the double door before giving her another, more passionate kiss. Then he stepped back a little.

"Lisbeth, you look stunning in your riding outfit—this green velvet is delightful on you. It doesn't match your blue eyes but goes so well with your dark hair."

"It was my mother's outfit, but it's as good as new, as she rarely wore it. You had better leave, Richard—one of Grandpa's horses just died. I feel very upset about it, but my grandfather will be in a filthy mood when he finds out. This is not the right time for your game—you'll just make things worse. In fact, what exactly *were* you planning? To make him think that you come here frequently on your travels, and have fallen in love with me? To ask him for my hand in marriage . . .?"

His amber eyes stared at her in astonishment. Elizabeth could often guess his thoughts.

"I had indeed contemplated something of the sort," he admitted. "It's as if you could read my mind!"

"Perhaps," she acknowledged, looking wistful.

She hadn't told Richard about her nightmares, nor about her intuition which verged upon clairvoyance.

Their time together was always limited, and they spent it lustfully savouring each other's bodies. Johnson was an energetic and insatiable lover, but he also knew how to be tender and attentive. Elizabeth drew strength from his athletic arms, feeling no need to bare her soul to him.

"You are no ordinary young woman," he declared. "That's what attracted me to you the first time I laid eyes on you in Central Park."

Germaine came in, carrying a heavy tray. Elizabeth was surprised at her speed.

"What efficiency, Germaine!" she remarked.

"I always have boiling water at the ready, Miss, and the coffee and tea sets are laid out ready, protected from dust by a clean tea towel," bragged the maid, gazing in awe at the handsome visitor.

What a shrewd manipulator, Elizabeth thought, knowing at once what was behind little Germaine's zeal. As a dejected-looking Bonnie entered the room, Elizabeth announced that she was going upstairs to change.

"I'll leave Mr. Johnson in your hands," she said calmly.

The sun flooded the vast bedroom that used to be her mother's room. An overwhelming scent of lilies took the young girl by surprise as she hastily undressed. Semi-clad, she went to freshen up in the powder room.

A large blue-and-yellow patterned Limoges porcelain jug contained water, which she poured into the matching basin.

Once again, Elizabeth became aware of the exquisite fragrance of lilies. Certain that it was a message from an invisible presence, she felt her heart start to pound.

"Mummy," she called out softly. "Are you here with me?"

Nothing happened. Suddenly Elizabeth decided she was being silly: through the open windows, she could see rambling roses growing down the walls.

I'm too sensitive, she thought, as she put on a mauve silk dress that revealed her shoulders. She completed the outfit with a satin shawl, arranged a strand of hair and hurried down to the drawing room. Richard was sipping a cup of tea, chatting away with Bonnie. Germaine was busy tidying up the music sheets that lay on the grand piano.

"I'll see you out, Mr. Johnson," said Elizabeth, in a formal tone. "My grandfather will receive you another day."

Richard gave in, looking disappointed. He said goodbye to Bonnie and Germaine. As soon as they got outside, the young lady was less gracious.

"For pity's sake, don't ever do that again!" she ordered. "Tomorrow, we're meeting in Montignac, in my parents' house."

I was looking forward to it, Richard. If Grandpa sees you, he'll be livid and might even forbid me to go out."

"Precisely—it's time to put an end to his tyranny!" he retorted, pointing angrily at the raised drawbridge, the thick walls and their huge masonry stones. "You'll become a prisoner of this fortress, Lisbeth, and that old lecher will end up tarnishing you forever!" he declared.

"He would never dare transgress certain limits, I'm sure. I should remind you that in France, as in America, wealthy young ladies have no freedom whatsoever at my age. I've given you a lot, Richard, and you know it. My virtue has fallen by the wayside."

"Do you regret it?"

"No. It was my decision—I'll explain another time!" she said. "Now, please leave. You could go straight to Montignac now— you'll easily recognize the house. It's about five hundred yards from the mill, near an oak wood. There's a green gate at the end of a path lined with boxwood, and an unusual mermaid weathervane on the roof—Daddy made it. My aunt Yvonne hides the key under a stone on the porch, on the left. I'll try to come tonight, and if I can't make it, tomorrow at noon. By the way, how did you get to Guerville?"

"You won't believe it. The headmaster lent me the motor car he purchased in June. It caused quite a stir wherever I went. If I park it near Montignac, it'll attract a crowd of curious onlookers."

He gave her a huge smile. Elizabeth, touched by his cheerful countenance and his accent that conjured up memories of faraway New York, stood on tiptoe to kiss him. Richard pulled her against him and kissed her back.

"I'll wait for you tonight, Lisbeth, darling," he whispered in her ear. "And tomorrow and the day after tomorrow, for the rest of my life."

A lustful tremor ran through her body as she reluctantly left his side.

Hiding at the corner of the stable building, Hugues Laroche had witnessed the whole scene. He was beside himself with rage.

Catherine and Guillaume Duquesne's house
Saturday, August 27, 1898, noon

Elizabeth tied up Pearl in the stall at the back of a small outbuilding where her father had built a workbench for his carpentry. Hearing the sound of hooves, Richard ventured into the dimly lit building.

"I was afraid you wouldn't come," he confessed, keeping a safe distance from the horse.

"I would've come last night," she replied with a sigh. "But Bonnie persuaded me not to, because of Talion. Strangely though, my grandfather remained indifferent when learning about the death of one of his favourite horses. He left the castle right after we told him, and didn't even blame Uncle Jean."

"Where did he go?"

"I don't know, Richard. We heard him come home after midnight. And this morning, he harnessed the carriage himself and went off again. I tried to talk to him, but he wouldn't reply."

Elizabeth unsaddled her mare and rubbed her down using a fistful of straw, then patted her neck gently.

"When I was little," she said, "Mummy had a grey donkey. It lived in this stall. For the past six months, I've made sure there is always clean straw, hay and grain here. I don't tell anyone, but I sometimes come here to rest. Our *cottage*, as my mother called it, is the only real home I have."

Richard's face was pensive as he nodded, admiring her elegant figure in her brown twill riding outfit. She handed him the tapestry bag that was hanging on a pommel of the saddle.

"I've brought a dress and some undergarments, but I didn't bring anything for dinner. I'm sure we'll find something to nibble on, though."

"Don't worry, I bought eggs and vegetables this morning. The car is parked in the mill courtyard. I took the liberty of introducing myself to your other grandfather, Antoine, and I also met your Uncle Pierre. I told them of my firm intention to marry you, Lisbeth. In spite of their poverty, they're very hospitable people."

Elizabeth couldn't curb her wrath:

"Wealth is no measure of a person's worth. Pops Toine is a devout and pious man!" she cried. "And you shouldn't have jumped the gun, defying common sense. We could have taken this step together, when I deemed it appropriate. If I were nothing but the granddaughter of an old miller, with no fortune, would you still want to marry me? Bonnie warned me about that in New York—she said you were a fortune hunter."

Richard grabbed her by the waist and hugged her, then covered her forehead, her cheeks and the tip of her nose in light kisses. Even so, she still eyed him with suspicion.

"Lisbeth, I would marry you even if I found you wandering along the roadside in rags, because I can't live without you. I love you with my whole being—you are all I want on this earth. I offended you by bringing up the Duquesnes' lack of means, but I was very touched by them. Do you know why? They are all so warm and cheerful—your Uncle Pierre, Yvonne, his wife, and your grandfather. The room they invited me into seemed to me . . . how do you say it in French? *Rustique*—yes, that's it. A smell of smoke lingered in the air."

"That never bothered me. I always feel more at home in the mill kitchen than in the castle's large drawing room."

She pushed him away and hurried out of the barn across the garden. He followed her at once. The young woman was captivated by the sight of so many beautiful flowers: dahlias, morning glories, buttercups and nasturtiums filled every inch of ground, and the walls were covered with roses, the branches of a hundred-year-old wisteria and a trellised vine.

"Mummy!" she whispered.

In her mind, she could see Catherine. Her mother used to stroll in and out of the little garden carrying a tin watering can, a blue apron tied around her waist. She loved planting different seeds, replanting seedlings, and arranging flower displays in the summer months.

"It's strange, Richard, but since my grandmother died, I can sometimes sense a presence—a very fleeting presence. Yesterday, I could smell lilies in my room, even though there are no lilies growing around the castle, and it's not even the season."

"These things happen—don't attach any importance to them, Lisbeth," Richard replied. "Let's go back inside and lock the door. People may be spying on us through the bushes."

Once they were back inside, Elizabeth regretted bringing Richard to her parents' house. Nothing had changed after all that time. The setting was so familiar, she felt as if she had been split into two: a six-year-old child on the one hand, and a young woman about to indulge in sensual pleasures on the other. Troubled, she looked at the light wooden furniture, the cheap trinkets on the mantelpiece, and the open doors.

"Oh my, how tiny it is!" exclaimed Richard.

"Yes—a kitchen, two bedrooms and a pantry. Daddy would most probably have built an extra room, had we stayed in Charente."

Richard detected a quiver in her crystalline voice. He swiftly pulled her to him.

"Stop thinking of the past, Lisbeth, darling. We're together, that's all that matters. Are you hungry?"

"No, not at all. Richard, it was wrong to bring you here. It would be immoral to make love under my parents' roof and in their bed, as the one in the nursery is too small. Besides, I'm not in the mood for it."

"You're overreacting somewhat!" he said, exasperated. "*Immoral*, you say? That's a bit strong, given that we shall soon be married. Your despicable grandfather Laroche is immoral, cajoling you and kissing you on the neck. Lisbeth, don't disappoint me. I think about you from morning till night, fantasizing about your beautiful naked body."

He took her right hand and placed it on his groin to show her how much he desired her. Then he seized her mouth, stifling her protests, kissing her with blatant intent.

"Come," he ordered. "And close your eyes—you'll soon forget where you are, darling. You know how happy I make you, each time."

Once again, Richard gave in to his powerful sexual urges. There would be no romance or tenderness until his sexual appetite had been assuaged. Elizabeth was his—she belonged to him and he would not tolerate any reluctance on her part.

Had she been more experienced, Elizabeth could have fought off her insistent lover. However, she was in the process of discovering a very primal aspect of a whole new world. Nobody had ever discussed romantic liaisons with her—the Woolworths, and even her parents had been very discreet about such matters.

Listless and dreamy, she let herself be carried into the next room and placed next to her parents' bed. As usual, he aroused her with an avalanche of rough stroking and fondling, before covering her nape and cleavage with kisses.

Excited at finally being alone with her, he tore off her riding jacket and skirt, tossing them on the floor. He went on to skilfully remove her bodice and petticoats.

"Be gentle, please!" she begged.

All that was left now was her pink satin corset, laced up at the back. Her legs felt like jelly and she longed to lie down, but he forced her to remain standing.

"And now your hair!" he said, panting.

The young man undid her braided bun, scattering her heavy brown curls over her bare shoulders. Then he contemplated her, a wild gleam in his eyes.

"When we're married, I'll photograph you in this kind of outfit. It makes you look mischievous," he said, his voice shaking. "Gorgeous, I want to pay my respects to you."

Richard pushed her into the only armchair in the room and crouched down, level with the soft dark fleece of her pubis. Then, with a head movement, he forced her legs apart and kissed her moist genitals, and the pink fleshy bead he hungered for. The tease of his tongue sent her into an erotic trance and she began to pant, her languorous little body trembling with pleasure as she offered herself to him.

"I want you inside me!" she moaned. "I want you right now!"

Richard helped her to her feet, and she fell across the bed as he shed his clothes. He straddled her slender body and quickly sank inside her, letting out a dull cry of delirious joy. Intoxicated by his burning desire, the young woman lost all track of time and place. She was breathing fast with her eyes shut, a slave to the jerky pumping movements Richard was making inside her. Then her pelvis arched, and she shuddered to a climax, lost in pleasure.

But Richard had been restraining himself. For the first time, he requested that she turn her back to him, getting on all fours.

"I can't—we're not animals!" Elizabeth protested.

He laughed mockingly as he stroked her round buttocks, the sight of which drove him crazy. Then he ripped off her corset and penetrated her with force. Elizabeth stifled a lascivious wail, in the grip of dizzying new sensations, before finally begging for mercy.

She endured a final onslaught and trembled with exhaustion. His deep shudder told her he had just climaxed inside her. Her lover rolled off her and stretched out, smiling blissfully.

"Are all men like you?" she asked after a short pause.

"I forbid you to ask such a thing," he snapped. "A woman must devote her body and soul to her husband and her husband alone—with the exception of widows and whores, of course."

Elizabeth stifled the sob that was choking her. She was a little ashamed, for her thoughts had turned to Justin.

Just last week, she had cried after they'd made love, and Richard had prided himself on it.

"You're crying tears of happiness, Lisbeth! I'm flattered."

Well aware that incest was a terrible sin—an age-old taboo, in fact—the young woman hastened to cuddle her lover, whispering sweet nothings in his ear:

"At this pace, you'll soon be pregnant!" exclaimed the American as she snuggled into him. "And then, Mr. Laroche won't be able to oppose our marriage. I'll be the perfect son-in-law—he'll realize that in time. My architectural background will be useful to him, as the castle needs restoring, but in a way that doesn't detract from its authenticity."

"But I'm in no hurry to be a mother!" she protested. "You're deciding for me. If it were only up to you, we would be staying in Guerville—but I've always wanted to live in my parents' house!"

"In your cubbyhole, you mean!"

Furious, Elizabeth sat up, covering her breasts with the satin bedspread.

"It's up to me to choose when I'll have a baby and where I'll give birth to it. I might as well tell you: I wrote to Maybel two weeks ago, to tell her about Grandma's slow and agonizing death. What's more, I told her how afraid I am of Grandfather. Her reply arrived this morning:

You can come back to New York anytime you wish, Lisbeth, my darling daughter! Edward and I will be the happiest people alive if you do. Send us a telegram in case you need money, and we'll arrange a transaction immediately.

"The rest of the letter would be of no interest to you."

"Go back to America . . .?" said Richard, astonished. "Why not, if we can get married before we leave."

She was about to reply when a dreadful crash resounded in the adjacent kitchen. Wood splintered and glass shattered. Both of them froze with shock when they heard heavy footsteps and the jingling of spurs.

Hugues Laroche was standing in the doorway of the bedroom. He went up to the naked couple, eyeing the clothes that lay scattered on the floor. Neither of them knew what to say. Then they noticed the horsewhip he was shaking along his right leg, and Elizabeth braced herself for the worst.

Richard, on the other hand, was in the throes of the most painful humiliation of his life. If he stood up to explain himself and defend the young woman, he would expose his genitals, but he also refused to cover himself, as if he were guilty.

"You have five minutes to get dressed and come with me, Elizabeth!" Laroche said coldly. "As for you, Sir—I advise you to leave the country as soon as possible."

"I won't go anywhere without Lisbeth," replied Richard firmly, reassured by the squire's apparent calmness. "I can't deny the obvious, but you should know that I intend to marry her. I visited the castle yesterday to ask you for her hand in marriage, Sir."

"You must be the famous Johnson then, are you not? The detective I paid a fortune for, and who still demonstrates tremendous zeal and dedication to his work!" shouted Hugues Laroche. "Don't get high and mighty with me. I could very well file a complaint against you, for taking advantage of my grand-daughter—even though I suspect she consented to it."

"And guess who is going to file a complaint against you if you harm my fiancée?" shouted Richard.

"Shut up, for pity's sake!" Elizabeth begged, her arms folded over her breasts.

Laroche stormed out of the room, and the young woman quickly jumped out of bed and pulled on her petticoats, under-wear, skirt and bodice, leaving her corset behind. She laced her boots with trembling fingers.

"Lisbeth, don't go back to the castle!" murmured the American.

"Don't make things worse, Richard—Bonnie's still there, I'll be safe."

She hastily tied her hair up with a ribbon and put on her felt hat. Richard grabbed her arm.

"I fear for you, my darling!" he breathed.

Elizabeth didn't answer, but gave him a quick smile. A myste-rious glow seemed to emanate from her, comforting him.

"I'm not afraid," she said softly.

The sight of the kitchen saddened her. The squire had smashed the French window, which had been decorated with macramé curtains. Pieces of broken glass were strewn over the red flagstones, and his forcing the lock had splintered the wooden door's green paint.

Hugues Laroche cast a disdainful glance at the humble setting. Elizabeth knew he was beyond anger, indignation, or even rage, which made him all the more dangerous.

"Hurry up!" he ordered. "This is the first time I've set foot in this damned shack, and I can't wait to leave. To think that Catherine settled for this! Your mother's heart must be bleeding from heaven, seeing you behaving like a whore."

On her guard, Elizabeth remained silent. She ran into the garden, followed by her grandfather. Richard Johnson caught up with them by the gate, dressed only in trousers and a crookedly buttoned shirt, his black hair a mess.

"Monsieur Laroche!" he shouted. "Don't be foolish. Let's discuss marriage! I'm prepared to stay in France and help you run the estate and restore the parts of the castle that are falling into ruin!"

"And I, Mr. Johnson, am prepared to kill you, if you ever touch my granddaughter again!" Laroche yelled. "Get out of my sight—I might forget myself."

The American stepped back, white as a sheet. Laroche had a deadly look in his eyes.

Guerville Castle
One hour later

They returned to the castle at a gallop. Galant was going so fast again that Elizabeth's mare couldn't keep up.

"Poor Pearl!" she muttered, patting the mare's sweaty brown coat.

She desperately scanned the surroundings for her Uncle Jean, but the stables were deserted by all except her grandfather, who was busy unsaddling the stallion. He had made no attempt to talk or even scold her, once they had slowed down at the park's entrance.

This deliberate silence frightened Elizabeth more than insults or violent shouting would have. Meanwhile, Laroche was struggling against his internal demons. The squire was haunted by the glimpse he had caught of his granddaughter's ravishing upper body. He couldn't stop thinking of her firm, young, white breasts, her arms, neckline, and the side of her hip, which reminded him of a smooth white pebble.

He clenched his teeth, his eyebrows furrowed, determined not to do anything he would later regret.

"Where is my uncle?" asked Elizabeth tentatively.

"I sent him packing to mix flour and wade in the mud!" he thundered. "And I hope it kills him, like it did poor Talion. After all, the poor beast died because of that jackass. Get out of the way, otherwise I won't be responsible for my actions. You deserve a good hiding."

Distraught, she fled, but not without noticing that the drawbridge was lowered—a rare occurrence. Elizabeth crossed it to reach the grand entrance hall directly. She normally appreciated the medieval hallway, except maybe the hunting trophies that had scared her as a child, but today it felt sinister and oppressive.

"The sky is overcast—it's going to rain, that's why!" she told herself, without conviction.

Old Leandre appeared in the doorway leading to the staircase that descended into the pantry. The gardener never normally ventured that far.

"Good morning, Leandre," she muttered, taking off her hat and gloves. "Sir won't be long; he's tending to the horses. Do you need anything?"

He shook his head, looking all around him. Elizabeth, eager to find Bonnie, headed for the stairs.

"Since you're here, Leandre, would you tell Germaine to make some tea and hot milk, and bring the tray up to my room— not to the drawing room?"

"Well, that's the trouble Miss—Germaine isn't here," replied Leandre, fiddling with his worn-out cap.

"How absent-minded of me—it's Saturday. Sir must have given her the day off."

"No, Miss. Germaine was supposed to go to her mother's on Sunday, not before!"

"How odd—Bonnie will know, though. Thank you, Leandre."

Elizabeth did her best to look relaxed, but she was still suffering from the extreme shock she had suffered an hour before. She needed to find Bonnie urgently, to tell her about her relationship with Richard and get the maternal affection she craved.

Instead of going to her own room, she therefore opened the next door, but there was no one there.

"Bonnie?" she called out. "Bonnie, Bonnie—where are you?"

She inspected the scene—everything appeared to be in order: the red quilted bed, the basket full of balls of wool, the shoes lined up under the wardrobe, barely sticking out.

She must have gone for a walk, or maybe she's with Uncle Jean, Elizabeth told herself.

While she was rationalizing her thoughts, an insidious fear engulfed her. The castle had never seemed so silent. Suddenly she thought she could hear noises overhead.

"Germaine and Bonnie are most probably upstairs."

The young woman felt unbearably lonely. She walked down the hallway and up the stairs she had climbed all those years ago with Madeleine, before finally opening the door to the nursery.

Everything is exactly as it was: the net curtains, the cot with bars, the pink marble fireplace, the large wardrobe, she observed.

The tall standing mirror, which had terrified her at the time, cast her reflection back to her. She studied her strained features, her unkempt hair and her mouth that was still swollen from Richard's kisses. But above all, she noticed her abnormal pallor and the panic in her eyes.

"Justin!" she called out softly. "If only you would appear and comfort me again!"

A light-brown cardboard box on the parquet floor caught her attention. She bent down to pick it up. Once she'd taken off the lid, she discovered toy soldiers inside, their colours faded with time.

If I only knew where I put the drummer ... she thought with a heavy heart.

She went through the figurines with her index finger. Something intrigued her: the box was lined with thick greyish paper that bulged on one side. She found a small schoolboy notebook hidden under the bulge.

Maybe it belonged to Justin?

She took it and was about to leaf through it when she heard footsteps. Without thinking, she slid the item into her pocket. Hugues Laroche burst in.

"What are you doing here?" he barked. "Go to your room immediately!"

"I was looking for Bonnie, and Germaine."

"I threw them both out. Tomorrow, a woman from the village will start work in the kitchens."

"What?! I don't understand, Grandpa! You had no right to throw Bonnie out. She is *my* governess. I pay her wages. Why on earth did you do that? I understand you're angry, after what happened, but this morning you didn't even know about my relationship with Richard Johnson."

"Is that what you think? I saw you, yesterday afternoon! That dandy was sticking his tongue into your mouth in the alleyway. I decided to leave, so as not to make a scene, but then this morning, after you ran off like a cat on heat, I questioned Germaine and Bonnie about it. They were both in on it, so I got rid of the riff-raff!"

Laroche had completely lost the plot. His language was vulgar and coarse, something he habitually claimed to despise. Elizabeth felt faint. She was now alone in the castle with this terrifying man.

"I'm your legal guardian, Elizabeth," he added in a bitter voice. "What does a respectable man do when confronted with a slut who gives herself to the first man to come along? A gorgeous little slut who happens to be his own granddaughter? He must clamp down on it—no one would disagree. Now go to your room."

But she was frozen on the spot. Laroche finally grabbed her by the elbow and pushed her in front of him. Five minutes later, sitting on her bed, Elizabeth heard the click of one lock, and then of another. Only her bathroom remained accessible.

"I'm doing this for your own good and your safety," her grandfather was saying through the door. "Tonight, you'll skip dinner—Aline will bring you bread and milk tomorrow."

Elizabeth didn't dare reply. She got up and went to undress behind her Japanese-inspired painted screen. She washed and put on her nightgown as if in a trance, and went to bed, even though it was still broad daylight. Soon, torrents of rain were streaming down the slate roofs and pouring into the gutters. In the large drawing room, the docile Alcide had lit a fire at the squire's request.

Germaine's parents' house, Guerville village
The same day, same time

Gustave Caillaud was a self-employed wheelwright. His work-shop adjoined the sombre room in which he and his wife slept, in a bed enclosed by curtains. Germaine's mother also cooked there. The girl was their youngest child and slept in the attic, on a straw mattress. Her two brothers had left the county to work for the railway company. Being married with children, they didn't send any money home.

"We were so happy she got a place, our lass!" groaned Amelie Caillaud to Bonnie, who was sitting by the hearth. "We'll have to find her a new one now."

The girl had run upstairs as soon as she got home. She had quietly begged Bonnie to explain to her father what had happened. The governess, who did her utmost not to stray too far from the castle, agreed to visit the Caillauds' humble dwell-ing. She paid Amelie for her lunch, then went to the village church to light a candle, before going to the cemetery to pray at Adela Laroche's grave.

Back beside the fire, which had been reduced to a few embers under the low blackened beams, Bonnie was lost for words.

"Mrs. Caillaud, I'm going upstairs to have a few words with your daughter. I can hear her crying."

"Our Germaine, she always was a cry-baby. But think about it—she was earning good money at the castle. It's hard for her."

"I'll see if I can comfort her in any way," said Bonnie, as she set foot on the first step of a narrow staircase.

Upon her arrival at the workshop, the wheelwright had been busy reinforcing a wheel with iron. Bonnie had told him right away that Mr. Laroche had dismissed them both.

"And that, in spite of me being Miss Elizabeth's official governess," she added indignantly. "I don't cost her grandfather a single penny."

"Well, he's the one in charge, isn't he?" answered the wheelwright, as he carried on hammering at the plate of iron. "For Germaine, things are quite different. I'll give her a good beating if she has misbehaved."

"Your daughter is an excellent worker—she mustn't be punished!" protested Bonnie. "When Mr. Laroche is furious, you can't reason with him. One of his horses died last night—a grey gelding he was very fond of."

"Would that be Talion? A fine beast! Understandable that it upset him. That man is ill-humoured, with a bilious disposition."

Bonnie thought back to this brief conversation as she entered the attic. It was warm there, and you could hear the sound of the rain pattering on the tiles. Apples and pears were lined up on racks, and there were ears of corn drying on an old sheet in a corner. Germaine's straw mattress had been placed under a skylight. A wooden frame completed the crude bed, and a box served as a bedside table, with a candle holder on top.

"My poor child, calm down—your father won't hurt you!" whispered Bonnie kindly.

Germaine was sobbing heavily, her face partly buried in a filthy pillow, her blonde hair all tangled up.

"Your mother is worried, and so am I, because you won't stop crying," sighed the governess. "Miss Elizabeth will talk Mr.

Laroche round, and we'll be able to return to our duties in no time, I'm sure."

"You, perhaps, but not me!" said Germaine anxiously. "Bonnie, I'm a fallen girl. Please don't tell my parents. Here, see what he gave me!"

The adolescent girl pulled a glittering coin out of her dress pocket. Without knowing much about French coins, Bonnie remembered the golden Louis d'Or piece Justin had received after being struck in the face with a whip. Elizabeth had told her about the incident quite recently.

"A Louis d'Or," muttered Germaine, "so that I keep quiet and leave the county."

An icy chill came over Bonnie. She wasn't very supple but she managed to sit down on the dusty floor.

"What has happened to you, my child?" she asked softly, stroking her cheek.

"Since Madeleine's arrest, I've been sleeping upstairs in her room. One night, a strange sound woke me, and . . . and there was Sir, standing by my bed with a lantern in his hand. He was staggering, and I'm sure he'd been drinking, for his breath reeked of alcohol. I asked him to go away, but he hung the lamp on a nail, pulled back my sheet and thrust himself on me. You can imagine what followed. He must have been afraid I'd cry out, for he rammed a handkerchief in my mouth first. He behaved like a madman, and it hurt—oh the pain, such splitting pain! While he was doing it to me, he kept saying, 'Catherine, Catherine.' It didn't last long, and he left in a hurry. Then, this morning, he sent me home with this golden Louis d'Or coin in my pocket."

Germaine sobbed until she choked on her tears. Finally, she added, with a frightened look:

"I won't be able to marry now. I'm a fallen girl—I will be despised. No man will ever want me when I grow up!"

"Good Lord, that's abominable!" moaned Bonnie. "My poor child. This man has no morals. He's depraved and mad, raving mad. Please be brave, Germaine! I'm going to tell the police."

"Oh no—please, Bonnie—if you do that, the whole village will know what happened. Please, I'd die of shame if anyone found out. With the money I can go to Poitiers, to stay with my brother Leon. He'll find me somewhere."

"And if you're pregnant?"

"No, that can't be. I'd just had my monthlies, and my grand-mother used to say you can't catch a child at that time."

The young girl paid less attention to her language, now that she no longer had to play the role of the accomplished servant.

Bonnie was deeply moved and saddened.

"I dearly hope so, my poor Germaine. Come on, stop crying, or your mother could guess what has happened. You'd better go somewhere far away from here—and I'd better return to the castle! Miss must be back, and I don't want to leave her alone with that dirty old man."

"He would never dare harm Miss—he loves her too much," said Germaine, sniffling.

"Let's hope God can hear you! He loved his daughter Catherine too much—and you, poor thing, have had to pay the price."

Guerville Castle
The same day, two hours later

Cowering in the hollow of her bed, after much thought Elizabeth decided to get up. She got dressed in a straight skirt and a round-necked woollen bodice.

The young woman felt vulnerable and at her grandfather's mercy—being the only one who had the key, he could enter the room at any time.

Elizabeth opened the window and leaned out; the yellowish grass seemed a long way down to her. Feeling despondent, she remembered the notebook she had found in the box of tin soldiers. She knew it was essential to occupy her mind, in order to remain calm and not give in to fear.

"Everything will be all right. Bonnie won't abandon me, nor will Uncle Pierre or Richard," she muttered half-heartedly.

The young woman settled in a pink velvet wing chair and opened the first page of the notebook. Upon reading the date, she immediately recognized her mother's handwriting: *June 9, 1875, St. Diana's Day. My secret thoughts.*

Elizabeth quickly calculated that Catherine had been seventeen years old at the time.

The same age as me when I left New York, she thought to herself, and her heart tightened. She suddenly knew that she had been beckoned upstairs to read this diary.

"My dear Mummy, if it was you who called out to me, please listen. I love you very much, and I ask for forgiveness for what I did with Richard. I will marry him, I promise."

Then she began to read.

Saturday, June 12, 1875

Mother's away again, visiting Aunt Clotilde. Is she doing it on purpose? She knows very well that I don't like being alone with my father, but doesn't seem to care. Just last month, he came into my room and sat in the armchair, asking me to sit on his lap. He stroked my hair, my cheeks, my shoulders. I didn't dare move or protest, yet I wanted to scream when his breathing changed while he stared at me.

I managed to break out of his embrace by pretending I wanted to go riding. Even so, he insisted on accompanying me to the stables. Thank God the grooms, Robert and Marcel, approached him to discuss a late grain delivery. I wish I could have galloped away, never to return to the castle that I hate as much as I hate my father.

The text was three pages long, because the pages were so tiny. Filled with fear and disgust, Elizabeth continued reading:

Friday, June 25, 1875

This morning, I begged Mother to let me spend the summer months in Arcachon, at the home of Marguerite de Maumont, my friend from boarding school. After much huffing and puffing, she finally agreed, but under one condition: my father had to agree.

I was so angry that I said: "Mummy, you know perfectly well that Father will refuse. Why let me get my hopes up?"

My mother stared at me anxiously. It was then that I realized that she knew what was going on under her roof. What a relief that was! She ended up helping me pack my bags and told me she would accompany me to Rouillac station, where I could take a train to Angoulême. Marguerite would pick me up there.

Thursday, September 2, 1875

I am back at the castle, after the most wonderful days of my life at the sea, far away from my terrifying father. At last I could sleep in peace, for he no longer sat on the edge of my bed, kissing my hands and the edge of my lips, or caressing my thighs through the sheet.

Marguerite advised me to get married as soon as possible, since I wouldn't be returning to boarding school. This is what young ladies of the so-called high society are faced with: I've been asked to devote my life to a man to escape the depravity of another, who happens to be my own father.

If I ever get married, it will be out of true love.

Elizabeth was on the brink of tears, thinking of her beloved father, Guillaume. Her parents had loved each other passionately, and she wondered if Richard would make her just as happy.

Thursday, October 14, 1875

This evening, in the tack room, my father overstepped the mark. He hugged me and kissed me on the back of the neck, nibbling a lock of my hair that was sticking out of my hat. His right hand grazed my breasts. Terrified and full of disgust and anger, I pushed him away with all my might and slapped him.

If only the grooms had been outside—they would have intervened, for they respect and like me. Father was shocked by my reaction and went all red. He grabbed his crop, and I was given a good whipping, but did my best not to scream. When he finally stopped, I threatened to tell on him, saying I would run away and never come back if he ever tried to touch me again. He begged me not to. I think I made my point: he seemed truly worried about losing me.

Monday, December 27, 1875
Approximately two months of respite. We celebrated my eighteenth birthday at home with my Aunt Clotilde and Uncle Armand. Mother gave me a sewing kit made of ivory and silver-gilt to keep me busy during the winter months.

My father bought me a magnificent horse. In front of her stall, he quietly promised not to bother me anymore on the condition that I help him out with the estate's business and start smiling again.

His greatest fear seems to be that I could fall in love and marry. Mother isn't allowed to throw any balls, and he insists on escorting me every time I go riding.

I don't know what the future holds for me, but I often dream of going to America, of sailing away on a ship and putting an ocean between myself and my father. Tonight, I have promised myself to one day set foot on the cobblestones of New York.

Those last words pierced deep into Elizabeth's heart. To her surprise, she had just discovered that Catherine had wanted to leave before even meeting Guillaume Duquesne.

"Mummy, my darling Mummy!" she said softly. "You never got to admire New York, nor walk on its cobblestones. It's so unfair you died on the ship, having suffered so enormously here! Why, in God's name?"

Blinded by tears, Elizabeth tried to decipher the last entry, which had been penned in miniature writing.

October 1878

Guillaume, Guillaume, Guillaume! It is he, Guillaume, my great love. I'd write this name a hundred times if I could.

I met him three weeks ago at the Montignac fair, where I went chaperoned by my mother and Madeleine. All it took was a look followed by a smile, and I knew he was my destiny.

Last night and with the help of Marcel, an old groom and a friend of Guillaume's father, I was able to spend an hour with the man I love.

My parents were invited to a neighbour's house—a rare occurrence—so I could escape through the kitchen door.

Nothing and no one will stop me from marrying Guillaume. He is twenty-five years old and already a skilled carpenter and a member of the Carpenters' Guild. He has the most beautiful grey eyes on earth.

Elizabeth noticed that two pages were missing at the end of the notebook. Ripped page fragments suggested they had been torn out. The young woman closed the diary and put it away in her skirt pocket. It was dark in the room, so she could easily discern a ray of light under the door. Someone was standing there behind the heavy oak door.

"Grandpa?" she called out. "Open up—I know it's you. Open the door, I want to talk to you!"

There was a click. The key turned in the lock. Hugues Laroche stood there, haggard, holding a lantern.

19

Turnaround

Guerville Castle
The same evening

Elizabeth could feel the blood pound in her temples as she stood on the threshold of her room, not daring to move, in case her grandfather noticed the slightest movement. She felt her fate was being sealed at that very moment: a single step forwards or backwards could tip the balance.

If she hadn't read Catherine's diary, Elizabeth might have backed down, but knowing her mother had managed to escape and find happiness, she felt a surge of renewed strength. No, she wouldn't be a victim. Bravely, she inched forwards.

"I'd like to have a serious talk with you, Grandpa," she said sharply. "Can we go into the dining room? I would like to have dinner, too."

Taken aback, the squire looked at her suspiciously. He hesitated. With his fury subsiding, he took stock of the heinous crime he had committed in abusing Germaine. Although the memory was blurry, he remembered raping the young girl under the influence of alcohol.

"Grandpa, did you hear me?" insisted Elizabeth. "I've got a lot to say to you. For starters, I will not tolerate being punished like a child—and I want Bonnie back."

Laroche opened the door. "Your governess is preparing a meal in the kitchen," he scowled.

"What about Germaine?"

"I've just learned from Bonnie that she has got a place to go to in Poitiers. As I already said, Aline will replace her."

Laroche looked broken and disorientated all of a sudden, and Elizabeth guessed he wouldn't try anything. She hurried out of the room, in her haste to see if her governess really was there.

Without waiting for her grandfather, she ran to the pantry, where delicious aromas were wafting through the air. Vegetables were being steamed and meat was sizzling in a pan.

The room was well lit, thanks to the three opaline lamps hanging from the beams. Old Leandre and Alcide were sitting at the table, holding glasses of wine. Bonnie, an apron tied around her rounded belly, busied herself at the big cast-iron stove.

Elizabeth ran up and flung her arms round her, trembling with relief. They held each other tightly.

"Oh Bonnie, I'm terribly glad you're here! I was so worried— I already imagined you lost and distressed in the middle of the countryside."

"No, Miss, I was in the village."

"With Germaine? Why is she leaving? My grandfather dismissed her in a fit of rage, but I would have made sure she got her job back."

Bonnie pretended to be tending to the soup. She hated lying to Elizabeth but had also promised Germaine not to tell anyone. Never would she forget her desperate plea: "Please, Miss mustn't know, nor my parents—you're the only one I've told, Bonnie. If anyone finds out, I'll throw myself into the Charente river, I swear to God."

"Germaine has her pride; she couldn't bear to be fired without just cause," sighed the governess. "Besides, she probably wanted to move to the city. Meanwhile, I'm back on duty and I must say, it's nice to pitch in again!"

But Elizabeth wasn't paying attention to Bonnie's deceptively cheerful tone. She knew she had to choose her battles, and joined Hugues Laroche in the dining room.

A fire was blazing in the hearth, and her grandfather had lit the large oil lamps they kept on the nearby shelves.

This is the room we were in twelve years ago, Elizabeth thought. *My parents, Grandma, Grandpa and I—all gone now, save for the two of us.*

"You said you wanted to talk to me. I'm listening," declared Laroche awkwardly.

He glanced at the silver tray that held a bottle of cognac and crystal glasses, but didn't go near it. Chilling images ran through his mind: the look of terror in Germaine's eyes as he forced himself upon her, her blonde hair on the pillow, her tears.

"To start with, I admit I behaved badly in seeing Richard Johnson," said Elizabeth. "I fell in love with him in New York, where I enjoyed his company. When I saw him again here in France, my overwhelming feelings got the better of me. However, you haven't stopped insulting me and my mother these last two days, even though you're not exactly a saint yourself, as you well know."

Hugues Laroche turned around and stared at her. He tried to be unpleasant but didn't quite succeed.

"Are you going to blame me yet again for being a little too affectionate with you? Or is there something else?"

Elizabeth felt unsettled, for she sensed her usually ruthless grandfather's panic.

"No, you haven't done anything truly terrible—at least not yet. But earlier on, I was reading Mummy's diary, in which she described your behaviour, and it could be called incestuous."

"Incestuous! Whatever next? It was love!" Laroche snarled, frightened. "Love and jealousy. I did nothing that harmed Catherine. And to prove it, she forgave me once she was married and became a mother. We discussed it at length on the evening of your third birthday. Adela had organized a tea party in the park, Guillaume was also there. Catherine and I went for a walk under the trees, and I told her how much I regretted my past actions. My daughter was nothing but goodness and intelligence personified—she forgave my wrongdoings and even kissed me on the cheek."

This confession reassured Elizabeth in her decision. She was fed up with conflict, fear and brutality.

"In that case, Grandpa, for Mummy's sake, promise me you'll make an effort. I agree to help you run the business, even though you could also do with Richard Johnson's invaluable assistance. The Montignac locals are already talking, and there's not just my reputation to think about, but also my uncles' and Pops Toine's. If we announce our engagement and forthcoming wedding, the gossip will cease. As for you, you've got your name to think about, and the estate. We must avoid a scandal at any cost. What will your employees and customers think if I'm stuck alone with you all day in your fortress? Grandpa, I'm eighteen years old and am keen to enjoy the fine life I could have here. Just think of the balls and parties we could throw!"

Stunned by his granddaughter's speech, Hugues Laroche went to sit by the fire. Deep down, he knew she was right.

"In her diary, Mummy mentions an Aunt Clotilde," continued Elizabeth. "Is she your sister or my grandmother's?"

"My younger sister. She has been widowed for six years now and writes to me once a month, complaining about how lonely she is—despite living in a beautiful house near Segonzac!"

"And it didn't even enter your head to invite her to meet me?" exclaimed the young woman, astonished. "Why didn't she attend Grandma's funeral? So very few people were there—just the locals, and your friends from Rouillac."

"Clotilde happened to be on the Riviera at the time, in Nice. I did send her a telegram, but she couldn't get away in time."

Elizabeth wandered around the vast dining room. By now it was almost nightfall. She lit the candles of a candelabra near a window and stroked the dark-green velvet of the double curtains. Against her will and in spite of everything, she had become attached to the ancient castle, and her energetic mind was busy making plans.

"If we call a truce, Grandpa, I'll help you restore our estate to its former glory. You should invite your sister Clotilde to come and stay here: I'm certain she would love to meet me. And we could celebrate my engagement! I'm still waiting for your response on this point."

"I don't care whether it's your American, or someone else,"

he sighed. "You're right—we may as well not leave ourselves open to gossip. And since you've lived in America for years, it won't come as a surprise that you're marrying an American. But you're forgetting one crucial detail: all this is happening terribly close to Adela's death. It would be the height of indecency to celebrate while we're in mourning."

He had scored another point over Elizabeth, but this simply emboldened her.

"Well, we needn't worry about the engagement, as we can settle for a formal dinner," she stated. "Then Richard would at least be able to visit me under your supervision. I'll teach him to ride a horse. As for the wedding, it can take place a year from now, next summer. These arrangements will allow me to stay— for you should know that I had planned to run away, like Mummy, and return to New York."

The squire's whole body was trembling. He buried his face in his hands.

"I don't want to lose you, Elizabeth. I'll get treatment, I promise you. Dr. Trousset prescribed potassium bromide, and I'll quit drinking entirely. Your plans sound good to me—whatever you do, please don't leave, I beg you."

Bonnie entered, looking daggers at Hugues Laroche. She glanced at the empty table and shrugged arrogantly—which was almost comical, given her messy auburn bun and the apron tied round her middle. She pulled a tablecloth out of the heavy cherry-wood dresser.

"*I'll* set the table, Bonnie, thank you!" cried Elizabeth. "Would you mind eating supper in the pantry, just this once? Grandpa and I haven't finished talking."

"I was planning to, Miss. In any case, I'll be better off in the kitchen—there's still heaps to do," replied the governess.

As soon as she had gone, Elizabeth set out everything they needed for their meal. When she cast a furtive glance in her grandfather's direction, she saw him brushing away a few tears with his fingertips. It was as if she had just knocked out a fearsome titan, without knowing exactly how.

"Are you crying?"

"A man is sometimes torn between his good and his bad side. Admittedly, my bad side often takes over, but the possibility of losing you has made me want to become a better person. Elizabeth, I lost Catherine, my beloved daughter, my flesh and blood, and now also my wife whom I loved so dearly, even though I made her suffer. I need you by my side, whether engaged, married, or a mother—I'll want for nothing as long as you're here with me."

Hugues Laroche's sincerity deeply moved the young woman. She wanted to make an affectionate gesture, but restrained herself immediately.

"I appreciate you letting your guard down, Grandpa," she said quietly. "Ah! Here comes Bonnie with our meal."

Sitting *tête à tête*, they enjoyed a thick tomato soup laced with fresh cream, followed by fried ham and peas. They dined in silence, savouring the peace and quiet.

"I ask just one thing of you," said the squire calmly when they had finished their dessert of peaches and plums. "Respect the engagement period. You must not give yourself to Johnson until you are married."

Elizabeth blushed, remembering her grandfather's intrusion that morning.

"Logic dictates a year of chastity," he added. "If you got pregnant before the wedding, all our plans would fall apart."

"I agree—we don't have a choice," she conceded. "I promise to comply, Grandpa."

"Very good. And now, a new era is dawning!" he declared, a shy smile on his thin lips.

Shortly afterwards, Bonnie made sure to remind him of his part of the deal. Once Elizabeth had retired to her room, the governess followed the squire into the smoking room, where he was about to light a cigarillo.

"Sir," she whispered, settling on a nearby chair, "as I already told you, I am in the know about what you did to poor Germaine. If Miss Elizabeth found out, she would loathe you for the rest of her life and leave the castle at once. As for me, I'm warning you: if you dare so much as lay a finger on your granddaughter, I know my plants as well as Madeleine did, and I'm not talking about culinary herbs. But meeting your maker would be too easy a way out for you—I'd much rather tell the police about your revolting exploits. On this note, I wish you good night, Mr. Laroche."

Laroche only nodded. There was no point in fighting a losing battle.

Guerville Castle
Sunday, August 28, 1898

Upon waking, Elizabeth was a little surprised to see Bonnie stretched out next to her. Then it came to her that she had asked her governess to sleep in her bed. They'd intended to have a long talk, but had dropped off in no time, exhausted from all the emotion.

Purple rays lit up the large bedroom. It was dawn, and the birds were singing cheerfully in the park.

"Bonnie, it's morning," whispered the young woman. "I have to talk to you."

"Yes, yes, I know," her governess grumbled drowsily.

When Bonnie turned around Elizabeth tried hard not to laugh. Messy auburn locks protruded from Bonnie's nightcap, and her cheeks were marked by the folds of the pillow.

"It's not very kind of you to mock me, Miss," she said. "I know I'm not a pretty sight in the morning."

"But on the contrary—you're cute, Bonnie! You look like a doll."

"Hum! A thirty-four-year-old doll with red hair, you mean? I don't know what your Uncle Jean sees in me. Anyway, I've changed my mind about getting married."

Elizabeth straightened up and patted her only friend's shoulder compassionately.

"Do tell me why, Bonnie. But first, you should know that I'll soon be engaged to Richard Johnson. Forgive me for keeping all these things from you lately—I worried that they might startle you."

"I always prefer to know, Miss!"

Elizabeth then quietly told her everything. She confessed to getting intimate with Johnson on board the liner, and becoming his mistress in July, a mere two days after Adela Laroche's funeral. Finally, she told her about the dreadful incident the day before.

"Good heavens! Your grandfather forced the door of your pretty little cottage and found you and Richard naked?" she cried, her eyes popping out of her head. "I must say, I'm very disappointed, Miss. I didn't know you had it in you to transgress the church's rules. How could you give yourself to this man without being married?"

"I was so unhappy, Bonnie. Justin had gone—you know why. I knew we would never be allowed to love each other. But it's not just that—you have to take my word for it. The night we slept at the Three Pillars in Angoulême, I had the same nightmare that I'd had on the boat. Again, I woke up terrified, but this time I put it all down on paper. I've been noting what I see in my dreams ever since, especially if they feel significant or threatening."

Bonnie sat up. She turned very pale and crossed herself, before responding:

"And what happened to you in these nightmares, Miss?"

"A man in black in a darkened room was raping me. He didn't have a face. It was a barbaric, horrific experience, and I remember wanting to die. At first I thought it was Richard, but then I recognized the man in the second nightmare. Do I need to tell you his name?"

"Probably not," said the governess, thinking of young Germaine, who had been brutally raped just the night before.

"I failed to save Daddy when I was a child. This is why I sought to change my destiny, by giving myself to Richard. And I succeeded, Bonnie! My grandfather wouldn't dare touch me now, and even less once I'm married. Had he rejected what I proposed last night, I would have told him about my dream."

Elizabeth then took Catherine's diary out of her bedside-table drawer.

"I want you to read it, Bonnie. I want you to know how strongly I felt Mummy's presence in the nursery and here in this room. Had I not read her words, I wouldn't have had the courage to confront my grandfather. I want to stay in France now, to look after my dear Pops Toine and my cousins, Gilles and Laurent. And you and Uncle Jean will get married, I'm sure of it. There—now I've told you everything, and a huge weight is off my mind."

"I wish I could say the same, Miss."

"What's bothering you? Tell me, Bonnie. If only you'd use my first name, it would break down that last barrier between us."

"I'm sorry, I can't—besides, I like calling you 'Miss' even though, alas, you're not a miss anymore. Oh, don't take it personally, but at barely eighteen you already know more about relationships than me. Don't you think I'd have to do *it*, if I were to marry your uncle?"

"I suppose so!"

"Well, bother! To tell the truth, it scares me. I asked one of my cousins, when I thought I was going to marry Harrison, but all she said was, 'You'll see when the time comes.' That really wasn't much help to me."

Bonnie kept staring at the muslin curtains that filtered out the sun, so as not to have to face Elizabeth. But the young woman whispered in her ear:

"The first time is a little painful, but I assure you, it becomes very pleasurable and even exciting afterwards. As I see it, the most important thing is that you truly love your husband."

Elizabeth held back a sigh and stood up. Barefoot, she trotted to the window and opened it. An enchanting landscape stretched out in front of her, its vivid summer colours slowly fading. A flight of swallows soared across the pale-blue sky, and the damp ground filled the air with its fragrance. In the distance lay the vineyards, and she could spot horses behind the oak trees in the meadow.

Elizabeth tried to convince herself that a peaceful future awaited her. The next few days would be so busy, she wouldn't even have time to think about Justin. At some point though, he would return—it was inevitable.

And I will love him, Mummy, since he is your brother and as gentle and kind as you were.

Bonnie saw her blow an invisible kiss and laugh softly, her delicate features outlined by the morning light.

The governess promised herself to keep Germaine's secret, to spare Elizabeth, who had been through enough already and deserved to be happy—even if that happiness was founded on lies and wrongdoings.

The Dakota Building, New York
Monday, January 2, 1899

It was snowing so heavily and was so cold that Maybel Woolworth had ceased to go for daily walks in Central Park with her neighbour Scarlett Turner. The two women were now best friends, spending hours chatting over biscuits and tea, and had even celebrated their forty-fourth birthdays together.

Whenever Edward wasn't there, they would take the tarot cards and seek answers to their respective problems. The two women had spent the late summer and early autumn studying the colourful images on the cards, trying to interpret what the future had in store for them.

Scarlett had stayed single to retain her independence, but was now keen to meet her soul mate. Maybel, on the other hand, was eager to learn when Elizabeth would return.

In August she had been absolutely certain her daughter would come home, but her frantic hopes had been dashed by the long letter she had just received. Elizabeth had announced her impending engagement to Richard Johnson in October, explaining that her grandfather had mellowed at the thought of losing her. She went as far as claiming he was a new man.

Maybel pondered over this particular sentence, curled up in a leather armchair and wrapped in a sumptuous angora wool shawl. Familiar footsteps resounded in the apartment's wide hallway, and she could hear the rasping voice of their servant, Norma, who was still working for them. Her husband entered the living room shortly afterwards and kissed her on the forehead.

"Darling, don't tell me you are re-reading Lisbeth's old letters?" he asked, stroking her hair. "Are you alone? Lucky me—I was afraid of finding Scarlett on the couch, talking to one of the ghosts she keeps seeing."

"Edward, it's not a laughing matter. You spend your days at the office and on Wall Street; I'd be terribly bored without her. She has a date on Broadway today."

"That's good news, because I have a surprise—a new letter, and judging by the thickness, it must contain more photos!"

"How wonderful!" exclaimed Maybel. "Don't worry about me poring over Lisbeth's delightful prose. I'll be overjoyed to see her again this summer, at her wedding in France. Mr. Laroche really has changed—he has invited us!"

She clapped her hands like a happy child. Touched, Edward handed her the envelope.

"And before we arrive at the *château*, we'll spend a few days on the famous French Riviera—the Côte d'Azur!" he reminded her. "You've taken your depression by the horns, Maybel, and it's a real pleasure for me to offer you this journey."

"I've been letting my imagination run away with me," she said, "although it's hard to believe, looking at the snow that's falling outside! And my feet are freezing, despite the central heating. Yet in July, I shall discover France, the Mediterranean Sea, and above all, I'll hold Lisbeth in my arms again. Don't forget, you promised me a whole new wardrobe. French women are at the very height of fashion!"

"Open the letter quickly!" he said in reply.

The Woolworths loved looking at the pictures Elizabeth sent them regularly. Her engagement to the handsome Richard Johnson hadn't come as a surprise to them, as they knew him to be an attractive, educated and imaginative young man.

"We have a real gallery of pictures now," remarked Maybel.

She had bought a large leather-bound album to keep the photographs neat and in chronological order. The couple grinned as they contemplated the pictures of harvest-time they'd received a while back, especially the one in which their Lisbeth was wearing a straw hat and holding a sackful of grapes. They also had a larger photograph which had been taken on the day of her engagement. Edward had had it framed, and it proudly dominated the mantelpiece.

Maybel pointed it out to her husband, nodding her head. She often admired the beaming young girl who was posing at the foot of the castle walls on Johnson's arm.

"She radiated beauty that day! It must have been sunny outside—her hair is shining in the light," she sighed, enraptured. "That long pleated dress with its lacy neckline suited her perfectly."

"We should be pleased she's marrying an American," added Edward. "Richard has family in New York, so they'll have reason enough to visit from time to time."

His wife tried to hush him by placing her index finger on his mouth, but he covered it with kisses.

"I'm about to read it, darling," she said, giggling.

Guerville Castle
December 18, 1898

Dear Mom and Dad,

By the time you get this letter, we will be in 1899, a new year that will see me become Mrs. Johnson. It will also bring me the great pleasure of seeing you again, my dear second parents!

I've grown quite fond of this term I've coined, as my love for you remains unchanged, and I am so looking forward to showing you around the castle, the vineyards, the wine cellars and the stables.

You would think that my life seems to be almost perfect now! The locals even take their hats off to me when I ride or drive past.

Sadly—and this will make you laugh—my fiancé is just no good at horse riding. He prefers motor cars and plans to buy one as soon as possible.

As I told you in my last letter, Clotilde, my grandfather's sister, has moved into the castle permanently now. She is a charming and extremely talkative lady who loves playing endless rounds of chess with Richard and Grandpa.

Her daughter, Anne-Marie, has also been living with us for the past month. She'll stay until New Year's Day. We get along well, although I can't say I envy her: at just thirty-six years old, she is already a widow.

I am still satisfied with Aline, the servant who replaced Germaine, though I do miss Germaine's sweet little face. We've hired a cook and a new maid, as the household chores have increased now that there are more of us.

Now to dear Bonnie. We're still waiting for her to get engaged or married. My Uncle Jean misses her, but since I managed to get him his job in the stable back, he keeps running into his "intended", as he refers to her.

It saddens me all the more, because I know why Bonnie can't bring herself to marry him. She doesn't want to be parted from me, even though I'm in good company and, admittedly, don't have much time to devote to her anyway.

This autumn, which was particularly wet, I had to keep a close eye on my Grandpa Toine's health, as his rheumatism was at its worst. He jokes about it though, telling me repeatedly that all millers suffer from this painful and crippling ailment because they live at the water's edge.

Mom darling, I believe you liked my powder-pink engagement dress. I'll see to it that my wedding dress dazzles you even more: Richard is the one designing it. My fiancé might be unable to stay on a horse for long, but he is a highly talented artist! As it will be hot in July, I thought of silk chiffon. I'll let you into a secret: the bodice will be embroidered with flowers made of mother-of-pearl.

What other news have I got? I have come to terms with my past—that is, my childhood and the death of my beloved parents. Richard tells me incessantly that I must look forward, distract myself and shine in society, so we go to balls at the homes of wealthy neighbours. Out of respect for my late grandmother, we haven't yet invited anyone to waltz in our drawing room, though we will, notably on the evening of our wedding. I'll save the first dance for you, Dad.

Just a few final lines to let you know that Grandpa and Richard are getting along reasonably well.

They discuss architecture and the restoration of the castle's Renaissance structure, and to make an even better impression, Richard has become involved in wine sales abroad. By that I mean the Laroche cognac, of course.

I promise to write to you once a month between now and this summer, when I'll finally have the pleasure of welcoming you here in Charente. I can't wait to introduce you to Grandpa Toine, who has already set aside a bottle of his best cider for the occasion.

I am enclosing a few more pictures with this letter. They show Bonnie, now slim and cheerful, my Uncle Jean, who is the spitting image of my dear father, as well as my cousins Gilles and Laurent. The boys are ten and seven years old, and never miss an occasion to cuddle me or beam at me. I help them with their schoolwork whenever I visit my Aunt Yvonne.

The time has come to decorate the giant Christmas tree in the dining room. Anne-Marie and Clotilde are waiting for me to do it, because I'm the only one who can venture all the way up the stepladder without getting vertigo. Bonnie has already devised the menu for Christmas Eve, and will spoil us with *roasted pheasant, truffles* en papillotes, *yule log and other delicacies. You must know that she is now also the castle's housekeeper, in addition to her duties as my governess.*

I picked out a greeting card for you both when I went to Angoulême with Aunt Clotilde. It will certainly please you, for it has been decorated with artificial frost that reminds me of Central Park in deep winter.

With all my love,
Your Lisbeth.

Maybel folded the two sheets of paper carefully and studied the greetings card. It depicted a frozen lake bordered by holly bushes, and in the background a small house with a snow-covered roof and an illuminated window. A robin was perched on an adjacent tree. Edward gently brushed over the silver glitter.

"How thoughtful and caring our daughter is," he said softly. "Our darling daughter."

"No one can hear us—we can call her whatever we want," Maybel reminded him. "Lisbeth seems to be happy there, at last. I'm not going to indulge in self-pity, although I must admit that I was thrilled when she announced her return, after Adela Laroche's death."

"She *is* happy there," corrected Edward. "I can feel her enthusiasm and energy, and she has a mountain of support from her family—from both her families, I should say."

"Yes, you're right."

The trader tenderly pulled her towards him. He was weary and sought rest in the warmth, lulled by the crackling of the fire and the sight of the heavy snowflakes falling outside of the tall windows of the Dakota Building. He would have been unsettled, had he been able to read his wife's thoughts.

Did Scarlett get it wrong, then? wondered Maybel. *When she draws the cards, she often claims that Lisbeth loves another man and is unhappy, deep down. I mustn't listen to her anymore, as Edward advised me.*

Feeling chilly, she took shelter in her husband's arms, dreaming of the beautiful summer day when they would embark for France.

Montignac
Thursday, April 20, 1899

The boat gently glided along the green waters of the Charente river. Richard had pulled a fashionable straw boater over his black hair and was rowing at a steady pace, without undue effort. Lost in thought, Elizabeth listened to the lapping of the current against the wooden hull. She was holding a satin parasol to protect her face from the sun.

"We must look like characters out of a Renoir painting," cried Anne-Marie, who was shielding herself with a yellow parasol.

The squire's niece was a keen artist, and eager to share this passion with Elizabeth, who would listen attentively. The charming young widow had stayed on after New Year's Day, and it was clear that she would delay her departure until the wedding.

"This boat trip was an exquisite idea," she added. "Thank you, Richard."

"My fiancé is full of bright ideas when it comes to pleasing me," agreed Elizabeth. "I hope we will end up finding that little island Uncle Pierre was telling us about. *The Luncheon on the Grass*—Anne-Marie, does that ring a bell?"

"Of course: it's a painting by Édouard Manet. Let's just hope that neither of us will be playing the role of the naked young woman!"

They burst out laughing, to Richard's annoyance. Although he was thrilled to be officially engaged to Elizabeth, the period of chastity she had imposed on him was making him very prickly.

"Renoir also painted his own *Luncheon*," added Anne-Marie, "but only years later, and the painting didn't cause a stir. Oh, dear Elizabeth, I would love to take you to Paris to visit the Louvre and Versailles!"

"We will go next year, in 1900," Elizabeth replied enthusiastically. "Richard will accompany us—he is thoroughly familiar with the capital, or so he tells me."

"Or so I tell you? Elizabeth, I spent three weeks there!" protested Richard. "You've been taunting me non-stop since yesterday—don't you agree, Anne-Marie?"

"Perhaps, but let's blame the springtime air and your beautiful fiancée's sweet and playful nature," she replied. "Would you rather she were morose and quiet?"

"Of course not," snapped Richard.

He quickened the pace, leaning back to plunge the oars deeper into the water. Elizabeth pretended to marvel at the yellow irises growing on the bank. She knew perfectly well what was making her future husband so irritable.

I have to say, I'm rather enjoying this long period of abstinence. Richard refers to it as "leaving you in peace", but I really don't want to get pregnant before our wedding, she mused.

Nonetheless, she had almost given in to him on several occasions, as he begged her and harassed her with kisses whenever they were alone. But so far she had managed to resist him, remembering the promise she had made to her grandfather.

"I won't betray my promise, Richard. You have easy access to the castle and I have a good dowry, which will allow you to buy that famous motor car," she said, trying to appease him. "My grandfather has kept his promise, too—he is nothing like his old self, you've seen it for yourself. So be patient."

The handsome American was patient, but she was such a delicate creature of rare beauty and charm that it felt like torture. He kept imagining the torrid love scenes they would act out, once she bore his name. They planned to spend their honeymoon on the Mediterranean coast, and even take the boat to Corsica, an island Elizabeth was keen to discover.

An hour later the trio were sitting on a large blanket, finishing off the picnic. Richard had rowed up a branch of the river, in the shade of ash and willow trees, and then docked on a small island. A wooden cabin daubed with whitewash sat on this small patch of ground.

The two women had tucked into the fresh bread, the hard-boiled eggs and Bonnie's pie at once, but the American had lit a cigarette before nibbling on some cheese and walnuts.

"What a romantic spot!" raved Anne-Marie. "Would you like some tea, Elizabeth?"

"Yes, please. But let me serve you—pass me your cup."

She opened the Thermos flask and smiled sweetly at Anne-Marie. Suddenly, a fish leapt out of the water and Elizabeth jumped, spilling some of the tea on her striped skirt.

"Oh no! I'm so clumsy these days," she sighed.

"You're jittery because your birthday is approaching, my dear," said Richard. "Really, what were you thinking, organizing a costume ball that will be more of a tea party in the park than an actual ball? I'd much rather we went to Angoulême to dine in a fine restaurant, the day you turn nineteen."

"Don't upset her," preached Anne-Marie. "You know very well it was my mother's idea, not Elizabeth's."

"Indeed. When she was a young girl, my great-aunt Clotilde couldn't get enough of masked balls, so we decided to celebrate my nineteenth birthday by dressing up. It will be held in the park, out of respect for my late grandmother, and we'll rely on a single violinist for the music. Even Gilles and Laurent will be there—can you imagine, Grandpa has agreed to invite them! Uncle Jean will fetch them in a horse-drawn carriage."

"Forgive me, Lisbeth," sighed Richard, taking her hand. "I'm more worried about how you intend to disguise me. I don't want to look ridiculous."

"I promise to settle on something by tomorrow at the latest, darling," she replied, giggling, "but I do see you as a pirate or a marquis, with a big feathered hat and white stockings."

This time, Anne-Marie burst out laughing, and Elizabeth soon joined in. Catherine's first cousin was such charming company that Elizabeth envisaged the forthcoming weeks as a series of cheerful moments, filled with literary and artistic conversations.

"And where do you think you'll obtain such an extravagant marquis outfit from?" said Richard, alarmed.

"I could easily sew it myself, with Bonnie's help," replied Elizabeth mischievously.

They continued to chat about the costumes and the elaborate wedding cake that the new baker, an expert in choux pastry, would make. Finally, Anne-Marie stretched out in the sun, her hat over her face. She was a pretty, brown-eyed brunette, with the Roman nose that was so common in the Laroche family.

"She has fallen asleep," whispered Richard, a quarter of an hour later. "Lisbeth, why don't we visit that cabin?"

He was begging her with his warm, amber gaze and pouted lips. Elizabeth got up quietly and followed him through the wild grasses and nettles. She felt dangerously languorous. Their boat trip on the river and the secluded setting of the small island had made her more receptive to her fiancé's seductive allure.

Richard had no difficulty in opening the rickety door. The cabin had been abandoned years ago, but had a surprisingly cosy interior.

Hand in hand, the young couple stared at the simple layout of the cabin: woodworm-eaten shelves, two stools made out of logs, a wooden crate, and two bamboo-handled fishing nets with holes in them, hanging from a nail.

"The fisherman who used to come here must have died," muttered Elizabeth.

"Have you nothing more cheerful to say, sweetheart? Am I at least entitled to a few kisses and embraces?"

The young man didn't wait for her answer, and firmly pressed his mouth against hers, cupping her right breast with the palm of his hand. He didn't hide his mounting excitement from her and mimicked the sexual act with his tongue. Then he slid his hand under her skirt, but Elizabeth escaped his clutches.

"Have you lost your mind? Anne-Marie might wake up! She will come looking for us . . . I know you, Richard—if I let you,

you'll lose control. In less than three months I'll be your wife, and you'll have me at your disposal day and night. Sometimes I wish you would cuddle me more, simply to be tender and romantic! I came here hoping for a moment of tenderness and bonding, but you're only interested in a hasty and furtive grope."

Disappointed and humiliated, Elizabeth ran off, hastily wiping away the tears that ran down her cheeks. She came to a halt in front an elm tree and sat down.

What a fool I was to think Richard would ever grow into a caring, affectionate man, she thought. *Oh, he can be, but only after he's had his pleasure. Admittedly, I yearn for it too. My legs start to tremble as soon as he touches me, and I go all weak, completely at his mercy.*

Gradually, the young woman calmed down. She had had the strength to resist her own desires, which were so strong, they alarmed her. Thinking she had inherited her grandfather's failings, she had adopted a more forgiving attitude towards Hugues Laroche.

Already, Richard came running, a sheepish look on his face. He helped her up and she forced a smile.

"I beg your forgiveness, Lisbeth. Come, Anne-Marie would like to go home."

The trip back was less joyful. The sky was overcast and all three were silent, plunged in their own thoughts.

Too bad—I'll go back into town tomorrow evening and stop by the brothel, pondered the American. *Otherwise, Lisbeth will loathe me and could go as far as cancelling our wedding.*

As for Anne-Marie, she was thinking about her late husband, who had died of tuberculosis six years, to the day, after they got married. She hadn't wanted to love another man after that.

There'll only ever be one man in my life. My only regret is that I don't have any children to care for. It must be my destiny.

Elizabeth was thinking neither of love nor of future children. She had had a strange dream two nights ago. It was not a nightmare, but she could tell that it was a premonition. Everything had taken place in the dark and she had been alone, looking for a huge chest in which she hoped to find some old disguises and costumes. Suddenly, she was crying and screaming, even though she wasn't being threatened by anyone.

Why on earth did I dream that? she wondered, as she skimmed the surface of the water with her fingertips. *I can still smell the dust, and feel the old wood of the floorboards beneath my feet.*

More intrigued than worried, she had been surprised to learn the next morning that the attic still housed a large leather chest.

"It came to my mind the day before yesterday, when we settled on a costume ball for your birthday," Clotilde had told her. "It will be just delightful! Our mother always threw a masked ball at the end of Lent for Mardi Gras. She had Hugues dress up as a knight once, and I wore a shepherd's robe. You should go up to the attic before your birthday—you might find a few nice things up there!"

Her great-aunt's words haunted Elizabeth until they reached the stables. They had used the carriage to travel to the riverbank and back again. Uncle Jean rushed up to them and patted the horse, a sturdy grey Percheron.

"Did you have a nice trip?" he enquired, helping Anne-Marie out of the carriage.

"It was enchanting," she replied.

"And we easily found the little island that Uncle Pierre had told us about, thanks to the little cabin that can be seen from the river," added Elizabeth. "Richard is a passionate rower—he should enter a few competitions!"

"Another dig," complained Richard, laughing. "In fact, Jean, it was rather hard going on the way back—my muscles were aching."

"Bonnie will be waiting to serve tea to you—you can relax now," said Jean, winking at his niece's fiancé.

Elizabeth took the time to go and stroke Pearl's filly, which had been born in February and was kept by the mare's side in a nearby paddock. Pearl greeted her with a soft whinny and was rewarded with a piece of hard bread.

*

Clotilde greeted the little troop with a broad smile. She was embroidering beside the fire in the dining room. She preferred this cosy room rather than the large drawing room.

"Tea is ready," she announced. "Anne-Marie, my dear girl, you look so well—it must be the fresh air! Bonnie will bring us some candied fruitcake."

"Where is Grandpa?" asked Elizabeth.

"My brother is unpredictable," sighed Clotilde. "He decided to go to Rouillac, on Galant. According to Hugues, the stallion needed exercising, but I assume it was an excuse, and that this unforeseen jaunt has something to do with your birthday."

Anne-Marie took Elizabeth by the waist and kissed her on the cheek.

"All of us here want to spoil you, dear cousin," she whispered in her ear.

"Indeed!" crowed Richard. "I've already bought your present."

A surge of happiness swept over Elizabeth. As the months went by, the shadows and grief of the past were fading, and the presence of her great-aunt and her daughter had greatly contributed to this. Elizabeth was now even able to divide her time between the Laroches and the Duquesnes.

Of course, she knew that her Pops Toine and Uncle Pierre would never set foot in the castle, or even its grounds, but it didn't bother her, since they preferred to welcome her at the mill.

"While you were out, young ones, I compiled the guest list," announced Clotilde. "There will be about ten of us on Saturday. Bonnie has agreed to wear a wolf mask, but refuses to disguise herself. As for Dr. Trousset, his wife and their three daughters confirmed their attendance by return post."

Elizabeth nodded, but was suddenly overcome by a strange feeling. She had been so happy earlier on but felt immensely distressed now, her chest tightening in panic. The young woman could no longer hear her great-aunt's words. What is more, her eyes were glued to a photograph of Catherine that had been taken on the day of her mother's twentieth birthday. The squire had shown it to her on Christmas Eve, the day he'd had it framed.

Mummy, my beautiful sweet Mummy, you're looking at me as if you were still alive!

Distraught and frightened, Elizabeth realized she needed a moment. By chance, Bonnie had just appeared with the warm cake and began to slice it. The distraction was timely: no one paid much attention to the young woman when she got up and hurried out of the room.

"I'm going up to my room to get a shawl!" she shouted back.

In reality though, Elizabeth made her way up to the attic as fast as she could. She knew only a part of it, the rest having been allocated to the servants for centuries.

I went up there after Justin left, to see where Madeleine used to hide him, she remembered. *It was a sad nook directly under the framework, with a straw mattress.*

She walked past the greyish partitions which divided the small rooms that had housed generations of servants, house-keepers and laundry maids. Beyond was a vast space flooded with darkness: the huge attic space.

"Mummy, why have you brought me here?" asked Elizabeth in a frail, trembling voice.

20

A Dramatic Turn of Events

Guerville Castle
The same day, same time

The castle's vast attic space was another hidden world within Elizabeth's reach; one she had overlooked so far. It contained damaged, dusty pieces of furniture, half-open chests—which she guessed contained old books—and disembowelled mattresses, as well as split bolsters in which mice had made their nests.

Old slate roof tiles and pieces of zinc guttering had been piled up under the sloping roofs. The young woman had hoped to come across the chest she had seen in her dreams, most likely the one her great-aunt had mentioned, but found nothing but discoloured cardboard boxes and open leather suitcases on top of old clothes and bits of shabby cloth.

"I'm wasting my time!" she whispered.

The flapping of wings nearby startled her. Disturbed by her presence, a white owl had fled the beam it was perched on.

Elizabeth watched it glide around the complex network of rafters that comprised the gigantic roof structure. With surprising ease, the bird weaved its way through the space between a door and its stone archway.

"This must surely lead to another attic room in one of the towers," she said under her breath.

Elizabeth had long since lost her bearings and couldn't tell which tower it led to, but her curiosity was piqued, and she hastened to follow the owl. She lifted the door latch, the wood of which was unusually well preserved.

"It's locked!"

Elizabeth examined the bolt, which wasn't even rusty. It seemed clear to her that she'd been led here either through her dream, or by a certain someone.

"Mummy, is that you?" she whispered. "What do you want me to do? They will start wondering where I am, downstairs, if I don't rejoin them soon."

Elizabeth was convinced that her mother could hear her, ready to lend a helping hand. Although ill at ease, she searched for the key in every nook and cranny at the bottom of the high tower wall, which was grouted with lime to the floorboards. The young woman even checked in the crevices of the ancient stone.

"What a waste of time. Whoever locked this door has also kept the key, and it can only be Grandpa. But will he give it to me? And what could he be hiding in here?"

Her thoughts were racing. Looking up at the rafters above her head, she suddenly had an idea. The young woman got on tiptoe and ran her fingers along the surface, which was thick with dust. About ten inches along, just when she was about to give up, her thumb grazed a metal object. It was the key. Relieved, she hastily opened the door. If anyone should find her, it would only be Richard or Bonnie, and she had her explanation at the ready:

I'll say that I wanted to bring the disguises down to them, so we could look through them together.

Despite the waning daylight, Elizabeth spotted the dreamed-of chest at once. It was massive, almost a miniature cupboard, but with a lid.

"So that's what it was all about?" Elizabeth exclaimed in amazement.

She was disappointed, having hoped to discover something more meaningful.

Leaning forward, she sifted through silky costumes that smelled of musty fabric, stiffened false collars and lengths of lace. But the dresses were small and mostly in tatters, as were the boys' outfits.

Exasperated, she seized a black hat adorned with a long red feather, and threw it with all her might against the adjacent wall. Then she stood up briskly, ready to return to the dining room.

"What's that?"

Elizabeth stared in bewilderment at two large wooden trunks, one of which was reinforced with leather, the other with iron. Her heartbeat slowed right down, as if about to stop, for she recognized these two trunks.

She could remember them from elsewhere, from years ago.

"Daddy labelled his trunk on the red flagstones of our kitchen—the one with iron reinforcements. And Mummy sat laughing on ours, which had leather reinforcements. Oh, God!"

Ice-cold with shock, she walked around the chest and knelt down in front of her parents' luggage, which had disappeared the day they boarded *La Champagne*. Her trembling hands undid the lock of the trunk in which Catherine had carefully stowed their belongings.

"Your doll will be safe, my princess. We'll give her some fresh sea air as soon as we're on the boat," she had said.

These words resounded in Elizabeth's mind as she looked at her mother's folded clothes, which lay next to her own, and her doll. Everything was still intact. She seized the puppet and crushed it against her chest.

Antoine Duquesne had made it for her with so much love, carving the body, arms and legs from fine lime-tree wood. For the head, the miller had used boxwood on which he had drawn a smiling face.

"And he had sewn the clothes himself, from striped cotton fabric, in pretty colours. I remember, Pops Toine warned me not to pull on the woollen braids he had glued on under her red hat."

Elizabeth couldn't breathe. She wanted to cry and scream, but the shock was so violent, she couldn't make a sound. The young woman hesitated, then put the doll back in its place and grabbed one of Catherine's bodices.

"It still smells of her perfume! Mummy, oh Mummy . . ."

The young woman blocked out all her thoughts and assumptions as to what it meant, lest she become hysterical. She went on to open her father's trunk. Beneath her wide-eyed gaze, she could distinguish the shape of the carpenter's tools, wrapped in tea towels to protect them.

Guillaume had packed them on top of his clothes—grey overalls and corduroy trousers.

"No, please, no!" wailed Elizabeth, who finally broke down and sobbed her heart out, releasing the explosive tension inside her.

Bonnie found her cowering, in tears. She tapped her on the shoulder.

"Miss? What's the matter? Your great-aunt sent me to look for you in the attic. She was right to think you'd decided to unearth the famous trunk. And you have! Is this the ancient chest full of rags? But why are you crying?"

"Bonnie, these two trunks belonged to my parents. We thought we had lost them, either on the boat or at the docks in Le Havre! But they're right here!" stammered Elizabeth, choking on her tears.

"There must be an explanation, Miss!"

"Bonnie, please lock us in: no one must come in until I find out exactly what happened. Look, this is the doll Pops Toine gave me to keep me company during the crossing. He gave it to me a week before we left, and I guarded it with my life."

"And I remember you asking for it during your first night at the Woolworths'," Bonnie said quietly.

"No, that was another one I'd lost, the tiny one that Mummy made on the liner, by knotting handkerchiefs together onto a piece of wood. Bonnie, we must think. How did these trunks end up in the attic space of one of the castle towers?"

With more ease than in the past, the governess settled on the floorboards and took a good look at the luggage.

"It's very simple, Miss. As they were lost, they were sent back to your grandfather. The people at the railway company must have inspected them and obtained your mother or father's name."

"But in that case, the trunks would have been sent back to the mill. The name Laroche is not mentioned anywhere on them, nor is Guerville."

Bonnie had no choice but to agree. Elizabeth wiped the tears from her cheeks with her forearm.

"Assuming the luggage somehow got returned here, Grandpa and Grandma should have told me, and even shown it to me."

"Maybe they were afraid of upsetting you?"

"Perhaps, but that's unlikely. Especially in my grandfather's case. I must admit, his behaviour has improved, but I'm not entirely reassured. It's as if he were making a superhuman effort to behave appropriately, but could still harm me."

"Don't torture yourself about that, Miss," said Bonnie fiercely. "Mr. Laroche wouldn't dare. If you think about it, he is as meek as anything in front of his sister. Bear in mind that he doesn't want to lose you."

Elizabeth sighed, plagued by intense nostalgia. With the back of her hand, she touched Guillaume's cap, then stroked a sachet of lavender buried between Catherine's nightgowns.

"And this leather wallet, did it belong to your daddy?" asked Bonnie suddenly.

"Where was it?"

"Behind his trunk—the one containing his tools. I'm afraid I'm starting to have my doubts. It's crocodile skin, which costs a fortune."

"Let me see!" cried the young woman. "No, I've never seen this wallet before. You think there are banknotes inside? It feels thick. No, it seems to be papers, receipts."

It took Elizabeth just a few minutes to figure it out. She examined the papers one by one, her mouth agape and her blue eyes filled with unspeakable horror. Bonnie watched her beautiful face turn a deathly white from the shock of her discovery.

"That can't be true!" she gasped in a voice that could barely be heard. "No, he couldn't have ... No, he wouldn't have dared ..."

She fell silent, about to faint. It took all her energy and adren-
alin-fuelled rage to keep her from passing out, so she lay down
on the floorboards.

"Look, Bonnie, look. Read it!"

So her governess started reading. The silence was interspersed by "Good Lord!" and "My God!"—but the worst was
yet to come.

"The most appalling part, Miss, is the two pages that were
folded into quarters! You haven't read them. I'm sure they're
from your mother's diary. They've been torn out, but the date
matches."

Bonnie helped her sit up, rubbing her temples and cheeks.
Elizabeth was barely able to decipher Catherine's handwriting,
which revealed her state of fear and panic.

*On December 10, 1878—cursed day and cursed night—I told
Papa that I was going to marry Guillaume in January, as I
will come of age in twelve days' time. He went berserk, while
my poor mother was bedridden on account of a miscarriage.
She heard us shouting, as the argument turned extremely
violent. He slapped me a few times, then the man who claims to
be a model father kissed me on the lips in an outrageous manner
and pulled me tightly against him. I felt he desired me, and it
was disgusting. He fondled my breasts, and even lower down,
through my skirt. I was terrified and found him so revolting
that I bit him in the cheek. When he let go of me, I ran upstairs
and locked myself in my room.*

*But the same night, he knocked on my door, begging me to
open it, saying he wanted to ask me for forgiveness. I already
knew what he really wanted, and didn't give in, but ran to my
mother's bedside.*

*I've made my decision: tomorrow I'm running away.
Antoine Duquesne will take me in until the wedding, and
Guillaume and his two brothers will protect me. My nightmare
will finally be over.*

"It must have been that very night that he went up to Madeleine's room," remarked Bonnie, once Elizabeth had folded up the pages.

"Yes, I suppose so. And there was I, starting to feel sorry for him. I will never, ever forgive him! The man is a filthy pervert— a madman and a villain."

"I know, Miss. Alas, I know."

"My poor Daddy—I can see him coming towards us, on the quay in Le Havre. He had been beaten up, his face was bleeding, and his money and his father's pocket watch had been stolen . . . Even his wedding ring, Bonnie! And the scumbags that my grandfather—no, I can no longer call him that—those thugs that Laroche paid to kill Daddy kept the jewellery in return for their work. Luckily, Daddy was strong and a good fighter, or I'd have lost him before we even got to New York."

"How absolutely dreadful!" stuttered Bonnie, flabbergasted. "His plan seems obvious: had your father died or been severely injured, your mother would have stayed in France and returned to the castle with you."

"You're right. That's the evil mind of an insanely jealous man who refused to let his daughter go, because he loved her as a man would love a wife," whispered Elizabeth. "And those same thugs must have stolen our trunks first. It all makes sense! They had to stop Mummy and me from going to America. Bonnie, I feel sick to the stomach—I want to kill him!"

"Hush, Miss—don't talk like that."

Elizabeth was shaking convulsively, obsessed by the run-of-the-mill words that could have signed her father's death warrant. Looming out at her on the beige paper telegrams she and Bonnie had read were the words, "*couldn't eliminate Duquesne*" and "*send large sum promised, without delay*". At a later date, Laroche must have given orders and instructions, because they replied that the matter would be settled quickly.

All these unscrupulous, shameless exchanges sent shockwaves through Elizabeth's body. She begged her governess to put the papers back in the wallet.

"What are we going to do, Bonnie?" she asked, her teeth chattering. "I can't go back down and face my great-aunt and Anne-Marie in this state. You go and make up some story—I knocked my head against a rafter and you brought me back to my room, or something."

"And your grandfather?"

"Don't call him that again, please!"

A click in the lock silenced her. After double-locking the door, Bonnie had put the key in the pocket of her white apron, without thinking.

Hugues Laroche pushed the door open. He appeared gigantic to them, as they were sitting on the floor.

"Female curiosity," he said in a hoarse voice, having noticed the open trunks. "I was careful to get a spare key cut. Please go, Bonnie—I want to talk to my granddaughter alone."

"Talk about what?!" exclaimed Elizabeth as she arose, helped up by her governess. "These trunks? I remember how distraught my father was, when he had to tell Mummy they were missing. And I remember Mummy trying to manage as best she could with the contents of her leather case, in which she had put the basic necessities. You tried to kill Daddy, without thinking of the pain you would have caused your daughter! Mummy was pregnant and no longer had her layette, or anything! *I hate you!* I'm going to report you to the police—I've got proof!"

The squire surprised Bonnie, who was hastily trying to hide the crocodile wallet under her apron.

"Give me that!" he ordered without raising his voice, his eyes burning with rage.

"I hated your father, Elizabeth, and I was right! He messed with Catherine's head, promising her the earth once they were in New York. Had it not been for him, she wouldn't have died in that storm. Had it not been for him, her body wouldn't have been tossed into the ocean, like some cumbersome package to be disposed of."

"*You* are the only one to blame!" she retorted. "And you know it, and it must be eating away at you. Did Grandma know about your vile shenanigans? By God, and to think I didn't listen to Dad's advice. He had a bad feeling about you, and he was right. You hated Daddy and now, because of you, I know what hate is, and how it burns inside, because I *hate* you! I curse you!"

"Be quiet," said Hugues Laroche, threateningly, locking the door behind him. "What would you know about the fate that awaits us at each moment of our lives? I decided to get rid of your father before the ship left—yes, and if the imbeciles in charge of the dirty work hadn't messed up, Catherine would still be alive today! She'd be here now, with you and her son. That little boy born before his time, likewise tossed into the ocean."

Bonnie was praying silently. She was hoping that Richard would start to worry where they'd got to and would discover the entrance to the tower attic.

"I know more than you think!" replied Elizabeth angrily. "I used to have nightmares before I left France, but was so young that I didn't understand what they meant. I never told you, but in my dreams I'd already seen the funeral scene, where Mummy's body was wrapped in cloth, and shrouded sailors threw it into the sea. I also saw Daddy being attacked in the Bronx, but didn't dare warn him—and he died, just like Mummy. Or maybe it was you who paid those men to kill him in New York too?"

"Little fool! When I set off for New York, I had no idea what had happened to Guillaume. One thing is for sure—I didn't care what happened to him. I was only interested in you!"

"I don't doubt it. You needed to replace Mummy, to have me at your beck and call, to fondle and kiss, like you did with her!"

"Just shut up!" snapped Laroche. "When it's your American fondling and kissing your naked body, you like it, don't you?"

He sprang forward, skirting around the huge chest, an insane look in his eyes. Terrified, Bonnie tried to block his way, but he punched her straight in the face and then dealt her a second blow in the stomach. The governess staggered and collapsed, her nose bleeding. Elizabeth saw her fall against the wall and sink lifeless to the floor, her forehead on the stones.

"Bonnie!" she moaned. "You filthy brute! Murderer!"

She was gripped by an urge to kill him. She hurled herself at her grandfather and began hitting him randomly in the chest and the face, hurling insults at him. He was panting like a rabid animal as he grabbed her wrists, crushing them between his fingers.

Unable to escape his grip and half-blinded by tears of anger and despair, Elizabeth suddenly realized the stage was set. The scene from her nightmare was about to come true. It was dark, and the towering figure of a man dressed in black was overpowering her.

Laroche knocked her down between the chest and her parents' trunks and pinned her to the floor.

No—please—no, not that! she thought.

Then, amidst a rustling of skirts and petticoat, he forced his way inside her body, and she felt a sharp, searing pain between her legs. Like a powerless, fear-stricken little animal, she wailed in agony at the viciousness of such a depraved act. Finally, she sank into a welcome state of oblivion.

A lantern in his hand, Richard Johnson stopped dead on the threshold of the attic, the door of which was wide open. He had been wandering around the attic space for several minutes before getting there, guided by faint murmurs.

"Ah, there you are!" he cried, aghast when his eyes fell on Bonnie's puffy, injured face.

The governess was clutching Elizabeth in her arms. They were both standing behind the chest, but Richard noticed that his fiancée's face was ashen and she seemed in pain.

"What the hell happened here? Darling, look at me!"

"My grandfather went mad with rage because I discovered my parents' trunks, Richard—and proof that he tried to have my father murdered twelve years ago," Elizabeth replied weakly. "In an attempt to retrieve the wallet containing the evidence, he punched Bonnie, thrusting her against that wall and knocking me to the floor, too. When I fell, my back hit the lid of the trunk."

"What? I don't understand. How could your grandfather have done that? I mean, he wouldn't have had time to climb up to the rafters. When he got back, he came to see us in the dining room, refused a cup of tea and went into the kitchen to talk to Leandre about some ornamental shrubs to be planted before Saturday. He stayed in there for a long time—I'm sure of it— before riding off again. Anne-Marie heard the sound of galloping hooves and was surprised, as it was starting to get dark. As for me, I began to get bored and decided to find out where you'd got to."

"A little late, unfortunately," whimpered Bonnie, shaking her head.

Elizabeth only shrugged. Though she clearly looked distraught, she didn't shed a single tear or tremble.

"I assume you told him where I was," she said.

"Your great-aunt did. She joked, saying that you would come back down disguised, to entertain us."

"It's quite simple," replied the young woman. "Justin told me that you can get from the pantry to the attic rooms by a narrow servant staircase built into the walls. As a small boy, he used it to sneak into the kitchens and back up that way. This is how that monster was able to get to us without attracting any attention, and escape in the same way. Richard, are you absolutely certain that my grandfather has gone out again?"

"Why yes, Lisbeth—and if I understand correctly, he was running away! What you're telling me is diabolical. That old lunatic deserves to spend the rest of his life locked up."

Elizabeth nodded her head, under the anxious gaze of Bonnie, who continued to hold her tightly.

"I'll take you to your room, Miss. You need to rest."

"Rest! How could I, Bonnie!"

The governess frowned nervously. Once she'd regained consciousness, Elizabeth had got up and called out to her. They were alone. Her first thought was to look for the crocodile wallet, but it had disappeared.

"I was terrified, Bonnie," she whispered. "I thought you were dead, and your head was split open."

"Enough of me—what about you?" her governess exclaimed. "Where does it hurt?"

In a calm and collected manner, Elizabeth reeled off the same version of events she would give her fiancé, but in slightly more detail.

"I was furious he had struck you, leaving you to lie motionless by the wall—and for everything else he did! I tried to hit him back, but he knocked me backwards so violently that I fell, and my head struck the floor. I was concussed for a few minutes, and he took advantage of it to escape with the evidence of his crimes."

This brief account didn't entirely convince Bonnie. She knew perfectly well what Laroche was capable of.

"Be reasonable, Lisbeth—you need rest," insisted Richard. "Let's start by getting out of this horrible place. And you, Bonnie—you need to see a doctor. It looks like your nose may be broken, and your forehead's still bleeding."

With that, he took Elizabeth's hand, but the young woman abruptly pulled away.

"Please don't concern yourself with that, Richard," she replied sternly. "We have arnica balm and camphor oil in my bathroom. Now, I'm begging you—listen to me without interrupting me or trying to change my mind. You must do exactly as I ask, and for once, don't take any action on your own. Promise me!"

Startled by her curtness and the compelling look on her face, Richard quietly agreed.

"Every evening before dinner, my great-aunt and Anne-Marie retire to their bedrooms. They must be waiting for me now. You're going to tell them that I hit my head on a beam, and that I am lying down for a while. Tell them we'll meet at dinner, and then wait until they go upstairs."

"All right," he said solemnly.

"Once that's done, go to the stables to check that Galant's box is empty, and most importantly, you must ask my Uncle

Jean to harness the carriage with two of his best horses. That will give Bonnie and me time to prepare our luggage. Wait for us over there and explain everything to Uncle Jean."

"But explain what, darling? Where are you going?"

"I'm leaving, Richard. To get as far away as I can from this castle. I'll never have a legal case against my grandfather because he is going to destroy the evidence. But be that as it may, I never want to see him again. I'm returning to New York—you can do as you please."

Johnson was smart enough not to ask her about their future or the money needed for the crossing. He had just one answer:

"I'd follow you anywhere, Lisbeth."

Once Elizabeth was back in her room, she set about preparing for their departure. The young woman was careful not to wince in pain as she walked down the stone staircase, and adopted an appropriate voice tone.

"Bonnie, take the large leather bags I bought at the fair last year. Put two or three bodices, two skirts, undergarments, a dress and my doll in mine. Where's my travel outfit? I'll get changed in the bathroom."

All wound up, she rummaged through her wardrobe in search of undergarments. Her governess handed her a brown velvet skirt, a matching jacket and a pink poplin blouse.

"Thank you, Bonnie. Now go and pack your own bag, please."

"Yes, Miss—don't worry."

Once she was alone in the small room, the bolt firmly across, Elizabeth tore off all her clothes in rage. She filled the large enamel basin with cold water and began to wash herself fiercely, using a square cloth.

With clenched teeth and a fixed gaze, she frantically scrubbed her aching genitals with soap, rinsing herself repeatedly, spilling water onto the polished parquet floor. Breathless, she poured the remaining contents of the jug over her body, took the soap and tried yet again to wash him off her. She was seething with rage at having failed to change the course of her destiny.

Bonnie was listening at the door, holding her breath. She had already guessed the terrible truth.

Yet her bodice wasn't torn, nor was her skirt. For a moment, I believed she was telling the truth when saying he had just pushed her hard! she thought.

On the other side of the door, Elizabeth was drying herself.

As she dressed, she looked bitterly at the pretty blue-and-white striped skirt she had put on for the boat trip.

My goodness, it all seems so long ago now, she thought. *I didn't know just how happy I was.*

On her way out, Elizabeth saw Bonnie fastening one of the leather bags. The young woman pulled on her best boots in silence. She had composed a straight face and plaited her long hair before leaving the bathroom.

"I'm almost finished—I won't be taking much with me," declared the governess.

"Thank you, Bonnie. Now, where is my velvet pouch—the one with the canvas lining?"

"In the third drawer of the dresser, Miss."

Elizabeth was void of all emotion. Bonnie saw her emptying all her jewels into the pouch, together with a thick wad of banknotes and a cheque book. She then slipped into Adela's room, which hadn't been touched since her death.

"I will take anything that I can sell," she declared, grabbing her grandmother's emerald ornaments, rings, and gold Louis d'Or coins. "Don't look at me like that, Bonnie—all this is my inheritance. I'm not stealing."

"But it hurts me to see you like this, Miss," Bonnie sighed. "He raped you, didn't he? Like in your nightmare."

"Of course not—what are you talking about?! His only concern was to escape as quickly as possible."

"Why did you spend so long washing yourself, then?"

"Am I no longer allowed to take my time bathing?" snapped Elizabeth indignantly, her voice strained. "You're getting on my nerves, Bonnie. If the timetable hasn't changed, we have a train for Paris in about three hours. I picked up some leaflets at the small train station in Vouharte last summer, when I first decided to run away. But that would have been too early. I had to stay to find out what really happened. I'm convinced it's what Mummy wanted."

"All right, Miss!" stammered Bonnie, taken aback.

"I know what I'm doing," added Elizabeth. "If a cob alternates brisk trotting with galloping, it can cover a distance of more than ten miles in an hour. We have no time to lose. I want to stop off and say goodbye to Pops Toine on the way, as this'll be the last time I see him. I'll leave a message for Clotilde and Anne-Marie, and then we must go. They'll find it later, when they start looking for us at suppertime."

Bonnie put on her frock coat and hat, while Elizabeth slipped on a slim-fitted jacket and tied a beige scarf around her neck. She hastily scribbled a few lines on a page torn from her writing pad:

> *Dear Great-aunt, Dear Anne-Marie,*
> *A serious matter has given me no choice but to leave the country immediately. I am sorry that I won't be able to say goodbye to you. Please accept my apologies. Maybe someday you'll understand. Please return to Segonzac without delay. I'll write to you there. Bonnie will accompany me, of course, as well as Richard.*
> *Elizabeth*

"Poor ladies—they'll be so upset!" moaned Bonnie. "The two of them are so kind, and they love you very much."

"I'm afraid I don't have a choice! We don't know if the monster who fathered my poor mother will return tonight, tomorrow or the day after tomorrow, but he will be back. Evil creatures like him always return to their lair, and if I ever come face to face with him again, I shall kill him. He himself taught me how to use a rifle."

Panic-stricken, her governess seized the two bags. She had taken care to hide the jewellery and money underneath Elizabeth's undergarments.

"In that case, let's get out of here quickly, Miss!" urged Bonnie.

On the route to Montignac
Ten minutes later

Frisky and excited by the outing in the chilly night air, the two horses were galloping so fast, the carriage felt like it was flying. Perched on the coachman's bench, Jean tugged regularly on the reins to slow them down a little. He had followed his niece's instructions without asking any questions, having listened to Richard's brief and confusing account of events.

The puzzled American held Elizabeth tightly against him. She was abnormally silent but had laid her weary head on his shoulder, which pleased him.

Bonnie was clinging to the door, talking to her intended. She raised her voice to make herself heard over the noise of the wheels and shod hooves.

"I hope you understand why we're going back to New York, Jean. You must be disappointed, but believe me, it's better this way. You'll meet a younger, prettier lady—and besides, I cannot leave Miss Elizabeth."

The handsome Jean Duquesne turned around and smiled, despite the gravity of her words.

"Bonnie, you don't choose a woman like you pick out a piece of fruit. For Christ's sake, I love you, and I love my niece. In remembrance of Guillaume, it's my duty to protect her. I have some savings, so I'm coming with you. I'll buy a third-class ticket and we can get married in America! Besides, it would be fun to see the ocean and roam around the streets of New York. It's also where my brother died, so I'll be able to pray for him. And in all honesty, if I stay here, I won't be able to keep myself from going after Laroche, to give him what he deserves for all the pain and suffering he has caused."

"Uncle Jean, are you serious? You are really coming with us? Oh, I'm so glad!" cried Elizabeth. "I can't wait to introduce you to Daddy's friend, Baptiste Rambert, when we get there."

"I did meet him once, when he spent the night at the mill," replied her uncle. "It's high time I left France."

Bonnie was speechless with amazement and joy. The draught generated by the sheer speed of the carriage dried the tears that had rolled down her face. Elizabeth hugged her governess and best friend.

"You're going to be my auntie," she whispered in Bonnie's ear. "No more calling me 'Miss'. I love you so much!"

Her body was trembling with her sobs. Bonnie hugged her even tighter.

"Have a good cry, my darling," she whispered. "I love you too, like a mother loves her daughter. Cry—it'll ease the pain."

Richard was feeling sick from the bumpy ride. He was fretting too, which didn't help. A dreadful thought had crept into his mind while running to the castle stables, and he couldn't get rid of it.

Why the hasty escape? he thought. *We could have told Clotilde and Anne-Marie, and blown the whistle on Laroche and asked the police to find him. This way, we're giving him the chance to destroy the evidence that would put him behind bars. For a start, Bonnie could press charges against him for assault, and he ill-treated Lisbeth and knocked her about, too. In fact, he might have done more than that, or she wouldn't be in such a hurry to get away.*

He couldn't get the thought out of his mind again. If his fiancée had been raped and had told him, his reaction would have been one of absolute revulsion, disgust and overwhelming jealousy. He couldn't picture himself being sympathetic—not for a second. Although a little ashamed, he quickly banished his doubts.

No, I refuse to even contemplate such a thing! That old pervert has bolted, to avoid rotting in jail. I'm merely getting carried away— Lisbeth was calm and composed. You could tell she hated her grandfather, but she wouldn't have remained quite so calm and collected, if he had raped her.

The handsome American was underestimating his fiancée's strength of character. What's more, he didn't realize how proud she was, or that she had clairvoyant powers. Though he wasn't aware of it, Richard cherished and desired Elizabeth like a coveted jewel. She was the most wondrous gift that had ever been bestowed on him, and woe betide anyone who might attempt to steal her from him.

The Duquesnes' mill
One hour later

Wracked with grief and sorrow, Antoine Duquesne cradled his granddaughter in his arms. He immediately sensed that disaster had struck under the centuries-old rooftops of the Guerville fortress.

Pierre, who was standing at an upstairs window, had announced that a carriage pulled by two horses was entering the courtyard. He then raced downstairs in alarm, Yvonne at his heels.

Jean stepped into the kitchen, holding Bonnie by the hand.

"We've come to say goodbye to you," he called out. "Daddy, please kiss my bride to be—I'm leaving for New York, where we'll be getting married."

Elizabeth appeared, looking dignified and pale, but with a faint smile on her lips.

"Pops Toine, hold me tightly!" she begged as she ran towards him. "I must go, and I won't be back. I would rather have stayed here with you, but I must let go of that thought. Forgive me—I have no choice but to leave you all."

Moved by his niece's distress, Jean took it upon himself to give a brief account of the terrible discovery she had made in the tower's attic space.

Pierre's horror-stricken face glanced over at Elizabeth with tears in the eyes. She huddled in her grandfather's arms, but the distressed old man gently pushed her aside.

"Poor little one, go quickly!" he urged. "We've discussed it before. Only one thing matters to me—not vengeance, not justice, just your happiness. I'd rather see you safe on the other side of the Atlantic than in danger here. Eventually Laroche will pay for his crimes."

A heavy silence fell, and Antoine Duquesne cupped Elizabeth's beautiful face in his wrinkled hands, his gaze full of love and tenderness. His bright-blue eyes met Elizabeth's.

"For *all* his crimes!" he whispered so softly that only his granddaughter could hear.

He could tell what she was hiding, from the frightened, hunted look in her crystalline eyes, and the way her wounded, bruised little body quivered. Then he said:

"You have my blessing, little one. May the good Lord watch over you! Now you must leave at once—all of you."

He held Elizabeth tightly, cuddling her as if she were still a child, before kissing her forehead. He also gave a fatherly kiss to Bonnie and his son Jean. Yvonne was distraught and weeping.

"Gilles and Laurent are at my mother's, as I'm going to the fair early tomorrow. They'll be so disappointed to have missed you!"

"I can imagine—they were so excited about coming to my birthday party," Elizabeth replied, hugging her aunt.

"Oh well, they'll soon get over that. What I meant was, they'll be sad about not seeing you again. They love you very much—we all do!"

Richard looked anxiously at the clock. He was adamant about retrieving his personal belongings from his room in Angoulême.

"Don't worry, we'll be on time," said Jean.

Elizabeth stepped back towards the door, looking totally despondent and sorrowful. She was taking stock of the devastation caused by Hugues Laroche over the years.

So many wasted lives, all that happiness doomed, she thought to herself. *My parents could have lived very happily, here or elsewhere, if it hadn't been for that evil man's hatred.*

Consumed by animosity, she blew a final kiss to her family before rushing towards the carriage, helped by Richard. Bonnie followed on her heels.

By now it was pitch black outside. Jean untied the horses and lit the carriage lanterns fixed on each side of his seat, before taking his place and adjusting the reins.

"And what will you do with the carriage and the horses?" asked Pierre, who had escorted them.

"There's a livery stable near the railway station. We'll leave them there with the castle's address," replied Elizabeth. "Uncle Pierre, please write to me. I'll send you a letter as soon as we get to New York, from Mom and Dad's apartment—my second parents' home. Farewell, and take good care of my Pops Toine. Oh! I nearly forgot—tell him that I found his doll in Mummy's trunk, and she's now accompanying me to America."

"I'll tell him. Look after yourself, Elizabeth!"

Jean shook his brother's hand and manoeuvred the carriage through the large courtyard and its entrance gate. Antoine Duquesne stood in the lodge doorway, watching the carriage disappear into the night. He caught a last glimpse of Elizabeth's face through the narrow porthole at the rear.

The old miller made the sign of the cross and prayed that they would have a safe journey. So many dangers could befall them on the way from Montignac to Paris, and from Paris to New York: accidents, storms . . .

But then, he decided not to give in to fear, and imagined the path along the Charente river, its dark waters reflecting the moonlight. He could almost smell the heavy fragrance of the springtime night air, and imagined how the horses' fast trotting would scare the birds nesting in the gorse bushes.

"Goodbye, my little Elizabeth," he said quietly. "Farewell, and be happy."